CONTENT WARNING

The following material contains discussions of self-harm, suicide attempts and ideation, childhood physical and sexual abuse, racialized and police violence.

RUN J RUN

BY

SU J. SOKOL

Renaissance
Diverse Canadian Voices

RUN J RUN ©2019 by Su J. Sokol. All rights reserved. No part of this book may be used or reproduced in any manner whatsoever without written permission except in the case of brief quotations in critical articles and reviews. For more information, contact Renaissance Press. First edition.

Cover image by Lin Lin Mao. Back cover art, cover design and interior by Nathan Frechette. Edited by L.P. Vallee, Myryam Ladouceur, Evan McKinley and Nathan Frechette.

Legal deposit, Library and Archives Canada, April 2019.

Paperback ISBN: 978-1-987963-51-9
Ebook ISBN 978-1-987963-52-6

Renaissance Press
http://renaissancebookpress.com
info@renaissancebookpress.com

Two are better than one; because they have a good reward for their labor. For if they fall, the one will lift up his fellow; but woe to him that is alone when he falls; for he has not another to help him up. Again, if two lie together, then they have warmth; but how can one be warm alone? And if one prevail against him, two shall withstand him; a threefold cord is not quickly broken.

ECCLESIASTES 4:9-12

CHAPTER 1

I clamped down on both hand brakes, hard enough that my bike's back wheel lifted off the ground, nearly pitching me into the late afternoon Lower Manhattan traffic.

Fucking Zak. How did he always manage to time it so that he went through the intersection just as the light turned red?

I waited for the green, watching Zak glide between lanes like some frictionless wonder—just the way he'd glided into the room that morning for staff orientation. I'd been standing in my first-day-back-to-school shirt, thinking about starting a conversation with the new 9th grade English teacher. Then Zak arrived and every head turned towards him, like he was a rock star instead of a high school math teacher.

The light changed and I stood on my pedals to close the distance between us. Zak grinned at me over his shoulder, then proceeded to accelerate his death-defying weaves through traffic, slipping between busses and darting cabs. After his third suicidal maneuver, I was tempted to ditch him. But if I did that, who would watch his back?

Earlier that day at school, I'd watched him too, this time as he worked the crowd. He shook hands, kissed cheeks, and clasped shoulders like a politician before an election—all the while smiling that smile of his. But throughout the kissing and handshaking, Zak was also peering over heads, searching for someone. When at last he found this someone, his smile was about ten degrees warmer than every other smile he'd smiled so far, and that was saying a lot.

How could I not have felt good, knowing that smile was for me? How could I not have felt lucky when he quickly navigated his way around chairs and clumps of people, and what *I* got from him wasn't a handshake, but a bone-crushing bear hug followed by an enthusiastic kiss on each of my cheeks, and a third one too, like we were in fucking Europe or something. The European-style greeting was probably Zak's idea of a joke, a nod to my summer spent in Paris working on my book and trying, once again, to get over Tara.

Zak's bike veered to the right. I followed and was nearly doored.

A guy would have to be an asshole to be jealous of his best friend; to think it isn't fair that someone with a partner as smart and sexy as Annie also had all these other women drooling over him; to resent the fact that the person voted "Most Popular Teacher" every year by our high school students was also so well-liked by his colleagues; to wonder why someone as good-looking as Zak also had to be such a math genius that it was frankly scary.

Well maybe I'm an asshole.

Yet, the thing of it was, if Zak could somehow have peered into my mind and seen what an egocentric, self-pitying, miserable excuse for a friend I was, he would have smiled that sweet smile of his and said, "J, you're too hard on yourself." Then he'd invite me out for a beer and lay out his newest, sure-fire scheme to help me meet someone new, get laid, fall in love again, forget my ex-wife once and for all, and live happily ever after.

The Green Bullfrog was a 19th century tavern located on a narrow street in Downtown Manhattan. I locked up my expensive touring bike—ill-equipped for the kind of rough use I'd put it through—and tugged at my good shirt now plastered to my back. Zak pulled off the helmet Annie probably made him wear, liberating his wild, black curls from their temporary prison.

"You almost got me killed three separate times," I said.

"Let me buy you a beer," Zak replied.

"Two beers. So both hands can be wrapped around something other than your neck."

"Sure Jeremy, as many beers as you like. But you have to tell me *everything* about Paris and who you met there."

Two Brooklyn Nut Browns were placed before me on paper coasters on the scarred wooden table. I reached for one of them, wondering how to best spin my story for Zak. I began by delaying it, asking instead about Annie and the kids. Though Zak wasn't yet thirty, he already had two of them, the older one nine. Sierra was a top-notch baseball player, the only girl on her team, and Brooklyn was a sweet little boy of five with his father's fascination for numbers. His kids were great, but in this I felt no jealousy. I had my own little 'Supergirl,' Kyra who at not quite three was already starting to read, though only Zak and Annie would believe me.

I finally launched into my tale of the woman I met at a café during the World Cup finals. We were both rooting for Brazil, me because the U.S. had already lost and Americans can't play soccer for shit anyway, and her because she was Brazilian.

"Describe her," Zak demanded.

"Beautiful, vibrant, smart, fun."

"But what'd she look like *exactly*? I want to picture her."

"Tall and curvy. Thick, curly dark hair."

"Like Annie's?"

"I said *dark*. But yeah, curly like Annie's."

"So, what'd you do?"

"I bought her a drink. Red wine. We finished off a bottle together."

"And?"

"We talked. She told me about her work—communications, for a not-for-profit. I told her about teaching high school English and my research on language acquisition in children."

"She must've been impressed."

"She was impressed an American could do something more than grunt monolingually. I didn't mind her attitude, though. It was provocative, sexy in a way."

"Yeah, and?"

"When Brazil won—"

"Brazil won?" Zak said.

"Of course Brazil won. Where the fuck were you?"

"You know I don't follow sports. C'mon, Jeremy. Get to the good part."

"OK. So Brazil won and we both cheered and before you knew it we were in each other's arms. I asked if I could walk her home."

"Good, good."

"She was staying at a small boutique hotel on the Rive Gauche. We were on the Rive Droite. Which meant?"

"You had to cross a bridge."

I gulped down the rest of my first beer and smiled at him, getting into my own story now, almost forgetting how it ended. "Exactly. And bridges ... "

" ... are romantic."

"You got it, my friend. So I kissed her. Right in the middle of the bridge."

"Were you equidistant between the two banks?"

"What the fuck are you talking about? Stop interrupting and listen. Picture a big bright moon, the Bateau Mouche slipping through the water, the golden reflection of the buildings on either side of the river. She leans into me and we start kissing." I stopped and took three long swallows from my second beer. He was staring at me, mouth slightly open, his own beer forgotten on the table. "She tells me what a good kisser I am and—"

"What were her exact words?"

"They were Portuguese. You wouldn't understand."

"Tell me anyway. Tell me I'm a good kisser in Portuguese."

"I will not."

"C'mon, Jeremy, please?"

I tolerated his childish banter because both of us knew this would be the highlight of my story, and most particularly, there'd be no happy ending. I could see this shared understanding in his dark eyes. Actually, I could hardly look him in the eye. I felt depressed, humiliated, thinking about how I'd been home for four days and Tara still hadn't made time to speak to me.

"Listen Zak, it didn't work out in the end. I guess she wasn't my type after all."

"Tell me what happened."

"We were a few blocks from the hotel when another couple passed us. They

4

had a little girl—about two years old. She was crying. The parents were oblivious—in the middle of an argument. So my date, she says something like 'what a spoiled brat' and I lost interest."

I could still picture the poor little kid, but now she had Kyra's face. How could I have fucked up my own family so badly?

"I get it, it's OK," I heard Zak saying. "Anyhow, long distance relationships suck. Look, I brought you here for the wine. Sit tight. I'll get us a couple of glasses of something high end."

Zak walked off with a determined stride. Like a man with a plan. It worried me. Couldn't he just leave it? It's true I'd agreed before going to Paris that it was time I got over Tara. "Plan P," Zak had called it. I'd work on my book during the day and make the most of the Parisian nights. I didn't want to admit to Zak that I'd spent many evenings composing heartfelt messages to Tara, hoping she'd take me back.

I took out my phone, wondering if she'd texted me in the few minutes since I'd last checked. I also wondered what was taking Zak so long. When he finally returned, he was carrying four glasses of wine balanced on a tray.

"Did you steal that from someone?" I asked.

"I got us a glass of Bordeaux and a sweetish white from Banyuls, France. The waitress—Camille—is coming with a grey wine from the, uh, Jura region. You're gonna like her."

"The bartender?"

"She's a foreign student from Lyon, working on a Master's in Cultural Anthropology. I mentioned yours in Linguistics. She's really into you."

"Zak, what are you talking about? She hasn't even met me."

"I told her all about you. How you teach English but love sports. How you've travelled and are a good judge of wines. She let me try six different types to decide which you'd like."

"She let you sample six types of wine? For free? She doesn't like me, she likes you."

"No, we talked about you the whole time."

"Zak—"

5

"Shh, here she comes."

Camille placed two glasses of wine onto our already crowded table.

"This is Jeremy Singer," Zak said, introducing us.

"Pleased to meet you," I said, extending my hand.

I could always count on Zak's good taste in women. She was tall and looked athletic, with a heart-shaped face and large, hazel eyes. She told us about the wines, speaking with confidence in a flawless but lightly accented English.

"Be right back," Zak said. "Gotta offload some liquids."

I watched him walk away, wishing he'd stick around to help grease the conversation. "So," I began. "You're studying anthropology."

"And you are a high school English teacher," she answered. "When I was in high school, English teachers didn't look like rugby players."

She smiled at me and I smiled back. This was actually going pretty well. I tried to think of something to say that was clever but light.

"That couldn't have been too long ago." She tilted her head at me. "That you were in high school," I finished.

"I'm twenty-seven. Your friend told me you are thirty-three."

"That's right," I replied.

"He said some very nice things about you."

"He's a nice guy."

"Yes, he seems nice. Are you very close?"

"We're pretty tight."

"Well, here is my number. If the two of you would both like to hook up with me some time, give me a call."

With the smile frozen on my face, I watched her return to the bar. I thought about tossing the cocktail napkin with her number onto the floor, but that would have been rude and I was raised to have good manners. That "the two of you" shit, though, what the hell was that? I stuffed the napkin into my pants pocket. When Zak returned, I said, "Let's go."

"But what about the wine?"

I drank the first glass in one long swig. "This isn't a Bordeaux, it's a Burgundy—

6

a Pinot Noir," I grumbled.

"Yeah, I know. I was hoping you'd correct me in front of Camille, so she'd know I wasn't kidding about how smart you are."

I drank down the other two glasses without comment, pushing them away one by one as I drained them. Zak took one look at my face and did the same. He went to pay while I left the bar. Once outside, he hesitated. "What happened? Didn't you get her number?"

"Yeah, I got it. How about you? You get her number too?" I asked him.

"Sure, J," he answered slowly. "For you, in case you forgot to ask."

He looked up at me, all innocence, like I was supposed to believe he didn't know what went down. I refused to meet his gaze. "For me," I repeated.

"Of course for you. Here."

He handed me a piece of neatly folded paper. I stuffed it into my other pocket without looking at it. While we unlocked our bikes, I told him he should get going without me, that we were headed in different directions. The smile slipped from Zak's face. He opened his mouth as though to say something, but stopped, chewing on his lower lip instead.

I felt guilty then. After all, it wasn't entirely Zak's fault that everyone wanted to sleep with him. I shoved my guilt aside, stoking my anger with images of Zak flirting with Camille while Annie waited for him at home. I knew they had this open relationship that allowed him to have his flings or whatever, but I couldn't help thinking it was fucked up. If Annie were mine, I wouldn't waste my time flirting in bars. Sometimes I regretted ever having introduced Zak to Annie, and for more than one reason.

After he rode away, I pushed my bike towards Chinatown, hoping to walk it off. The night was wet and grey, the susurration of light rain combining with the alcohol to press on my senses. When I got to the Manhattan Bridge, I started riding, shaky on the narrow path as I crossed the East River. I thought again about Zak, riding home alone with his reckless style, less able to hold his alcohol than I am. I shoved my worry aside too. It was me, not him, who was accident prone, despite all my efforts at caution. Like a cat, Zak always landed on his feet.

When I got home, I emptied my pockets, the folded paper Zak had handed me falling onto the bed. I opened it up and saw Camille's name and phone number in big loopy handwriting. Below it, in Zak's careful, tiny print, were the words "For J" written inside a drawing of a heart.

I really am an asshole.

CHAPTER 2

I lit up a joint and took a long hit before washing it down with the rest of my second beer. Though I didn't usually mix pot and alcohol, even on weekends, this morning had called for exceptional measures.

The downstairs buzzer rang, and I let Zak in. When I'd called to see if he could come over, he hadn't even asked why—probably because I was the only one stupid enough not to have seen this coming. I took a final toke before carefully stubbing out the roach and placing it in my antique cigar tin. I opened my window to clear out the smoke, then closed the curtains. The unobstructed view from my high-rise apartment made me wobbly.

Standing in my socks in the hallway, I heard Zak rounding the stairs. Zak never used the elevator. Running up twenty-four flights was his idea of fun.

He asked me how it went, adding that Annie had been surprised the lawyers would meet on a Saturday. I shrugged and offered him a beer, though it wasn't quite noon. Zak sat down on the couch, placing his beer on the coffee table next to the open Scrabble board. I swallowed more beer, fussed with the music, and continued pacing the room.

"Hey, J, could you put on something else that's less ..."

"Nihilistic?" I supplied.

"I was gonna say suicidal, but nihilistic's a better word."

After I changed the music, Zak patted the spot beside him.

"Tell me what happened," he said.

"Well, at first it was going fine. They agreed to fifty-fifty custody."

"OK, good."

"Tara was even being nice to me, touching my hand when I told her about my aunt's stroke. She made actual physical contact with me twice."

"Not that you were counting ..."

I took another swig of my beer. "So I did what I always do—read too much into it."

"You asked her about getting back together."

I nodded. "And she lost it."

Staying seated was impossible. I went into the kitchen, rinsed out my empty beer bottle, and grabbed a full one. I returned to the living room to drink it while standing.

"Zak, you had to see her. It was like the idea of getting back together was ... unthinkably horrible. She shouted at me, and ..." I leaned against the wall near the entrance to the kitchen, a little dizzy. Maybe the second joint was one too many. Or this fourth beer.

"And?" Zak asked, startling me out of my reverie.

"Her lawyer whipped out this document. A legal agreement to never talk to Tara about reconciliation again."

"You're kidding me."

"I can show you. It's around here somewhere." I knocked over some papers on the mail table by the door, checked under the couch cushions. "Maybe I threw it away."

"You know you didn't throw it away, Jeremy. What'd it say?"

"I ... I can't ask Tara if she's seeing anyone, or say how lonely I am. And there's a whole list of words I'm barred from using with her. It's like a verbal restraining order. No 'sweetheart,' 'baby', 'love'. Yeah, 'love' is at the top of the list."

"What about your lawyer?" Zak asked.

"What?"

"Your lawyer, J. What did she do?"

"Oh, she objected, said it was irregular. Then she took me aside and told me to sign it. They must think I'm sick to have come up with this."

"They're the ones who're sick. You, an English teacher, helping kids communicate better, while this tool gets paid a ton of money to list all the loving words he can come up with that you shouldn't be allowed to say ..."

I was half listening, satisfied by his tone of outrage, but thinking of tomorrow and the next day and the next, my family broken with no hope of repair. On top of that depressing reality was humiliation for the lengths they'd needed to go for me

10

to accept the situation.

"Tara's right to not take me back. I'm an asshole. I actually stalked her."

"You're being too hard on yourself."

"I'm ... I'm fucked up, Zak. I *stalked* her. Did I mention that?"

"Look, you just ... call her too much. Without waiting for her to call back."

"I sent her one hundred and thirty-seven text messages from Paris."

"OK, that wasn't a great move but—"

"I can't say the word 'love'! It's in the agreement. And you know why? It's because I don't know how to love."

Zak moved towards me. I had this weird notion he was going to hit me, though I'd never seen Zak hit anyone. Instead, he pushed me against the wall and kissed me hard on the lips. I shut up, shocked and calm at the same time, like there were two of me, one who shoved Zak away while the other watched from a distance to see what would happen next. What happened next was that he kissed me again, this time, very tenderly. I thought of shoving him but remembered having done that already and that it didn't work. When he released me, I looked around the room, searching for an ally. I spotted Zak's beer and lunged for it, knocking it over instead. I was startled by how full it was, by this clear demonstration that Zak was stone-cold sober.

I retrieved the bottle and upended it, more or less over my mouth. Zak moved towards the kitchen, but I waved him off and grabbed at one of those new micro-strips, the kind that my daughter Kyra loved to watch get bigger as they absorbed liquid. I awkwardly slapped the strip onto the spill and stared as it plumped up to eighteen times its original size, unable to look away despite an uncomfortable answering bulge in my pants.

"Why would you do that?" I finally asked.

"Because I love you."

I considered this, answering carefully. "I love you too. We've been best friends for thirteen years. You're ... like a brother to me." An impulsive, queer younger brother.

Zak's arm was around my shoulder but it was weird because I hadn't seen him move. "Well listen, brother," he said. "It's been too long since you fucked."

I shrugged his arm off and turned towards the kitchen. Zak graciously moved back a pace, clearing the way between me and my alcohol stores. I grabbed a beer from the refrigerator and twisted it open. Zak was still talking.

"If you're not attracted to me, just say so. My feelings won't be hurt." He paused as I squinted at him, his familiar form going from sharp to blurry. "I can find a dozen people—women if you prefer—who'd be happy to have sex with you. I can think of two teachers from our school right off. Want to know who?"

"No! Stop talking!" I said.

"Alright, no colleagues. Someone you don't know, maybe?"

"No. I—"

"Good, 'cause I'd rather it be me."

I shook my head, trying to figure out how to steer this conversation away from that wacky parallel universe known as Zak-land, and fast, before the additional alcohol I'd just consumed made its way to the part of my brain that processed language.

"Listen, Zak," I said finally. "You're very ..." I got lost completing this sentence while I wondered, and not for the first time, how a feral child like Zak could have survived this long among normally socialized people.

"Very what?" Zak asked.

Weird. Whacked. Wackadoodle. I started giggling. It wasn't a pretty sound. I tried to remember what I wanted to say. "Sweet. You're very sweet." I cleared my throat and concentrated harder. "You also probably know that you're a very attractive, um, person, but what you're suggesting ..." I hung on tightly to my train of thought. "That is, what I believe you're suggesting—this isn't the kind of thing you offer a friend because they're ... hard up. Do you understand?"

"If you think I'm just being nice, you're wrong. See?"

He grabbed my hand and pushed it against his crotch. I pulled away, wondering whether to be angry or flattered. No, not flattered. Zak could get a hard-on watching the sun rise.

"Shut the music, J," he said.

12

I turned to him to argue but something in his eyes stopped me. I turned off the depressing blues number that had been playing. Zak stepped forward and leaned his whole weight against me. I watched my arms close around him, hoping he wouldn't be stupid enough to try this on someone else, because if he pulled this on the wrong guy, he'd get the shit kicked out of him. I was actually seeing it, Zak on the floor, blood coming from his mouth and ears, and all because I was too stoned to explain it properly. The only thing I could do was fold him into my arms and protect him, in order to keep someone, someone like me, from kicking the shit out of him.

Zak started kissing me again. This time I gave in, gave in to everything—the pot, the alcohol, my emotional exhaustion, my rapidly slipping sense of reality. Pushing him away again was too much trouble. Besides, that would have involved letting go of him. Zak and the wall were the only things keeping me upright. I felt safe between these two hard surfaces, one in front and one behind, and the main difference was that the one in front, the one that was Zak, was very, very warm. I could feel his heat through the thin cotton of his t-shirt, and especially through his jeans. I liked how warm he was and how he smelled—like freshly laundered cotton and sandalwood soap and something else, very distinctly him.

My mouth was kissing and being kissed, my arms were holding on tight, but my brain was on sleep mode. I closed my eyes, drifting pleasurably, but Zak moved his mouth away from mine and I had a lungful of oxygen, which cleared some smoke from my head.

"Tell me what you want," he whispered, his breath hot in my ear.

What did I want? To not answer questions. To not make decisions. To not want things and then fuck those things up. What else? I wanted to not fall down or throw up. I also didn't want Zak's warmth to move away from me. I focused my stoned brain on some sort of coherent response and came up with: "This is good. Let's keep doing this." Hugging. Kissing. It's OK for best friends to hug. Maybe even kiss a little? I decided it was nothing to worry about.

Zak smiled at me. I had to admit, he had a pretty sexy smile.

"You wanna lie down, maybe?" he asked.

13

Yeah, that was probably a good idea. Once the thought of lying down had entered my brain, I couldn't stop myself from sliding down the wall. What was the point of resisting gravity? Somehow, Zak managed to re-choreograph my fall so it became a graceful tumble into his arms. I rolled onto my back, pulling Zak on top of me. He was at least thirty-five pounds lighter than I was, but still a good solid weight on my chest and legs. It was reassuring, like being between him and the wall again, only this was horizontal, which was more restful. At the same time, lying there on the floor, passively accepting Zak's ministrations, I felt like the victim of a tragic event—like a drive-by shooting. Or a tsunami. And Zak was a foreign doctor, practicing an alternative medicine I wasn't sure I believed in. Still, it felt good to be getting some kind of care.

Zak tugged off his shirt and slid his belt out of its loops. He gazed down at me with eyes that were an ordinary brown, but there was nothing ordinary about their intensity. His eyelashes were dark and very long. He was much too beautiful, especially for a man. And this was not my fault. I grasped his face between my hands and pulled his mouth down onto mine again.

There was a deep, exquisite ache low in my stomach that moved down to my balls. My breath was coming short and hard. I didn't know how long we'd been lying together, our jean-clad legs tangled up on the floor. Zak's tongue and lips moved along my throat. His hip pushed insistently into the crotch of my pants. When he repositioned himself on top of me and rubbed the length of his cock against my own, it all became too much, even through all that fabric. I flipped him onto his back and ground myself into him. One, two, three, and it was all over.

I shuddered and climbed off of him, then stumbled into the bathroom, locking the door. I cleaned myself, sitting on the edge of the toilet, and waited until I could no longer hear the blood pounding through my veins. When I was capable of it, I took a piss that seemed to last a good fifteen minutes. The walls gradually settled into place around me.

My plan was to stay in the bathroom until Zak left, but even in my state, that seemed like atrociously bad manners. I walked back into the living room, eyes down not only out of embarrassment, but to make it less likely I'd trip. Zak was

14

sitting on the floor with his back against the wall, still shirtless, his arms wrapped loosely around his knees. I slid down next to him.

"I'm sorry," I mumbled.

"What for?" Zak answered.

"For acting like I was fourteen, fumbling around for the first time."

"Well, it is a kind of first time for you. Besides, it's flattering you couldn't wait."

I felt a flush moving up my neck.

"Hey, I've got an idea," he said, tracing my lips with a fingertip, a smile spreading across his face, "We could go at it again, and this time, you set the pace. I'll do whatever you say."

I knew I should tell him to go home but making him leave wasn't going to erase what happened. To have done what I did was embarrassing enough, but to have done it so incompetently too … I thought about his offer. It appealed to my pride. I didn't want my best friend thinking I was such a pathetic lover.

I stood, using the wall to brace myself. Zak remained sitting, waiting, I realized, for me to tell him what to do.

"Get up," I said.

He scrambled to his feet, eyes bright beneath dark, tangled curls. He was beautiful and wild and ready for anything and, for once, there was the promise he'd be under my control. I put my hand behind his neck and kissed him roughly. Then I pushed him into my bedroom.

The remainder of Zak's clothes lay in an untidy heap in the corner of my bedroom. I had a small urge to fold his jeans the way I'd folded mine when I'd removed them, but I left them there, feeling careless and defiant. My right hand was laced in Zak's hair while the other explored his body. I have unusually large hands, which tended to make me careful when making love. With Zak, I was less careful, knowing it would be harder to hurt him. To be honest, I was letting myself be rough. It didn't occur to me to wonder if I was angry. Or what emotion I was experiencing. I thought I'd put my emotions on hold. Wasn't that the point of all the pot and beer?

Though my head was clearer, the room was still spinning slowly. I crushed Zak against me to get him to stop moving. He squirmed, so I squeezed tighter until he went still. That was better. I closed my eyes and concentrated on his warm, smooth skin as my hands slid down his body. I kissed him some more, his teeth sharp against my tongue. I realized my palms were cupped around his ass. He had a sweet ass, as soft and as hard as an unripe peach. What was I doing? I pulled my hands away and tried to think.

I needed to exert some control over the situation, but every time I let my mind wander, my hands found their way back to his ass, like metal to a magnet. My heart was racing; my breath was short; I kept losing track of my hands. The third time this happened, Zak rested his head on my shoulder and hummed a strange, beautiful melody into my ear. There was something so odd about this, but peaceful too, that I stopped worrying. It's like I'd been transported to a parallel universe, a secret place inhabited by only Zak and me where I could do as I pleased because it was somehow unconnected to the real world.

I turned him around, lowering my mouth to the back of his neck. His skin was warm and tasted slightly salty. I pushed myself against him and he moaned, saying something. He turned his head towards me, repeating what he'd said. I kissed him hard from the side, swallowing the word where it vibrated in my throat and out to my ear. The word was "condom."

I had a moment of panic trying to calculate the average shelf life of a condom. I pictured them decomposing in my drawer and was relieved to find some intact packets of grey and blue. Lubricated, good. I took out two—two guys, two condoms, right?—and handed one to Zak. I tried opening the packet, but my hands were shaking. Zak took it, dropping to his knees to roll it onto me. He tilted his head up, the expression on his face one of total trust. It nearly undid me. I thought, *what am I doing?* Zak licked his teeth, now wearing a complicit look that challenged me to continue this adventure. I put my hands in his hair and he grinned and asked where I wanted him. I pushed him onto my bed on all fours. He tossed his own, unopened condom onto the floor.

Zak had a strange tattoo on his lower back. A map or maze, it seemed designed for an insane mathematics genius. I ran my finger along a pathway. It warmed to my touch, like an interactive game. I pressed my finger against a spot towards the bottom left of the tattoo, where there was the symbol of a key. *Ready player one*, I thought to myself. Zak shuddered violently. I removed my hand and wrapped my arms around his chest. "Alright?" I asked. He didn't answer but seemed to calm.

Zak began rubbing himself against me and all rational thought was pushed from my mind. I shoved his shoulders against the bed and told him to stop moving. He complied at once. I waited a beat, then ran the tip of my finger along his crack. He trembled. I traced the same path with my cock before pushing into him, testing, while he clutched at my pillow. I pulled out again, then pushed further in. Zak turned his head and moaned. His tongue peeked out from between his teeth and his eyes were half-closed, long lashes brushing his cheeks. I pushed in again, harder, penetrating deeply as he clenched around me.

Grasping his upper arms tightly, I moved out and in again, closing my eyes, my emotional and physical exhaustion allowing me to slip into a dreamlike state. We were on one of our wild bike rides, Zak just ahead of me. I was flying, pressed against him, the two of us high enough to see all of the bridges of the City, like a set of diamond necklaces joining borough to borough. As I pumped, the sky exploded with a brilliance I felt rather than saw. Then, after a long, drawn-out moment, everything began to softly dim as my body, weightless with pleasure, slowly floated down, Zak clutched in my arms.

When I came to myself, we were both collapsed on the bed. Zak was lying so still beneath me that, for a crazy moment, I wondered if I'd somehow killed him. I rolled onto my side, placing my hand lightly on his back. I was relieved to find him breathing.

"Did I hurt you?" I asked.

Zak turned over, a beatific smile on his lips.

"That wasn't a moan of pain you heard, brother."

"You're not going to let me forget that brother comment, are you?" I asked, but

17

was reassured. I fetched a washcloth. When I returned, Zak looked up at me with sleepy eyes. I cleaned him off and dried him with the blanket. My limbs felt wonderfully relaxed, like after a good workout. Zak turned his back to me, pulling my arm around him. What the hell, if he wanted to cuddle a little, it was the least I could do after he let me fuck him.

I drifted, his back against my chest. His skin was smooth, and unlike mine, almost hairless. My arm seemed pink against his darker skin, my muscles thick where his were leaner and more articulated. It had felt incredibly good to let myself go like that. I was so relieved I hadn't hurt him that it took me a few minutes to worry about other things—things that were harder to ignore as my head got clearer.

"Zak," I finally said. "You can't ... you're not going to tell Annie about this, are you?"

"Why not?" he responded. "You know we have an open relationship."

"Yeah, but we're talking about me, not some random ... some woman at a bar."

"She'll be happy. We've both been worried about you."

I shook my head, exasperated. To him it would make perfect sense that Annie wouldn't mind that we'd had sex because she, too, had been 'worried about me.'

"Think this through," I told him. "Why risk upsetting her?"

"I don't like keeping things from Annie ..." he said, but must have seen how panicked I was because he added, "OK, I'll think about it."

"Thanks," I answered, relieved.

"J, would you mind if I slept a little?"

"Oh ... sure," I said, starting to get up.

"Stay here. I'll sleep better," he said, grabbing my arm.

"Are you having trouble sleeping again?"

He shrugged. This concerned me, because Zak never lied, so shrugging was the best he could do to hide what was probably a not-very-encouraging response. Before I could frame a follow-up question, Zak snuggled against me. My arms went around him automatically. I decided to let it drop. Less than a minute later, I experienced that familiar dead-weight heaviness on my shoulder that any parent

18

recognizes.

I was surprised by how quickly Zak fell asleep, a poor sleeper like him in a strange bed. It made me happy, like a sign he trusted me. I felt a wave of tenderness towards him and wrapped my arms around him more tightly. Unsatisfied, I pushed some stray locks of hair from his eyes and pressed my lips to his forehead, kissing him gently. A tightness in my chest let loose, so I kissed him again, rubbing my cheek against the softness of his hair. It was only then that I thought to ask myself when it was exactly that I'd managed to fall in love with my best friend.

CHAPTER 3

The next day was Sunday and I spent it cleaning. I emptied the trash, carried out the recycling, stripped my bed, did the laundry—everything I could think of to remove all traces of yesterday from my apartment. If only it were as simple to remove the day from my life. At least it seemed I'd gotten through to Zak about how bad an idea it would be to tell Annie. I was now more worried about what would happen at school. Would Zak know to act normal in front of our colleagues, the principal, our students? Did Zak even know how to act normal?

On Monday, I got to school early, hoping to have a quick word with him. He wasn't in yet, so I settled down on the sagging couch in the teachers' lounge, my students' compositions spread out on the low table in front of me. The air was redolent with the smell of old refrigerator and fresh, strong coffee. I took a second cup, hoping the caffeine would help me focus, but my mind kept wandering from my students' musings on Ellison's *Invisible Man* to a critical reexamination of my thirteen years of friendship with Zak. I was wondering if there was something I'd missed, something that should have alerted me to the danger that one day we'd end up in bed together. Then Zak arrived and plopped himself practically on top of me.

I put my hand on his shoulder and shoved him over a foot, then glanced over to see if my shove had pissed him off. He laughed at me. I felt relieved but annoyed. Did he have to be so cocksure of himself?

I wondered if anyone noticed anything. Our friend Robyn was bent over her laptop preparing a worksheet for Spanish class, her dark, straight hair curtaining her face. She glanced up and smiled indulgently, the kind of smile I imagined she gave her four and six-year-old sons when they were horsing around. With a flash of insight, I realized that this type of physical interplay between Zak and me was nothing new, that Zak was acting as he always did while I was the one in danger of blowing it.

The rest of the morning was uneventful, except every so often I'd fantasize about going into the male teachers' bathroom, finding Zak there, making him drop his pants, and drilling him against the wall. I told myself to get a grip, that there were more than enough hormones raging around the building without adding to the mix.

At lunch time, I went into the concrete yard beside the school to monitor the kids. This time of the year especially, an extra adult presence wasn't a bad idea, and the fresh air would do me some good. There was a nice crispness to the weather, and the sky, instead of looking like the usual low-hanging bruise, was a striking dark blue against bright white clouds. A beautiful sky like this appeared rarely in New York City, almost always in September or October, and usually presaged some kind of disaster, like 9/11.

I leaned against the red brick of the building, my eyes automatically noting potential trouble spots. Zak came and stood next to me, too close again, but this time I ignored it. Not far from us, two 10th grade girls—one tall and skinny, the other shorter and curvier—were speaking in raised voices. Another girl came over and the argument seemed to ebb. Some boys joined them and one of the girls laughed. I turned to say something to Zak when I saw a quick movement out of the corner of my eye. Before I could react, Zak was there, pulling two boys apart who were swinging at each other. The smaller of the two, a wild kid named Dez, managed to land a glancing blow across Zak's chin. The whole thing was over as quickly as it had begun. I moved to haul Dez into Malika's office.

"Leave it," Zak said. "It was nothing."

Ignoring him, I reached for Dez's arm. He shrunk from me, a terrified look on his face that stopped me cold. I dropped my hands quickly and walked off in the other direction, making a complete circuit around the school building. By the time I got back, the group had dispersed. I approached Zak, my eyes sweeping him for signs of injury.

"I'm fine," he said. "What's the matter with you?"

"I don't know," I said, but maybe I did. "Do you have time to talk after school?"

"Sure. You wanna grab a beer?"

"Maybe the coffee shop would be better."

"OK. Catch you later."

Zak left to mingle with the students. He blended right in, like he was one of them.

We were meeting at The Muffin Café. I was thinking through what I would say when I saw Zak biking down the street while texting. I thought about chewing him out, but we had more important transgressions to discuss.

"Annie says hi," he said.

"Um, hi back," I answered, uncomfortable. "Do you want a coffee?" He shook his head as I remembered his recent insomnia. "Or an herbal tea, maybe?"

"No thanks," he answered.

"Something to eat? They have bagels."

"If you need to spend your money on me, how about a muffin? Apple cinnamon."

"Done."

Zak chose a table by the window and picked up a local paper. The small seating area was about half full, people sitting in ones or twos, sipping lattes and tapping on laptops or phones. I came back with my coffee and a muffin for each of us. Steeling myself with a bite of muffin and a sip of black coffee, my fourth today, I jumped right into my planned speech.

"Thanks for being such a good friend the other night. But I want to make sure you know that ... that what we did, we're not going to do it again. It was a one-off, alright?"

"Sure, Jeremy."

"I've thought about it a lot and have several good reasons for this decision."

"You don't need reasons," Zak said, digging into his own muffin.

"Reasons are important," I answered, frustrated he was so easy to convince.

"No one's going to force you to have sex with me again, so stop worrying," Zak said.

"I'm not worried, but could you keep your voice down?"

"I'm not speaking loudly," Zak said.

"One of my reasons is about protecting our friendship. And it's clear I'm right because it's already affecting our friendship. We're arguing."

22

"We're not arguing. I'm saying it's cool, with or without good reasons."

"Normally you'd be interested in my reasons."

"OK, fine," he said, putting his muffin down. "Tell me your reasons."

"Reason number one is that I don't want anything to negatively affect our friendship."

Zak was absorbed in surgically cutting his muffin into bite-sized pieces.

"Reason number two is I'm not gay. I'm not homophobic, it's just that I'm straight."

The corner of Zak's mouth quirked as though he were struggling not to smile.

"Reason number three is Annie. Maybe that should have been reason number one. I know you say you have an open relationship. And it's not that I don't believe that *you* believe it's fine. It's only that I don't know how it could really *be* fine. With Annie, I mean."

I let out my breath and waited, but Zak kept eating.

"Aren't you going to say anything?" I finally asked.

"Thanks for the muffin. It's good. But your homemade ones are better."

"Zak, now you're supposed to tell me if you agree with my reasons or not."

"I told you already. You don't need reasons. You should do what feels right to you."

"Tell me what you think! Is that so much to ask?" I gripped my mug tightly.

Zak sighed. "OK, fine." He leaned back and began counting off with his fingers. "Number one: I don't see how having a physical relationship is bad for our friendship. As far as I'm concerned, it makes me feel closer to you. Number two," he continued, "I'm not saying you're homophobic, but I think you're a bit too concerned about putting people, including yourself, into some kind of binary box. The question shouldn't be 'am I gay or straight?'—and by the way, there are way more categories than that—but 'does this feel good?' And it sure felt good to me." He popped the last piece of muffin into his mouth and chewed it with relish. "As for reason three, which you think is your best reason, it's really your worst. Annie was totally into it. She said—"

"You told her," I said. "You fucking told her after I'd asked you not to."

23

"I never said I wouldn't tell her. Only that I'd think about it. And I did."

"For how long, three seconds?" I shot back at him.

"Listen, Jeremy," Zak said, a rare anger tightening his jaw. "I'm sorry you're upset, but no one, not even you, gets to say what I should and shouldn't tell Annie. What's between Annie and me ... You may think you understand it, or us, but you don't."

He shoved his chair back and said, "I gotta go," tossing a ten-dollar bill onto the table. I wasn't sure if he was giving me money for the muffin I'd paid for or if he simply meant to leave a ridiculously large tip at this place that doesn't even offer table service. The latter would certainly be in character, but I feared the first explanation was more likely. But fuck it, if I wanted to buy him a muffin, I'd buy him a muffin. I left his money where he'd tossed it.

CHAPTER 4

Zak wasn't one to hold a grudge, so when he began keeping his distance from me, I knew it was to respect my need for space. I kept my distance too, mainly because it was hard to stick to my decision about our relationship when he was too close. I told myself things would go back to normal soon. Instead, our distance became an uncomfortable habit.

When Zak started calling me 'Jeremy' like everyone else, I didn't notice at first. Zak often used my given name instead of his nickname for me. Sometime in November, though, I realized I couldn't remember the last time he'd called me 'J'.

Growing up, I didn't have a nickname, at least not after I was eight years old. My parents were formal, well-mannered, socially conservative. They considered nicknames crude. My older sister, Jennifer, had no problem pronouncing my name. The only one who had was gone now and having anyone else call me 'Jemmy,' as he had, would have been too painful.

I don't know why Zak called me 'J,' but I liked it. I knew he meant *J* the letter, rather than 'Jay' because I'd seen him write it, but also because of how he said it, like I was some big fucking letter with a hook on the end. When he said my name like that, I imagined myself like the Catcher in the Rye, using my big hook to make sure no one fell off the cliff. It made me feel useful, like someone with the power to protect.

Maybe this was what I was after when Zak and I and our friend Robyn organized an after-school club for at-risk kids. We were a good team—me, with a background in psychology; Robyn, cool and hip and maternal; and Zak, so popular with the kids and with a natural affinity for those who were troubled.

I was thinking about the kids in our club on that dark, cloudy morning in November when I saw the police cruiser parked outside our school. Seeing a police car in front of your school is worrisome enough, but the way the car was sticking out made me even more uneasy—like the situation were too urgent to bother with parallel parking.

I wanted to check on Zak, but I was late and his classroom was on the second floor. Instead, I concentrated on my lesson, knowing it was important to maintain a calm routine. At some point, I glanced out the window to see the police car driving away, an extra passenger in the back, a figure I thought I recognized.

Third period was a prep time for me, but I was too anxious to concentrate. I took the stairs two by two towards Zak's classroom. The hallway was empty. I peeked through the door's glass transom. Zak was sitting on the corner of his desk, juggling Rubik's Cubes. He did this sometimes when teaching geometry, but juggling was also something he did when agitated.

At lunch break, I went to the teachers' lounge. Zak wasn't there, but everyone was talking about what happened. I learned the police had indeed come to arrest one of the kids in our club: Dez, the one who'd taken a swing at another boy earlier that year. He was in Zak's homeroom, and more than once, Zak had signaled a suspicion of abuse to Child Protective Services. The rumor circulating now was that Dez had stabbed his stepfather.

"The arrest happened in Zak's classroom," said Jon, who taught science.

"Has anyone seen Zak?" I asked.

"He hasn't been by," Khalil, the tenth-grade history teacher, answered. Maria, who taught math like Zak, shook her head with the others.

"You should look for him," Robyn said, her voice worried.

I went upstairs to Zak's classroom. It was dark. I went back down to the principal's office. Malika was sitting at her desk, her usual smooth demeanor ruffled as she told me she'd be meeting with Zak later. I looked for Zak in the cafeteria, then checked to see if he'd gone out for some air. The clouds were finally emptying their load and the cold rain was falling in depressing grey sheets. Zak's bike was still outside.

Returning to the teachers' lounge, I grabbed my lunch from the refrigerator and decided to try Zak's classroom one last time. It was still dark. Too dark. Why were the venetian blinds down? I pressed my face against the glass, straining my eyes, then forced myself to relax, to adjust to the darkness. There, in the front of the classroom, I could make out a form sitting on the floor. I tried the door. It was

26

locked. I rapped on it, calling Zak's name, then used my keys. Stepping inside, I relocked the door and left the lights off, following an instinct. I found Zak sitting with his back to the wall and slid down next to him.

It was quiet but for our breathing. Beneath the scent of Zak's freshly laundered shirt and the clean smell of his hair was the tang of sweat. The odor wasn't unpleasant, but it told me he was scared. He shifted so his shoulder was touching mine. I didn't move away.

"What happened?" I asked.

"There were two of them, with guns. They took Dez, put him in handcuffs. I tried to protect him. I tried, Jeremy."

"I'm sure you did what you could."

"What will happen to him?"

"That depends. They'll assign him a lawyer."

"They didn't find the knife so maybe they'll release him."

"Maybe."

"I was thinking. We could adopt him."

"What?" I asked, startled by this non-sequitur.

"Annie and I. You know what foster care's like. More of what he's been getting at home. Only strangers'll be doing it to him instead. If we adopted him—"

"Zak, you haven't thought this through. You're ... you're too young."

"I'm not. He's fifteen. I'm almost twice that."

"This isn't a math problem."

"I'm old enough to be his father. I am."

"They're not going to let a teenager like Dez, especially if they confirm there's been sexual abuse ... They won't give him to a young guy like ... to his teacher to adopt."

"I need to help him," Zak said, sounding desperate.

"There are limits to what we can do for our students. Talk to Annie. She's a social worker. She'll know how these things work."

Zak was silent for a moment. "I keep imagining him in jail. What they'll do to him. But ... maybe they won't put him there. Since they didn't find the knife."

27

There was something about what he was saying that bothered me. Something about the knife. This was the second time he'd mentioned it. And he'd said *the* knife rather than *a* knife.

"Zak, was there a knife?"

He didn't answer.

"Where's the knife, Zak?"

He still didn't answer but now I was sure. I slipped my arm around his waist. Zak leaned against me, his breath escaping in one long exhale. I felt a stab of guilt because my arm was around him not for comfort but so I could slide my hand into his pocket and pull out the knife I knew I'd find. He reacted quickly, grabbing my wrist before I could raise my arm.

"Let go, Zak," I said in a calm, firm voice. "I need it. To cut my sandwich. I brought my lunch to share. I bet you haven't eaten all day."

He wavered, confused, just enough for me to rip my arm out of his grip.

"No, J," he said, "There may be blood on the knife."

I froze, still holding the blade. It was about the length of my hand, lightweight and retractable.

"He cuts himself sometimes," Zak added.

This was crazy, Zak was crazy, and what the hell did I think I was doing? But he'd called me 'J' for the first time in over two months. And Malika would be questioning him after school. Something about this was triggering Zak and there was no way he'd get through a meeting with the director carrying the kid's knife in his pocket. I dropped it into my lunchbox—real metal, with a superhero motif. It made a solid clunk when it hit the bottom and I felt Zak's body jolt in response. I took out a cream cheese and jelly sandwich and broke it into two approximate halves. "Here, eat something," I said.

His hands remained on the floor on either side of him. Our bodies were still close enough that I could feel him trembling next to me. I tore off a small piece of the sandwich and offered it to him. After a moment, he opened his mouth and I pushed the piece inside. His tongue grazed my finger. He swallowed and I broke off another piece.

Little by little, I fed him the entire sandwich half. When I started on the second half, he shook his head. "Your turn, J," he said. So I ate it while he studied my face in the darkness. When I was done, he pulled my finger into his mouth and licked away a bit of jam, sucking on the tip of it. I closed my eyes and tried not to think.

I sat with him a few minutes longer, the ticking of the old clock on the wall sounding loud. I wanted very much to put my arms around him, to tell him everything would be OK. I don't believe I'd ever wanted to do anything so badly, but if I let myself do that, there'd be no resisting everything else I wanted to do to him—like shake him, kiss him, fuck him, hide him someplace where he'd be safe from the world. Instead, I closed my lunch box and stood.

"You gonna be OK?" I asked.

"Yeah," he said. "Thanks, J. Thanks ... for the sandwich."

I stayed late that day, grading, eventually seeing Zak leave the building and get on his bike after his meeting with Malika. This would have been a good time to call Annie, to ask her how Zak had been sleeping lately and what he'd said about Dez. I didn't call her. I told myself it was to respect his privacy, but this was a lie. The real reason had more to do with the fact that when I touched myself at night, it would be with the thought of Zak's lips and tongue on my body. I couldn't speak to Annie with this guilty knowledge weighing my words.

I left the classroom, but Malika stopped me in the hallway.

"Dez," she said, her hands clutching a manila folder. Her face was set, but her dark brown eyes were liquid. "He's dead."

My insides turned to cold acid. "What? How—"

"He was shot ... shot by the police. They say he had a knife."

"It's not true," I said, clinging to this, as though it could also make Dez's death untrue.

"I don't want to believe it either, but Dez was ... troubled. He may have been carrying something. Even so, they had guns. Two grown men against a scared child with a pocket knife."

"There was no knife," I repeated. Malika regarded me curiously. I shook my head, unable to explain my certainty. "How ... how did Zak take it?"

29

"I've never seen him so upset. It's admirable how Zak—and you and Robyn too—have forged such strong bonds of caring with the students in your club. I hope it will help get us through this tragedy."

She spoke to me for a few more minutes about counseling resources and organizing a school assembly. I needed to speak to Zak, so when Malika mentioned the letter to the school community she was drafting, I told her I'd let her get back to it.

Walking to the subway, I dialed Zak's number, but there was no answer, so I texted Annie to tell her what happened. After, I took the subway to York Street. When I first moved to the City, I loved my neighborhood and its acronym—DUMBO: Down Under the Manhattan Bridge Overpass. These days, I wasn't sure the brickwork and impressive views of Manhattan made up for the ubiquitousness of hipster culture.

Walking towards downtown, I found a hole-in-the-wall bar where having a switchblade knife in my bag felt less out of place. Annie had texted me back, thanking me for the message and telling me that Zak was safe at home. Relieved, I sipped a beer as the remaining natural light leached from the sky. When it was as dark as it gets downtown, I left, taking Jay Street to the Manhattan Bridge walkway. Mounting the stairs, I made my way towards the center. The wind blew the rain into my face; it felt like needles against my cheeks. With my low tolerance for cold, I was miserable, but glad for the solitude the nasty weather gave me. I walked until I believed myself to be equidistant between the two ends, remembering what Zak had said that night in the bar when I'd talked about Paris. "And bridges," I'd begun, "are romantic," Zak said, completing my thought. That night seemed so long ago.

I glanced around to be sure I was alone. Shivering in the cold wet, I wondered if I was doing the right thing. *It's OK, J,* I imagined Zak saying, hands on my shoulders, that look of trust on his face. I leaned back and flung the knife as far as I could into the rough waters, picturing it sinking into the depths, the blood coming free from the blade and dissipating, no way any longer to know whose blood had stained it. In my mind, though, it was Zak's own blood.

CHAPTER 5

November slipped by, the once bright leaves brown and wet and trodden. When I think back on that month, what I recall is Zak's boundless energy. He was everywhere—spending time with the kids in our club, planning special activities, speaking with students and their families, and, when Malika was too busy to do so herself, meeting with counselors and crisis workers and the press. There were also the demonstrations. This latest police killing of a young man of color had reignited a righteous anger in the community. Malika asked that teachers avoid anything too radical, but I believe she knew Zak attended all the protests.

Zak showed only compassion and strength to our students; with his colleagues, he expressed more fury than anguish. Anguish, though, was his true emotional state. Aside from me, only Robyn seemed to sense how deeply Dez's death had affected Zak. His lively energy hid his distress like a bright sweater hid a bruise, but I'd seen how dark the bruise was and was concerned that, by concealing it, Zak was letting it fester.

The two of us didn't speak of the incident with the knife, but it was never far from my thoughts. How it affected our relationship was complex. It joined us, yet at the same time, it reinforced my instinct to avoid him—the way people tend to avoid others with whom they've shared a morally ambiguous experience. I watched him from afar, waiting with both longing and dread for the moment he'd turn to me for emotional support. That moment never came.

As winter arrived, school gradually returned to normal. Out of respect for Dez, Malika canceled the holiday talent show. Last year, Zak had juggled, and I did my magic act. If I could really do magic, I think I'd have made this whole semester disappear.

Holidays were never easy for me. Family tragedy is a powerful transformer, turning the best times of the year into the worst. Kyra's birth had temporarily reversed that, but I'd managed to destroy my new family too. To add to my loneliness, I hadn't had a normal conversation with my best friend in three months, and my next best friend—Annie—probably hated me.

I'd considered not coming to Zak and Annie's annual party, but Annie had both texted and called me, urging me to attend. Plus, I'd faithfully spent New Year's Eve with Zak for the past thirteen years, ever since that first time when—cold, drunk, lonely, and in the midst of an existential crisis—I'd decided to make a bonfire of my psychology textbooks. The campus had been empty, with almost everyone home for the holidays. Zak—a freshman at the time—had listened to me talk all night while he kept the fire going, feeding it a wooden chair he'd smashed to bits, and his own t-shirt. When campus security showed up, he took the blame for the bonfire while I was puking in the bathroom.

This New Year's, I was sequestered behind the closed door of Annie and Zak's bedroom accompanied by my third vodka and the guests' coats. I sat on the edge of their king-sized bed, which occupied most of the small bedroom's floor space, and reread my sister's text. I had counted so much on Jennifer's promised visit; her last-minute cancellation was a hard blow with everything else in my life imploding.

I listened to snatches of conversation, sudden laughter, the repetitive beat of the music, and wondered if I could slip out of the apartment without anyone noticing. The talk and laughter grew louder and soon came the inevitable countdown: four, three, two, one, "Happy New Year!" I drained the remainder of my drink. Zak was standing in the doorway with two flutes of champagne. Perfect timing with my glass currently empty.

"So this is where you been hiding," he said, closing the door behind him.

"I'm not hiding. I'm just … yeah, hiding."

I reached for one of the flutes, toasted him silently, drank it down. Zak did the same then placed both our glasses on the bedside table. He sat beside me on the bed. I could feel the heat of him where his thigh brushed against mine. I thought I should leave but didn't budge when he put his hand on my shoulder. Instead, I slid mine around his back. Zak took me in his arms.

I grabbed hold of him and fell backwards, onto the pile of coats. I breathed in

32

the smell of leather, of perfume and aftershave, of lilies and chrysanthemum. Of death.

I was a young child again, lying on the bed in the guest room under the pile of coats, imagining what it felt like to drown. Was it like this, the weight on my face and limbs, the lack of air, the desire to disappear and never resurface?

My parents had pulled me out from under the coats and brought me to the funeral. They made me look at the coffin, alarmed at my insistence that my brother and I still played together. The coffin was so small, even for me. At eight years old, I was already big for my age. I could picture my little brother inside, his white-blond hair wet from the river, traces of mud on his little face. I'd told him to stay put, but I knew he'd followed me.

Now Zak's hands stroked my cheeks while he murmured soft, reassuring words. I opened my eyes to my brother's face, but this was wrong. Zak was tall and dark and strong, not blond, not frail. But he was beautiful like my brother. And with the same sweet innocence. My fingers reached to push a lock of hair from his eyes. Zak leaned over and began kissing me. I kissed him back, then turned my head away. "No, please. Please don't," I begged.

Zak stopped, lying quiet in my arms while I held him against me in a death grip. My sweet friend. So good, so alive. I buried my nose in his soft hair, his scent replacing the odor of leather and perfume and death. I breathed deeply, gathering my strength before pushing him off me. I sat up, wiping at my eyes with a sleeve.

"It wasn't your fault, J. You were just a little kid yourself."

I nodded, noncommittally.

Zak repeated, "It wasn't your fault."

"I know. My parents spent a lot of money on a child psychologist just so I'd know that. But I still get sad sometimes. It's OK to be sad when something bad happens. Like with Dez."

I watched Zak carefully. His face was a mask, still and impenetrable. "But your brother—it was so long ago," he said quietly.

I shrugged, letting him sidestep my question. "Yeah. I barely remember his face. I know he was beautiful, though. Everyone said so. I was jealous of the attention he got and ... I was cruel sometimes."

"Sibling rivalry is normal."

"You don't have siblings, do you?"

Zak shook his head slowly.

"You don't like to talk about your childhood," I observed.

"I don't need any brothers or sisters. I have you and Annie."

"And Annie's probably wondering where you are. You should go back out."

"Come with me."

"I will. In a couple of minutes. First I need to pull myself together."

After Zak returned to the party, I smoothed out my clothes and texted my sister before exiting the bedroom to walk down the hall. The living room was decorated with aluminum foil stars, and numbers representing the date were hanging from the ceiling. Annie was the first to notice me, her large eyes concerned rather than angry. She sat with Zak on the couch while he told the story of how he'd climbed naked up the water tower to protest abuses at a nearby detention center. The guests were arranged around them, faces oriented towards Zak, like planets orbiting a bright, hot sun. Zak motioned me over, moving away from Annie to pat the space between them on the couch. As much as I would have liked to bask in the warmth of his physical presence, I couldn't bring myself to get between them.

"I'm heading out. I've had too much to drink," I said.

Robyn, who'd given me a lift to the party, offered to drive me home, but I caught the annoyance on her husband Carlos' face. I told them I'd prefer to walk it off.

"That's a long, cold walk," Annie said. "Let's at least call you a cab. Or crash here."

Crashing at their place would be a very bad idea, so I grabbed my coat and left. As Annie predicted, I was shivering before I was halfway home. I thought about how, with all their insistence that I understand what happened to my little brother, my parents had allowed me to believe he'd drowned. I'd eventually learned he'd died of hypothermia from the river's icy waters. It was Jennifer who'd told me the truth, claiming our parents were protecting me, but even she couldn't explain why they thought imagining my four-year-old brother drowning rather than freezing to

34

death was preferable. Maybe they were right, though. I never developed a phobia of the water, but I still can't bear to be cold.

CHAPTER 6

After New Year's, the weather turned mild. I even got sunburned on my annual ski trip with Robyn and Khalil and the gang. The Sunday afternoon in February when I ran into Annie, though, winter was back with a vengeance.

"Howdy, Jeremy, what brings you to these parts?" she drawled in a fake western accent. It was hard not to smile, hearing this from a totally urban New Yorker in her East Village black.

"Howdy yourself," I answered. "What's with the cowboy talk?"

"It's how you're hunching those big shoulders of yours."

"It's freezing out."

"Come inside and have a coffee with me."

I couldn't politely refuse, so I followed her into an overpriced java joint.

"So," she said, openly looking me up and down. Her cheeks were rosy from the cold and her bright curls spilled out of her stylish wool hat.

"I was dropping Kyra off," I said. "One of her little friends from daycare lives nearby. Tara is supposed to pick her up later."

I glanced out the window, wondering if Zak would show up too. If Annie noticed my discomfort, she didn't say anything. She drew me out about Kyra and how the new custody arrangements were going. I asked her about Sierra and Brooklyn. I'd forgotten how easy it was to talk to Annie. Finally, there was a lull in the conversation. I fastidiously cleaned the muffin crumbs from my plate, picked up my cup. No help there—it was empty.

I hesitated, then asked, "How's Zak?"

"He's been better. He misses you," she told me.

"I've been busy," I mumbled, unable to meet her eye.

"Jeremy," she said, touching my arm. "Can we stop pretending? I realize you're uncomfortable with me knowing what happened between the two of you. But you've had some time to sort things out. Why the distance? Are you angry with him?"

"Angry? No. I mean, he was trying to help me in his own nutty way. And I was drunk and stoned and really ... really fucked up that night. I admit I'm annoyed he said anything. I didn't see the point in upsetting you."

"Why would I be upset? You know we have an open relationship."

"Yeah, but ..."

"But what?" Her tone was suddenly sharp. "Do you think we're shitting you?"

"No! It's only ... I'm sorry, Annie. I don't get it."

"Let me ask you something. When you were with Tara, how often did you have sex?"

I thought about telling her this was personal but that might have sounded a bit hypocritical considering I'd fucked her husband. Partner. Whatever. Besides, Annie was like this—the type of person who could get you to talk about anything. So I answered her frankly.

"On average I'd say maybe two, three times a week?"

"Not bad. When I asked my girlfriends the same question, it was once a week tops. For those with kids, anyway. For me and Zak, it's at least twice—twice a day, I mean."

"Seriously?"

"Yeah. Don't get me wrong. I love having sex with Zak. He's a very sexy guy. But I guess I don't have to tell you that," she added.

I felt my face grow warm.

"Zak's right. You're adorable when you blush," she said, pinching my cheek.

"I guess I deserved that."

Annie laughed. "Yeah, you did. Anyway, what I wanted to say is that I get tired sometimes, so if Zak can go somewhere else to satisfy his needs, why should I have a problem with that? Aside from the fact that I believe in this type of freedom."

"I hear what you're saying, but it's one thing if Zak has occasional sex with some random woman. But with me? How could you be cool with that?"

"Because you're a guy? You think that freaks me out?"

"It freaked me out. You should know, I'd never ... I mean aside from—"

"Have you considered a woman might feel less threatened by that? Or even get off on it?"

"Um. OK, but Zak and I are best friends. It's not like we're just ... getting our rocks off."

"Do you think I should worry?"

"Of course not. Zak would never leave you."

"Damn right he wouldn't," she said, and now I saw she really was angry.

"Annie, I'm sorry, I don't know what I'm saying. This is exactly the kind of conversation I was trying to avoid."

"This conversation is important, if for no other reason than to get any stupid notions out into the open. Jeremy, you need to talk to me. And to Zak."

I made myself look directly at my old friend. My friend who, if I admitted it to myself, I'd always regretted not dating myself.

"Tell me what worries *you*," she said.

I thought hard about how to put this. "Being with Zak ... it couldn't just be casual for me. Maybe I'm not a casual guy. And Zak and I are already best friends. Having a physical relationship too might make it easier to ... I don't know. Accidentally fall in love or something."

I realized I was staring at the table again. I lifted my head to her gentle smile.

"Oh, honey, I reckon you're trying to close that barn door after the horses have done gotten out," she said.

"Being from Upstate New York doesn't make me a cowboy, you know." I was going for lightness, but I felt like I was standing in front of her naked. "Please don't tell Zak about this part of our conversation," I said in a quiet voice.

"No, I don't need to do that. Anyway, I understand now what you're concerned about. But even if Zak were to fall in love with you ..."

"I wasn't talking about him. I was talking about me."

"You don't think Zak would love you back?"

"Zak isn't like other people. Sure he loves me. He loves everybody."

"Alright, I'm not going to argue with you, but only because this is a conversation you should be having with him. Anyway, let's suppose, theoretically, that you and Zak fell in love. I'd be glad. You're a good influence on him. Zak can be hard to deal with sometimes."

I didn't answer her. What was I going to say? Deny I loved him? Tell her I thought this whole conversation was crazy? Annie wasn't stupid. Plus, I understood what she meant about Zak being hard to deal with sometimes, with his moods and unconventional behavior.

"Remember when you used to babysit for Sierra, in the beginning when she was so jealous of her baby brother?" Annie asked.

"Sure."

"We told her that even though we loved Brooklyn, we'd never love her any less—that the more people you love, the bigger your heart gets."

"Did Sierra buy that?" I asked.

"Yes. After all, she loved her mommy *and* her daddy. But what closed the deal was that she loved Brooklyn too."

"I'm so scared of fucking things up," I told Annie quietly.

"Doing nothing is a choice too. Zak needs you. He needs his J. You know how he gets sometimes. And since Dez's death, he's been low. Really low."

I stared at my clenched hands, torn between desire and propriety, with guilt on both sides of the equation. Annie laid her small hands on top of my fists.

"Just go to him. Whether as a friend or as a lover, I don't much care. For that matter, I don't understand why you think being lovers should make me more jealous than you calling him your best friend. Zak's my best friend too."

"I hadn't thought of that."

"So, what are we going to do about our best friend?"

"Where is he?"

"At home. Reading Gödel, Escher, Bach: An Eternal Golden Braid."

"Shit, I better get over there before he does permanent damage to his mind."

"I knew I could count on you, J."

39

CHAPTER 7

The pub we chose was quiet; the loudest conversation was between servers changing shifts. I carried two pints of stout from the bar and seated myself across from Zak. He'd seemed pleased when I'd stopped by, but now I was having trouble reading him. Lifting my mug, I toasted our friendship. I meant to clink glasses but Zak pushed his mug against mine and kept on pushing. I pushed back, matching him push for push, like a reverse tug of war. Finally, he leaned in, like an acrobat moving into a headstand, and sipped from the top of my mug. I returned the favor and took a sip from his. He released the pressure.

"So, I guess we're blood brothers again. Or beer brothers. Or something," I said.

"Yeah, something," he replied, his serious expression belied by the foam mustache on his upper lip. I couldn't resist cleaning it off with my fingertip. He responded with a smile that left me warm all the way through for the first time this winter.

"I've missed you. I haven't been around lately, but that's going to change."

"OK," Zak said happily, like all was forgiven. I felt like such a shitty friend.

"Did Annie tell you … did she mention I ran into her?"

"Yeah, she said she saw you walking up 7th. I guess you were on your way to our place?"

"Yeah," I lied. "I was on my way to see you. We ended up talking about … Well, I understand better now about your relationship and … and everything."

"Cool," Zak said.

We made small talk for a while. When I'd finished my beer and Zak had nearly finished his, I reached for my wallet.

"You want another one?" I asked.

"No."

"Oh," I said, disappointed. "Do you need to go home?"

"Nope."

"So maybe we could hang out or something."

"What'd you have in mind?"

"I don't know. You could come to my place and ... now that I understand about you and Annie, maybe we could, like, see each other."

"See each other?"

"You know. Like we did before?"

"See each other like in seeing your big fat cock up my ass? Is that what you mean?"

I stared down into my mug, my voice low. "Is this the part where you punish me?"

"Don't worry. I'll put you out of your misery soon enough." He swirled the beer around in his mug before drinking the remains down. "You ready?"

I stood quickly, nearly knocking over my chair, grabbed my coat and Zak's arm, and walked us both to the door without a backwards glance. I didn't let go of him until we'd reached my building.

In the elevator, I pulled him towards me. His skin was hot, like someone with a fever. When I put my tongue into his mouth, the fever spread to my body. What if the elevator broke down? I'd take him right here; I needed to have him that badly. My hands moved over his body as I counted the seconds until we got to my floor. The elevator slowed, but too soon. Someone was getting on. I shoved Zak away from me as the doors were sliding open.

Zak's eyes seemed to flash, but in one graceful movement he bent over his sneaker to retie his shoelaces, his body curled around itself. An older woman entered the elevator with a young child, her eyes widening as she took in a boner the size of the state of Florida pointing towards her from my pants. I turned my back, mumbling, "Excuse me, um, we're going up," but she was already smacking at buttons. When the elevator stopped again two floors later, she pulled the kid out the door with a look of disgust.

Zak was making no attempt to hide his laughter, asking if I was sure I was going up and not down, but when I reached for him he slipped out of my grasp.

In the apartment, I wanted to take him in my arms but he kept his distance, looking around as though he hadn't been to my place a million times. He picked up

41

a photo from Kyra's first birthday. Tara and I were on either side of her, me stooped over so Kyra could hold onto my finger. Zak examined the photo thoughtfully before replacing it on the shelf.

"Hey, come here Zak. What are you doing way over there?"

"I haven't been here in a while. Should I drop my pants as soon as I get in the door?"

My face flushed. "Of course not. Excuse my manners. Would you like a drink?"

"No. The pint at the bar was enough for me."

"Something to eat?"

"No, thank you."

"I could put on some music."

"Leave it off. We need to talk."

"I thought we'd talked at the bar. That we were cool now. Talk about what?"

"What the fuck you want."

"I want you. Please, Zak. Come here and I'll show you how much I want you."

"Maybe your body wants me. But what about your head? There's no way I'm gonna have us trade a few minutes of pleasure for another six months of estrangement."

"That won't happen. You took me by surprise the first time. Now I—"

"Describe the kind of relationship you want with me."

"I ... I thought we could be like friends with benefits."

"Do you have any idea how adolescent you sound?"

"It's what they call it. If you have a better name—"

"Fuck-friends, friends with benefits. Whatever. The problem is, you're clueless about the options. Do you even want to be friends?'

"Of course! You're my best friend. I don't want that to change. It's just ... I thought we could be more than that. You're ... you're very important to me."

"OK. We could be like a romantic but asexual couple, physically close but without sex. Maybe that'd be best since you don't think you're bisexual. Wanna hug and see how that goes?"

"Sure." Anything to get him in my arms. "This is nice," I said, holding him, and it was. Even before we'd slept together, we'd been physical with each other. I missed that. I pulled him in tighter and breathed in his scent. It felt so good to have his body next to mine—the softness of his hair, his smooth, hard muscles ...

Zak shoved me with sudden violence. "You're doing it all wrong, Jeremy. I said *not sexual.* You think I can't feel your hard-on?"

"I'm sorry! If this is about what I did in the elevator—"

"It's about knowing what you want."

"I want you. Please. Just, just ..." I was starting to get desperate, which makes me a little stupid. "Take off your clothes. That way we'll know for sure."

A small smile played on the corners of Zak's lips, but it wasn't a nice smile. He took off his pull-over in one smooth motion, then moved away from me before unbuttoning his pants and slowly pulling down the zipper. Each time he removed an article of clothing, he increased his distance from me. When he was totally naked, but now as far from me as he could get while still in the same room, he lifted his arms above his head and turned around. "What do you think, Jeremy? You like what you see?"

"You're beautiful," I whispered, throat dry.

"Yeah, but I'm a man. You get that, right?"

"Yes, but ... I mean, just come here, OK? Please."

"No. You haven't convinced me you're sure yet."

I rubbed my shoulder where he'd shoved me, starting to get angry. "I have an idea. How about you get your ass over here, I fuck you, and then *you* decide if I'm sure."

"I got a better idea. Try to catch me."

I licked my lips. "Why are you doing this? You can't hide from me in my own apartment."

Zak wandered over to the low table where I had a Scrabble game set up and fingered some of the tiles.

"Stop moving those around," I said. I walked towards him and he upended the board. "What the fuck!" I yelled.

"Let's find out how anal-retentive you are. Do you go for me or the tiles?"

I got down on my hands and knees. "I don't have to choose. I'm coming for you too and when I do, you'll be sorry you messed with my game."

Zak laughed and took off towards my bedroom. I watched his ass disappear with a feeling of loss, but I'd have him soon enough. There was no way now I wouldn't have him.

Once the tiles were counted and put away, I searched for Zak in my bedroom. There was no sign of him, so I entered the adjoining bathroom, opening the glass door of the shower. Empty. I exited the bathroom through the outer door that led to the hallway and then Kyra's unoccupied room. When I'd assured myself he hadn't snuck out that way, I returned to the bedroom. I checked the closet, pushing aside my button-down shirts lined up like reluctant soldiers. My skis were propped up in the corner, a few bulky sweaters on a shelf in the back.

I checked under my bed, the only other spot a grown man could hide. All I found was a large dust bunny. I flattened myself out to grab it but only managed to knock it further away. Sensing movement behind me, I stood. Zak seemed to come out of nowhere, shoving me hard and knocking me onto the bed. We immediately started wrestling.

Zak had the advantage at first, both because of his surprise attack and my initial reluctance to fight all out against someone who was naked, smaller than I was, and who'd never previously shown me even the slightest aggression. Once I realized he was fighting for real, I threw myself into it, managing to reverse our positions, but Zak used the momentum to roll us right off the bed. I landed with a dull thud onto my hardwood floor, him right on top of me.

The fall jolted my back painfully, fueling a growing anger. The weird thing was, I was also enjoying myself. I'd always liked contact sports. These days, my sole outlet was the basketball league where I played with Khalil and some other teachers. With his pathological dislike of competition, Zak refused to join us, though he was a natural athlete. Even so, I was surprised by his strength. And his apparent willingness to fight dirty.

Zak jabbed his fingers into my armpit and stomach, which both hurt and

44

tickled. I struggled to immobilize him, shouting, "Fight fair! That's not allowed!"

"I don't have to play by your fucking rules," he responded, pulling out of my grasp.

I scrambled to my feet, backing up a few steps while I pulled off my shirt. It felt wrong to be fully clothed while he was naked. Just because he had no sense of honor didn't mean I had to stoop to his level. I circled him, waiting for the pain and pleasure of the impact of his body against mine. Despite Zak's surprising ferociousness, I was confident I would win. I outweighed him and knew how to fight. I imagined Zak's body pinned under mine while I made him apologize for teasing me. I wanted this with an urgency that was both emotional and physical.

His attack didn't come so I lunged at him. He side-stepped me with a grin. Fuck, he was fast! He spun, kicking me, alarmingly close to the balls. "You sure? You sure about what you want?" he taunted.

That was it. I crouched and drove my shoulder into his stomach. He went down. I picked him up and threw him against the wall, then did it again. While he was still reeling from the impact, I spun him around and pinned him against the wall, grabbing his wrists and pulling his arms outward. I body-slammed him against the wall again, anger and excitement making my heart pound. I locked my right arm around his throat, undoing my pants with my left. I pinned him by the wrists again, my cock pushing up against his ass.

"I think we know what I want now," I said, my voice low and rough, "The question is, what the hell do you want?" When he didn't respond, I body-slammed him again. "Answer me because as angry as I am, I won't fucking rape you."

"Please ..."

"Please what?"

"Please, J ..." he panted. "Condom."

I pawed at the drawer, pulling it off its tracks before finding one. I rolled it on clumsily while keeping Zak pinned to the wall with my hip. I entered him in one savage thrust. Zak arched his back and screamed my name. "J!" he cried in time with my thrusts. "J! J!" His knees buckled and I had to hold him up while I finished.

I leaned against the wall with my head in the crook of my elbow and my eyes closed, blood pounding in my temples. I opened my eyes to cum smeared on my wall and Zak crumpled to the ground. "What are you doing down there?" I asked, almost to myself. I hauled him up and dumped him onto my bed. He didn't stir. I carefully lay down beside but not touching him. My body was covered in sweat but cooling quickly. I began to tremble. What had I done?

Zak's hands were on my shoulders, warm and firm. I couldn't meet his eyes but when he laid his head on my chest, I immediately stopped trembling. An emotion resembling remorse kicked me in the stomach. I wrapped my arms around him.

"Zak, I'm sorry. I'm so sorry." I don't know if I was apologizing for what I thought might have just happened or for what I'd put us through during the last four months.

"Shh," he soothed. "You keep apologizing, I won't let you have sex with me anymore."

CHAPTER 8

Zak lay with his head on my chest while I stroked him carefully, the way I would a wild animal I'd lured and tamed but was afraid might go feral again. I wanted to ask if I'd hurt him but resisted, remembering what he'd said about no more apologizing. I also wanted to ask why he'd acted that way. Zak was far from stupid. He'd known he was provoking me beyond reason. I kept silent, though. I didn't want to risk this moment of peace.

It was Zak who spoke first. "So how've you been lately?"

I started laughing. "You're something, you know that?"

He kissed me gently on the lips. "Tell me how you've been, J."

So I did, attempting to cram the past four months into one evening. He listened as though everything I said was unusually interesting. I spoke about Kyra, about some of my more challenging students, about my book, about my sister Jennifer's new exhibit, about my aunt's recovery from her stroke and theories I favored concerning brain lateralization. I even talked about Tara, but simply to indicate I'd truly gotten over her.

Zak talked too, though less than I did. He didn't speak about Dez but brought up our after-school club. He had some crazy notion about using found materials to create musical instruments and forming a street protest band. I smiled, enjoying the lively expression on his face as he explained his ideas. His lips were about two inches from mine and he interspersed his words with kisses. After a while, when the kisses were coming more frequently than the words, we began to make love again. As rough as I'd been before, this was the measure of how gentle I was now. I took pleasure in how he pushed his body against mine, like a cat begging to be stroked, in how he moaned and sighed under my hands.

I rolled on top of him. He held me tightly, enveloping me in his warmth. I longed to bury myself inside him, but I didn't want to be deprived of the sight of his face and the feel of his tongue moving against mine. When I didn't think I could hold myself back any longer, he wrapped his legs around my hips. Reaching into my drawer, he pulled out a condom and some organic skin lotion I hadn't remembered putting there.

"My hands too rough?" I breathed.

"Not at all," he answered, showing me what he wanted.

He guided me inside him and I moved in and out in a slow, steady rhythm. It was a smooth, smooth ride and I heard myself let out a long, low groan of pleasure. My hand was on his warm neck. I imagined I could feel his blood pulsing. My other hand slid into his, our fingers lacing together. He squeezed hard, just once.

"That was amazing," I said when I was ready to speak. "I never knew you could ... come in the back door from the front like that."

Zak laughed. "You got a way with words, my friend. Yeah, I thought you'd like that. More what you're used to. Like when you're with a woman."

"No, it's because I want to see your beautiful face when I make you come."

My denial wasn't completely honest, but it wasn't a lie either. Though Zak's physique made it hard for me to think of him as anything but masculine, I liked that he wore his hair longish and how soft it felt. He smelled good too, not like how most men smelled. More than that, there was a sweetness to Zak I associated with women, though I'm not sure why. Tara wasn't particularly sweet and even Annie wasn't sweet as much as she was generous and good.

Zak's limbs loosened around me and I slipped out of him. He was already more than half asleep. I stroked his face with the side of my thumb as his eyes closed and opened, more slowly each time. I pulled him on top of me. He burrowed his head in the crook of my neck, sighing.

I didn't want to sleep yet. There was too much to think about. I found thinking easier when Zak was asleep: his wild impulsiveness, his crazy, irresistible ideas temporarily at rest. Though my body was sated and a warm ball of happiness was spreading in my chest, my mind was troubled. "I don't want to hurt you," I whispered into his hair. Zak mumbled something back but I hushed him, telling him I had his back. He sighed again and fell into a deeper slumber.

I tried to imagine what my life would be like now, with him fully in it again, and in this way. My imagination failed me. Instead I thought back to the past few months. In retrospect, it was like I'd been half alive, trying not to feel, resisting and denying my most basic desires. I pushed my mind to the present. It was so good to lie here, letting my hands touch and stroke as they pleased, my lips placing small kisses on Zak's head while he slept, compliant.

I fought sleep but was tired and comfortable with his warm body against mine. My eyes closed to dreams of summer and sun and gentle waves lapping over my body. Much later, I awoke to late night darkness, my bladder full and my right arm asleep. I didn't want to disturb Zak—it was clear he needed this rest—but the longer I lay there the more desperately I needed to pee. Also, there was Annie. What if she were wondering where Zak was? Keeping her guessing wouldn't be a good way to reward her trust. But what if she were asleep? I decided to text her.

I carefully rolled Zak off of me, grabbed my phone, and made my way to the bathroom. My right arm flapped uselessly at my side, a heavy rubbery thing. I made a fist, the pins and needles starting.

After emptying my bladder, I sat on the toilet seat and tapped out a simple message: *Zak's with me. We fell asleep. Didn't want to wake him.* Her response came right away. *No prob, J. I'll see Z at home.* Relieved, I shut my phone. Annie hadn't seemed worried or put out. Then again, she had still been awake.

Returning to the bedroom, I found Zak sitting up, blankets around his hips.

"Sorry I woke you," I said, but he didn't answer. Something seemed off.

"You OK?" I asked. He still didn't answer, so I put my hand on his shoulder. His body was trembling. "Zak, what is it?" I clicked on the bedside light. Zak's eyes were open, pupils dilated like he was drugged. I thought he might be asleep, but then he mumbled my name.

"That's right. It's me. You're at my place."

"J," he repeated. And then, "I killed him."

"What are you saying? Who?"

"J. I killed J!"

A chill went through me, but I took him into my arms. "Shh, it's OK. You had ... you're having a bad dream."

"J," he wailed, trembling.

49

I held him tighter and rocked him, reminded of the night terrors Kyra used to get. I'd never heard of adults experiencing them. I tried to recall what I'd learned from my Internet research. I knew night terrors were a type of sleeping disorder. I thought I remembered something about being too deeply asleep, your brain telling you you're dying. But he wasn't talking about his own death. He was talking about mine.

He continued to silently shake as I rocked him. With Kyra, singing helped when nothing else would, so I began to hum, a tune I'd learned recently but couldn't place. Zak calmed immediately. I remembered where I'd learned the tune—from Zak himself, the first time we'd had sex. He'd put his head on my shoulder and hummed into my ear—a beautiful, haunting melody.

Zak's breathing became slow and regular. He was sleeping peacefully again, but I kept rocking him, nervous the terrors would come back. When at last I laid him down, he murmured my name again.

"I'm here. Sleep now, sweetheart." Disconcerted by the fact that I'd just called Zak 'sweetheart,' I almost missed his next words.

"J," he mumbled, insistent. "... need to keep away from him."

"Who?" I foolishly asked, knowing from his voice he was still talking in his sleep.

"Zak," he answered. "So he doesn't kill you again."

It was a long time before I slept.

When I next woke, I was alone. It was morning, but very early. The bed was still warm where Zak had lain and I could hear the sound of the shower. I relaxed.

Zak came in, body slick and wet hair hanging over his eyes. He gave me a dazzling smile and all my uneasiness evaporated. Still, I felt the need to say something.

"How you feeling this morning? Sleep OK?"

"I slept great. How 'bout you?"

50

"You had a bad dream. Remember?"

His smile faltered. "I never remember my dreams. I ... I should be getting home now."

"Why don't we go to work together?" I said, suddenly desperate to keep him with me. "I could lend you a toothbrush. I have a fresh one, still in the box."

He laughed. "I spent the night with your tongue in my mouth. I'm not worried about using your toothbrush."

"I have some clothes that would fit you too. No need to go all the way back home."

"You really want me showing up to school wearing your clothes, bro?"

"Yeah, you're right. We wouldn't want to ruin your fashion reputation," I replied, ashamed of how he'd zeroed in on my real concern. "It's just ... I don't want you to go yet."

I grabbed his wrist and he let me tug him back into bed. I kissed him roughly, already knowing how to read his moods. I reached for the condoms and took him on his stomach, teeth against his neck. In the shower, he knelt in front of me, sucking and tugging until I reached a shuddering climax again. Zak left with me still in the shower. I let the hot water pound over me, reenacting our sex play in my mind, remembering how he'd laughed and fought as I pinned him to the bed. I carefully avoided thinking about what he'd said in his sleep.

CHAPTER 9

Sundays and Thursdays became Zak days. At first, we mostly had sex, often two or three times in a row. I made a trip to the pharmacy to restock my condom supply, adding a giant pump bottle of water-based lube to my purchases. After a time, Zak and I expanded our routine to include an activity and meal. I'd choose a game like bowling or Scrabble, or sometimes a film. Zak favored long bike rides or walks where we explored far-flung neighborhoods like Dyker Heights or Canarsie. On the weeks I had Kyra, while I prepared supper, the two of them would play together, totally engaged in imaginary adventures. Once Kyra was asleep, I'd work on my book, Zak leaning against me absorbed in some intricate math puzzle, until anticipation of the night's pleasures made concentration impossible.

Zak made love with an intensity and fierce joy that moved me. Though he liked it rough, I developed an ability to sense and satisfy his needs before things went too far, and afterwards, he'd let me be gentle. This pattern seemed to reassure him in some way I didn't fully understand. My only complaint was his fanatical insistence on using condoms. One time, frustrated, I asked him if he thought I'd give him a disease.

"It's not me I'm worried about," he answered, without heat.

Too late, I realized how stupid I was being. "Are you still ... seeing other people?"

"Sure I am. You know that." He smiled patiently, waiting for me to understand. I felt like one of his slower students. "For one thing, there's Annie," he finally said.

"Yeah but Annie ... I mean ... Is she also..."

I was way out of my depth. Zak took pity on me, kissing me gently. "Tell you what, J. Annie's got enough on her plate. And as for me ... I reckon I don't feel much like sleeping with anyone but the two of you right now. How 'bout we all get tested again? Then we'll talk more about the condoms."

Eventually, Zak began inviting me to supper on Fridays. I declined, thinking I should leave the weekend to Annie and the kids. It wasn't until Annie repeated the invitation for three consecutive weeks that I finally accepted. I arrived with a bottle of merlot, two pints of Chunky Monkey, and a bouquet of roses. Annie took the gifts and then my arm, leading me to the table as though I were a VIP. Soon, Friday night at their place became a habit too. Annie, Zak, and the kids made me feel like Kyra and I were part of their family.

Once, after a late night of Monopoly, Annie suggested I stay over. Brooklyn clapped his hands, saying "hurray, a sleepover!" Sierra, however, watched me carefully as, flustered, I refused the invitation. She was nine going on ten and not much got by her—not when she played catcher for her baseball team and not when it came to social interactions either.

I continued to insist our relationship remain secret. Zak wasn't happy but went along. Aside from this small friction point, my life, though unorthodox, was full and happy. I had Kyra, a meaningful job, friendship, a good sex life, and something that felt like a family. My contentment was obvious enough that even Tara noticed. I was at her place one Sunday waiting for Kyra to put some toys in her Supergirl backpack when Tara commented that I seemed happy.

"I'm fine," I answered politely. "How are you?"

"Seriously, Jeremy, what's going on?"

I shrugged, turning towards Kyra's bedroom door.

"You're seeing someone, aren't you? You've got a girlfriend!"

"Is Kyra almost ready?" I asked.

"You're not getting off that easily," she said, dark eyes sparkling. "Tell me about her!"

"You're not standing there asking me about my love life, are you? Not when you have a legal injunction prohibiting me from doing the same?"

Tara had the grace to look uncomfortable but said defiantly, "There's no injunction against *me* asking *you*." I stared her down. "Well there isn't!" she insisted. "Because I never sent you hundreds of texts and called you all day long. I never followed you around when you were meeting someone or—"

"Alright, that's enough. Yes, I did those things and I'm sorry for it. It doesn't mean it was right to use our daughter as a weapon, or for you to humiliate me. And it doesn't mean I'm going to sit here and discuss my private life with you."

"I'm only asking if you have a girlfriend. What if Kyra has questions?"

"Don't worry about Kyra. I'll take care of her."

"Yes, you're a good father. Otherwise, I wouldn't have agreed to joint custody."

"Eventually agreed," I corrected.

Tara sighed. "I know I hurt you."

"You don't know anything—" I stopped, surprised at how angry I still was. "I never would have put you through anything remotely like what you put me through," I finished.

"No, instead you ... Oh, never mind. This isn't getting us anywhere. I'm asking because I'm happy for you. I *want* you to be happy without me."

"I am." I should have left it at that, but in her own way, she was trying to be nice and I was never comfortable being rude. "I want you to be happy too, Tara."

"Thank you," she said, and brightened. "I know! I'll tell you about my love life and in return you can tell me about yours. So, I'm seeing Todd again."

I didn't trust myself to speak, but she must have seen the look on my face.

"I know you never liked him but take it as a compliment. I'm attracted to big men."

"I don't trust him. And there's a difference between being big and being a bully."

"And there's a difference between being a bully and being strong," she countered. "Women like guys who know what they want, not who—"

She saw my expression and didn't finish. I turned my back on her and knocked on Kyra's door. "Come on, Supergirl, it's time to go." Kyra came out, already chatting a mile a minute. "Kiss Mommy goodbye," I told her. Then I hoisted her onto my shoulders and left.

CHAPTER 10

I grabbed one of the sandwiches Annie had packed and settled myself onto the grassy slope running parallel to the first base line. The sky was a hazy blue but cloudless, and there was a good crowd, the opposing team's fans sitting on the opposite side of the field. Annie chatted happily with some other parents, Brooklyn snacking on pumpkin seeds by her side. Zak stood sullenly apart from everyone. I motioned him over. He hesitated, then sat behind me, back to my back, facing away from the baseball field.

"Sierra's pitching today. What will she think with you facing the wrong way?" I said, taking a bite of my sandwich. I knew Zak hated baseball, and I was used to his moods at the end of the school year, but these last few months had spoiled me, with his emotional state ranging from upbeat, to very upbeat, to extremely upbeat.

"I'm hungry," Zak complained, sounding like a petulant child. "Gimme your sandwich."

"No. Not unless you face forward like a normal person."

Zak got up and sat himself right between my legs. I was about to yell at him again when I noticed how shaky he was. Seeing Brooklyn had wandered over, I called out to him: "Tell your mommy to come here. Let's see how fast you are."

Brooklyn took off on his skinny legs and soon returned pulling Annie by the hand.

"What's up?" she asked.

"Could you sit down in front of Zak?"

Annie's eyes went from me to Zak. She did as I asked without questioning. With his body pressed between us, Zak let out a long sigh. Using Annie as a shield, I put my arms around him. "What's the matter?" I whispered.

Zak rested more of his weight against me. I was conscious of his breathing, the smell of his sweat, how his jaw worked as he chewed on my sandwich.

"What are you playing? Can I play too?" Brooklyn asked.

"We're playing sandwich," I said, with sudden inspiration. "Me and your mommy are the bread and your daddy is the meat."

"Daddy's vegetarian. He can't be meat."

"He's the smoked tofu," Annie said, squeezing Zak's hand.

Brooklyn sat down in front of his mom. "Now I'm bread!"

"Then what am I?" Annie asked.

"You can be pickles, Mommy. You like pickles."

Amazingly, as this was going on, Zak fell asleep, head against my shoulder.

In between the third and fourth inning, the coach called Sierra over. She sprinted to the dugout to grab a ball and one of her teammates—a short, solid boy whose black dreadlocks hung to his shoulders. With him trailing behind her, Sierra walked towards us then hesitated, but it was too late to turn away.

"Is this your family?" the boy asked, his eyes sweeping from Brooklyn back to me.

"Some of them. That's my dad and mom and brother." She pointed at me. "The guy in the back's my dad's friend, Jeremy. He ... He's a good ballplayer."

"OK," the boy said. "You wanna go warm up?"

"I'll be right there. I gotta tell my dad something."

Sierra waited until her friend was out of earshot before zeroing in on Zak. "Do you stay up thinking of ways to embarrass me?" She had somehow, and not without reason, decided whatever was going on was her father's fault.

"We're playing sandwich," Brooklyn piped in. "Do you want to play too?"

"This is a *baseball* field so I'm going to play *baseball*. Why don't you do something normal like play catch?"

"Sierra ..." Annie started.

"It's OK," Zak said, yawning and sitting up. "Wanna play catch, Brooklyn?"

Brooklyn scurried away to find his ball and I went in search of another sandwich. I ate it standing behind the backstop. It was the best place to watch Sierra pitch, and here there was no danger Zak would sit on my lap in front of the other parents.

Sierra stood on the mound, her frizzy brown hair pulled away from her face, eyes intently focused on the catcher's glove. She zinged one in, hard and fast, better even than when I'd practiced with her. The reaction of the other team's coach to seeing a girl on the mound changed from smug underestimation to concern. I saw similar reactions from the opposing team's parents, though many of the moms seemed pleased—as if they'd switched allegiances from their kids' baseball team to the feminist solidarity team.

The dads were another story. One particular guy—beer-bellied, broad of shoulder, and with florid cheeks—glared at Sierra with something close to hatred, but when he came to stand behind the backstop too, his white-knuckled grip on the fence made him seem more nervous than aggressive. The other team's pitcher, a big freckled-faced boy with more strength than control, was up at bat. The family resemblance was unmistakable. I had a moment of sympathy for the man when his kid struck out looking and the coach proceeded to ream him out. My sympathy turned sour when the dad started making motions behind the backstop obviously meant to break Sierra's concentration.

"Please stop that," I said. "It's not fair to the pitcher."

"What's it to you? She your kid?"

"She's my friends' daughter."

"Your *friend*," he said. "I saw you over there. Is that what you call it? Sick."

I thought about punching him in the face. I glanced over at Zak. He was alternating between throwing the ball to Brooklyn and swinging him into the air and tickling him. I decided to leave it alone since the guy had stopped trying to distract Sierra. His palpable hostility increased throughout the inning, though, especially when Sierra struck out a third batter with a change-up pitch that seemed to float to the catcher's mitt.

"Fucking girl. Should be playing with dolls," I heard him mumble.

I walked away in search of a beer. That's how I missed Brooklyn's throw that went out of control and hit the asshole, but I saw Annie's eyes widen and heard his curse. I turned. Zak was approaching the guy, holding Brooklyn by the hand.

"Keep your brat away from me," the man said, rubbing his chest.

I took some steps in their direction, but Annie put a restraining hand on my arm.

"Apologize to the man for hitting him, Brooklyn," Zak said.

Brooklyn tried to hide behind Zak's legs. Zak held him gently but firmly by the shoulders, repeating his request in a voice that was kind but allowed for no argument. I turned to Annie. She seemed nervous yet very definite about not interfering.

"I'm ... I'm sorry," Brooklyn stammered.

Zak released him and he ran to his mom. Annie held Brooklyn in her arms, but all her attention was on Zak, so I knew this wasn't over yet.

"Now it's your turn," Zak said to the man. "Apologize for calling Brooklyn a brat."

"Yeah, right," the man said, brushing Zak off.

Zak persisted. "Apologize. You've hurt his feelings. And frightened him."

The man poked his finger into Zak's chest. "You, get out of my face. Maybe someone should teach your son how to throw. And to act like a boy instead of a pansy."

"You're just upset because my daughter pitches better than your son."

The man shoved Zak. I started moving towards them, but Annie grabbed my arm. Zak smiled as he walked up to the guy again. "Apologize," he repeated.

This time the man punched him in the mouth. Zak spat at his feet. The man lunged for Zak, but I was on him before Annie could stop me. I grabbed him by the shoulders and smashed him against the chain link fence of the backstop. It made a metallic groan as it gave under our combined weight.

"You want a fight? Well you got one," I said. I backed up a few steps, standing lightly on the balls of my feet, arms loose and ready.

Conversation around us ceased. People glanced at each other for a clue about how to react. The asshole's eyes darted around nervously. "My fight's with him," he said, pointing to Zak.

"You know he's not gonna hit you back. You get off on that? And you called *me* sick."

I took a step towards him, but now that his opponent was not only willing but anxious to fight, he'd lost interest. He mumbled something about us all needing to cool off, but I wasn't letting him off that easily. Before I let him walk away, Brooklyn had his apology.

At Annie's suggestion, Zak and I left the park. Maybe she thought he and I needed to talk. Or maybe she simply didn't want to deal with him in the mood he was in.

I knew Zak was upset with me, so to please him, I suggested we go on a long walk. He agreed. We ended up walking through some of the scariest neighborhoods I'd ever seen in all my years in New York City. I walked close to him, copying his studied indifference while passing groups of tough-looking young men on street corners. He stopped to talk to one group. I tensed up until I realized he knew one of them. I couldn't decide if this made me feel better or worse.

No one bothered us. I felt almost exultant when we returned to my place late that evening, but Zak still seemed wound up. He grabbed hold of the scaffolding outside my building, looking as though he'd rather scale it than use the elevator. I led him inside, my hand on the back of his neck. Once upstairs, I took down the Scrabble, hoping to distract him. I noticed him playing "cock" and "thrust" and other words with double meanings, but when he wasted another *s* on the word "sex" instead of hooking onto a high-scoring plural, I lost patience.

"You know I hate it when you don't even try," I said.

"I'm trying. I'm just not following your rules."

"They're not 'my rules.' They're the official rules of the game."

"Fuck the official rules."

"It's not fun to play with someone who's following arbitrary, personal rules."

"Sorry you're not having fun. Why don't we say you won?"

"We didn't have to play Scrabble. What do you want to do?"

"Fuck," he said, and walked into the bedroom.

When we were done, I held him, my pleasure making me feel tender towards him. I stroked his lips with my fingertip, kissing them lightly where they were swollen from the punch. "I'm sorry about what happened in the park but don't be so upset. I didn't even hit the guy."

"Would you have, J? If he hadn't've backed off?"

I decided to be honest. "Absolutely."

Zak didn't answer, but his face reflected a strange combination of satisfaction and fear. It had always struck me that Zak's horror of violence came with an equal measure of fascination.

"I know you and Annie are pacifists. I don't share your views, but I respect them."

"J, promise you'll never hit anyone because of me."

"I'm sorry, but you can't ask me to sit there and watch someone hurt you."

Zak got out of bed and began to pace, counting his steps as he walked first the length then the width of my room. I took him by the shoulders to stop his pacing. "Let me get you some ice."

He twisted from my grasp and went to his knees, pressing his face into my crotch. My breath got heavier as he took me into his mouth. I'd rather have held and soothed him, but his warm mouth felt too good around my cock. I came in a sudden, intense spurt, my fingers entwined in his dark curls.

I led Zak back to bed but though it was very late he couldn't sleep. He pushed himself against me, begging me to hold him tighter, to fuck him harder. I could tell he wanted something rough, but I didn't think this was a good idea. I couldn't resist him completely, though, and afterward, I lay spent and exhausted in his arms, sweat and cum making us sticky, my back sore where he'd been digging his fingers into my flesh.

I dozed for a few minutes before waking to Zak's restless turning in bed. I turned with him, spooning him from behind. "Try to sleep," I said. He lay still but I could tell he was wide awake. He guided my hand down to his cock and as tired as I was, I felt mine stiffen in response. I moved against him with my eyes closed, willing him to relax, willing this next time to be the one that satisfied him enough to sleep off his dark mood.

I woke to the sensation of falling. It was 3:13 a.m. and Zak was gone. I called out to him. There was no response. Thinking he might have gone home, I was ashamed to feel a small relief. I got out of bed and pulled on my shorts. His sneakers were still in the hallway. I walked into the kitchen, opened the refrigerator door, closed it. Something seemed out of place. Stepping into the living room, I noticed a slight draft. I turned towards the window. That's when I saw Zak outside on the ledge. I was suddenly wide awake.

"Zak, what are you doing out there? Come inside."

He didn't answer. I put my head and torso out the window. Zak sat shirtless and barefoot, his legs casually dangling over the ledge, like he was sitting on his own stoop rather than over a twenty-four flight drop.

"Zak, come in now! You could fall," I said, as though to a child. I didn't hear an answer, but his lips seemed to be moving. "Zak, please, what are you doing?"

He finally looked towards me. "I'm counting. Now I'll have to start all over again."

A chill ran down my back. "Don't move. I'm coming out."

Without waiting for a reply, I climbed out the window, settling myself carefully onto the outer sill. It was very narrow, too narrow for a man my size. Holding the ledge, I dragged myself sideways, the scrape of my shorts sounding loud as it caught on the rough concrete. When I was close enough, I grabbed hold of Zak's elbow with my left hand. A siren wailed in the distance.

I sat beside him, trying to breathe, trying not to look down. There was a bitter taste at the back of my throat.

Zak touched the side of the building with his hand, caressing the brick as though it were the skin of a lover. He stopped and turned to me like he'd forgotten I was there. "Let go of my arm. You're hurting me," he complained.

"I'm sorry," I answered, without loosening my grip. Zak shifted his weight forward.

"Please, Zak, don't ... don't fall. If you do, I'm going down with you."

He stilled, leaned his head back carefully, and closed his eyes.

"Zak, what are you doing?" He didn't answer but his breathing had slowed. "Fuck, are you falling asleep? Zak!"

"Shh, Jeremy, I can hear you."

I took a long, shaky breath, checked my grip on the ledge, squeezed Zak's arm harder.

"Please, Zak. Can we ... can go inside now? Please!"

He opened his eyes and looked down with a hungry longing that made my blood run cold. He leaned forward again and I pulled back on his elbow, nearly slipping from my precarious perch. If he pushed himself off the ledge, there was no question that I'd be falling right behind him. Still, I couldn't make myself let go. Zak turned to me, an immense curiosity on his face, and blinked. "OK, J."

I swallowed, carefully scooting over to my right, leading him by the elbow. When I was in front of the open part of the window again, I climbed inside, still holding his arm and guiding him. As soon as he was past the open glass, I grabbed him around the chest and hauled him through the rest of the way, slamming the window closed and locking it. I dragged him into the bedroom, threw him to the ground, and closed the bedroom door, sinking down in front of it. My face was in my hands and my chest was heaving. "Oh God, oh God," I kept repeating.

Zak crawled towards me. "Don't come near here," I shouted, a breath away from losing control. "Get on the bed and ... go to sleep. Do what I tell you."

Zak climbed up into the bed but couldn't lie still. He finally sat up with his arms wrapped around his knees. "J," he whispered. He was shaking so violently I could see his teeth chattering from where I sat. I walked towards the bed, reaching for the extra blanket. I saw his quick movement and tackled him halfway to the door. He struggled with the desperate strength of someone fighting for his life. Only it was the reverse.

I tightened the choke hold I had on him. His pulse fluttered against my forearm. "Stop struggling!" I shouted. "If not, I swear, I'll knock you out." He strained against me. "I beg you, Zak, don't make me hit you. If you have even the smallest feeling for me ..."

He went limp. I waited, not trusting him, until he began to sob. "Lemme go," he begged.

I folded him carefully into my arms. "I'm sorry. I can't."

"Please, please ... I need to go outside. You don't have to watch."

"Shut up. Don't ... don't talk."

I held him, trying not to listen to his sobs because the sound made my stomach

62

twist. I rocked him and said, "It's OK, it's OK," but it wasn't OK. Nothing was OK. "You're just tired," I tried. "Very, very tired. It's why you're not ... not yourself. You need to sleep. Everything will be OK. Shh, shh, sleep now. I'll hold you and you'll sleep."

Zak quieted. "You're getting heavier," I whispered into his ear. "Your arms and legs are heavy, your head is heavy, your body wants to rest." I knew where these words were coming from—from my hypnosis act. "Sleep now. Sleep," I said.

Long after his breathing told me he was asleep, I held him against me, rocking us both gently. I was exhausted, though, my back aching, so little by little by little, I slowed my movements and pushed myself, with Zak, along the hardwood floor towards the bed. I leaned against it, resting there for a few minutes before somehow pulling us both up onto it. Zak stirred. I rubbed his back until he quieted.

I needed to sleep badly. I told myself it would be safe, that he wouldn't wake, but each time I started drifting off, my heart lurched in my chest, the start of a full-blown panic attack. Finally, I flipped us over so that I was on top. With my weight pressing him to the bed, it would be hard for him to go anywhere, and if he tried, at least it would wake me up.

Sometime later, I woke to find my cheek against Zak's chest. "It's OK, J," he whispered. "Go back to sleep." I closed my eyes and slept to the sound of his heartbeat.

CHAPTER 11

When next I opened my eyes, it was light. Zak pushed against my shoulder. I rolled off of him but caught his wrist as he tried to get up.

"I have to pee," he said.

"I'll come with you."

In the bathroom, I refused to release his wrist. He gave me a half smile and asked, "You gonna hold my cock for me too? If not, you need to let go of my arm."

I let go but stood in the doorway while he peed. "How can you joke?"

Zak sucked on his lower lip. "It's my way of saying I'm OK now."

I waited until we were out of the bathroom before responding. "You need help, Zak."

"I've had help. It didn't work."

"We'll find you a good therapist—an expert in suicide."

"I wasn't trying to commit suicide."

"What the hell were you doing on my window ledge, then?" I took a deep breath, repeated more quietly, "What did you think you were doing?"

He hesitated. "Trying *not to* kill myself."

"I don't understand."

"I was ... delaying, hoping the urge would pass. Something Annie taught me. To resist, to delay. Even when I'm sure you'd all be better off without me, my kids especially. It's why— " He pressed his hands together nervously. I noticed something I hadn't seen in the dark—the multiple cuts running up his forearms.

"Talk to me," I said, newly shaken. "Tell me everything that happened."

Zak sat cross-legged on my bedroom floor. His stillness might have been mistaken for relaxation, but I knew his body, could practically feel his tightly-held stress.

"I waited until you were asleep, then went into the kitchen," he finally began. "I saw the knives. Thought about slitting my throat. I decided to see which knife was sharpest." Zak touched his forearm with his fingertips. "The truth is, I could do it with a butter knife, but I tested all your knives to pass the time, to convince myself not to use them. I thought about how you'd have to clean up the blood. Of how upset you'd be with my blood all over your kitchen. I felt ... bad for you, even though I thought you were stupid for caring about me."

I glanced at him sharply but he avoided my gaze.

"Then I thought of the window," he continued. "I'd jump and no mess. Someone else would find the body. I climbed out but resisted a little longer. I decided to count off three minutes for each of you—Annie, Sierra, Brooklyn, Kyra ... I thought I could wait fifteen more minutes. I started with Sierra, thinking about how she'd feel when I was gone—angry as well as sad. I remember myself at that age, I remember ..." He swallowed hard, Adam's apple bobbing. "When you called my name I'd just gotten up to you."

"Why ... why didn't you jump?"

"It's how you held my arm. At first, I wasn't worried. Figured you'd let go when I started falling. It'd be a reflex, a survival reflex. They've done studies. Related to car seats. People think if there's an accident, they'd hold onto their baby, but they wouldn't. They couldn't help themselves. But when I moved forward on the ledge, you just held on tighter. I worried you wouldn't save yourself in time."

My breath was short with fear, imagining how things could have gone. I slid off the bed to kneel in front of him, grabbing him by the shoulders. "Promise you'll never do anything like that again! That you'll get professional help!"

My fingers dug into his arms, but Zak didn't flinch. He gazed at me with compassion, like I was the one who needed help. "OK, J," he finally answered, but I wasn't convinced.

"Zak, please. I keep seeing you on that ledge."

He pried my hands from his shoulders and kissed my knuckles. I pulled him against me and held him tightly enough that I had trouble taking a full breath. When I finally loosened my hold, Zak lifted his head towards the morning sun slanting through my window. He smiled at me and his face seemed full of light. I flushed with desire, even knowing it was wrong. I should be calling doctors, specialists, Annie. But Zak's fingers moved over my body, igniting it with a gentle fire, and his mouth was against my ear, his whisper airy with passion. "Don't think about what happened. Don't think about what might happen. There's no past, no future. That's the secret I've learned. It's all there, in the math. There's only now."

His tongue moved to my mouth and there were no more words. Just our limbs melting together. Just our heat and our need. Just now and now and now.

Annie stood beside me as I did the dishes. Zak had texted her, then proceeded to cook a huge meal, using most of my groceries and all of my pots and pans. When Annie walked through the door, her pale face and darting eyes told me she knew what had happened. She had no more appetite for Zak's post-suicide-attempt brunch than I did.

"Was there anything that seemed to have triggered it?" she asked me quietly.

"I don't know. Maybe."

"Tell me everything, even details that don't seem important."

I went through the events of the evening, my voice sounding mechanical, emotionless. Meanwhile, my thoughts were going in circles, looking for somewhere safe to land. The same egocentric question kept flashing in my mind: *How could he do this to me?* It was accompanied by an anguished fury so huge I felt I might explode into a thousand tiny pieces.

I shut the water, listening for Zak in the other room. "Your turn, Daddy," I heard Brooklyn say. Then, Zak's voice. "I got a three." I picked up another dirty dish.

Annie chewed on her nail, pushing me for more details. I had glossed over the sex marathon, finding myself tongue-tied, twisted with shame and guilt and other less nameable emotions. I shut the taps again and walked into the living room to check on Zak. The Scrabble tiles were still on the board, the words COCK and THRUST screaming at me in accusation. I swept the tiles into the box and returned to the kitchen and Annie.

"The point is this: nothing I did satisfied him, and I was too tired to keep going. I keep thinking maybe ..." My hand was balled into a fist around the sponge. I spit

66

my words out at her. "Maybe if I could've gotten it up one more time—"

"My God, Jeremy, don't go down that road. I've been down it myself and it's a dead end. This isn't about you."

"It happened on my watch."

Annie touched my arm. "Did you know though? That it was 'a watch,' as you put it?" I didn't respond but she was observing me closely, her green eyes bright. "You didn't, did you? You didn't know Zak had tried to commit suicide before."

I shook my head. Annie's composure broke all at once. "I swear, if I'd known he was ... but I should have." Annie twisted the towel in her hands. "It's just ... I've been so tired. And he's been better since you and he ... And in the park—you're so good with him, Jeremy."

"And I let you down."

"No. You saved his life. I don't know how you did it, but you did."

"I ... I just wouldn't let go of him."

Annie looked at me with wonder, but beneath it I saw the desperation. I felt that way myself, like I was locked in a dark room with no doors but dozens of broken windows. Is this what it felt like to be mentally ill?

"Annie, Zak needs professional help. Maybe ..." I lowered my voice to a whisper. "Maybe you should bring him to the hospital. I could watch Brooklyn, or if you'd rather—"

"Stop whispering. Zak knows we're talking about him. He's crazy, not stupid."

"I didn't want Brooklyn to hear," I said, flushing.

"I'm sorry." Annie tugged at her hair. Her curls were flattened on one side, like she'd just gotten out of bed. "But hospitalization ... it's not an option. I did that once and ..." Annie shuddered. "It was a bad mistake."

"What happened?" Annie didn't answer. "When was this?" I tried instead.

Annie shook her head, carefully polishing a glass from the drainboard before responding.

"I almost lost him. After, I promised Zak I'd never hospitalize him again. And I won't."

I squeezed some more soap onto the sponge and decided to try another approach.

"What do you know about Zak's childhood?"

"Not much more than you do, I guess," Annie said, seeming relieved I hadn't pressed her just before. "That he was born in Iowa and grew up in Nebraska. His mother died giving birth to him and his dad ... He sounded like a strict disciplinarian, but Zak claims he was a bad kid. That doesn't sound like the Zak I know. Wild maybe, but I picture him as sweet."

"Zak told me he was an orphan."

"I've wondered about his father, whether he's still alive, but Zak won't talk about him. I gave up asking because he'd get so upset." She paused. "It's weird, when he refers to his childhood, it's like he's reciting memorized facts. And there are these big gaps. I don't even know his parents' names."

"Some of what you've said does sound strange. Like his mother dying in childbirth. It's like a story from the olden days. Zak's never spoken to me about his mother. He liked to say at college that he was raised by wolves, but I've also heard him say his father was a wolf."

Annie paled and the glass she'd reached for dropped from her hands with an explosive crash. Zak burst into the kitchen, Brooklyn behind him, and stooped down to pick up the broken pieces. "Don't touch that!" Annie shouted. Zak jerked his hand back. "You might cut yourself," she said, color flooding back into her face.

Zak took her in his arms as she began to sob. "Shh, shh," he soothed.

I grabbed the broom while Annie continued to sob against Zak's chest. Brooklyn hugged Annie's legs. "It's OK, Mommy. Jeremy's cleaning it up."

Zak went with Brooklyn to search Kyra's closet for more board games and to let us finish our conversation. I tackled the last sink full of pots.

"This must be a huge shock for you," Annie said, as though it were me, not her, who'd just been crying. "You should take some time to ... to process it. Zak will understand."

"Is that what a friend does? Run when things get difficult?"

"It's what I'd do if I could."

"No, you wouldn't."

"It's exactly what I did by suggesting ... when I let you ... " Annie trailed off.

I waited her out, methodically rinsing the inside and outside of the pot, and shaking the excess water into the sink. I took the towel from Annie and dried the pot too.

"Jeremy, I'm scared. What if I can't help him, stop him? I'm so tired. I ... I can't do this alone anymore." Annie's face crumpled, but she kept herself from crying.

I carefully placed the pot on the range and replaced the towel on the rack. I wanted to hold her in my arms, the way Zak had, but I didn't want to disturb her hard-won equilibrium. Instead, I took her two hands in mine.

"You're not alone. I'm here. I'll do anything."

Annie squeezed my hands. We stood there for a long moment. Finally, her face cleared as though she'd come to some decision. "What's all the scaffolding downstairs?" she asked.

I shrugged at the non sequitur. "My asshole landlord. Trying to drive us out with his bullshit renovations so he can jack up the rent."

"What are you going to do?"

"Stick it out, I guess. I have nowhere else to go and the rent is affordable, by New York standards anyway. Why?"

"Maybe you should move in with us."

"Move in? I don't think ... I mean, I couldn't impose—"

"We could share childcare. I always wanted to live in a communal household."

"I don't know, Annie."

"I'm sorry. I just got through saying you ought to take some time to yourself."

"It's just that it would be ... complicated."

"I'm not suggesting you give up your apartment. We won't ask you for any rent—"

"I'm not worried about the rent—"

" —just chip in for household expenses. You can bring some of your stuff. Our apartment's pretty minimalist. But don't decide right away—"

Brooklyn came into the kitchen to ask if we could have the apple pie à la mode now. I took out the ice cream, welcoming this break from the drama. When it was time for them to go and pick up Sierra, I lifted Brooklyn up into the air to do our airplane trick before hugging Annie goodbye. I hugged Zak too, but a little too long and a little too tightly.

CHAPTER 12

The next morning, I left my apartment at dawn and began to walk. I was physically and emotionally drained, but I sensed the adrenaline pumping through me. *Fight or flight.* Annie wasn't wrong about the urge to run from this situation. I wasn't sure I could handle it, especially with my history.

I tried to think—about Kyra, about school, about my book—about anything other than Zak's body lying broken on the sidewalk. My mind kept drifting back to college, where we first met. In my senior year, I began playing poker as a way to practice risk-taking, something that was hard for me since my brother's death. I enjoyed the slap of the cards, the chink of chips being tossed into the pot, the steady but minimal conversation. Then Zak began to play with us. I'd never met anyone who could calculate odds so quickly or who'd grin no matter what hand he was dealt. Most of all, I'd never seen anyone as outrageously lucky as he was. He loved to go 'all in.' Sometimes he'd do this when he was ahead, but when he was losing and there was no other way to stay in the game, he'd invariably toss in all of his chips.

Recalling this now on the Manhattan Bridge pedestrian path, I nearly smiled. Was it merely six months ago I'd stood here and tossed what I thought might be criminal evidence into the river? I used to believe that I lived by certain rules, yet for Zak, I'd systematically broken more of these rules than I could name. And I'd do it all again to wake up to his sweet smile, to feel his strong, lively body move under mine. Who was I fooling? I was already all in. It remained only to own up to it.

I called Annie and told her I'd move in with them. She suggested I wait a week to be sure, but I was already sure. I would fight, not run.

I used the week to prepare. Zak hadn't taken time off after the incident and, at least at school, he somehow seemed fine. Perhaps he was more subdued. If anyone had known our true relationship, they might have suspected a lovers' quarrel.

After each work day, I poured my attention into Kyra, and once she was asleep, I did research. While Annie sought professional help for Zak, I read about suicide, depression, bipolar disorder, trauma—bookmarking the more interesting articles to reread later. It made the situation seem less out of control.

At the end of the week, when I was dropping off Kyra, I casually mentioned the move to Tara, emphasizing its temporary nature.

"They have enough room for you?" she asked.

"Yeah. You know them. Aside from the kitchen table, the only real furniture they own are futons. Plenty of places to sleep. Kyra can stay on the bunk bed in Brooklyn's room."

"Can't she stay with Sierra? Brooklyn's a boy."

"He's six years old, for fuck's sake."

"And I don't want her sleeping on a top bunk. She could fall."

"The bedrail is three feet tall—more a crib than a bed."

I knew I was being argumentative, but I preferred having the discussion focus on Kyra's sleeping arrangements than on mine. I couldn't have said where I'd be sleeping.

I packed a small valise of clothes but brought my guitar, reasoning that I didn't want to risk damage during the renovations. For the same reason, Annie said I could bring the antique chaise longue belonging to my great grandparents. I added some towels, my toiletries, my baseball glove and ball, a basketball, a frisbee, and my computer. Feeling like I'd overpacked, I put back my shaving kit. Maybe I'd grow a beard.

Our first night together, I took everyone out for pizza. After, Sierra asked me to do a magic show like I'd done for her birthday last year. Brooklyn jumped up and down, saying "Please, please!" Since Annie and Zak had no objections, I did a few card tricks and other simple sleight-of-hand, but Sierra wouldn't rest until I did my hypnosis act. I lined the four of them up on the couch and proceeded with some relaxation exercises.

Annie and Zak sat close together, leaning towards one another. While Zak seemed genuinely relaxed, Annie was obviously keyed up, her attention moving from one family member to another. Sierra was also distracted. "Stop wiggling so much, Brooklyn!" she complained.

"Breathe deeply," I said. "Close your eyes if you like. Imagine something pleasant. Clouds. Floating. A meadow filled with flowers."

Brooklyn stopped wiggling.

"As your body begins to get heavy, count down from one hundred. Ninety-nine, ninety-eight .... Your arms are getting heavier .... Eighty-six, Eighty-five .... Your legs are very heavy .... Sixty-five, Sixty-four .... Your head is heavy on your neck. Let it fall back."

Brooklyn leaned his head against his sister's arm and his eyes began to close.

"Look, Mommy! Brooklyn's hypnotized!"

"Am not!" he said, sitting up. He yawned.

"It's past your bedtime. Come." Annie lifted Brooklyn up and carried him to his room.

I turned my attention to Sierra. "You must be sleepy too."

"That won't work with me. I'm staying to watch you hypnotize Daddy. Make him bark like a dog or something."

"Just because someone's hypnotized, it doesn't mean you can get them to do whatever you want." Sierra looked at me skeptically. "Or that you should," I added.

"I have an idea! Daddy once told me he used to play baseball, but when I asked him what position, he wouldn't say. Let's make him tell!"

I glanced over at Zak. He looked comfortable, a small smile on his lips, probably playing along for Sierra's benefit. She'd been grumpy at supper, obviously ill at ease with my intrusion into her family's home. Maybe if I proved entertaining, she'd tolerate my presence better.

"Zak, I want you to imagine your mind drifting through time. Before your children were born. Before you were a teacher. Before college. Let your mind fall backwards."

He seemed to melt into the couch, his chest rising and falling slowly.

"That's good. You're a boy again. The sun is bright. You're in a field, a baseball field, surrounded by your friends. Can you see it?"

73

"Yeah."

"Tell me about it."

"The sky's blue. It's dry and ... I can smell dust."

"It's your turn in the field. Take your position."

Zak stood and moved to the middle of the room. He brought his hands to his chest, his left one clutching a phantom ball. He reminded me of Sierra when she pitched, not only because they were both lefties but because they shared the same look of fierce determination. Zak wound up and let loose. His stance was perfect, his mimed throw powerful.

"Yes! He was a pitcher. I knew it!" Sierra said.

Annie came back into the living room, a look of inquiry on her face.

I winked at her. "We're doing a little demonstration for Sierra."

Sierra grinned as her dad pitched another fast ball. "What's his team called?" she said.

"Tell me the name of your baseball team, Zak."

"The Wolf Cubs," he answered without hesitation.

"How old were you when you started playing?"

"Six," he said. The same age Sierra started.

"And what was the name of your team when you were seven?"

"The Wolf Cubs."

I wondered about this. Kids usually have different teams each year, but I don't know how they did things in Iowa or Nebraska or wherever. "What's your coach's name?"

He hesitated. "John Wolf."

Ah, I thought. "Were you also a *Wolf* Cub when you were Sierra's age?"

I waited, but Zak didn't respond. "Go back in time. You're nine years old. You—"

I stopped. Zak was shaking his head back and forth, his breathing rapid.

"Jeremy ..." Annie said.

"Zak. The game's over. Sit down on the couch and relax," I told him, puzzled.

His eyes darted to the couch, then back at me, blinking rapidly. Sierra noticed his agitation and was beginning to look troubled.

"Why don't you sit on the chaise longue instead. It belonged to my great grandparents." Zak obeyed. In a slow monotone, I told a long, pointless story about my great grandmother's apple muffins, reciting the recipe and describing how my great grandfather would sit on the chaise longue and eat them. Zak relaxed as Sierra shifted with boredom.

I turned to Sierra. "Time for bed. Right, Annie?"

"Right. Go get ready. I'll come tuck you in."

"What about Daddy? Are you gonna leave him hypnotized?" she asked me.

"Don't worry. Your dad's fine."

Satisfied, Sierra left to get ready for bed. Annie followed, shooting me a look over her shoulder. I turned my attention to Zak.

"How do you feel now?"

"Mmm," he said sleepily.

I wasn't sure what was going on. I'd assumed Zak was play-acting for Sierra, but it's true some people are easily hypnotized. It's largely a matter of deep concentration and Zak was certainly capable of that. If Zak were hypnotized, maybe I could learn something about his childhood that could help him.

"Listen carefully. You're safe and relaxed and your mind's clear. You'll hear everything I say and respond 'true' or 'false.' Understand?"

"Mmm," he said.

"Your name is Zak."

He hesitated. Maybe 'Zak' wasn't his full name. He could be very literal-minded. I rephrased the question. "Your nickname is Zak."

"True."

All this time, I'd assumed that 'Zak' was his given name. It was the name on his work I.D. and any document I'd ever seen, though Zak didn't have a drivers' license.

"Your name is … Zachary?"

"False."

"Zachariah?"

"Mmm."

I decided to take that for a yes, sort of. "You're twenty-nine."

"False."

I stopped, surprised, and switched to something else. "You live in Brooklyn."

"True."

"You're a teacher."

"True."

"You teach ... elementary school."

"False."

"You teach high school."

"True."

"You teach math."

"True."

"You're twenty-nine years old," I tried again.

"False."

"You're twenty-eight," I said, thinking he seemed younger than he said he was.

"False," Zak said again.

"You're twenty-nine," I said for a third time.

"No. No." He swallowed and licked his lips.

"What are you doing?" Annie asked as she entered the living room.

"How old is Zak?"

"Twenty-nine," she said.

"False," he whispered to himself.

I hesitated. "Are you ... thirty?"

"True."

"Your birthday is November 13th."

"False."

I couldn't imagine a reason Zak would have lied about both his age and his date of birth. I wondered if Annie had a copy of his birth certificate somewhere. I turned to her, but she seemed confused and nervous.

"You were born in the fall," I ventured.

"False."

"You were born in the spring."

"False."

"The summer."

"True," he said.

"You were born in ... in July."

"Yah," Zak said, his voice barely above a whisper.

"You're Zachariah Heron, thirty years old, born on July—"

Annie grabbed my arm. "Stop it. It's enough."

Zak was counting to himself in a young, breathy voice, his face taut with concentration. I realized that the counting seemed to be calming him, so I decided to use it. "Zak, I want you to close your eyes and begin counting backwards from one hundred. One hundred, ninety-nine," we said together. "Very good. The lower down you get, the better you'll feel...."

When he got down to fifty, he again seemed completely relaxed. I continued.

"You're floating in a quiet place. Stay there and count back silently. When you reach zero, you'll be conscious of your surroundings. When I say your name, you'll sit up feeling fine, alert but sleepy and ready for a good night's rest. You won't think about my questions."

Zak finished counting and opened his eyes. I waited a beat, then said his name. "How are you feeling?" I asked.

"Fine." He got up and stretched. "Tired. I think I'll get ready for bed."

"Good idea," Annie said, following him to the bedroom.

I stood up, not sure what to do. Zak paused and turned back to me. "Coming?"

I looked towards the couch. Annie peered around Zak's shoulder.

"You wouldn't be very comfortable there," she said.

"The chaise longue then," I said.

"Roll over once and you'd be flat on the floor," Zak said with a smile. "C'mon, Jeremy. There's plenty of room on our bed. It's a king-sized."

Annie was watching me with an amused smile on her lips.

"Um, OK. I'll be right in. I'm going to, um, clean up first."

I went into the kitchen and put away the dishes drying on the rack. There was a plate, a butter knife and three glasses in the sink, so I washed them and wiped the counter. I used the broom to sweep up some crumbs. Finding nothing else to do, I sighed and told myself to grow up. I walked down the hall to the bedroom.

Zak and Annie were already under the covers. Zak scooted over to the middle, leaving me the right side of the bed. I closed the door and flipped the light off to undress in the dark. I left on my boxers, slipped into bed beside Zak, and lay perfectly still on my back.

Zak took my hand and pulled it to his chest to press it against a smaller hand—Annie's. I could picture him as he brought his two hands to his chest, exactly as he had when he was imagining himself pitching. I turned to him, but it was too dark to make out his expression. Instead, I pictured the happy smile he had on his face when he recalled being a pitcher. I contrasted this with the look of despair and self-loathing he'd worn the night he'd climbed onto my window ledge. I vowed that no matter what it took, I'd find out what or who had done that to him.

CHAPTER 13

I woke curled around Zak's back, my morning wood throbbing against him. I rolled away and headed for the bathroom. Stepping gingerly over the lip of the claw-foot tub, I closed the heavy, wrap-around curtain and turned on the cold tap. A few seconds later, I heard the bathroom door open.

"Um, I'm in here," I said, wondering if it was one of the kids.

The shower curtain moved, and Zak stepped in.

"Brrr," he said, wrapping his arms around me.

"You've completely reversed the effects of all that good, cold water."

"That's no way to treat your body, J. I have a much better idea."

Zak turned on the other tap. I sighed as strong hands rubbed soap into the back of my shoulders and down my spine. His fingers were gentle on my neck, firm on my arms, playful as he soaped up my chest hair, slow and languid on my hips and cock.

"Now let me do you," I said, voice husky.

I took the soap bar and rubbed it between my palms, turned him around, and soaped him inside and out. He leaned over the tub and I pushed into him, first with my fingers and then with my still-soapy cock. My hands moved over his body as I slid in and out, deeper and deeper. I shuddered with pleasure and relief, the night of tossing and turning a distant memory.

As we were rinsing off, I heard a knock.

"I need to use the bathroom," Sierra said on the other side of the door.

I gave Zak a panicked look. He addressed Sierra.

"Fetch me a towel from the linen closet, K?"

"OK, Daddy."

Zak stepped out of the shower and quickly pulled on his clothes. When Sierra returned with the towel, he was waiting outside the door.

"Thanks, sweetie," I heard Zak say. "Can you get the new oatmeal soap too?"

By the time Sierra was back with the soap, Zak was in his bedroom and I was at the sink brushing my teeth, towel wrapped around my waist.

"Sorry, I didn't know you were in here," Sierra said.

"I'm just about done."

"But where's Daddy?"

"In his room, I guess," I said innocently.

During breakfast, Sierra said, "I don't see your pillows and blanket on the couch."

Before I could improvise, Zak said. "Jeremy slept with us."

"But—" Sierra seemed shocked and I felt ambushed, but Annie met Sierra's eyes without discomfort. "Jeremy wouldn't be comfortable on the couch."

"What about your ... your privacy?"

"You weren't worried about our privacy when you used to sleep with us."

"I was three the last time I slept in your bed!" Sierra said in an outraged voice.

"You slept with us a few months ago," Annie countered.

"That's 'cause I was sick. Are you sick, Jeremy?" Sierra asked, turning to me.

"I gotta get to work," I said, gulping down my coffee. "See you there, Zak."

To avoid awkward questions, I'd already decided not to commute with Zak, despite my desire to keep an eye on him. At work, I put all my mental energy into my teaching, studiously not thinking about the suicide attempt. I think I was still in shock. I displaced my worry to the mystery of Zak's date of birth. By focusing on this puzzle, I could block out the image of him on my window ledge. In any case, watching Zak make jokes, energetically teach, play with our kids, eat with good appetite, it was hard to imagine he wanted to end his own life.

At Zak and Annie's place, too, much was going on to allow time for contemplation. I'd gone from living alone or with one small child to being in the middle of an active family life. Annie and Zak must have spoken to Sierra because she was carefully polite to me, but I could tell that underneath was a storm of suspicion, resentment and confusion. For my part, I bought a lock for the bathroom door, kept to my side of the bed, and woke up early to shower—early enough that Zak could join me and I could be in and out, no pun intended, before little fists were pounding on the door.

I wondered if this was what my life would be now: sleeping on the edge of a bed, only having sex in the shower, dealing with the moral outrage of a ten-year-old. I kept dreaming of falling off beds. The smell of soap and shampoo gave me a boner. At least there was something about my situation I could try to improve. I concentrated on winning over Sierra.

On Friday, Tara asked if I could pick up Kyra from daycare. She had a date with that creep, Todd. I told her yes if I could keep Kyra through the week. To my surprise, Tara agreed.

Kyra was so excited about staying with Brooklyn and Sierra that it was after eleven before I could get her to sleep. Zak came into the bathroom while I stood at the sink getting ready for bed. He slipped his arms around my ribs, peering at us in the mirror.

"Trying out a beard?" he asked. "I like it."

I shrugged. "Too lazy to shave. You really like it?"

"Mmm," he answered, rubbing his face against mine. "We make a nice couple."

"You and Annie make a nice couple," I responded.

"A triple, then."

"You're a couple. I'm a third wheel."

Zak sucked on his lower lip.

"Don't be upset," I told him. "I was thinking, though. When Annie proposed this, she'd talked about sharing childcare. Why don't you two go out tomorrow and let me watch the kids? You guys used to love to go dancing on Saturday nights."

"You don't need to do that."

"You'd be doing me a favor. The thing with Sierra's bothering me."

"Sierra'll get over it. She's always been crazy about you."

"Yeah, but she's not a little kid anymore. If I could spend some time with her..."

"Well, if you really don't mind. It'd be fun to go dancing."

The following night, I left with the kids while Zak and Annie were still dressing for their evening out. I was happy with my plan. Dancing was an ideal activity for Zak since both exercise and music were proven to fight depression. Meanwhile, I'd have some time with Sierra.

We began with a ride on the Roosevelt Island Tramway followed by a restaurant I was confident Annie and Zak would never take them to since it was famous for its footlong hotdogs and violent video games.

"So, what do you want to eat, kids?" I asked after we'd played a few rounds of Skee-ball.

"Ice cream!" Brooklyn answered. "They have 49 flavors! That's seven times seven."

"That's a lot of flavors," I said.

"Are there more flavors here than anywhere in the world?" Brooklyn asked, wide-eyed.

Sierra was watching, like she was waiting for me to trip up.

"I don't know," I answered carefully. "I think they invent new flavors every week."

"Can I invent a flavor?" Brooklyn asked.

"Sure. Go ahead," I told him.

"Banana chocolate jelly bean!"

"I want the flavor Brooklyn adventured!" Kyra said, chubby hands clutching her share of redeemable tickets we'd won earlier.

"That's invented, pumpkin, but supper first, ice cream later."

"You didn't invent that, Brooklyn. It was at the frozen yogurt place," Sierra said.

"Ice cream and yogurt are different!" he said.

"You stole the idea," Sierra insisted. Brooklyn started to get upset.

"Brooklyn didn't steal anything," I said. "But Sierra may be right that you were *inspired* by something you saw at the other place. Artists and inventors are inspired all the time. You're very clever, Brooklyn. And it was also clever of Sierra to realize what inspired you." There, I thought, argue with that.

Sierra scowled, but then her face smoothed. "Can we order anything we want, Jeremy?"

"I suppose, but those foot-long hotdogs—your parents might not approve."

"You wouldn't have to tell them," she said.

Another test, I thought to myself.

82

"I don't want meat. I want pizza," Brooklyn said, coming to the rescue.

"Me too!" Kyra echoed.

"I'd like to order pizza as well," I said, turning to Sierra.

"You like meat. Stop faking it."

"I'm not faking anything. Just because I like meat doesn't mean I can't eat vegetarian. I respect your parents and their beliefs."

Sierra pressed her lips together and looked around, like she was searching for a new target—or inspiration—for her anger. I cut her off. "Since Brooklyn and Kyra know what they're ordering, they can go play. You and I will stay here while you figure out what you want."

I brought the two younger kids to the nearby racing car ride—the type where you steer while desperately avoiding high-speed, dramatic, bloodless traffic accidents. I placed a token in the slot for Brooklyn. In Kyra's case, I didn't bother. The repeating loop of sample race tracks was amusing enough for a kid her age. Returning to our table but keeping my eyes on Kyra and Brooklyn, I addressed Sierra.

"Alright. I've had enough of you trying to pick a fight. Say what you have to say."

"Why do you have to live with us?" she said accusingly.

"Your parents invited me. Because of the renovations. We explained this."

"That's not the real reason. Who are you having sex with, my mom or my dad?"

I almost choked on my root beer. I'd told her to speak her mind, but still. "I'm not going answer that. First of all, my sex life is none of your business."

"I bet it's my dad. Did you hypnotize him? So he'd turn gay and fall in love with you?"

If I hadn't been so angry, I would've laughed. "Second, that's a very rude question. And third, your question includes a hidden assumption. Questions like that are not only rude, they're misleading. It's what sleazy lawyers like—"

I'd been about to say, "like Tara's lawyer," but stopped myself, seeing Kyra happily pretending to drive. Somehow Sierra followed my train of thought.

"You're gonna make me a divorced family, like you! And like my friend Ashley, who never sees her dad anymore, or my friend Nelson whose parents say mean things about each other." Sierra had gone from too-smart-for-her-own-good to a scared, confused kid.

"That's absolutely not going to happen to you. Your parents are the most in-love people I've ever met. You know I introduced them?"

Sierra's face softened. "Yeah. Daddy told me that's one reason you're his best friend."

"Your parents are both my friends. I would never, ever do anything to hurt them. Plus, I wouldn't want to wreck my own perfect fixing-people-up record, would I?"

"I guess not."

Sierra was a bright kid, with good intuition, and could probably sense I was hiding something. I thought about what to say. As all good dissemblers know, if you can't tell a complete truth, tell a partial one. "There is something I haven't told you, but you have to promise not to say anything to your brother." I glanced over to Brooklyn. "He's too young to understand."

"I promise." She leaned towards me.

"Well, your dad hasn't been himself lately. Have you noticed he doesn't sleep well?"

"Yeah. Mommy tries to make him take naps."

"Did you know I almost became a psychologist?" She shook her head. "I studied psychology but decided to become a teacher like your dad. That's how I know not sleeping well can affect your health."

"So that's why you're staying in the bedroom? To help Daddy sleep better?"

Though skeptical, I could tell Sierra wanted to believe this.

"Yeah. Your mom and I, we're trying out a technique. To help him sleep."

"What kind of technique?" she asked, glancing over to Brooklyn and Kyra. She was getting bored with this conversation, which was a good sign.

I thought of that day in the park, how Zak had relaxed against me with Annie sitting in front of him and how I'd called it playing sandwich. "It's called ... sandwiching. And speaking of sandwiches, what do you want to order?" I ventured.

"Can I get that hot dog if I want?"

I hesitated, disappointed. "Sure. I promised. Go ahead."

84

"Nah, I don't feel like a hot dog. I'm gonna get pizza too."

"Good choice," I said, smiling at her.

CHAPTER 14

After our night out, the kids went to bed without an argument—at least once I'd threatened to cancel our plans for ultimate frisbee the next day. I spent the evening with my laptop, as I had for the past few days. I was trying to get my hands on a copy of Zak's birth certificate. Zak had told me the original was lost in a fire but when I attempted to learn more, Annie went from shooting me warning looks to kicking me under the table.

The problem was, without knowing Zak's city of birth, I couldn't make an online request, and applying by mail presented even more obstacles. Luckily, I'd found some family genealogy websites that were tolerant of partial information.

I thought I now knew Zak's real year and month of birth, and Annie said he was born in Iowa, though grew up in Nebraska. I listed 'Heron,' Zak's last name, as his father's surname. If I were Zak, I'd be able to use permutations and combinations to calculate how long it would take to guess right, with thirty-one days in July, two possible states, and several alternate spellings of Zak's name. I went through the possibilities methodically, starting with Iowa.

Although it was slow, tedious work, I refused to get frustrated. Besides, my late-night research gave me something to do while Annie and Zak made love without me in the way. I figured we had the shower; it was only fair they had some time alone between the sheets.

By two a.m., I'd tried all the dates in July using Iowa and various spellings of Zak's name and was about a quarter of the way through Nebraska. I wanted to continue, but my vision was beginning to blur. I closed the computer and went to brush my teeth. Zak and Annie came in the front door as I was undressing in the bedroom. I dove into bed to pretend I was sleeping.

Zak and Annie entered, whispering. I concentrated on breathing evenly. When the light clicked off, I felt the newly darkened room as a coolness on my eyelids. The bed creaked and shifted. I heard more whispering, then wet and breathy sounds. Unable to suppress my curiosity, I opened my eyes a crack to the sight of

Zak moving energetically against Annie, his mouth on one round breast. The streetlamp outside the open window highlighted the musculature of his shoulders, his dark curls bobbing as he sucked on a nipple. I quickly closed my eyes but couldn't help imagining that mouth on my own skin, sucking and licking and taking small nips. I also allowed myself to imagine the opposite—that it was *my* mouth on that soft breast, that hard nipple. I wished I'd had the foresight to turn to the wall.

When they were finished, I waited long minutes before daring to roll onto my side, away from them. As tired as I'd been, I couldn't sleep now with the almost painful hardness between my legs. I felt Zak turn too. He pressed himself against me, his hand finding my cock.

"Let go. I need to use the bathroom," I whispered, pulling away.

"That's not what you need right now," he whispered back.

"Leave it," I insisted. "I don't want to wake Annie."

"Don't worry about Annie," he said, reaching for the lube.

"Zak ..." I said as he pushed me onto my back and straddled me. "Don't."

"Shh. I thought you didn't want to wake Annie."

He pulled me out of my boxers and slid his hand up and down my shaft. I grabbed hold of his arm, squeezing hard. I wanted to push him off but my hands had other ideas. They grabbed his hips. I concentrated on not making a sound as he rode me up and down. I turned my head away from Annie, hoping she couldn't see what we were doing. It was childish, magical thinking—as though by turning away I could keep *her* from seeing *me*.

After we were done, my physical satisfaction was replaced by anger. I turned my back on Zak but he wrapped his arm around my chest.

"Leave me alone," I said.

"Don't be angry."

"I told you to stop. You should have left me to sleep," I whispered.

"You weren't sleeping. You were awake the whole time Annie and I were fucking."

"I ... It doesn't matter. I told you no and you kept right on."

87

"I didn't want you to waste yourself in a handful of toilet paper when there were human beings right in your bed ready to make love with you."

"It's not my bed and I said no."

"J ..." he began, but I turned away again.

The next morning, I was still furious. I went to shower, locking the bathroom door behind me. I ignored Zak during breakfast, instead chatting with the kids about ultimate frisbee while Annie and Zak prepared a picnic lunch.

With three adults and three kids, how to form balanced teams wasn't obvious. I decided Zak and Annie should be together. Kyra would be on their team while I joined forces with the two older kids. This way, I could bond more with Sierra and Brooklyn; also, it might give me a chance to tackle Zak into the dirt. The bonding worked out fine, but most of the tackles found me on the bottom of the pile.

Frisbee was followed by a late picnic lunch. I tried to get Kyra to nap.

"I'm not tired, Daddy," she complained, rubbing her eyes.

Zak yawned ostentatiously, stretching out on the grass. "Come nap with me."

"But I'm not tired," Kyra said, less sure this time.

"Maybe your daddy will tell us a story." Zak winked at me.

I didn't respond to Zak's wink, but began a story about Supergirl and a mermaid fairy. There was no real plot—just a lot of flying and swimming and meeting up with talking animals. Zak took his t-shirt and wrapped it around my sleepy little girl, cradling her against his bare chest. I couldn't say who fell asleep first.

While Zak and Kyra napped in the sun, I gave Sierra some pitching pointers. Brooklyn sat on his mom's lap with a coloring book of the fifty states. He was looking from his book to his father's back, his head turned sideways.

"It's a map," Brooklyn said. "I used to think it was a math puzzle but it's really a map."

"Shh," Annie said, but she turned her head sideways as well.

"What do you mean, Brooklyn?" I whispered.

"That's Nebraska and that's Idaho," Brooklyn whispered back, pointing to Zak's tattoo.

I knelt down beside Brooklyn. Zak's back was illuminated by a sun that had moved lower in the sky. In the brightness of the sun's rays, I realized the tattoo on Zak's lower back wasn't one big form as I'd always seen it. Rather, there were two separate, distinct shapes, each one colored slightly differently.

"Mommy, it's time for practice," Sierra said.

Annie left with Sierra and Brooklyn while I waited for Kyra and Zak to wake up. Sitting cross-legged behind Zak's back, I studied his tattoo. By turning my head sideways as Brooklyn had done, I could now easily discern the two shapes: in the middle was Idaho; below and slightly to the left, where Wyoming should be, was the more regular shape of Nebraska. I straightened up. With Zak horizontal and me vertical, the tattoo took on a whole different form. It looked like a gun, and the gun was pointed to his head.

I wanted to shake the image of the gun, but like those optical illusions of the young woman who turns into an old woman, once you see it, it can't be unseen. I lay down on my side to try to see Idaho instead of the gun. The sun was dropping in the sky and the more indistinct the shapes and colors became, the more I saw the gun and not the state. I had an urge to cover Zak's back, to cover that gun, with my own body. I imagined the smoothness of his skin, my face against his curls, kissing his warm neck and that sweet spot behind his ear.

I remembered last night and stayed where I was. I'd said no and he should have listened. Sometimes the things he made me do to him in bed ... it didn't seem healthy. It was up to me to set some limits.

I concentrated on the mystery of his birthdate. Idaho. Not Iowa, but Idaho. If Zak had really been born in Idaho, maybe I could finally find his birth certificate, the first step to learning about his childhood. I knew there was something dark buried in his past and was sure that if we could find out what it was, we'd be able to understand and treat his mental health problem.

As it got later, the wind picked up. I thought I should wrap my arms around Zak, keep him warm. After all, it was the least I could do with his shirt wrapped around my child. I inched up towards his back but stopped short. No, I shouldn't touch him. It would be sending the wrong message. I lay down a couple of feet behind him to serve as a windbreak. I forced my arms to remain at my sides, my hands clenching into fists. I think I slept a little.

I opened my eyes as Zak was turning towards me. He touched my face and my breath caught in my throat. "Stop," I said gruffly. "I'm ... I'm being a windbreak."

He pulled back. The absence of his hands on me made my chest ache.

"I only wanted to say I'm sorry," Zak said.

I let out a second breath, this time without pain. "Tell me what you're sorry for."

"For last night. And for ... for the nightmare I've made of your life."

"Don't say that." I put my finger on his mouth to stop his words. His lips were smooth and dry. I stroked first his upper lip then the lower one. "Don't ever say that. I'm thankful for every day I have you in my life. Every fucking day."

Zak didn't speak but his eyes were bright with emotion. I moved my fingers from his lips to stroke his eyelids. "It's alright, Zak. I'm not angry anymore."

"I know. I just ... I don't ever want to hurt you."

"Then don't." He didn't answer. I watched him struggle to shake off his darkness. "Zak, it'll be OK. Do you trust me?" He nodded, sucking on his lower lip nervously.

Leaning forward to kiss him, I glanced around at the sloping expanse of the park, clumps of trees marking small, private spaces. Most picnickers had gone or were far off. Satisfied no one was watching, I took Zak in my arms, running my hands down his smooth back—something I'd been wanting to do all day. My anger dissolved. With his mouth on mine, my body felt like it was melting into a sweet, thick liquid.

We made out for a few minutes on the grass, but I had a growing sense of being watched. I turned my head to see Kyra sitting up, her big eyes observing us closely.

Following my gaze, Zak turned his head as well. "Hi, Kyra-Kyra!" he said cheerfully.

"Hi Zacky-Zacky! Watcha doin'?"

"Kissing your daddy."

"Cuz ya love him?"

"Yes," he answered simply.

"Can I have ice cream now?"

That was it. A conversation I'd been dreading was over.

"Supper first, ice cream later," Zak said, unknowingly echoing my words from last night.

"But I am so, so hungry!" Kyra said, in full drama-queen mode.

"We'll fly home very fast," Zak answered for me. "Let's put on your Supergirl cape."

Zak tied his t-shirt loosely around Kyra's shoulders. We each took a hand and ran at full speed towards the exit to the park with Kyra airborne between us.

Later at home, while Zak took the kids for ice cream, I opened my lap top.

"How's the book coming?" Annie asked.

"I'm not working on the book now. I'm searching for Zak's birth certificate."

"How are you doing that?"

"There are these sites for family tree research. But it doesn't help that you told me he was born in Iowa instead of Idaho." It was frustrating, all that wasted time.

"Iowa, Idaho. Geography's not my strong suit," Annie said dismissively. "But what are you using as his date of birth?"

"I've been trying every date in July with various spellings of Zak's name. I used Iowa as the state of birth and now I'll do it all over again with Idaho."

"It must be taking you forever. Let me have that." I hesitated before handing her my laptop. "Zak must know his real date of birth," Annie continued, "even if it's buried in his mind. So, I've been thinking about whether there's a day in July when he behaves strangely."

"Zak always behaves strangely." I was still annoyed about Idaho but I relented, interested in her reasoning process. "He is especially moody when the school year ends. He worries about the kids who aren't coming back."

"But you don't think there's any day in particular?"

"Well, there's the fourth of July. But that's because he's so anti-American."

"Anti-nationalist, you mean."

"He also hates fireworks."

"Zak loves the fireworks on New Year's Eve."

"That's true."

"And there's his tattoo," Annie added. "Brooklyn's right about it being a map, but that doesn't mean it can't be a math puzzle too. You know that string of figures running from Iowa—I mean Idaho—to the Nebraska part of his tattoo? One squared, two squared, three squared. I was trying to make sense out of that."

"And? Come on Annie, Zak will be back with the kids soon."

"One, four, nine. What date is one year, four months and nine days before the date he always claimed was his birthday?"

I did the calculations. "July 4th. This is crazy."

"In my opinion, it's less crazy than shooting in the dark."

"Fine. Let's try."

Annie entered July 4th as the birth date, Idaho as the state, and Zachariah Heron as the name. She moved the cursor to the field where you enter the parents' names.

"I've been entering Heron as the father's last name," I told her.

Annie shrugged and typed 'Heron,' before pressing the enter key. No match.

"I'm going to put Heron as his mother's last name," Annie said.

Red text this time, stating that the first name was a required field.

"Well, that's different," I said. "Any ideas about his mother's first name?"

"No. Did Zak ever mention his parents' names to you?" she asked.

I shook my head. "Like I said, Zak told me he was an orphan, joked that he was raised by wolves." I thought back to the night I did the hypnosis act: The Wolf Cubs, John Wolf, Zak's terrified reaction to some of my questions. I felt a prickle on my neck. I reached for the laptop and typed 'John Wolf' in the field for father's name, pressed enter. There, on the screen, appeared:

Zakarya Heron Wolf, born July 4th to John Wolf and Simza Heron.

"Bingo," I said.

CHAPTER 15

On the fourth of July, the date I now knew was Zak's birthday, I surrendered to an inner voice that ran contrary to the cautious, methodical me everyone saw. The voice spoke for the me who secretly thrilled to Zak's dangerous bike rides and wild, unpredictable nature—the same me who'd tear Zak apart rather than lose him. This voice urged action, to push and see what might shake loose.

The kids were both out and Kyra was with her mother, so Annie and I were using the time to reorganize the apartment. Zak, meanwhile, stared out the window looking morose. I didn't like to see him by the window. I also didn't like the vibe he was giving off—like a trapped animal ready to chew off his own leg. After a while, I suggested to Annie and Zak that they take a walk in the park. I said I'd appreciate a little time to myself, but I had another motive.

When the two of them returned, Zak seemed calmer but no happier. My heart urged me to forget what I'd planned and show some patience, but I forced myself to remember the night he climbed out my window and how useless patience had been then. I brought Zak and Annie into the kitchen and showed them the cake I'd baked.

"Happy birthday, Zak," I said. A look that might have been panic flashed across his face.

"Jeremy," Annie said. "What—"

"Zak must have a good reason for pretending his birthday's in November, but I thought it might be nice to celebrate on the real date. Especially since we missed his thirtieth."

"Stop, Jeremy," Annie said, putting her arm around Zak protectively.

"I ... I don't understand," Zak said, eyes darting nervously around the room.

"Look, I even have a copy of your birth certificate."

I took Zak by the wrist and brought him to the table where the document lay waiting. Zak's finger went to the lines of print, touching his mother's name. He sat down heavily.

"You remember your mom at all, Zak?"

"What? No. She died. When I was born."

"Yeah, that's what Annie told me you'd said. But it's not true, is it? I looked into it. I thought November 13th might be significant since you claimed it was your birthday. Turns out it's the date your mom died. I saw the death certificate."

"I ... but I killed her."

"What are you saying? You were only a toddler when she died."

"Zak, are you OK?" Annie asked.

"Yeah. I'm sorry. It must seem pretty weird, but J's right. My actual birthday is July 4th. I guess I got used to celebrating it in November and forgot about the real date."

This made no sense as an explanation, but Annie's eyes were shooting me such sharp daggers that I didn't press it. Instead, I went into the kitchen to get some plates and forks, and a knife for cutting the cake. I handed the knife to Zak but Annie grabbed it out of his hand and cut the three pieces herself. We waited while Zak took a bite.

"Chocolate—my favorite," he said, trying to smile despite being shaken up.

Annie gripped her fork tightly, like she wanted to use it on me as a weapon. Zak stood up and quickly ran towards the bathroom. Annie and I took off after him but she beat me, arriving just as Zak dropped to his knees in front of the toilet and threw up. He heaved long after there was anything left in his stomach.

Annie made Zak lie down, though he insisted he was fine. He apologized three times, saying the cake was delicious, that it must have been something else that didn't agree with him. He was quiet after that, and when Sierra returned from her outing that evening, Zak seemed like his old self. He even joked about his birthday, telling us we owed him thirty-one kisses.

I was glad Brooklyn was having a sleepover with Robyn's two boys; it was hard enough getting Sierra to bed with all the firecrackers. Annie convinced Zak to turn in soon after. I stayed up, wanting to learn more about Zak's mother. There was something familiar about her name so I googled it. It turned out it'd been used in a Sherlock Holmes movie for a gypsy character. I was intrigued by the idea Zak might have Romani blood. Couldn't that tune he'd taught me be a gypsy melody? The style seemed to fall between Eastern Europe and Italy. I was so absorbed in thinking about music I didn't notice at first when Annie stepped into the living room. I pulled off my headphones and smiled. She didn't smile back.

"Is he OK?" I asked.

"You tell me, Dr. Freud. You're the one who decided to unilaterally bushwhack him with his real birthdate."

I swallowed hard. "Well, he seemed relatively OK."

"Except for the part when he was puking his guts out."

"I'm not saying there was no reaction. He's obviously submerged something deep, some trauma presumably. I thought we'd agreed—"

"What made you think that? Was there a conversation I missed?"

"We talked about his childhood. And searching for his birth certificate—"

"Another thing you started doing on your own."

"Luckily you helped. That was genius, the way you figured out the date."

"Jeremy, stop. This isn't about my pride, it's about Zak. You can't mess around in his head like a bull in a china shop."

"I'm just trying—"

"You need to consult me. Not rush in like ... some damn cowboy! Look, Jeremy, don't you think I might have given Zak's situation some thought?"

"You're right," I said, unable to deal with Annie being upset with me. "It's just that I ... I'm scared. And I can't explain it, but I feel responsible somehow."

"Why would you feel responsible?"

"I don't know," I answered, looking down. To my horror, I felt tears behind my eyes.

"Jeremy ... J," she said softly. "We need to work together. That's all I'm saying."

"You're right. You're absolutely right. I'm sorry."

"It's OK. Just don't let it happen again, cowboy." She smiled at me. Annie had a short fuse, but once the explosion happened, it was over.

She went back into the bedroom. I told her I'd be in soon, but it was another two hours before I got ready for bed. I spent most of that time listening to Romani music. Finally, I took out Simza Heron's death certificate and read over the cause of death for the third time: Intracranial hemorrhage from a blow to the head.

CHAPTER 16

Jemmy, help me! I swam towards my brother's voice as he disappeared into the depths. I wouldn't give up, not this time, even as the cold stabbed at my chest like ice picks, even as his limbs became translucent and his bright eyes went out like a blown match.

Jeremy, help me! My body surged to the surface and I sat upright. I was alone in the bedroom and it was Annie who was calling me. I was out of bed and stumbling into the kitchen before I was fully awake. The light was on and the birthday cake sat on the counter, surrounded by knives of different sizes. My stomach clenched. I bolted down the hall and found Annie in the bathroom. Zak lay naked in the tub, a knife in his hand.

My body lurched towards him and he pressed the blade against his throat, drawing blood. "No!" Annie shouted. Zak and I both froze. I tried to calculate how much more damage he'd be able to do to himself in the time it would take me to wrest control of the knife. *Don't be a fucking cowboy,* I told myself. *Just follow Annie's lead.*

I carefully dropped to my knees, hands in plain view, as Annie resumed her steady stream of words aimed at talking Zak down. "Tell Jeremy the three things you're doing to delay. There are always three," Annie said, her eyes flicking to mine for an instant.

Zak's voice was toneless. "One, I'm counting for everyone. I'm up to Kyra now."

I flinched at the mention of my daughter. Zak watched me, clearly wary.

"Number two, the knife. I took a long time choosing it," he said evenly. "And number three, I've made the water cold," he finished.

"How ... how does that help?" I asked.

"You bleed more slowly in cold water," he said.

I turned to Annie, feeling a fresh wave of sick panic. All her attention was on Zak. Her knuckles were white where they gripped the side of the bathtub, but it was the blue tinge to Zak's lips that spurred me to action.

"Let's add some warm water," I said. Annie seemed confused, but I persisted. "Please, Zak. Seeing you wet and so cold ... it's like seeing my brother all over again."

Zak sucked on his lower lip, then nodded.

I turned on the hot water tap, moving slowly and deliberately. "I'm sorry, Zak. I've taken away one of your ways to delay. You'll need another now."

"Jeremy's right. You need three. Your lucky number," Annie chimed in.

"I ... I don't know what else to do," Zak said hopelessly.

"Let me hypnotize you," I told him.

"You said hypnosis can't change a person's will."

"I only want to help you relax."

Zak hesitated, testing his grip on the knife before agreeing.

It was hard to put him under until it came to me to use the fact that he was in a bath. "You're floating. Floating in peaceful waters," I said. I thought about how he'd claimed his mother had died in childbirth. "You're in a womb," I continued. "Nourished and protected. They say some people can remember their birth. Try to think back to before you were born."

I talked about how infants are bathed in tepid waters, the same temperature as their bodies, so they feel nothing at all. That's what Zak needed right now. To feel nothing. His psychic pain lit his eyes like a terrible fire.

The images of wombs and floating, of peace and safety, eventually seemed to do the trick. Some of the stress left Zak's face. His eyes were locked to mine, attentive and trusting. I began a full relaxation litany, focusing on his muscles one by one. Finally, I got to his arms.

"Your arms are heavy. Let the muscles relax, your arms drop, your hands loosen."

I dared not move as Zak's arms fell to his sides, fingers opening as the knife slowly slid from his grasp. Annie's hand darted into the tub. She grabbed the knife and left the bathroom with it. It was then that Zak realized what had happened. He folded his legs to his chest and pressed his face to his knees, letting out a muffled wail.

"It's OK. Everything's OK now," I said.

Annie returned a few minutes later. I assumed she'd checked on Sierra. I supported Zak in the water as he lay curled in the fetal position. The water was a cloudy pink from the blood, reinforcing the image of childbirth.

"It's time to come out now, Zak," I said.

I moved to help him out of the bath, but he twisted out of my grasp like a man-sized, slippery fish. I reached for him again and he arched his back, smacking his head against the taps. As he lay stunned in the water, Annie and I together managed to pull him out of the tub. I held him immobile against me while Annie wrapped him in towels.

"Help me get him into the bedroom," she said.

"I got it. Just open the door." He was limp as I lifted him and carried him to bed. Annie patted him with a towel, attempting to simultaneously dry him and staunch the blood from his wounds. Soon, he'd recovered enough from the blow to his head that he began to thrash around. I held him tightly and tried to quiet him. Once again, I hummed the tune he'd taught me, Annie looking on helplessly. "Sing with me, Annie," I said.

I began again. Annie sang along haltingly, an octave higher. Zak reached for her, pushing his face into her breasts.

"Your mother sang that song to you, didn't she?" I said.

He lifted his head up. "I killed her." The calm certitude of his voice gave me a chill.

"How could you have?" Annie said, stroking his face. "You were a baby."

"Who told you that, Zak? Who said you killed her?" I asked.

Zak's demeanor changed completely. He began to tremble. "No one. Don't say that."

"Don't say what?" I asked.

Zak remained silent. I reached for his shoulder. His body folded like a collapsible chair, knees to chest and forehead to knees.

"Please, Zak. Talk to us. Tell us what you remember," I begged.

"I can't," he whispered into the space between his knees. "I can't think about it."

"It's alright," Annie said. "Relax now."

Zak lifted his head and tentatively reached out to touch a lock of Annie's hair.

"Your mother," I said. "Did she look like Annie?"

"Yes," he whispered. "Her hair was dark and curly. She was tall."

Annie had reddish hair and was of average height, if that, but I didn't contradict him.

"I'm sorry, I'm sorry!" Zak said, staring at Annie.

"Hush now. You didn't do anything," Annie said, voice taut with tension.

"I didn't listen," Zak whispered. "I came out from hiding. He saw me."

"Who saw you?" I couldn't keep myself from asking.

"It was the bad man! He made her red!" Zak's voice was filled with terror.

"It's OK, Zak," Annie said. She tried to take his hands though her own were shaking.

Zak pulled away, clearly petrified. "Please, please, please," he said. "I need to hide."

Annie glanced at me. She was pale, shaky; her nerves seemed shot.

"Calm down, Zak. Don't think about it," I said, but it was too late. I'd meant to help Zak face his past but what I'd done was submerge him into a nightmare. The only thing to do was meet him where he was. "I ... I can hide you," I said.

"Where?" Zak said, sounding hopeful.

"Right here. Come to me."

I opened my arms and Zak crawled into them. I rolled on top of him.

"Can he see me?" Zak asked in a small, childish voice.

"No. I'm hiding you. No one can see you now."

"Are you sure?" His body shook beneath mine.

"Hide your arms," I said, and he obeyed, tucking them beneath me. "That's good."

"I'm little now," he whispered. "He can't see me."

"That's right, you're safe," I assured him. "I won't let anyone hurt you."

Annie sat white-faced with her arms wrapped around her chest, but after a moment, she seemed to come out of it. She grabbed the blanket and tucked it around us. Zak's trembling stopped and I concentrated on the rhythm of his chest expanding and contracting under me. I think my mind shut down for a few minutes. I don't remember falling asleep but the next thing I knew, Annie was shaking me awake.

"What?" I said groggily, squinting my eyes against the bedside light.

"I need to take care of Zak's injuries."

I tried to roll off of him but my t-shirt stuck to him where the blood had clotted.

"Annie! Help me," I said.

"Stop twisting around like that. Just take it off."

I awkwardly pulled my head and arms through the holes, the t-shirt still sticking to Zak. Annie carefully peeled it from his skin.

"I'm going to get some first aid supplies from the bathroom. You OK?"

"What?"

"Jeremy, look at me. Does blood make you squeamish?"

"No. Yeah, a little."

"Don't look, then."

I nodded, but when Annie left the bedroom, I turned to Zak. He lay on his back, eyes closed. His chest was smeared in blood, darker around the wound in his neck, like an obscenely wide mouth surrounded by badly applied lipstick. A clump of his hair was stiff with blood, and blood had dripped around his ear. Seeing him like that made me light-headed and nauseated, but I forced myself to not turn away from what my cowboy tactics had done.

Zak woke, moaning softly, as Annie cleaned his wounds.

"Where does it hurt?" she asked. "Your head? Your throat?"

Zak shook his head, shivering.

"Zak, Annie can't help if she doesn't know what's hurting you."

"It burns. My back. I ... I shouldn't have told." A violent shudder shook him.

I held him, hoping the physical contact would be calming. As was often the case, his skin temperature was noticeably warmer than mine. I touched his back. It felt like he had a fever, or a bad sunburn, and it was particularly hot on his lower back, where his tattoo was.

"I understand the problem. It's your tattoo. You've filled it with clues, with information, with ...with things you're not allowed to remember, haven't you?"

Zak didn't answer but he pushed his back against my cool hands. I used my forefinger to stroke the three figures in red Annie had noticed: One squared, two squared, three squared.

"That's good that you did that. But don't think about it now," I said.

We helped Zak to get comfortable. I continued to talk while stroking his back. What I said was mostly nonsense, but my voice seemed to calm him enough that he slept. I wrapped my arm around his chest. Annie was facing him, thigh against his thigh. The bedroom was very quiet. My eyes began to close.

I dreamt I was in a horse-drawn buggy, like in an old cowboy movie. The carriage was pulled by a team of wild horses, and I was fighting to maintain control. Zak sat between Annie and I, whooping and laughing, blood from multiple gunshot wounds reddening his white shirt. I handed Annie the reins and held Zak tightly in my arms.

CHAPTER 17

I read Annie's text and mentally crossed psychiatrist number five off the list. Annie had been going with Zak to all his first sessions. Apparently, today's psychiatrist had been of the "medicate first, ask questions later" variety, a problem since Zak had a deep-seated aversion to meds. This was the third we'd eliminated for this reason. Annie had eliminated two others for being "too easily charmed by Zak." I think I knew what that was code for.

Since the birthday cake incident, I'd been deferring to Annie on all matters related to Zak's mental health. She'd been right about not pushing him too hard, just as she'd been right to let him go into work so soon after his latest suicide attempt. Zak always managed to pull it together for his students.

Zak taught summer school every year, but this was my first time. I'd wondered how he'd handle questions about his injury. Though the head wound didn't show under all his hair, the gauze taped to his neck was bound to draw attention. I'd thought about suggesting he wear a button up shirt, or even a tie, but Zak dressing that way would've stuck out more than a bandage wrapped around his throat.

In the teacher's lounge, Robyn and Maria had looked up, Maria seeming more curious than concerned. Khalil was the first to ask about it. "Cut yourself shaving?" he said.

"Maybe I should grow a beard like Jeremy," Zak answered, smiling easily.

Khalil was a buddy and knew when not to press, but Jon could never resist an opportunity to be an asshole. "I doubt you could," he said. "Besides, Annie's your beard."

"What the fuck's that supposed to mean?" I said, getting in Jon's face.

Robyn put her hand on my arm. "Easy, Jeremy. It's just one of Jon's dumb jokes."

"Yeah," Khalil added. "Save that aggressive shit for the basketball court."

I had let my friends calm me down, wondering how much of what I'd done was an act, a way to divert attention from Zak's injury to my bad temper. The anger felt good, though.

With all of Annie's connections to mental health professionals, I'd been confident that we'd find a good psychiatrist quickly, but now I was beginning to despair. I decided to do what I always did when something important was at stake. I took out my laptop and did some research.

I located a number of websites with search engines for finding a psychiatrist: Psychhealthgrades, Psychology Today, Psychiatrist Search—even Yelp had one. Next, I created a spreadsheet organized by type of mental health problem, screening for factors such as experience, education, and patient satisfaction. Annie and I had both noticed that Zak did better with women, as long as they weren't too young, so I filtered by gender and age too. Given Zak's past negative experiences with mental health treatments, we were particularly interested in a psychiatrist who was willing to stray from standard approaches. The person should also be intelligent, preferably as intelligent as Zak, which wasn't easy. I sometimes forgot what a powerful mind Zak had because of how childish he acted, a trait that had recently become more pronounced. Finally, the psychiatrist had to be willing to accept the presence of Annie or me at Zak's sessions, at least at first.

I soon had a small list of candidates, with my preferred choice at the top. Her name was Laisha McQueen. She was 48, educated at Columbia University but originally from New Orleans. She'd written a number of well-received papers and had collaborated with a psychiatrist in Sweden to explore alternative treatments for bipolar disorder. I smiled when I learned she was multi-lingual, with fluency in Spanish, French, Creole and German.

At home that day, Zak seemed calm, anxious to please—offering to make Annie and I tea after the kids were in bed. While he did that, Annie asked me to check my calendar.

"An appointment with a psychiatrist opened up, but I have a meeting," she explained.

"Forget that appointment," I told her. "I think I found someone good."

"Jeremy, I made the appointment already—"

"Listen, she's a woman, she went to Columbia—"

"Mine's a woman too, and mature. And she's cool, I can tell, and—"

"Mine's published research papers on relevant topics. She speaks five languages."

"I have a positive feeling about this psychiatrist. I think she'll understand Zak better than the others. Like Zak, she's not from the East Coast, and she's from a racialized group ... "

"A racialized group?"

"Well, I don't know what Zak is but he's often taken for Latino, or Native American, or part Black. The psychiatrist I found is African American."

"Oh. Well mine is Irish. Her name is Laisha—"

"McQueen," Annie finished.

Zak chuckled in the kitchen where he was making tea. I hadn't realized he was listening.

"Laisha McQueen?" I repeated. Annie nodded. "But ... how do you know she's Black? There's no photo on the site."

"I met her. I was near her office and decided to take a chance and stop in. In any case, her name's a dead giveaway."

"McQueen?"

"Jeremy, your cowboy's showing. Haven't you noticed Irish surnames aren't uncommon for African Americans? And how many white Laishas do you know?"

Zak, now hooting with laughter, joined us in the living room with three steaming mugs. "She got you good, J. The two of you crack me up. Like an old married couple."

"Whatever," I said ungraciously and entered the appointment into my phone.

Dr. McQueen had an office on the Upper West Side of Manhattan. The furnishings were comfortable, the art adorning the walls interesting yet somehow non-threatening. Perhaps it was the colors—all earth tones with subtle blues and greens—nothing red, nothing frightening. There was one piece that struck me: an image of a tree with a broad, brown trunk, the sky behind it like a turquoise sea with three bright orange suns. I pulled my eyes from this strange, oceanic sky and scanned a set of tastefully framed diplomas and certificates hanging behind the doctor's desk. Lastly, I regarded the doctor herself. She was a large, attractive woman who, like Zak, seemed charged with energy, but unlike Zak, also seemed calm and grounded.

She invited us to sit wherever we wished. I followed Zak to a small, fabric-covered couch. Dr. McQueen went through the usual preliminary questions but seemed more attentive than the others had been. When a response interested her, she'd lean forward slightly, her eyes bright and sharp, and sometimes she'd turn those eyes on me. It made me uncomfortable, but Zak seemed to like her. His smooth, easy responses were gradually replaced by a slight awkwardness, a hesitation as he searched for words. I found it reassuring. I admired Zak's social skills, his easy ways with people, but now I also viewed those things as a kind of armor against the world. It was when he stumbled that I knew he was opening up.

"I understand you were born in Idaho," Dr. McQueen said.

In a flash, Zak's slickness returned. "Annie likes to call Jeremy a cowboy, but I reckon it's me who grew up in the Wild West," he joked.

Dr. McQueen switched gears, asking Zak about his goals and expectations from therapy. If this was intended to put him at ease again, it was brilliant—a subtle reminder that he had a role in controlling the form his therapy took. After that, Zak seemed to relax again, and they were soon chatting like old friends.

"What in your life makes you feel good?"

"Teaching. Being in the classroom."

"And when you're not at work?"

"Playing with my kids. Running. Biking. Dancing with Annie."

"What do you like to do with Jeremy?" she asked.

"Eat his homemade apple muffins," Zak answered, smiling at me, but the smile was all wrong. Why had the slickness returned?

"What do you fear most?" Dr. McQueen asked, changing subjects again.

Zak's smile dimmed. "Hurting my kids. I ... I don't mean physically. I mean ... like if they see me when I'm not well. Or if I try to hurt myself. Or ... " Zak faltered.

"Or what?" she asked gently.

"If I ... leave them without a father."

"What about Annie? Do you fear leaving her too? Do you worry she'd be angry?"

"Angry? No." Zak glanced at me quickly. My chest felt tight with tension, but Zak seemed relatively relaxed. "Annie'd forgive me. Of course I don't want to hurt her. It tears me apart, the thought of hurting her, but she could meet someone else. Someone better than me."

I wanted to shout, to shake him. How could he say these things, imagine these things? How could the doctor let him? I opened my mouth to argue, but Dr. McQueen shut me down with a single look. I swallowed my words and clenched my fists.

"What about Jeremy? Annie said you call him 'J.' Are you afraid of hurting J?"

For an instant, I saw what looked like panic in his eyes.

"Yeah. Jeremy lost his brother when he was very young. He's never gotten over it."

This session suddenly seemed very long to me. I checked the time.

"And?" Dr. McQueen prompted.

"And Jeremy thinks of me as his brother. His little brother."

"Is that so, Jeremy?" She turned to me. "Do you think of Zak as your brother?"

"Yes," I said, clearing my throat. "Yes. Zak is like a brother to me."

"Yet the two of you have a sexual relationship."

I shifted in my seat. "This isn't about me," I mumbled, remembering having heard those words recently.

"No," she said. "But you're important to Zak. You're his best friend, you're his lover, and it seems you're also a kind of brother to him. That's a lot for one relationship. Maybe you both need to think about that, about what you really are to each other."

I wasn't sure if this was a question, but I answered it anyway. "Zak is everything to me."

"I understand. But relax, Jeremy. I'm not going to eat him."

"What—"

"It's your body language. You've interposed yourself between us, like a shield."

She was right. I could have sat in one of the wing-chairs next to the couch but instead I'd chosen to sit right next to Zak and was leaning forward, effectively getting between the two of them. "I ... It's just ..." I restarted. "If you can help Zak, anything I have is yours."

"That's very kind, Jeremy," she said gently, "but unnecessary. This is my job." Then she winked at me, and for a moment, she reminded me of Zak. "But if you like, for the next session, I'd be obliged if you could send Zak or Annie with some of your apple muffins."

CHAPTER 18

nnie and I began to share a cautious optimism about Zak's prognosis. Though there was no breakthrough, the sessions with Dr. McQueen were going well. One of Dr. McQueen's short-term goals was resolving Zak's inability to sleep at night. She put a lot of stock in sleep, claiming she'd seen cases where a mental health problem all but disappeared when the person began to get sufficient rest. It's true the three of us could hardly think through our exhaustion—and fear too. Each time Zak stirred in his sleep, I jolted awake, wondering if he was preparing to climb out the window or grab a knife from the kitchen. For this reason, I was relieved when Dr. McQueen convinced Zak to take a mild sleeping pill at night.

At first, the pills seemed to be working, but soon Zak began to suffer night terrors. He stayed up later and later, claiming he wanted to tire himself out, but I believe it was more to postpone the inevitable moment when he'd have to face whatever horrors awaited his sleeping mind. The first time Zak said he wanted to take a run before bed, Annie signaled that I should go with him. A new ritual developed. While Annie stayed home with the kids, I'd follow Zak to the park. When we got home, sweat soaking my shirt from trying to keep up with him, I'd hold him tightly in my arms until he slept.

Earlier in the year, I'd been invited to participate in a colloquium in Montréal on multi-lingualism in children. With all the drama of the past few months, it had mostly escaped my mind. Had it not, I would have cancelled, but with the conference now the following week, Annie and Zak both urged me to go.

I wondered if Zak might do better without me around, if perhaps the complexity of our relationship was causing him stress. Isn't that what Dr. McQueen had hinted at during our first session? For this reason too, in the end, I decided to go as planned.

I'd expected to miss Kyra while I was away but was surprised by how much I missed Sierra and Brooklyn too. The biggest shock was how much I missed Annie.

I'd gotten used to her calm, loving presence in my life. As for Zak, being away from him was like a constant ache in my chest—a hook in my heart that pulled inexorably.

Despite this, I was glad to have attended the conference. I made some helpful contacts and felt more rested. I hadn't realized how draining it was to be around someone you constantly feared might hurt himself. On my return, I suggested to Annie that she take some time off too. She decided to take Sierra and Brooklyn to see their grandparents in Massachusetts. Since Kyra was with her mother, Zak and I would have the weekend to ourselves.

We decided to treat our time alone as a weekend-long date. We took turns planning activities like we used to do. Saturday would be his day and Sunday would be mine.

Early the next morning, Zak woke me for an all-day bike trip. In less than twenty minutes, we were on the Brooklyn Bridge bike path rising towards pillars that stretched above slate grey water. Once in Manhattan, we pedaled hard uptown. I followed Zak from neighborhood to neighborhood, architecture changing with demographics. Central Park was filled with joggers and dog walkers, a rectangle of green in the middle of an asphalt world.

The sun was high in the sky when we reached the George Washington Bridge. Zak was bursting with energy and high spirits, smiling at me over his shoulder. Gazing down at the vast Hudson River sparkling below, I felt something expand in my chest.

By the time we got to the Palisades Park, we'd pedaled over twenty miles at a breakneck speed, but this was only the beginning. Zak took us through the park's bike trails, choosing the longest routes and most punishing uphill grades. I shifted my gears, stood on my pedals, and refused to ask him to slow down. In the afternoon, we stopped to eat a picnic lunch under the shade of some hemlocks. I pulled off my helmet, sweaty hair plastered to my forehead, happy we'd soon be on our way home. That's when Zak announced we'd be hiking the cliffs.

At first, being off the bike was a relief, until I found myself clinging to sharp stones and small, uprootable trees as Zak scrambled fearlessly up the rock face.

110

After a series of switchbacks, I called out his name. The only response was the echo of laughter riding the wind. I made myself move faster, shouldering the sweat out of my stinging eyes. As I cleared the last rise, I saw Zak standing alone at the precipice. With a rush of adrenaline, I sprang towards him, grabbing and tugging him backwards.

"J, you made it. Hey, you're shaking."

"What ... what were you doing up here?"

"Waiting for you. The view's phenomenal." He pulled at my arm.

"I don't like heights."

"But it's beautiful. And being close to the edge is exciting."

He moved behind me, guiding me to the lookout, hands on my shoulders. I gazed out, oddly level with the sky, the land spread below us. Zak wrapped his arms around me, his chin resting on my shoulder. I leaned back against him and let out a breath, remembering the joy I felt climbing trees as a kid and looking out at the world from above, the branches holding and protecting me. I took a last look, then turned to take Zak's face in my hands.

"You're all the beauty I need. And all the excitement too."

I pushed my tongue into his mouth, simultaneously pushing his body, one step at a time, away from the ledge until we were safely on the main trail again.

When we got home that night, I was clumsy with fatigue, but I knew the exercise was good for Zak. I also knew he'd want something rough from me now. I wouldn't disappoint him, but as exhausted as I was, I'd grab whatever advantage I could. Steeling myself with thoughts of how he'd laughed at me on that last heartbreaking climb, I kicked his legs out from under him. Zak fell sprawling. I yanked his shorts down to his knees and took him right there, pounding him to the floor while he let out gasps of pleasure and pain.

I could happily have fallen asleep right there on the floor with my face in his soft hair, but as soon as I could force myself to move again, I hauled him into the

111

bedroom, his knees still caught in his shorts. He kicked them off while I removed the rest of my own clothing. We hit the bed wrestling. I was grateful for its king-sized surface; if I fell off the bed, I wasn't sure I'd have the strength to climb back up. Zak, though, seemed tireless as he laughed and twisted beneath me. I grabbed him in a bear hug and squeezed his ribs hard, bashing him against the headboard. Putting my hands under his jaw, I pushed his head back and took his throat in my mouth. Zak went completely still.

I shifted until he was fully beneath me. My palms pressed against the base of his jaw, my hands almost covering his face. Even though we'd been exerting ourselves all day in the hot sun, he smelled good to me. I took his Adam's apple in my mouth like a large walnut, and bit down gently. The scar from his suicide attempt was thin and white, luminous in the faint light. I ran my tongue along it. Zak trembled beneath me, his erection pressing against my stomach.

"Be still," I said, and he obeyed. I licked and bit at his throat while I moved against his hot body, slick with sweat. I ran my hands down his torso to his slim hips. He struggled to remain still as I caressed his thighs. They were hard as steel but warm and silky under my fingers. Placing my hands behind his knees, I folded his legs up and outward, forcing his lower back up a few inches. I entered him, pushing hard and deep. He lifted his chin higher as he cried out, exposing more of his naked throat to my hungry mouth. All my exhaustion was forgotten while I thrusted. My body felt strong and whole, every cell vibrating with pleasure.

When we were done, I drifted off to sleep, the movement of air cooling my sweaty body, reminding me of the payoff from those long climbs: the wind on my face and chest as I flew downhill on my bike, Zak ahead of me, arms spread wide, his whoops of joy making me laugh with pleasure.

I woke to the smell of coffee and cooking. My stomach growled plaintively, but there was one thing I wanted more than breakfast: a long, hot shower. I made my way to the bathroom, grateful Zak was in the kitchen and couldn't see me limping. I smiled. Now that I'd survived Zak's Saturday date, I could enjoy the plans I'd made for Sunday—staying home.

Late afternoon, I suggested a nap, remembering my promise to Annie that I'd get Zak to sleep as much as possible. Zak stretched against me, moving his lower body against mine, a warm, frisson of pleasure radiating outward from my cock.

"God, that feels good. Is there a name for this? This rubbing up together?"

"Yeah, it's called frotting."

"Frotting. That makes sense. Like the French *frotter*—to rub."

"It's nice having a linguist in the family."

"You're sweet, you know that?" I said, stroking his cheek.

"What do you mean? You speak at least five languages and—"

"Only four fluently, but I don't mean the linguist part, I mean the family part."

"Of course you're a part of my family. What do you think?"

"I don't know why you'd need me in your family. You already have a family."

"I don't know. You smell right, I reckon," he said. I laughed. "I mean it. Like nutmeg." Zak ran his warm tongue across my lips. "And you taste like apples."

"I sound about as sexy as apple pie," I said, hiding the effect of his words on me.

"You're like a tree—"

"An apple tree?"

"A tall, strong tree," he said, ignoring my tone. "And I love how you talk. The strength. The confidence." He paused but I'd stopped trying to joke. "But most of all," he said slowly, "is the way I feel in your arms. Like in this world of grief and anguish, maybe I can be safe."

I wrapped my arms around him. "You are safe. I won't let you be hurt. I swear."

"You can't keep a person from being hurt. All you can do is help them bear their pain."

"That's not true. I—"

Zak put his fingers to my lips. "Shh, let's not argue. There are other things I'd rather do."

I resisted, my worry for him now utmost in my mind. "You should sleep."

"Soon. But I want you to relax too. Lie on your stomach."

He grinned at me and flexed his fingers. Zak had given me a massage once before and it had been heavenly. I rolled over, sighing as his fingers moved along

113

my muscles, pushing and pressing and rubbing away the tightness. When my back and arms felt as light and smooth as well-worked clay, he moved to my legs. The last vestiges of soreness disappeared under his strong hands. I was so completely relaxed that Zak had to help me turn over to work on the front of me. He massaged my chest and arms and thighs, even my feet and hands. Then he lay on top of me and massaged my temples.

"Sleep now, J," he whispered. "Sleep and dream and I'll be with you."

I was already floating somewhere between sleep and wakefulness. He brushed my lips with his and my mouth opened in response. Kissing him was like breathing—something vital and natural, as necessary and easy as air passing into my lungs.

"Zak," I whispered, wanting to thank him, but I was so sleepy the words slid back down my throat. I moved my hand up his back, hoping he'd understand what I meant: that I loved him, that I was grateful for every day I had him beside me. My hand closed on a lock of his hair as I fell into a deeper sleep.

While I slept, I was conscious of Zak's body on mine. Every so often he would rub against me and it would send a warm wash of pleasure through my veins. I'd surface a little from my sleep, enough to appreciate the sensation, then drift back into slumber, bringing the pleasure with me. Zak would begin a movement, and in my dream, it was completed.

All at once, the fuzzy edges of my drifting visions were replaced by an almost surreal lucidity. I was back at college, where I first met Zak. The fire I'd made of my psychology textbooks was blazing. Zak sat before the fire, his back to me, but turned as I approached.

"I've been waiting for you," he said.

"How could you be waiting for me? The dream just started."

"Nah, you're late as usual."

He smiled good-naturedly, so I shouldn't have minded, but for some weird, dream-logic reason, I believed he needed to understand. "Look, Zak. This is my dream so it couldn't have started without me. I'll prove it. You're about to throw your t-shirt into the fire."

Zak took off his shirt and flung it into the flames. "How'd you know I'd do that?"

"Because you're not real."

"Not real?" he said, sounding hurt.

"I mean this is a dream. *My* dream. We're both asleep."

"Together?" Zak smiled mischievously. I couldn't get over how heartbreakingly young and beautiful he looked. Had I been in love with him even then? I decided to tell him.

"We became lovers. Later on. When we were both living in New York."

"Cool!" he said, seeming pleased. "Hey, J, let's be lovers now! We can change the past, do some kind of time-travel sex paradox."

"You're ... you're not real," I insisted again, feeling troubled.

"I am real. It's me. Zak."

"If you're real, tell me how old you are," I challenged him.

"That's a trick question, isn't it?" The color drained from Zak's face, leaving him a ghostly grey. My heart beat a panicked rhythm in my chest.

"I take it back. Don't answer."

"I have to answer. That's how the game works. You and Annie each get one question." He swallowed hard. "I'm ... I'm seventeen."

Blood began to pour from Zak's throat, bright red against the sick pallor of his skin. He lifted his chin and exposed his neck to me. I was afraid of the blood but knew what I had to do. I leaned over and licked it from his throat. His skin was icy cold against mine.

"I've lost too much blood. Come into the fire with me," he said. I tried to move but my feet wouldn't budge. "Don't be afraid. I'll keep you safe. Fire's my element. Yours is water."

When he took my hand, I could move again. We stepped into the flames together and a wave of pleasure hit me all at once. I pulled Zak against me as the pleasure burned through. Zak began to go translucent in my arms as I realized I was waking up.

"Wait," I cried. "Come back with me!"

"You were right. I'm not real," he whispered through lips turned to smoke.

115

I woke with Zak clutched in my arms, still asleep. I tightened my grip, reassured by his solidity. He stirred and yawned. "I had the weirdest dream," he said.

"Really? Me too."

"What kind of dream did you have?" he asked.

"A wet one, obviously," I said. "But you first."

Zak told me he'd dreamed there was a huge fire and when there was nothing left to burn, he'd decided to throw himself in. I felt a preternatural chill. "What happened then?" I asked.

"I started falling. It was peaceful. You screamed at me not to let go, but I was tired. Then my body began to disappear and I had a horrible thought. What if I wasn't real? I asked Annie to grab hold of me, but she couldn't reach."

"Annie was there too?"

"Yeah. When she realized she couldn't reach me, she asked you to help. 'Cause your arms are longer. But you couldn't reach me either. Then I looked down and you were below me, waiting. I landed right on top of you."

"And then?" I asked, mesmerized.

"I came all over you."

I waited a beat to see if there was more, but of course that was how Zak's dream ended. I started laughing and he laughed with me. I got up and headed for the bathroom.

"Pretty, weird, huh?" Zak said, following me.

"Actually, you should tell Dr. McQueen about it. Dreams can be important. Let's record it while it's fresh."

Zak was reluctant, but back in the living room, I handed him my laptop.

"Is it C-U-M or C-O-M?" he asked a few minutes later, bent over the keyboard.

"What?"

"Like in 'I was coming all over him.' How do you spell it?"

"Zak, that's not the important part of the dream."

"For me, it was the climax."

"Very funny. If you don't want to write the dream down, you don't have to, but you should at least think about what it might mean."

"It means Annie ought to watch us while we fuck."

"Seriously, Zak? That's what you got out of the dream?"

"Yeah. But you're dying to tell me what it *really* means, so go ahead."

So I did. I told him it meant he didn't want to die. That he wanted Annie and me to help him. I waited for Zak to either admit I was right or argue, but instead he just sat there smirking.

"You're such a fucking child sometimes. Can't you take anything seriously?" I snapped.

I turned my back on him to get a hold of my temper. I wanted to fight him, anything to get a real reaction out of him. I spun around and caught an unguarded expression on his face. Not mirth, not anger, but raw, animal fear. "Zak," I said, and the look disappeared as quickly as it came, replaced by that expression of trust that so undid me the first time I saw it. My anger dissolved. "Sorry. I'm probably hangry. Let's get some supper, alright?"

We ordered Chinese takeout—enough for four people. Zak spent the rest of the evening being adorable. He horsed around and kept touching me like he couldn't keep his hands off of me. When the food arrived, I teased him about not knowing how to use chopsticks.

"I'm from a small town in Nebraska," he said, making a rare reference to his childhood.

"I thought you were from Idaho."

"That's where I was born. But I grew up in Nebraska."

I wanted to ask more questions but noticed the subtle tightening of his facial muscles. "No excuses," I said instead. "You've lived in the City for a decade."

I showed him how to use chopsticks, laughing as he ran around the apartment picking up inappropriate objects—like the salt shaker—with his sticks. I told him he was a hazard to both the Eastern and Western worlds and ought to simply let me feed him. He agreed if we retired to the bedroom. "But be careful. Annie'll kill us if we get food in the bed."

I told him not to worry and showed off my forkless prowess, using precise control to place a shred of cabbage, a pea, or a few grains of rice into his open, waiting mouth.

When Zak had his fill, I hungrily shoveled food into my own mouth, but even I couldn't finish all we'd ordered. Soon Zak curled up with his head on my chest and fell asleep—the third night in a row he'd slept without taking anything. It was just past 10 p.m. and Annie and the kids were due home in less than an hour. I told myself I'd get up soon and clear away the remains of our meal, but my full stomach, yesterday's intense physical activity, and Zak's warm body against mine all combined to lull me, the takeout boxes on the bedside tables standing as silent sentries to our unguarded sleep.

CHAPTER 19

I jerked awake to the sound of rattling keys and high-pitched voices. Before I could stir, Sierra appeared in the doorway of the bedroom. She stopped short, her mouth o-shaped as she took in the scene. Annie was behind Sierra, a sleepy Brooklyn against her hip. I carefully slipped out from under Zak, who turned onto his back and stretched. When he saw Annie and the kids were back, he sprang out of bed to wrap his arms around them.

"I missed you, Daddy," Brooklyn said, rubbing his eyes.

Zak lifted him into his arms and kissed his forehead. "I missed you too." Taking Sierra by the hand, he brought the two of them to bed. Sierra peered at me over her shoulder, as though to say she'd deal with me later.

Annie raised her eyebrows, clearly waiting for a report on the weekend. I told her we'd had a good time. Remembering the great sex, I felt myself blush. She regarded me with frank, curious eyes, like she knew what I was thinking and was waiting for details. Instead, I told her Zak had a dream that might be important. Thinking about it, I felt guilty about how I'd lashed out at him. This hadn't been the first time Zak spoke about wanting the three of us to be together, or at least to not hide our lovemaking. I'd assumed this was simply a sexual desire, but perhaps there was more to it, an emotional as well as a physical need he was expressing.

"Annie, let me ask you something. How did you feel, seeing Zak in my arms just now?"

"Good. He looked safe. It made me feel safe too."

"Really? That's ... nice. But how about if ... you know, you saw us—"

"Fucking?"

I blushed again. "It's only that Zak's always asking."

"It wouldn't bother me. Actually, the idea is kind of hot."

I didn't pursue it but thought about this conversation on and off during the week. Zak seemed upbeat following our weekend and excited about the new school year around the corner. I felt able to spend more quality time with Kyra and to work on my book.

The following Friday night, I was at a café glancing through my notes about Montréal's French immersion program when I received a text from Annie.

The kids are at sleepovers. Z and I r waiting for u. Airing a bottle of Merlot.

I put the phone back into my pocket to complete the section I'd almost finished. The phone vibrated again.

Zak says to tell you he's wearing his tight black briefs.

I packed up my laptop. I'd need to hurry; otherwise, the wine might get too oxidized.

Zak sat in bed brushing Annie's hair. Her curls bounced under his ministrations and her cheeks were a rosy pink. She let out a tinkling laugh in response to something Zak whispered as I entered the bedroom. I froze halfway between the door and the bed.

"Sit down, stay a while," Zak said. Annie laughed again and offered me some wine.

I walked slowly towards the bed and took the glass, drinking it down without noticing the taste. Zak refilled my glass, grinning. This time I sipped more slowly. Zak stood and kissed me, his lips and tongue tasting of merlot. Annie put on some music and I brought the wineglass to my lips again. Before I could take more than a couple of sips, Zak had his hands on me. I stepped back, almost spilling the wine. Everything was going too fast.

Zak took me in his arms. "Relax. I know, let's dance." His eyes sparkled with mischief.

"You know I can't dance." Nevertheless, I carefully placed my wineglass on the bedside table. The small, round surface was cluttered with the hairbrush, a box of tissues, a cell phone, and Zak's Rubik's Cube key chain. There was also an old photo from college Zak had recently dug up and mounted inside a heart-shaped paper weight. Annie was on the right, Zak's arm draped around her shoulder, the two of them grinning happily. I stood behind them, stiff and awkward, a hand resting lightly on each of their shoulders. I touched the heavy glass of the paperweight, searching my memory for the day the photo was taken.

Taking my hand, Zak pulled me to the center of the room, but I moved us to the corner farthest from the bed, next to the heavy wooden dresser Zak and I were sharing. There wasn't much space for dancing in the small bedroom, let alone for hiding, but even this slight increase in distance from Annie made me less self-conscious. Zak helped by drawing the attention to himself. He made dramatic dips and spins and seemed to be having so much fun that soon I was laughing and messing around too. The warmth from the wine made me mellow. The warmth of his body held me in the present. I brought my hands to his hips and pulled him against me.

I was relieved that Zak seemed calm. He rested his head on my shoulder and I let him slide his hands under my shirt. Then I let him take it off. I followed him a step at a time as he drew me closer to the bed. He laid back on it and waited, his eyes bright under thick, dark lashes. The intensity of his attention on me made my entire body flush.

Annie shifted over to give us more room. With Zak's eyes locked to mine, I'd been able to push all else into the background, Annie included. I turned to her now. I thought about what it would be like to kiss those full, rosy lips. I kissed Zak's instead, tasting hints of the wine again, and beneath was the taste of Zak, a taste I loved. The idea of performing for Annie still made me self-conscious, but it was also exciting. In any case, I'd decided to go through with this and my general philosophy was that if you're going to do something, you may as well do it well. I wanted to show Annie how much I cherished Zak, that she wasn't wrong to trust me.

My fingers felt heavy as they stroked Zak's face. "So beautiful," I murmured.

Zak's mood changed abruptly, his composure dissolving like a sand castle too close to the waves. There was a nervous tension in his body. If we were alone, I'd know what to do. I'd grab his wrists and pin him to the bed. I didn't want to do this with Annie watching, but I'd have to settle him down somehow, so instead of grabbing his wrists, I held both of his hands in mine and pressed them into the mattress. I lay on top of him, kissing him hard. Bringing my mouth to his ear, I bit down a little, whispering that everything was OK. I felt his muscles relax.

121

I loosened my hold on him and kissed his mouth, his neck, making my way slowly down his body. I wanted to taste every inch of his warm skin, to feel him react to the touch of my lips. I kissed each of his nipples, moved my mouth down lower to his stomach, slipping my tongue along the soft, dark hair curling up from his crotch.

"That tickles," he said, laughing. I marvelled at how innocent it sounded, how full of joy and wonder, so unlike how most adults laughed. I pushed the strangeness of this into a corner of my mind and let my heart feel light with happiness, the way it always did when he laughed.

I made love to him slowly, using my lips and hands more than my cock, but I found use for that too, at the end, when we were both almost more than ready.

When we were finished, I placed small kisses on his neck and back while he fell asleep beneath me. I kissed his tattoo, hot against my lips but cooling now like the beach at sunset. The numbers there swirled around in my vision, a set of nines, the figure 1001.

Annie shifted on the bed. I felt shy, thought about pretending to be asleep, as Zak was. Instead, I looked into Annie's eyes. To my surprise, they were shining. For a moment, I panicked, believing she was upset, but she smiled. "I knew watching the two of you would be hot, but I never imagined it would also be beautiful. You were so ... so tender, so gentle with him."

I should have been happy, or at least relieved. Instead, I felt shame, realizing I'd put on a performance after all. In that moment of intense intimacy, this seemed wrong. Before I could lose my nerve, I told her, "I'm not always so gentle."

"What do you mean?"

"You know," I said, faltering. "Just that Zak likes it rough sometimes."

"No, I don't know. Do you hurt him?"

"I ...well, I mean ... not too much. Annie, it's OK. He—"

"With what we suspect about him being abused? You think it's alright to hurt Zak while you're having sex with him?'

"It's not my fault, it's Zak," I blurted out. "He ... he likes it." Even as I spoke, I felt ashamed, like a kid pinning the blame on a younger sibling.

"And you, Jeremy? How do you like it?" she asked me.

I hesitated, then told her the truth. "Any way he wants to give it to me."

Annie's face twisted with distaste before she turned onto her side, away from us. I went to the bathroom to wash, wanting to feel clean again.

CHAPTER 20

In the beginning, our late night runs in Prospect Park made me nervous, but I gradually began to enjoy them. There was something magical about being in a park in the middle of the night while everyone else slept. Zak and I didn't speak, but we were together—wild, fast, reckless—our bodies pounding in rhythm to our twin exertions, the dim old-fashioned lamps lighting the twisty paths. The way Zak pushed me to my physical limits recalled the rough sex we were no longer having, and the solitary nature of our runs made me feel close to him.

Things were tense between Annie and me since the night of my admission, but with September and the return to our busy back-to-school routines, there was little time for brooding. The start of the term was a good time for Zak. In fact, to judge from outside appearances, there wasn't a happier man on the planet. On top of his usual excitement about the new academic year, he took obvious pleasure in being able to openly make love with either of his partners with the third party present. If Zak noticed that a certain distance had opened up between his two lovers, he didn't show it. I think he believed that this was a first, awkward step to a new openness, that soon we would go public about everything.

I should have been honest with Zak about my intention to continue keeping our relationship secret, but I avoided admitting this in the same way I avoided explaining why I refused to be rough with him in bed anymore; and in the same way I avoided admitting to myself that I missed the rough play.

By October, Zak's energy level had gone from impressive, to mildly manic, to scary. He was sleeping less and less. Dr. McQueen had suggested mood stabilizers, but Zak was resistant. For now, the strategy seemed to be therapy, patience, and exercise, exercise, exercise. The kids loved the weekends spent hiking and playing sports and Annie enjoyed dancing with Zak once or twice a week. I understood my responsibility was to accompany him on his nighttime runs.

Eventually, the broken sleep and non-stop exercise began to take its toll. I became short-tempered with my students. I had trouble concentrating. To add to my misery and exhaustion, I caught a cold. I told myself this couldn't go on. How could Zak, who was sleeping less than I was, even put one foot in front of the other?

A night arrived when I couldn't continue. When Zak began climbing out of bed, I grabbed his arm. "Stay here," I said.

"I need to run. You don't have to come."

Because I couldn't say I didn't trust him to be alone, I remained silent, holding his arm in the darkness. His muscles twitched under my fingers. I felt as though he could read my distrust, and that this hurt him. I slid my hand behind his neck to pull him down on top of me and kissed him tenderly. He kissed me back hard, tugging at my hair with both of his hands. I rolled onto him, groaning. He struggled under me, an even surer signal he wanted something rough, but I couldn't do it. Not with Annie lying in bed beside us.

He climbed out from under me and dressed. I followed him outside, into the darkness.

That night, the run felt torturous. My legs and chest were aching before we reached the park. My nose was running and I began to cough. Zak spoke to me over his shoulder. "J, go home." I shook my head and continued. Zak accelerated. It seemed so effortless. The more I slowed, the faster he went. Had he been holding back all this time? I couldn't squeeze one more ounce of energy from my heavy legs and heaving chest.

To push myself, I imagined being mugged. I pictured three guys, two of them hitting me while the other pulled the wallet from my pocket, the same wallet Zak teased me for carrying on our runs, as though I planned to stop for a latte. Frankly, the thought of being mugged didn't seem so bad. At least I'd have an excuse to stop, to lay on the ground. It was what would happen next that frightened me enough to keep me going. I'd struggle to my feet but Zak would be long gone. Perhaps it would be morning before I'd find his body. Maybe his throat would be slit or he'd be hanging from a tree. And it was all because I hadn't kept up with him.

Though Zak hadn't talked about hurting himself lately, I knew that people who were serious about suicide would do it in private, without the possibility of interference. Ensuring that Zak was never alone was why I was out here in the middle of the night, wheezing and coughing.

At the end of the run, I found Zak leaning against our building.

"So, you finally made it," he said, not moving from the wall. Zak seemed calm, relaxed, but there was something about his careful stillness that told me he was angry. Like the stillness of a taut bow right before the arrows were let loose.

"Why didn't you wait for me in the park?" I complained.

"You should have stayed home." Zak spoke these words calmly, but now I was sure he was angry. Otherwise he'd be teasing me about how slow I was.

"So why didn't you go upstairs without me?" I asked.

"First you ask why I didn't wait, now you ask why I did. Make up your mind!" I looked at him. "Fine," he said, dropping his careful pose against the wall. "It's 'cause I knew Annie'd be upset if she thought you'd lost me."

That *I'd* lost *him*. Funny he put it that way, when technically, it was Zak who'd 'lost' me, left me in the dust. But yes, that's how Annie would view it.

"Come on," I said, taking his arm. "Let's catch a few hours of sleep."

The next morning, I woke up with a hacking cough. Annie looked at me doubtfully as I swung my feet to the ground, doubling over to cough some more.

"You should call in sick," she said.

"I need to go in."

Zak came in from his shower, trailed by Kyra.

"Morning Daddy!" she said. Another bout of coughing hit me. "Daddy, you're sick!"

"From the mouths of babes," Annie said, catching Zak's eye. "Why don't you get Jeremy some tea. Maybe Kyra would like to help."

"Can I lick the honey off the spoon?" I heard her ask, as Zak brought her into the kitchen.

"Stay home today, get some sleep," Annie repeated.

"I'm fine."

"You're far from fine." I didn't say anything. "You'll get your students sick." I

126

glanced out the bedroom door, in the direction Zak had gone with Kyra. "Jeremy, following Zak around isn't the answer. It's not ... sustainable."

"So make him take the meds."

"How would you propose I do that? Force them down his throat? Threaten not to have sex with him unless he does what I say?"

"That second one might work." I began coughing again.

"Stay home. We'll figure something out. Dr. McQueen is working on it."

Zak returned with Kyra and the tea.

"Someone needs to take Kyra to daycare. And pick her up later," I said.

"I want Zacky!" Kyra said, jumping up and down.

"Kyra, Zacky—I mean Zak—can't. His name isn't on the list of grownups who are allowed to pick you up from school," I told her.

"Make his name be on the list!" She sounded as furious as a four-year-old could be.

"There can only be four names on the list and they already have me and Mommy and Annie and ... and Todd," I explained.

"Take Todd's name away. I don't like Todd."

That makes two of us, I almost said, but I didn't want any new problems with Tara. She'd been strange about me putting Annie's name on the list. I explained I chose Annie because Zak and I have similar schedules, so she was more likely to be available when I was not. I didn't mention the mental stability factor.

"How about if I take you and pick you up from daycare today?" Annie said. "We can stop on the way home to buy some special tea for your daddy's cold."

"We'll buy a magical tea!" Kyra answered, taking Annie's hand.

Annie left to help Kyra dress. I let Zak push me back into bed. He fluffed my pillows and brushed the hair from my forehead, leaving his hand there for a long moment.

When everyone left the apartment and I'd finished my tea, I closed my eyes, feeling Zak's phantom fingers in my hair. I slept until almost two in the afternoon.

Dragging myself into the kitchen, I couldn't believe how tired I still felt. Maybe it was because I'd been running in my dreams, chasing Zak. I made myself something to eat and tried to plan how to keep him safe at night. I took out my laptop and listed the possibilities:

1. Make him take meds.

2. Keep following him on his runs.

3. Every time he wakes up, simultaneously fuck him and beat the crap out of him.

I considered these choices. Annie was right about the difficulty of forcing him to take the meds. I imagined holding his mouth open while Annie tossed pills down his throat. As far as following him on his midnight runs, it had become clear I couldn't keep it up. And idea number three would completely ruin my relationship with Annie, though it was otherwise tempting. I stared at the list. What would happen tonight when Zak got up to run? Maybe we could lock him in the bedroom. I laughed bitterly, started coughing, thought about it some more. I showered, dressed, and walked to the hardware store.

A bell jingled when I pushed open the door. I found the aisle with the locks and inspected each one. I needed something that locked from the inside and only I could open. I found something at the end of the row, the instructions clearly stating that interior locks requiring a key were a fire hazard. I hesitated then took it from the rack.

The guy at the register had wavy hair and big, meaty hands. "Want an extra key for that?"

"No thank you," I said. "One key is all I'll need."

It was 4 o'clock by the time I began to install the lock. I heard the apartment door open. No one had been due back until later. Sierra walked down the hall.

"I thought you and Brooklyn both had play dates," I said to her.

"I don't have *play dates*. I get together with friends. What are you doing?"

"Could you hand me a screwdriver, please? No, not that one, the Phillips-head."

"Why are you putting a lock on my parents' door?" she said, handing me the screwdriver.

"What is it with your family's allergy to locks? You don't even lock the front door."

"Are you scared, Jeremy? Maybe you should move back to your apartment."

"That was uncalled for."

"Then stop lying. You're putting on a lock so you can have sex with my dad."

The screwdriver slipped as I began another fit of well-timed coughing. "What is this door frame made out of, lead?" I wiped my nose with a handkerchief.

"Admit it! Admit you lied to me!"

"There's nothing to admit. I know you're upset about what you thought you saw when you came home from your grandparents, but don't you remember what we talked about when I first moved in? Your dad's having a lot of trouble sleeping."

Her shoulders slumped. "I know. He gets up in the middle of the night sometimes."

"I thought putting a lock on the door might make him more secure."

"My daddy's not scared of anything."

"In case he sleepwalks."

Sierra seemed to consider this. "Does Daddy have nightmares?" she asked, sounding more like the kid she was.

"Some pretty bad ones. Hey, have you ever used a power tool?" I asked.

"No. My parents won't let me," she answered.

"When was the last time either of your parents used a power tool?"

"When I was about seven," she said.

"Oh well, that was ages ago," I said, winking.

"You'd let me?" she asked, brightening.

"I'll tell you what. I'll agree to trust you with the drill if you'll agree to stop suspecting me of things. What do you say?"

"OK," she answered, putting out her hand to shake on it.

I took her small hand in my own. She had a strong grip for a kid her age.

"Go wash your hands. I don't want you to catch my cold."

CHAPTER 21

Give her the fucking keys!" I shouted at Zak.

It was Saturday afternoon and it had been raining for forty straight hours—a little longer than the number of hours Zak had been awake. If he didn't sleep soon, we'd all lose our minds. We'd sent the kids to friends so the apartment would be quiet, and when Annie mentioned she needed to work on some file notes for a client, I encouraged her to go to the office for a few hours. But then Zak grabbed her keys and his childish joke devolved into a struggle that had Annie on the verge of tears.

"I'll trade you," Zak said to me. "Annie's keys for yours."

"You know what you need to do for me to give up that key." I was picturing the bottle of mood stabilizers Dr. McQueen had prescribed and which sat, unopened, in the drawer of the bedside table, right beside the unused condoms.

Maybe the lock had been a mistake, but at first Zak had accepted it. Perhaps he was humoring me; I was still pretty sick. A few nights later, he'd asked me to remove it. I refused. He didn't openly fight me but spent the next night sitting against the wall, reading mathematical textbooks with a flashlight. Then last night at around 2 a.m., he'd began throwing himself into the door. I grabbed him around the waist while Annie tried to calm him. Sierra had called out tentatively from the hallway. "Daddy? Are you sleepwalking?" Zak went slack. "It's OK, Sierra. I just can't sleep." I'd almost laughed when Sierra suggested he take a sleeping pill or something.

"Please, Zak," Annie said now in a flat voice. "I'll only be a couple of hours."

"Make J stop locking the door." Zak was jumping on the bed like a two-year-old.

"If you don't get your ass down here and give her the keys ... " I warned.

Zak stopped jumping and climbed down. "Go ahead, take'm."

I reached for Annie's keys. He slipped away with that incredible speed he had, poking me sharply in the stomach with his finger.

"Quit that," I warned. "I'm not playing."

He dangled the keys in front of me before stuffing them into his pocket, laughing like a maniac. Annie, exhausted by weeks of broken sleep, began to cry.

I lunged for Zak but he evaded me, somehow managing to poke me again. I went still, Annie's tears turning my anger from hot to cold. I waited, knowing Zak would come close again. When he did, I made as though to grab him with my right hand. With my left, I punched him hard in the stomach. He doubled over and I reached into his pocket for the keys.

"What the fuck, Jeremy!" Annie shouted.

"Annie, I—"

"No! Don't even—"

She turned and ran out.

It took Zak a moment to recover and then he was all over me. His hands were reaching, pulling; his tongue pushed against my teeth, his body pressed against mine. This change of strategy unbalanced me, and his attack was on too many fronts to resist. First his tongue slipped inside my mouth, next his hands were pulling down my zipper. Soon we were on the floor, wrestling, his body hot and fierce under mine, but he wasn't trying to hurt me anymore. Part of me wished he would, remembering with remorse the impact of my fist against his stomach, the same stomach I'd kissed so tenderly while Annie watched.

An insight flashed. Was there something Zak felt bad about that made him provoke me until I hurt him? The truth was, I had no idea what was going on in his head. No matter how gently I probed or how hard I pushed, he wouldn't let me in. I could penetrate his body, as deeply as I was doing now, but I couldn't touch his mind. It was closed up tight, keeping me out. The thought filled me with grief.

I lay on top of him, spent, and looked up to see Annie in the doorway.

"I thought you'd left," I said, embarrassment sharpening my tongue. "Get an eye full?"

"My keys, Jeremy."

My left fist was full of Zak's hair. My other hand was clenched too, something poking painfully into my flesh. I let go of Zak and opened my right hand. Annie

131

stepped into the room, gingerly snatching her keys from me while I stared at the imprint they'd left on my palm. The apartment door slammed closed.

Zak began to laugh.

"You think it's funny, making me look like an animal in front of Annie?"

"Don't tell me you didn't enjoy yourself." Zak stroked the damp hair on my chest.

I slapped his hand away. "Leave me the hell alone."

"Come on, hit me some more. You know you want to—"

I grabbed him. Released him. "Why do you do this? I just want to know why."

Zak's smile disappeared. He sucked on his lip. "Don't worry about Annie. She understands."

"What is it she understands? Explain it to me so I can understand too." Zak remained silent. "Is it because you were hit as a kid? Do you equate being hurt with being loved?"

Zak smirked.

"Or low self-esteem. You think you deserve it or something. Or a control thing. You want to be dominated because you're afraid. Afraid that—"

"Shut up or—" Zak stopped.

"Or what? You'll hit me back? That would at least be normal."

"I'm not normal. You want normal, there's the door," Zak said, gesturing with his chin.

I looked at the door and thought about using it. Instead, I took Zak's jeans from the floor where he'd shucked them and threw them at him. "Get up," I told him. He ignored me. "I told you to get the hell up. Put your clothes on."

"Why?"

"Because we're going out."

"Where are we going?"

"I'll tell you when we're outside."

I dressed, put on my jacket, and grabbed an umbrella. Zak wandered into the hallway coatless. "Put on a rain slicker or something. Do I have to fucking tell you everything?"

132

Zak returned with his windbreaker. I pulled the hood over his head and shoved him into the hall, locking the door behind us. I had my umbrella in one hand and Zak's upper arm in the other as we made our way out onto the street. The rain was falling steadily.

"Where we going?" Zak asked again.

"The Brooklyn Parkside Museum," I said, deciding. "There's an exhibit I want to see."

I had no idea what exhibits were showing, but it seemed like a good choice—somewhere that was indoors and dry, with interesting things to look at, lots of space to walk around in, and no need to be sociable. Zak shrugged his acquiescence.

He was silent as we walked up to Eastern Parkway, a boulevard impressive even in the rain, even following decades of City neglect. I let out a breath. Leaving the apartment had been a good idea. I felt Zak relax in small increments the longer we were outside. I'd gotten used to monitoring his mood and could tell how he was feeling by the set of his shoulders, his tone of voice, and other signs I couldn't even name. It was like there was a device inside my head giving me readings on Zak's state of mind, but like all devices, it sometimes failed.

Inside the museum, Zak's natural curiosity and exuberance slowly replaced his dark mood. He was still quiet and moody, but calmer. I put my hand on his shoulder. He shrugged it off with a note of impatience, but no real hostility.

We wandered around, Zak always a bit ahead of me. I'd be reading an explanation of a piece of art; he'd peer over my shoulder, scan the text, move on. He regarded the objects in the room in no particular order, flitting from one thing to the next as it caught his attention. He especially loved oddities. When he discovered one, he'd pull me by the arm until I came over to see what had caught his imagination.

There was an exhibit entitled *Women and Bicycles: Cycling to Suffrage*. In the center of the room, high above our heads, was a wire replica of one of those old-fashioned cycles with a giant wheel in front. Seated on the bicycle, back straight and proud, was a papier-mâché woman in a big hooped skirt striped purple, green and gold, reddish curls spilling from the bun on her head. "Annie!" Zak laughed in delight. "Look, it's Annie!"

The crowds were thin, most people probably snug at home watching videos or playing games, not worried a loved one was going to bounce off the ceiling and self-destruct. Could the other museum-goers tell that Zak was unstable? The air around him seemed to buzz—pulsating waves of heat and jangly vibrations emanating from his body. Maybe they could sense his energy. The truth was, people always looked at Zak. He was striking, a pleasure to look at. My arm reached for him again, as though to lay claim. "Mine!" my body wanted to say. I pulled my arm back and followed him out of the room.

I was reading the guide I'd picked up to decide where to go next. Zak, about ten feet ahead of me, turned the corner. "Strange fruit," he called out. "I like weird food."

"Wait, Zak," I said, but it was too late.

It still astonished me how little Zak seemed to know of popular culture. As an activist, I'd have thought Zak would be familiar with Billie Holiday's 'Strange Fruit,' or at least its historical connection to the movement to end the lynching of Black men in the South.

Inside the exhibition room it was dim, like a night club. Or a tomb.

"We should go," I said.

I walked over to Zak, but he moved to the first image. I repeated my suggestion that we leave, but Zak seemed to be in his own dark space as he slowly walked around the room. He minutely examined each painting, photo or image of a man hanging from a tree. Some of the bodies were bloody, some were burnt, some had been shot or hacked or disfigured.

Towards the middle of the room was a short biography of the person who'd written the song—a man by the name of Abel Meeropol. He was a white, Jewish, high school teacher from the Bronx who'd also been a song-writer, a communist, and a political activist.

"Look at this, Zak," I said, calling his attention away from the disturbing images. "The guy who wrote this song was a teacher like us. Not only that—listen, this is fascinating—he and his wife adopted the orphans of Julius and Ethel Rosenberg. You know, they were the ones who were executed by the government for treason in the nineteen fifties."

Zak's eyes were like big, dark puddles. He returned to the images. I began talking again to distract him. "I wonder what the Rosenbergs must have felt like, knowing their actions had made their children orphans." Zak swallowed hard, his eyes filling. Why had I said that? "We should go," I repeated softly. Zak shuffled over to the last image. I followed him, placing my hands on his shoulders. I tried to steer him towards the door, but he wouldn't budge. On the other side of the room, a man and woman, both white, were reading a caption and laughing. What could they possibly be laughing at?

I looked up at what was holding Zak's attention. The image was not of a hanged man but of a house on fire. It was hard to tell whether it was a photograph or a painting. There was something disturbingly surreal about it.

"Are they still inside?" he asked me in a small voice.

"Who?"

"The people. The people who live in the house."

"I ... I don't know. I mean, it's a picture. We don't even know if it's real."

"It's real," he said with certainty.

"Then ... no, they got out. They escaped." I thought, incongruously, of *The Little Prince*, with the sheep safely inside the box. I still had my hands on Zak's shoulders, felt when he began to tremble. "Zak," I said gently, turning him towards me. He pressed his face into my neck. "Sweetheart," I murmured as he began to cry—wracking sobs that convulsed his body. I wanted to soothe him, but what could I say? Remind him that Black men were no longer lynched in the South? But he might remind me that unarmed people of color, including our own student Dez, are routinely murdered by the police. No, I had no comforting words, so instead I simply held him. One of the museum staff gave us a look. I gave him a look of my own. "The geniuses who run this place, they ever heard of a trigger warning?" I said angrily.

I led Zak out of the room, through the corridors, and downstairs. At the exit, I pushed him ahead of me through the revolving doors. As soon as he was outside, he began to run. I took off after him. "Zak, wait up!" I called, but he ignored me. The rain had stopped for the moment, but the sky was gray and the ground slippery with wet leaves. At Grand Army Plaza, Zak turned towards the Archway. He entered a small door at the bottom of the monument. I didn't realize there was a way in. "Zak!" I called again, following him inside.

There was nowhere to go but up, so I scrambled after him, nervous about where it led. The archway overlooking Prospect Park was a smaller, less grand version of the Arc de Triomphe in Paris, but a fall—or jump—from the top would be no less deadly, a man's neck broken as surely as a neck in a noose.

I accelerated, no longer able to hear Zak's footsteps. A few long seconds later, the stairs ended and I burst into a small space. An elderly man sat behind a desk with an old-fashioned cash register, cheap souvenirs beside it. There was a narrow corridor beyond him. "Go on," the man said. "Weekends are free." I hesitated a second, then ran down the corridor.

I stumbled into a low-ceilinged rectangular space, empty of people except for Zak. In the center was a glass-enclosed exhibit containing small objects—historic, military, nautical. Zak pushed his hands along the stone walls. "What are you doing?" I asked.

Zak looked up at the ceiling, his eyes moving all around as though searching for an escape. Or a way further up. He glanced down at the glass display. "Another museum," he whispered, with something close to horror in his voice.

I walked towards him from the entranceway. Zak charged, knocking me to the ground, and ran out of the room. As soon as I was on my feet, I was chasing him again. I flew past the old man—who stared at us with bewilderment—and made my way downstairs. I exited the archway right behind Zak, spinning around to see which way he'd gone. He sprinted across the plaza and I followed, passing food trucks selling smoothies, french fries, Lebanese food, and soon found myself on a paved path of rough, hexagonal tiles that took me into the park. Zak turned off onto a smaller dirt path that led to a stone archway.

The sky was dark and overcast, and it was even darker under the broad arch

136

where Zak had gone. I squinted to make the shapes and forms resolve themselves into something recognizable, something Zak-like in form. "Where are you?" I called out.

I saw a dark shadow an instant before I felt the impact of his body. The two of us fell onto the uneven surface. Zak's voice echoed in the chamber. "Hold me," he begged, though his limbs still flailed as though seeking escape.

"I've got you. It's OK." My heart was racing. I wasn't sure what the images in the museum had triggered—Zak's general sensitivity to violence, his grief over Dez, or something else, even more personal. I thought about the burning house, Zak's sad, childish question, our mutual dreams of fire. "Fire is my element," he'd said to me once. But that was in the dream, wasn't it?

"The rain will put out the fire," Zak murmured.

The hair on the back of my neck seemed to stand up. Could he have read my mind somehow? I held him against me more tightly. "Relax, Zak. Take some deep breaths." I followed my own advice, counting out loud as I exhaled. Zak counted with me. "I'm going to ask you a question now." I paused. "When you were younger, did you watch a house burn down?"

"Yes," Zak whispered.

I felt a combination of horror and excitement. "One more question—"

"It's Annie's turn," Zak objected, remembering the game we used to play in college.

"Annie said I could ask for her," I improvised. "She wants to know ... was it the Bad Man? Did the Bad Man burn down your house?"

Zak let out a long exhale. "No," he said, with obvious relief.

"Then who—" Zak put his fingers to my lips and I knew I'd get no more out of him.

"Listen, J. Listen to the rain."

I cocked my ear. At first, there was nothing. Then I heard the rough, wet whispers of water falling on grass and dirt and perpetually thirsty stone. I realized I'd asked the wrong question.

CHAPTER 22

Annie was waiting for us when we got back, her expression stony. She'd been busy. The lock had been removed from the bedroom door, and it hadn't been done gently. Where the lock had been, the wood was scarred, an ugly hole where I'd had to drill.

"Zak and I are going for a walk," Annie said to me, without preamble. "Do something about that door. Also, you need to pick up the kids."

Zak meekly followed Annie outside.

By the time the two of them got back, it was late and the kids were fast asleep. Zak went directly to the drawer of the bedside table and retrieved the medications Dr. McQueen had prescribed. Annie and I followed him to the kitchen where he poured himself a glass of orange juice and made a big show of swallowing a pill down. I tried to catch Annie's eye, but she avoided my gaze.

The next day, Annie arranged to meet me at a café on Smith Street. I ordered a large coffee and a muffin, brought them over on a tray, and sat down across from her. Annie's hands were wrapped around a brown ceramic mug of tea—mint, from the smell—and she'd seated herself by the window. I asked her how she'd convinced Zak to take the meds.

"We'll talk about that later," she said. "I asked you here so I could apologize."

"Apologize?"

"About my reaction to what you told me about the sex you and Zak have."

"Don't apologize," I said glancing around. "Your reaction was totally understandable."

"No, hear me out. Yesterday, after I left, I spoke to Laisha—to Dr. McQueen. We talked about relationships and expectations and ... and boundaries."

"Did you—" I'd been about to ask if she'd told Dr. McQueen about the rough sex, but I caught myself. It was none of my business what she discussed with Zak's psychiatrist. Yes, it was getting increasingly difficult to work out boundaries. "Go on," I said, instead.

"Laisha helped me understand that my reaction was inappropriate. You see, I've always seen you as Zak's protector, a kind of big brother. I'd counted on you to keep him safe. My image of this didn't include you hurting him in bed. Your admission freaked me out, and it wasn't even the thing itself, but more the idea that your relationship wasn't under my control after all."

Annie paused, took a sip of her tea. My coffee sat, untouched, in front of me. Not sure what to say, I joked that if it made her feel any better, it wasn't under my control either.

"Why would that make me feel better? That means Zak— the one with the mental health problems— is in charge."

"You're right," I said. I slurped down some coffee, liquid courage in the absence of booze. "But just so you know, he's not totally in control. There are limits to what I'll do."

"That's good to know," she said, laughing.

I laughed with her, but the laughter sounded strained so I stopped. "So how did you get Zak to take the meds?"

"I told him that otherwise I'd have him hospitalized."

I was impressed by the strength that must have taken but wondered if such a threat had been a good idea. "You did the right thing," I said, hiding my doubt.

"I broke my promise to him."

"You didn't. You promised you wouldn't hospitalize him and you haven't."

"You're splitting hairs. I can't play fast and loose with the truth the way you do."

That hurt, but I pushed it aside. "Zak knows you want what's best for him."

"You didn't see his face. It was like I'd stabbed him in the back. And the truth is, I didn't do it for him. I did it for the kids. When Sierra came to the bedroom door the other night .... It was the same when I had him hospitalized. Brooklyn was a baby and Sierra was four. I couldn't take care of both of them plus Zak. There's not enough of me to go around."

"I don't know how you manage, balancing everyone's needs. I wonder what I'd do if Zak were having an episode and Kyra were there. I worry about that all the time."

"Don't worry. I'd take care of Kyra. You take care of Zak."

"But—"

"You still don't get it, do you? That's why you're living with us. I had it all worked out. You'd take care of Zak so I could take care of the kids. I manipulated you. And then I had the gall to get all self-righteous about the kind of sex you were having. And here you're imagining I'm so open-minded, so generous."

"Annie?"

"What?"

"Have some of my muffin."

She raised here eyebrows in pleased surprise as I pushed my plate towards her.

"You told us the meds would stabilize his mood gradually," I said, focusing on the painting with the three orange suns hanging in Dr. McQueen's office. I tried to keep the accusatory tone out of my voice, but as soon as Zak began taking the medications, it was like we'd chained a lead ball to his ankles and tossed him into a black abyss.

Dr. McQueen answered me calmly. "It could be that Zak was already on a downswing and would have begun a period of depression even without the medications."

"That's the other thing," I continued. "You're assuming he's bipolar, but I'm not convinced. Zak's always been very upbeat, full of energy. That doesn't make him manic."

"I understand that he was throwing himself against a locked door."

"That was my fault. I shouldn't have locked it." Dr. McQueen remained silent, waiting.

"OK, yeah. Things were a bit out of control, and I know why he seems bipolar

140

to you, Dr., but Zak's dark moods have always been strictly episodic, linked to real events in his life, like Dez getting shot. You know his mom died practically the same date in November that Dez did? And there's July. These are always hard times for Zak. He's ... very sensitive. Annie agrees with me. She thinks it's also linked to the kids' birthdates, like when Sierra turned nine."

"That there are episodic reasons for Zak's depression doesn't mean he isn't suffering from bipolar affective disorder. I agree that there are unique elements to Zak's case, but it's important to treat his symptoms, given their severity. Has there been any improvement at all?"

"No, he's worse. He's managing to keep it together at school, and when the kids are around, but it's costing him. He's so low, especially at night. I've never seen him like this."

"Does he talk about suicide?"

"Not in front of me. He knows ... I think he knows how angry that'd make me, so he keeps quiet. I figure that's good, right? Don't let him fixate on dark thoughts."

Dr. McQueen's face was unreadable, but before I could question her, she asked me how I was doing. I deflected her question, preferring to return the discussion to Zak's meds.

"I am considering other drug combinations," she told me. "Meanwhile, I've given Zak some tools for identifying how he's feeling—a kind of warning system. He's supposed to rate his mood on a scale of one to ten. What we're aiming for, ideally, is for him to be at around five."

"Zak's an eight. Normally. Why force him to be a five?"

"It's the lower numbers we need to be concerned with. Three is worrisome. If he rates his mood as two or lower, you bring him to the hospital and call me. Understood?"

"How do we know he'll tell us the truth?"

"Because it's Zak and it's about numbers."

I acknowledged this with a nod. Perhaps she knew Zak better than I thought.

CHAPTER 23

November 13th fell out on a Friday, and this was the day Malika chose for the afternoon assembly. In the year since Dez's death, relations between the police and the community had further deteriorated. Though the two community officers who worked in the neighborhood were reasonably well-liked, the cops from the School Safety Division were not. Malika had agreed to invite them to an assembly only after negotiating for a presentation that wouldn't be the standard "the police are your friends" rap. She'd asked Zak to speak first and planned to give her own speech at the end.

The auditorium was full, and emotions were running high. I stood at the back where I had a clear view of everyone. I'd already broken up a fight, and Robyn—sitting with our after-school club—was comforting two girls who were crying intermittently, setting each other off. Zak stood on the scuffed stage beside Malika. He was wearing black jeans and a white button-down shirt. He seemed calm as he looked out over the assembly, making eye contact with students and teachers, and even briefly glancing at the two cops standing in the back. His eyes found mine last of all and he nodded slightly, not quite smiling. I nodded back. Malika motioned to Zak and he began to speak.

"It's been a year since Dez died ..." Zak paused, glancing up from his paper. "No. Since he was killed," he continued, regarding us steadily. A collective sigh seemed to pass through the assembly. Zak's voice was perfectly pitched—warm and empathic but confident—so his words came across not as a provocation but as a simple truth that needed saying.

"For some of us, the pain of this loss is still sharp. When you're in pain, it can seem like it'll never end, that this is the way you'll always feel. The future—it's hard to imagine it as different from the present. But here's the thing. You kids are the future. This is a factual truth. One day, it'll be you standing up here talking, or in the back watching over everyone; it'll be you working late at night, like Malika does to make this school the best place it can be; you who'll be voting, having families, screaming at the politicians from your offices or from the streets. One day, maybe you'll have a gun in your hand, deciding whether or not to use it." Zak paused to let that sink in. "Yeah, this'll be your world, and you need to decide whether it'll be full of hate and violence and ignorance, or love and justice, hope and learning. When I think about what you're capable of, I'm so proud."

Zak paused again while his eyes moved over the crowd, and you knew these weren't merely words. You could see the pride on his face. The love.

"Let me take a few minutes to talk about your classmate Dez ..."

I brought my forearm to my face, surprised by the pressure of tears behind my eyes. I blinked the tears away and surveyed the room again. Everyone was paying close attention to Zak, even the biggest hotheads in the school, and right then, they looked like kids who thought they might have a future, some agency over their own lives; that they were worthy of love and respect. Like Zak, my heart felt full of pride for them, and for Zak too, who'd managed to dig himself out of the dark place he was in to say these important words.

I leaned against the back wall of the auditorium and listened to Zak. A year ago, I might have been jealous that Malika hadn't asked me to speak. What an asshole I was. I could never have made a speech like this. Maybe I could've written down similar sentiments, though expressed less plainly, but I never could have delivered them like he was doing. And even if I could have, what excuse was there ever for jealousy?

When the assembly was over, I made my way to where Zak was standing. Malika wanted to introduce him to the two police officers who'd spoken and were patiently waiting in the aisle. Zak lifted his chin slowly to glance in their direction. The movement was full of grace and strength, reminding me of a young deer, but when I saw his face all resemblance to such a pacific creature dissolved. Zak regarded the two cops with an expression of raw fury. I put my hand on his shoulder and squeezed hard until I felt his muscles relax.

"Zak should be with the club right now," I said. "Couldn't you chat the officers up with one of the other teachers? How about Khalil?"

"They asked for Zak specifically. I don't need to tell you how important good relations with the police are for our school." Malika turned to Zak, whose expression was now unreadable. "Just be your usual charming self. Can I count on you?"

"Sure." Zak licked his lips and set them into the approximation of a smile.

"I'll come too," I said, catching Robyn's eye and mouthing "five minutes."

If the police thought it was odd that I had my hand on Zak's shoulder the whole time we talked with them, so be it. They could attribute any awkwardness to that.

Knowing it would be an intense day, Annie arranged to do all the after-school pick-ups. Zak and I worked until it was time to meet Robyn and our club for a sit-down supper of cayenne pizza at Mama Lula's. Afterwards, the three of us were supposed to get a beer, but Robyn bailed out because one of her boys was sick. Zak looked like his battery was on its last 3% of charge, so I gave him the chance to back out too. He insisted he was still up for it. I was pleased. It had been a long time since the two of us had gone out alone together.

Zak brought us to a place I'd never been to before. From the outside, it didn't seem like much, but the inside boasted exposed brick and beautifully worked tin ceilings. It was surprisingly large too, with a horseshoe-shaped bar and a dance floor. I ordered us a couple of glasses of IPA. Dr. McQueen had said an occasional beer was fine.

We sat at a table on the far side of the bar. Zak was quiet so I kept up my end of the conversation. I told him about a play Kyra had 'written' and insisted everyone in daycare perform, including the teachers. Zak gave me his first real smile of the evening and asked how things were going with Tara.

"Fine," I told him. "She's stopped asking if I have a girlfriend and has figured out I don't want to hear about Todd, so our conversations are mostly about Kyra, which suits me."

"You don't think it's time to tell her what's really going on? Aren't you afraid

Kyra's gonna say something about our sleeping arrangements?"

"No. First of all, Tara would never talk to Kyra about anything like that. Plus, that's why I do all the change-of-custody pickups and drop-offs— this way she doesn't have to see the apartment and wonder."

"But she knows you're living with us."

"Tara has no imagination. If anything, she might suspect I have a crush on Annie."

"I think you're underestimating Tara."

"Well, look, if she suspected anything, I'd know."

"But is she right?"

"About what?"

"About you having a crush on Annie."

"You know I've always had a thing for Annie. I figured if I couldn't have her, you having her would be the next best thing." I winked.

"Annie's crazy about you. If you wanted it, I'm sure she'd ..."

"Whoa, slow down. Life is complicated enough. Besides, I don't agree Annie would want that. And ... I don't know. When I'm with someone, I can't think about other people. You remember how it was with Tara."

"But now you're over her."

"It's true. I still care about her, but not in the same way."

"And if I were out of the picture, you could get over me too. Love someone else instead. Love Annie, for instance."

The beer went sour in my stomach. I kept my voice level. "We don't need to worry about that, because you're *in* the picture. You will never be out of the picture. Understand?"

"Jeremy, you need to be realistic. If one day I'm gone—"

"Shut up."

"The two of you would be great together. And my kids love you too. If—"

"I told you to shut the fuck up. What part of 'shut the fuck up' don't you understand?" Zak closed his mouth and hung his head. "That's right. Now you listen to me. I am not your fucking exit strategy. You want to imagine me and Annie

145

together with you dead? You want to imagine us in each other's arms? Then imagine this: The two of us holding each other, crying our hearts out, knowing we'll never be happy again. Next picture your kids, the kids you imagine might love me but who we both know worship the ground you walk on. Picture them crying too. And you can add my little girl to the picture, the one who considers you her best friend and a fairy prince rolled up into one. Even if I could forgive you for breaking my heart, I could never forgive you for breaking hers."

"I'm sorry," he mumbled.

"I don't care about sorry. You take your sorry ass and think about the promises you made. You said you'd try. You said you'd stay positive. That you'd tell us when you were hurting, having suicidal thoughts. Dr. McQueen broke it all down for you into numbers. All you had to say was one or two, or two point seven two three whatever the fuck."

"I'm sorry. It's not ... I mean, I thought .... I'm ... I'm so tired ..." Zak's voice was hitching as he struggled not to cry.

"I understand," I said, my own voice icy calm. "We're all weak sometimes. I know it'd be comforting to imagine your actions wouldn't hurt anyone. That we'd all live happily ever after. It's understandable you'd want to view it that way. Selfish, maybe, but understandable."

Zak put his face in his hands.

"Tell you what," I said, "You pull yourself the fuck together while I get us another beer."

I walked off to the other side of the bar where he couldn't see me but I could watch his back. His face was still in his hands and his shoulders moved to the rhythm of his sobs. I shifted so I could see him better. I forced myself to absorb every detail of his suffering, welcoming the intensity of the pain this caused me. I glanced around the bar in case anyone else was watching Zak. I saw men in tight jeans with longish beards, women wearing black, or in blousy vintage dresses—no one who seemed likely to bother him. Maybe there was someone who was just being an asshole, someone I'd have an excuse to hit.

"What'll it be?" the bartender asked. "Another IPA?"

"No, something darker. Two stouts."

"Doesn't look like your friend finished his first beer."

"He will. He starts slow, but he's a good closer."

"Whatever you say. That'll be—"

"I'm not done. Give me a whiskey too. Neat."

"Two of those?"

"No. Just for me. I'll drink it here."

By the time most of the whiskey was in my stomach, Zak had stopped crying. He was searching for me. I swallowed the rest of the whiskey and crossed the floor with our two beers.

"Here you go," I said. "Finish that one up and you can start on this one."

Zak finished his beer, looking up at me for approval. He showed me a courageous smile. It took all of my strength not to get down on my knees and beg his forgiveness, but I was afraid to show even the slightest weakness, to risk giving him any excuse to think his death was something he was allowed to ponder, to plan. Zero tolerance. But I didn't even believe in this philosophy. Or in tough love. I didn't believe in any of that crap.

"What type of bar is this?" I asked.

"What do you mean?"

"I mean, is it straight or gay or what? I can't tell with all these fucking hipsters."

"Oh. It's not one or the other. I guess it's anything goes."

"Good." The DJ was playing something upbeat but not too fast, major and minor chords weaving together. "Do you want to dance?" I asked, to please him.

We walked onto the dance floor and I pulled him in close. My insides felt tender and vulnerable, like new skin under a blazing sun. I pressed my cheek against his soft hair and put my mouth near his ear. "If you knew how much I loved you, you wouldn't ... you wouldn't ..." I stopped, unable to go on.

Zak put his head on my shoulder. "If it were about love, I'd live forever."

I didn't answer. This wasn't an argument to be won with words. It would have to be won some other way. I simply needed to figure out how. For the moment, I concentrated on the beat of his heart against my own chest and tried to live in the moment, the way Zak was always asking me to. His shirt smelled like clean cotton and the weight of his head on my shoulder felt reassuring and familiar. I moved my hands up and down his back as we swayed to the music, surrounded by other couples.

"This is nice, J, but it's not dancing. It's more like dance floor groping."

I laughed. The music changed.

"Listen!" Zak said. "It's a tango. Come on. You can do this. You've watched Annie and me enough. Just let me lead."

It wasn't a tango, but the rhythm and intervals reminded me of one. And I was familiar with some of the basic moves; plus, following was easier than leading, once you gave into it. It was like guarding someone on the basketball court, but less aggressive.

I began to get the hang of it. Zak added small flourishes and people began to notice us. Some moved away to give us more room. Little by little, dancers trickled off the dance floor to watch us. When I noticed this, I faltered, feeling self-conscious, but being watched only encouraged Zak to perform more complex and daring moves. Soon I stepped back to join the spectators that had gathered, leaving him to finish the dance alone. The DJ segued into another song, similar in style to the first but faster. Zak spun and moved all over the dance floor, gorgeous and graceful and full of energy. This was my Zak, the real Zak, beautiful and lively, all eyes on him, everyone smiling and wanting him. Fuck the depression, the drugs, the suicidal thoughts. This was the true Zak and I was going to save him.

When the song ended, he put his arms around my neck and whispered, "Let's go home." We left our unfinished beers on the table and headed outside. Zak couldn't tolerate being underground, so we walked to the bus stop. It was unseasonably warm that day, like a global warming Indian summer with rain. We ducked into the shelter as the rain got heavier. I stood behind Zak, my arms around him. He leaned back against me and I rubbed his shoulders.

"Your dancing was amazing. No one could take their eyes off you. You're ... beautiful."

148

I felt Zak stiffen in my arms.

"Did I say something wrong?" I asked.

"No." Zak pushed his ass against me. "How about I give you a lap dance?"

I felt myself swell against him. "You're going to get us arrested."

"How can you stand to wait? Come on, J, let's run home."

"Run home? It's over three miles. And it's raining. Hey, Zak, wait for me!"

I sprinted after him. He ran like he danced, graceful, beautiful, full of joy. I wanted him in my arms again, wanted it with a hot, desperate need the rain couldn't cool. I turned the corner and saw him ahead of me, spinning with arms wide as though to embrace the rain, the world, me. Lightening flashed, illuminating Zak's features like an old-fashioned camera bulb, freezing his look of ecstatic joy and etching it into my heart. I ran towards him and he laughed as he pulled off his shirt and threw it at me. I caught it as he ran off again.

"Zak!" I called.

He turned and slowed, running backwards until I'd caught up. When I was in reach, he grabbed my hand and brought it to his mouth, sucking the rain from my fingers. I couldn't see an inch in front of me through the curtain of water falling from the sky but I could hear the sound of his voice, whooping and laughing, feel the pressure of his hand, tight and hot in my own. We ran past people in bus shelters or cowering in doorways, their umbrellas turned from convex to concave as the wind had its way with the flimsy wire skeletons. Zak and I were impervious to the storm, invulnerable. Before, my feet had pounded the wet pavement, splashing awkwardly into puddles. Now, like Zak's own feet, they barely skimmed the surface of the sidewalk. While I held Zak's hand, I was flying, my chest beating with joy rather than exhaustion.

When we reached our building, Zak turned and faced me, rain streaming into his open, smiling mouth. I ran my hands over his wet torso and he pulled me up the stairs. Once in the apartment, we slipped quietly into the bedroom. It was late and Annie was already asleep. We silently helped each other peel off clothes clinging to our skin. When we were both undressed, Zak pulled us onto the bed. I rolled on top of him and kissed him deeply. He smelled of rainwater—fresh and wild and delicious. Zak pulled back. "J, you taste like whiskey."

There was no condemnation in his voice, but something in the tone disquieted me. "I'm sorry," I said. "Let me brush my teeth."

"No," he said, grabbing me. "Don't go." He seemed anxious, frightened.

"What's the matter?" I whispered, not wanting to wake Annie.

."We're wet, J!" he said, ignoring my question. "The rain made us all wet!"

Zak's voice sounded strangely childish and disconnected. Annie shifted in the bed.

"Everything OK?" she murmured sleepily, echoing my own question.

"We're wet, Annie! Me and J got wet from the rain."

"It's been a long day. Let's go to sleep now," I suggested.

"No! It's time for you to fuck me."

"You're ... You're tired."

"I'm not tired!" he said, sounding exactly like an exhausted child. "You said I was beautiful. You said you wanted me."

"I do. But you're ... you're not yourself right now."

"Please!" Zak begged. "I'll be good." He pushed himself against me.

I only wanted to hold him until he slept, but my body betrayed me. I knew it was wrong. It was like having sex with a child, or someone who was ill. But the body pinned under mine was not that of a child. It was the beautiful, flawless body of an adult whom I loved.

When we'd finished, Annie spoke quietly to me. "What's the matter with Zak?"

"I don't know," I said.

Annie clicked on the light. Zak lay on his stomach breathing deeply. I placed my hand on his back. His skin was very hot.

"You can ask me your one question," he murmured, half asleep.

Annie turned to me, raising her eyebrows in inquiry.

"It's like that game we used to play in college. I think ... I think he wants to give us clues, like with the tattoo." I pointed to the center of Zak's back. "See. Here we are, in the middle of Zak's story. We're in Nebraska, past the one squared, two squared, three squared. We're still above the flames, at the nines. And that other number. 1001. I don't know—"

"You don't need to ask about that," Annie said softly. "That's nine too. In binary code."

"That's good. That's good to know." I kept stroking Zak's back. "Zak, when you were a kid, let's say nine years old, did someone drink whiskey? Did your father drink whiskey?"

"Yes," he whispered, as a minute shudder shook his body.

"Annie? Your turn," I said quietly, hoping she'd follow my train of my thought.

"Did your father ..." she began, but then she faltered. "Did ... did he beat you?"

"Yes!" Zak said, almost too quickly.

Another wrong question, I thought to myself.

I went into the bathroom and examined my reflection in the mirror. Weight loss had left the broad bones of my face sharper. My beard needed trimming, and with the thick hair on my chest, gave me the air of a wild man, the one in the film who lives in the woods and kidnaps children. What other new things would I learn about myself this year? That not only was I capable of non-stop lying, but of cruelty to those I loved?

In the mirror's reflection, I saw the door open and Annie walk in. I didn't turn.

"What happened today?" Annie asked.

"Is Zak sleeping?"

"Fast asleep. Did the assembly go alright?"

"It went fine. Zak was brilliant."

"So, what happened?"

"I ... I made him cry, Annie," I said to her reflection.

"Zak cries easily these days."

"You don't understand. I did it on purpose."

"Why?"

"I can't tell you."

"I understand. Let's try this." Annie turned around so only the back of her head was visible in the mirror. "Talk to the hair," she said. "She'll keep the secret from Annie."

I cracked a small smile, and shifted around so I was facing her. "He said something. I can't tell you what, only that ... he was having suicidal ideation. Very specific—"

Annie became alarmed. "Should we—"

"No. I don't mean like that. He didn't have a concrete plan for killing himself, but he was saying things that showed he had no hope. And the way he showed me that ... I had to shut him down. You understand? You understand why I had to do it?" I put my head down, unable to continue making eye contact with Annie. "I made Zak cry! But later he was fine. He was great! He had us run all the way home and ... I couldn't wait to get him into bed. And then ... You heard him. I had a whiskey. Earlier, while he was crying."

I slid down the wall to the floor of the bathroom, wrapping my arms around my knees. "I'm sorry. I know I'm not making any sense."

Annie sank down next to me and took my hand. We sat there for a few minutes.

"Jeremy, you need to talk to someone. But maybe not me. Take my appointment with Laisha this weekend."

"I couldn't—"

"It's fine. You need this right now. But Jeremy? Don't waste your visit. You need to talk to her about what's going on with *you*. Agreed?"

"Yeah, OK," I said.

Already my mind was racing ahead, planning a new strategy for curing Zak that I could present to Dr. McQueen.

CHAPTER 24

So maybe it's time to change Zak's meds or take him off the meds entirely while we put together the rest of the puzzle about his past. Hypnotism works well on him, I can—"

"Jeremy, slow down. Are you telling me you've been hypnotizing Zak?"

"Well ... yeah."

"How many times?"

I glanced up from my notes, wondering if Dr. McQueen was angry. Her voice sounded calm, but she was leaning forward over her desk and gazing at me intently. I turned to the set of diplomas on her wall. The upholstered chair creaked as I shifted my weight. I decided to answer her question as precisely as I could.

"Um, four. No five," I amended. "If you include Sierra's party when I did it by accident. But we learned a lot. That's how we know his real birthday, and what happened to his mom more or less, and just the other day we confirmed that his father beat him. But we need to keep probing. There's a big mystery at the base of Zak's problems. He wants to tell, but someone's messed with his head and I think I know who. So I was thinking we should bring you in now and—"

"Jeremy, listen to me. I need you to promise that you won't hypnotize Zak again until we've had a chance to talk about this in greater detail."

"Um, OK. Do you want to talk about it now?"

"No. I want to talk about what brought you here today. Annie said you needed to speak with me about something that happened."

"Yeah. It's all related." I tried to slow down. I felt like I was on speed, but I was actually very, very tired. I took a deep breath and dove directly to the critical part. "I made Zak cry."

"Go on," she said gently.

"I did it on purpose. Because he was saying things he shouldn't have been saying. Zak figures it's OK to kill himself because I'll have Annie and she'll have me. But it's not OK, it's the opposite of OK, and I needed to make that clear. And on top of all that, a few weeks ago, Annie confessed that she'd orchestrated my whole relationship with Zak with an idea in mind too. She wanted me to take care of Zak so she could take care of the kids. All these people with these ideas for me, but what about me? Do I get to decide anything?"

"What about you, Jeremy? How do you feel about all this?"

"Oh, I have no objection to what Annie had in mind. I mean to take care of Zak. But what Zak was thinking? Not that I don't love Annie. But now I can't if he'll use that as something that makes his suicide more thinkable. I had to shut him down. Hard."

"How did it feel to make Zak cry?"

"How the hell do you think it felt?" I stopped, surprised at myself for swearing in front of Dr. McQueen. "I'm sorry, Dr., it's just that you can probably guess how I felt. I ... I was very upset."

"Any other emotions while this was happening?"

"Like what?"

"Well, for instance, you sounded pretty angry just then. Were you angry with Zak?"

"I had to *act* angry. So he'd get the message. We can't let him believe that planning his own death would ever, under any circumstances, be OK."

"So, you weren't really angry. You were acting."

I looked down at my laptop, which I was holding in a death grip. I put it down carefully on the table and closed it, letting my breath out slowly.

"Because if you were angry," Dr. McQueen continued, "that would be understandable. You're allowed to be angry." I didn't say anything. "Well, does he understand now that he shouldn't have thoughts like that?"

"I ... I don't know. I never know what he's thinking."

"That must be frustrating." Dr. McQueen looked at me, eyebrows raised, but I didn't have anything to say. "Can we try something? Tell me what you like to read."

"Lately, I'm reading non-fiction. Psychology textbooks, actually," I said sheepishly.

"How many have you read?'

"In the last six months or so, about twenty-five. Maybe thirty." Dr. McQueen raised her eyebrows, so I asked her if I should check the exact number from the list on my laptop.

"No, it's fine," she said, writing something down. "What do you read for fun?"

"When I was younger, I read a lot of sci-fi and fantasy."

"Alright. Let's pretend your life is a fantasy story. Who's the hero?"

"Zak of course. He's like the beautiful princess in distress. Or prince, in this case. I have to save him. I'm his knight."

"Isn't the knight usually the hero of the story?"

"No, not that kind of fairy tale. The kind where the hero is someone who has the power to save the world but has a fatal flaw. You know the type of story I mean. Let me think ... "

I glanced around the room for inspiration, fixating as usual on the painting of the tree and the three suns. I pictured an ancient forest. "Here goes," I said. "Z is being raised deep in the forest by an honest, hard-working family of modest means. Little does he know that ... that his mother was Queen of the Gypsies. But ... she was killed. By Z's evil, redneck father. Z is beaten by his father and ... partially loses his memory. His friends have to help him discover the secret. So Z can bring peace and prosperity to Middle-earth. "

Dr. McQueen smiled. "Good job. But who are you exactly in this story?"

"I'm Z's knight and sidekick. Annie is too. She's the smart and generous one— like Hermione in Harry Potter. I'm loyal but with more brawn than brain."

"More brawn than brain? Someone who reads thirty psychology textbooks?"

"I didn't say I was illiterate."

Dr. McQueen shook her head. "What happens at the end of the story?"

"We all live happily ever after, of course."

"What does that mean to you in this context?"

"We restore Z's memory, kill his father, Middle-earth enters a period of peace ... and Z and his two knights enjoy passionate sex on a regular basis for the rest of our long lives."

"Let's try something else. You and Zak are fond of games. What do you like to play?"

"Oh, pretty much anything. My favorite board game is Scrabble, but it's more fun when we play chess. He's better than me, amazing when he concentrates on the long game, but I'm more competitive and can usually at least give him a run for his money."

"Alright, what if your life were a game of chess. Who would be which piece?"

"Zak's the king, the most important piece and the one needing protection. I'm the rook—the castle. That's because I can move fast and far but only straight. Annie is the bishop because she's clever enough to move diagonally. The kids are the pawns. Unfortunately. Oh! And you're the queen, Dr. McQueen. Because you have the most power. You can best protect the king."

"Thanks for your confidence. What if Zak weren't the king? What would he be instead?"

"The knight, I guess. Because he's always moving in unexpected ways."

"And could you be the king?"

"No. I'm not the king."

"Usually, when folks create a narrative for their own lives, they're the stars."

I shrugged. Dr. McQueen seemed disappointed in me. I tried to explain how I felt. "I have to play whatever role is needed. For Zak. I'll be his knight. Or his pawn. I'll be his castle and spread my walls around him so he'll be safe. I'll ..." I trailed off.

"What is it?" Dr. McQueen asked.

"He's trying to castle. That move when the king and rook change places? It's done to put the king in a more protected position, but Zak's doing it to bow out. Fucking Zak. He's been playing the long game all this time and I didn't see it." I shuddered, suddenly cold.

"... Jeremy?"

"What?" I answered, realizing she'd been talking to me.

"I was asking what you've learned from this," she said.

"I don't know. That life isn't like a fantasy novel. Or a chess game."

"I think we both know you're a clever guy, and you don't need to be told that real life is messy and complicated and doesn't always end well. But reminders can be helpful sometimes. The fact that right now your emotional life—and it's a very deep, very complicated emotional life—is largely a secret from most of your friends and family, might make it easier to treat it like a game, like a fantasy that doesn't need to conform to rules."

"I guess it's back to the psychology textbooks for me." I wondered what time it was.

"Have you considered confiding in a close friend or family member?"

"About our relationship? I know Zak wants us to be ... out. But it's buying trouble."

"What about the simple fact of your sexuality?"

"My sexuality? I don't know what to say about that. Love is love. Why do I have to think about my sexuality? Zak agrees with me about this, by the way."

"Zak is precisely aware of his own pansexuality and is quite comfortable with it."

I shifted on the chair. "I'm not Zak."

"Let me ask you something else. What will you do if your story doesn't end well?"

"It has to. Otherwise it's all garbage. There's no beauty, no goodness, no justice."

"Real life has it all. Garbage and beauty, justice and injustice."

"Not without Zak. All the beauty would be finished for me."

"So maybe this story *is* about you, at least a little bit."

For the rest of the session, we spoke of other things. I know Dr. McQueen wanted me to talk about my brother, but I didn't oblige her. I was frustrated at her attempt to focus on me. I understood there was a connection between my guilt about my brother's death and the situation with Zak, and I realized I'd projected some of the love I'd had for my younger brother on Zak. Yes, I felt brotherly towards him, yes I felt protective, yes this was complicated since he was my lover. But I thought she was missing the point. The important thing was saving Zak, not worrying whose story it was. We needed to be knights—all of us. We needed to be knights for Zak.

At the end of the session, Dr. McQueen said something that made me wonder if she understood after all. "Jeremy," she said. "Zak is surrounded by friends and family who love him deeply. We'll all do whatever is possible for him. This may involve great courage in the end. We'll need to be strong and play our roles."

She looked at me like she was waiting for something, but I wasn't sure what. I remained silent, hoping she'd give me a clue. Instead, she took my hand. "Maybe you and Zak should spend some quality time together."

"Sure. That's a good idea."

She paused again, looking at me carefully. Finally, she sighed. "Have a good week."

"You too, Dr. McQueen."

I waited awkwardly in the doorway for her to release my hand.

CHAPTER 25

I can't believe you've never skied before," Jon said to Zak.

I was detaching my skis from the roof rack of Robyn's car. Zak pulled our bags out of the trunk before turning to Jon. "It wasn't a thing where I grew up."

"Where'd you grow up, Africa?"

I stepped between Zak and Jon. "Apparently, they don't have Chinese food where Zak grew up either," I joked. We'd just arrived, but Jon was already pissing me off.

"Anyway, I'm glad you're here," Robyn said to Zak, deflecting the subject away from his childhood. "We've been asking you to come with us for years. Are you taking a lesson?"

"Nah, Jeremy said he'd teach me. He's been skiing since he was a little kid."

"Just because Jeremy can ski doesn't mean he can teach," Jon said.

"After we're back home, maybe you can give me some career advice," I responded.

"I mean teach skiing. Jeez, you're so sensitive. Come on, let's find our suite."

Robyn, Zak, and I followed Jon as he weaved around the cars parked in the icy lot fronting the ski lodge complex. The style of the buildings was a bit kitschy, like a storybook German village, but the mountain views were gorgeous. It had been worth the longer drive to Maine to stay here instead of the crowded, commercial resort where we usually skied.

Khalil and Maria had gone ahead to check out the accommodations. They were waiting for us inside. "Problem," Maria said. "There aren't enough beds."

"Oh yeah," Jon said. "I forgot to tell you. The last three-room suite available included a room with only a double bed. But no big deal. The girls can take that room."

"The *girls*?" Maria threw her arms up. "Why is it always the quote unquote girls who end up having to share a bed? Why don't you share with Khalil, if it's no big deal?"

"You girls are smaller."

"You're at most two inches taller than Robyn, and my hips are wider than yours."

"Khalil snores," Jon said.

"How would you happen to know that?" I asked, frankly curious.

"Me and Jeremy can take the room with the double bed." Everyone turned and looked at Zak. "We don't mind. Do we, Jeremy?"

Now everyone turned to me. I hesitated, deciding on a strategy. "Actually, I've been looking for an excuse to share a bed with Zak," I said, putting my arm around him and acting like it was all a big joke. Everyone laughed except for Robyn, who gave me a funny look.

"You guys are such clowns," Jon said. "Let's go eat."

That night, Zak seemed distant. He was probably angry about the act I'd put on, but I hoped to make it up to him in bed. I nuzzled his ear. "Lucky Jon screwed up the reservation. Sharing a single bed would've been tight."

"We should have told them the truth," Zak said, pulling away.

"We did. They didn't believe it."

"Jeremy—"

"Can you imagine what Jon would have said? He's such an asshole."

"He can't help it. But you can. You should be nicer to him."

I stroked his face, then kissed him. "Right now, I'd rather concentrate on you."

And that's what I did, my hands and my lips finding their way to the parts of his body that most loved to be touched. He grabbed me hard and arched his back in pleasure. I covered his mouth with mine so he wouldn't cry out and wake the others.

Predictably, Zak took to skiing like he'd been born to it. The only thing he had any trouble with was the chairlift. I showed him how to let the moving seat scoop him up, and at the end, how to slide to the edge of the seat and let it push him to his feet. The first time, the two of us fell in a heap when I grabbed his arm to steady him and our skis tangled up. They had to stop the lift while we righted ourselves, the teenagers in the chair behind us snickering.

It didn't matter, though. Everything made Zak laugh or smile: the panoramic view of the mountains; the cold, clean smell of the air; how the chairs on the lift swung in the wind; the corny music playing in the background; the blinding whiteness of the snow in the sun. Most of all, though, it was the speed that drew Zak, something I could easily have foreseen had I given it three seconds of serious thought.

Zak had been off the mood stabilizers for a week now. His platelets had plummeted to a dangerously low level and Dr. McQueen was waiting for the results of another blood workup before prescribing anything new. Zak was in no hurry to be back on meds. As soon as he stopped taking them, his mood began to lift, like a helium balloon released from a heavy, metal net. It was such a relief, I felt my own mood swing up with his, though I tried to remember that being too high could be as dangerous as being too low.

On the afternoon of our third day on the slopes, this came to a head. We'd agreed to meet up with the others for lunch at noon, but Zak begged to do one last run. The pleasure he took in skiing—a sport I'd taught him myself—warmed me, and it was hard to say no to his infectious smile and bright eyes. We headed for the top of the mountain.

We sat on the lift in companionable silence. Halfway up, we stopped. I buried my face more deeply in my neck warmer, shivering a little. The morning had dawned sunny and bitingly cold, but now the clouds had moved in and it began to snow. I turned to Zak. His face was lifted to the sky, his mouth open to catch some flakes on his tongue. He looked like a kid in his blue cap with the yellow smiley face, his red kerchief hanging loosely around his neck. He was wearing one pair of jeans over another because he didn't have ski pants. I had an urge to put my arm around him but held myself back. Though our lift chair—hanging mid-air and surrounded by swirling snow—felt like a private space, I knew it wasn't. There were other chairs, dozens and dozens of them, following ours up the thick wire of the lift.

With a hard jerk, our chair began to move again and soon we were at the top. Once off the lift, I was anxious to finish the run. The snow was coming down hard and visibility was poor. I looked forward to putting something warm in my stomach.

"Can I lead this time?" Zak asked.

"Sure." I actually preferred that he lead. It made it easier to keep my eye on him.

Zak pushed off onto the intermediate trail leading to the left, skiing with confidence and grace. I felt a surge of pride. I hung back a little to leave him enough space to maneuver, but accelerated when I realized how fast he was going. The wind was blowing against us and the coldness was like a wet towel on my chest.

Zak lifted his right arm and pointed with his pole to indicate he intended to take the expert path branching off to the right.

"Wait, Zak!" I called out. "That trail's too difficult."

My voice was lost in the wind. I followed Zak down to a series of moguls. I weaved around them, but Zak took them head on, whooping as he soared.

"Careful!" I yelled. I had to ski hard as Zak picked up more and more speed. Soon we came to a part of the trail that led to a slope so steep I couldn't see beyond it. Zak flew over it, not bothering to cut his speed. I flew over the lip too, a sense of foreboding in the pit of my stomach. I looked out ahead of me to spot Zak, but all I could see was white powder everywhere. Why did I ever let him talk me into this last run?

When I landed, I cut hard to the right. The next part of the trail was a nasty bit—a steep grade, prone to ice, very little maneuverability. I strained my eyes for Zak, catching sight of his red kerchief in the whiteout. I accelerated, confident I'd soon be close enough to tell him to slow down, but my skis went over a mogul I hadn't seen. I flew into the air and landed badly on a patch of ice. I struggled to regain control, realizing with horror that I was headed straight for the edge. Panicking, I threw my body weight to the right; my skis went out from under me. I fell hard, wrenching my shoulder, but the momentum still had me moving, head over heels on the hard, icy surface towards the gulf. "Zak!" I called out as one of my skis caught on something. I heard a loud snap, not sure if it was my ski, a branch, or one of my bones. My body swung around, and my head bashed against something hard. Everything went black.

When I came to myself, I was disorientated. Slowly, I became conscious of my surroundings. I was wedged against a rock, my right arm wrapped around a small tree. Below me was a bowel-loosening drop studded with rocks and branches, ice and snow. With a sick feeling of vertigo, I realized my head hung lower than my feet. "Zak," I whimpered. Where was he?

"Can you climb back up?" Zak's voice came from directly above me.

"Climb where?"

"This way," he said sliding down beside me. "Use your knees and feet."

I did as he said but gasped as a nauseating pain shot out from my ankle.

"Where are you hurt?" Zak asked.

"My ankle. I can't climb," I said, my panic mounting. "I'm gonna fall."

"No. I won't let you." Zak strengthened his grip around my shoulder. "Stay calm. I need

to let go of you for a minute."

"No!"

"Just for a second so you can climb onto my back. You say when."

I turned my head towards him. I was having trouble seeing out of my left eye. That side of my face felt wet and stiff and hot. I let go of the tree I'd been clinging to and grabbed Zak's opposite shoulder. Slowly, I maneuvered myself onto his back. After that, I don't remember much, only that everything seemed to be spinning. I pressed my face into the crook of his neck and was comforted by his familiar smell. I don't know how he managed to get the two of us off the mountain, just that the ski patrol met us and put me on some kind of sled. Then Robyn was there too, and it was she, rather than Zak, who rode with me to the hospital.

I returned to the lodge a few hours later, with some protests from the hospital staff who thought I might have a mild concussion. I'd managed to cut my brow during the fall. There was a lot of blood and seven stitches, but they'd x-rayed me head to toe and found no broken bones. Aside from the stitches, some bruises, and a badly sprained ankle, I'd come out of it pretty well. I was tired of the fuss and wanted to get back to Zak.

He was waiting for me downstairs. I convinced Robyn to find something fun to do for the rest of the afternoon. Zak and I went up to the suite. He helped me change into a fresher pair of long johns and a thick sweater. I felt chilled to the bone.

"I wish Jon reserved something with a fireplace," I groused. "Well, at least there's liquor. Check the stock, will you? If there's brandy we can make a hot toddy."

Zak rooted around in the mini-bar in the common room and plugged in the pot to boil some water. When it was ready, he brought it over with some honey. I took a sip of my drink. It warmed my throat and stomach, but the rest of me still felt chilly. I drank down some more. The room began to spin. I put my hand to my head.

"You should lie down," Zak said, gently pushing me onto my back. "I'll get a blanket."

Zak returned with a blanket from the bedroom. I felt sick and dizzy. Maybe I did have a concussion. I closed my eyes and tried to sleep but jolted awake from a nightmare of a bottomless pit, Zak tumbling into it and me after him. I closed my eyes again. Now Zak was squatting a few feet in front of me, his back bare, his tattoo like an animation. The 1^2, 2^2, 3^2 were marching across his back, the three 9s doing cartwheels diagonally from his hip to his armpit. The flames at the base of the tattoo were moving, crackling as he fed the fire in front of us with skis, boots, books. His own right arm. "Zak!" I screamed, sitting up, my eyes flying open.

"It's OK, it's OK," he said, hands on my shoulders.

"Don't leave me," I blurted out.

"I'm here."

"No. I mean ... " My heart was beating hard. All my dread for him, it was suddenly more than I could bear. "Zak," I moaned. "Please don't leave me."

He covered my body with his own and held me tight. "I'm here now. I told you. There's only now and I'm here."

I grabbed hold of him and gradually fell asleep again.

In what seemed like minutes later, I woke again, covered in sweat. I wasn't sure where I was. I imagined I was in my childhood bedroom. It was warm and sunny, but I'd lost something important. But no, I was grown now. I lived in the City. My consciousness fast-forwarded. I was here, on a ski vacation with Zak and our friends. I'd taken a fall. There was Jon, Robyn, the others. What were they doing in our room? I pushed Zak off of me. I realized I was in the common room, on the couch. Zak was rubbing his eyes, groggy too, still partially on top of me. Our friends stood rooted in place. Khalil appeared embarrassed, but Maria was struggling to keep herself from smiling. Robyn seemed unsurprised, but Jon seemed both shocked and furious.

I glanced down at myself. Were my limbs intact? Was I dressed? Did I have a hard on?

Khalil broke the silence. "Hey man, how you feeling?"

"Better, now that I've slept. I was wiped out. No pun intended."

"Yeah, that was some wipe-out. Robyn said you had frozen blood all over your face."

"I'm fine. Nothing's even broken."

"You sure you're OK?" Maria's 'I know a secret' smile was replaced by concern.

"Yeah, except I'm starving. You guys eat yet?"

"No," Robyn said. "We wanted to make sure you were alright. If you feel up to it, we can go downstairs to the lodge's restaurant."

"Sounds good. Let me get dressed."

Zak moved to help me up, but I waved him off. "Can someone hand me the cane the hospital gave me? Yeah, that ugly thing in the corner."

Supper was an awkward affair. Jon didn't say one word to me or to Zak. Khalil and Maria made small talk and Robyn asked three times how I was feeling. I turned to her, exasperated. "I'm fine. More embarrassed than anything. I haven't taken a spill skiing since I was ... I can't even remember when."

"Then what happened?" Jon said, breaking his silence.

"I lost control. I guess I was going too fast."

"You're the best skier of all of us, and you never ski out of control. You're too much of a control freak for that. What really happened?" Jon asked.

I looked away and shrugged. Picked up my fork.

"Where were you when this happened?" Jon asked, turning to Zak.

"A little ahead of Jeremy."

"Going pretty fast, I guess," Jon said.

"I like to go fast."

"Jeremy doesn't, particularly," Jon commented.

"Everyone makes errors in judgment. That's what happened. I lost control. End of story," I said with what I hoped was sufficient finality.

"No, here's what really happened," Jon said, face flushed. "Zak's ahead of you. It's snowing hard. You can barely see. But Zak doesn't care. *He likes to go fast*. You got nervous. Your *boyfriend*'s going too fast. You're scared he'll fall down and hurt himself. So you go too fast."

"That's not what happened." I turned to Zak. He was staring at Jon, biting his lower lip. "It's not what happened, Zak."

"Of course it's what happened," Jon said. "Even Zak knows it. Look at him. He knows."

"Shut up," I said.

"OK, that's enough, you two," Robyn said.

"Yeah, take a chill pill," Maria added.

"Excuse me," Zak said quietly, standing. "I ... I need to use the bathroom."

"Zak ..." I tried to stand.

"It's OK, I'll go," Robyn said, and followed Zak out.

I turned to Jon. "When Zak gets back, you say one fucking word to him, I'll kill you."

At that moment, Zak's phone rang. It was Annie.

"Hey, Annie, it's me. Zak's in the bathroom."

How are things going?

"OK. Well, I had a small accident. I'm fine, though. Nothing's broken."

What happened?

"I fell. Twisted my ankle. But listen. Zak's upset. He's blaming himself because we were skiing together and ... well anyway, one of our so-called friends ..." I stared pointedly at Jon. "He decided it was all Zak's fault and told him so and now he's pretty upset."

Can I talk to him?

"Robyn went to find him. Here he comes now." I handed Zak the phone. "Annie," I said.

He put the phone to his ear. The others at the table ate silently, as though chewing and swallowing took all their concentration. I didn't even pretend to be interested in my meal.

Zak listened for long moments before speaking. "But it was my fault. Jeremy wanted to take a break, but I convinced him to do one more run. It was snowing hard and there was ice, but I wanted to go fast." Zak eyes filled with tears. "He was trying to catch up to me. There was blood all over his face. He almost fell off the cliff." Now Zak was crying full out, wiping his eyes with his sleeves. "He could've died. It was all my fault."

As Zak sobbed, I thought about killing Jon. Beating him to death with my fists would be more satisfying, but using that ugly cane would be quicker. I stared at him with as much menace as I could manage. He met my gaze, quickly looked away.

I heard Zak say, "Me? Only once. The first day, on the lift. We both fell. Skiing's easy." A pause. "Because he's angry. He found out we're lovers and we hadn't told. I mean we sort of did but Jeremy made it seem like a joke."

Zak wiped his eyes, listening carefully. All ears were on his conversation with Annie. Whatever she was saying, it was working. He seemed less upset. Finally, he said, "OK, I will." Then, "I love you too." He turned to me. "Annie wants to talk to you."

"Hi," I said, then listened for a long spell. She told me that the way everyone found out about Zak and I sounded pretty shitty, that pretending it was a joke and later finding out it was for real must have made our friends feel like fools, and if it were her, she'd be pissed off. She suggested I apologize. Then, as with Zak, she told me she loved me. "Um, me too," I mumbled, ending the call and handing the

167

phone back to Zak.

I cleared my throat. "I ... I want to say something." Khalil put his fork down and the others gave me their attention, but Jon wouldn't meet my eye. "Zak and I have been lovers for ... for more than a year. And I've been living with Zak and Annie since May—"

"Zak *and* Annie?" Maria said.

"It's complicated. Everything between Annie and Zak is fine. I'm just ... It's complicated. Anyway, I know we should have said something. I mean, Zak wanted to. I insisted on keeping it a secret. I guess I was worried. About our jobs. And what you'd think. And ... I don't know. But it wasn't because I was ashamed."

I turned to Zak. "Never ashamed," I repeated, before addressing the others. "Three and a half days skiing and he didn't fall once. I got hurt and I got you guys mad at me for the same exact reason. Because I have a hard time trusting sometimes. Not because ... Zak," I said, facing him again. "You ... you believe me, don't you?"

There was an uncertainty in Zak's expression that shamed me. I reached out and touched his cheek, tracing the sharp line of his jaw to where it tapered to his elf-like chin, and I willed him to trust me, to trust my love for him. He leaned forward, still uncertain, and I kissed him, first gently and then with a passion fueled both by desire and a desire to make things right. I thought of our friends watching and felt the blood rush to my face, but I refused to pull away until Zak finally did.

"I think I'd like to go back to bed for a bit. Zak, would you come with me?" I resisted the urge to wink, but the tip of my tongue slipped out to touch my upper lip.

Zak stood abruptly, nearly knocking over his chair. "Um, anyone want the rest of my fries? We're going upstairs." He reached down to help me up. I left the ugly cane under the table.

Making love with Zak that evening was different. Normally, I enjoyed the opportunity to dominate him physically, but this time I was focused on his strength. I couldn't get over how he'd saved my life, carrying me down the mountainside with me outweighing him by so many pounds. I left the light on, filling my eyes with the sight of his flat, muscled stomach, running my fingers over his pectorals and biceps, his rock-hard thighs against mine. Zak was slim and wiry, but his shoulders had a nice broadness to them. I squeezed them and ran my hands down his arms, something he often did to me. This seemed to trouble Zak.

"What is it?" I asked gently.

He was unable or unwilling to explain. I let him press his head to my chest. "J," he murmured, his mouth moving down my body until it found what it sought. I shuddered with pleasure. We both wanted more, but I wasn't up to it. My body was hurting and I was exhausted. I fell asleep in his arms.

I woke a little later to voices in the other room. Zak was no longer in the bedroom. I strained my ear for the sound of his voice. When I didn't hear it, I pulled on some clothes and limped out into the common room, sore flesh and muscles protesting.

"Where's Zak?" I asked, my eyes squinting as they moved around the room.

Everyone seemed more relaxed now, though Jon still avoided my eye.

"Maybe he went out for a cigarette," Maria joked, but the smile died on her lips when she saw my expression.

"What is it?" Khalil asked. "He said he needed some air."

I hobbled to the door then limp-jogged down the hallway, Robyn following me and the others following her. Zak had gotten as far as the elevators. He was sitting on the floor, his back to the wall. His arms were wrapped around his knees and the pain in his eyes made me forget my own. I dropped to the floor beside him and took his hand. He stared at the indicator on top of the elevator showing the floor, his lips moving to the numbers as they ascended.

"What are you doing, Zak?"

Robyn raised her hand in a halting gesture as the others came down the hall.

169

"I'm … I'm counting. The floors. The elevators. There are three of them. And nine floors. Nine plus nine plus nine is twenty-seven, two and seven, which makes nine again. The elevator in the middle stopped on our floor three times. The one on the right too. But the one on the left only stopped two times. When it stops on our floor again I—"

"Zak," I interrupted. "I need your help. My ankle hurts; I've lost my cane. We have to get back to the room." Zak licked his lips, looking up at the elevator with longing. I followed his gaze. It was two floors away. "Please, Zak. Help me up."

He stood, pulling me up with him. I leaned on him heavily. We slowly walked back to the room, the others following behind us, like children and rats behind a silent pied piper.

"Get the Scrabble," I told him. "And the pills. You'll be on my team. The others will team up too—Jon with … Robyn. Maria and Khalil will be a third team."

While Zak went into our room, I asked the others to go along with me, explaining that Zak sometimes had these episodes but the important thing was to stay calm. My friends' expressions were uncertain. Before anyone could ask questions, Zak returned with the Scrabble set. As everyone arrayed themselves around the low table, I had Zak pour a glass of water. Dr. McQueen had prescribed powerful tranquilizers to be taken in case of emergency. I had him take two. I sat on the floor with my back against the couch and Zak in front of me, my right hand on his shoulder. "We drew the blank, so we go first. Pick seven letters for us."

Zak pulled some letters out of the bag, hand shaking.

"J, something's wrong! The letters have numbers on them!"

Robyn's head shot up while my heart beat fast from the panic in his voice, the crazy things he was saying. Remarkably, my voice was even. "It's the point value. You know that."

"I'm afraid of the numbers."

"You love numbers. Don't be afraid, I'm here."

"It's infinity I'm scared of," he whispered. "Is that what the blank means? Infinity?"

I thought about the night he tried to jump. *There's only now. The math proves it.*

"Do you remember what you told Brooklyn once? How infinity means forever? Forever," I repeated. "That's how long I'll love you."

He was trembling, so wrapped my arms around him. I stared at my tiles, then at the board, then at our friends, feeling as though my world were being shaken apart by some vast, heartless, entropic force. Finally, I felt Zak's muscles relax, the trembling still. His head went back, heavy on my shoulder. When I was sure he was sleeping, I placed all seven of our tiles on the board. 'ENTROPY' I spelled out. "82 points. Your turn," I said to Jon and Robyn.

Everyone sat staring at me, Maria's eyes big and dark in her face.

"He has a small mental health problem," I said. No one spoke. "OK, maybe not small."

"We could help you get him to bed," Jon offered, reaching towards Zak.

"Don't touch him!" I said. Jon recoiled. "I'm sorry. I'm sorry. I want him close by. Let him stay here. With his friends. You're his friends."

Jon sat back down and fingered the tiles.

"Please. Don't say anything at school," I stammered. "Zak's work ... it's so important to him. It keeps him on track. He'll be alright. He's in treatment and his psychiatrist is very good. And ... you know he'd never let this ... You know how good a teacher he is. You know—"

"No one's gonna say anything," Khalil said, turning to Maria for her agreement.

"What happens at school and in your personal life are two different things. As long as—"

"Maria's right," Robyn said. "No one should gossip. But we also need to be sure Zak's alright. That his problems don't enter the classroom. We owe it to our students. To Zak too."

I nodded my head numbly before finally meeting Jon's gaze. To my surprise, he didn't seem angry—just upset. Even in my misery and fear, I realized something.

"Zak has always liked you, Jon," I said. "He told me ... The other day he begged me to be nicer to you." I continued swallowing my pride and it went down like the prickly, lumpy mass it was. "I should have listened to him. I was being an asshole."

171

"Don't worry," Jon said. "We care about Zak too."

I stared at my tiles, eyes swimming, trying not to cry in front of my friends.

CHAPTER 26

Winter rolled into spring, each month marked by a new side effect from Zak's medications. These side effects were so variable, and often so strange, there was little question but that they were psychosomatic. Even Zak understood this, which is why he let Dr. McQueen remove the labels from the bottles so he wouldn't know what counter-indications to expect. It made no difference. Zak suffered nausea, vomiting, a ticklish feeling inside his head, muscle cramps, imaginary birdsong, a racing pulse, a burning sensation, loss of appetite, synesthesia, and, regardless of which medication he took, a crushing depression nothing could lift.

Zak was uncomplaining. No matter how he felt, each morning he'd drag himself out of bed and swallow down the prescribed pills, and he always made sure Annie or I were present so we wouldn't worry if he'd taken his meds. He'd smile or make a joke. If he also winced as the pill went down, we tried to ignore that.

At school, Zak taught with his customary zeal, but the cracks were beginning to show. Other teachers began watching him with concern during staff meetings or whispering when he passed in the hall. Of course, our closest friends now knew Zak had mental health problems, and while I was sure they hadn't gossiped, their knowledge had somehow been absorbed by the rest of the staff. Even Malika noticed. She took me aside one day to ask if Zak was alright.

"He's going through a bit of a rough patch," I said.

"Problems at home?"

I shrugged. "He takes things too much to heart."

"Dez's death was difficult for him. It's been over a year, but he hasn't gotten past it," Malika said, surprising me with this insight. "He should talk to someone. Annie's a social worker, right? She could find him a therapist."

"I'll discuss it with them," I answered with a twinge of guilt for my lack of candor.

That night, after Zak put the kids to bed, I brought him and Annie some tea.

Zak took a sip and wrinkled his nose. "What type of tea is this?"

"Cinnamon apple," I said. "You usually like that."

"It tastes weird, more like ginger."

Annie took the cup from him and tasted the tea. "It seems fine to me. You could be catching a cold. That affects your taste buds. Why don't we go to bed early?"

"You guys go," Zak said. "I need to be alone for a little while. I'll come to bed soon."

I reluctantly stood and walked with Annie to the bedroom as Zak sniffed his tea suspiciously. Psychosomatic or not, the drugs were clearly affecting Zak physically. His hair had lost its luster; he was thin and ill at ease in his own body. He didn't even smell right. Zak had a very distinctive odor—clean and sweet, like laundry that's been hanging all day in the warm sun, but lately Zak's body had taken on an almost chemical taint. At night, I'd hold him against me. His sexual appetite had diminished, but his body sought mine or Annie's for animal comfort. His skin was always hot, like it enclosed a blazing chemical fire, one which caused Zak to thrash and moan with wordless, internal pain.

Annie's eyes sought mine across the space where Zak usually lay.

"Go to sleep," I said. "I'll make sure Zak comes to bed."

She hesitated, then smiled gratefully, turning onto her side. I shut the light and listened for Zak. I tried to stretch my mind out to him, penetrate that barrier between us. Was it possible to truly bridge the divide between people? Maybe our fellowship was an illusion to make us feel less lonely. The idea depressed me. I got up and went to the living room, longing for Zak's presence. He still sat on the couch, but Brooklyn had crept out of bed and was sitting on his dad's lap, looking like a miniature Zak, his small hands stroking his dad's cheeks.

I heard Brooklyn whisper, "Are you sad, Daddy?"

"I'm never sad when I'm with you," Zak answered.

"Maybe I should stay with you all the time."

"Maybe," Zak answered. "But you need to go to school."

"So do you, Daddy."

Zak laughed, and Brooklyn with him. Zak kissed the top of Brooklyn's head. "Go

174

to bed now, my love." He glanced up at me. "Maybe you can talk Jeremy into telling you a story."

I think Brooklyn would have preferred that his dad put him back to bed, but with a maturity beyond his seven years, he reached his arms up to me. I lifted him, spinning him around in the air like I did when he was little—a time that was less than a year ago. It felt like we'd both aged enormously since then, that a period of innocence had ended.

When I returned to the living room, Zak was staring into the distance. I sat beside him, only then noticing his face was wet. He was crying without making the slightest sound.

"How bad are you feeling, Zak? Tell me the number."

He wiped his eyes with his sleeve. "Two point three."

"Are you sure? Not one? Not even one point nine?"

He shook his head, wrapping his arms around himself.

"How can I help you?"

"I don't know." He paused. "Tell me a story. The one you told Brooklyn."

In April, while Sierra's baseball league was putting together its rosters, Malika was putting together her team of teachers for the summer. I was leaning towards working on my book instead. I'd talked to Tara about her vacation plans. She was still seeing that asshole Todd and was waiting to see if he could get time off. If I wasn't teaching, I'd be more available to Kyra as well as Brooklyn and Sierra. What gave me pause was Zak. Last summer, I'd been able to keep an eye on him by teaching summer school too. In the past couple of weeks, though, Zak seemed slightly better, and me having more unstructured time would take some strain off him and Annie.

It was a bright, beautiful morning on the day I was scheduled to give Malika my final decision. Zak was in a good mood, more relaxed and cheerful than I'd seen

175

him in months. He got up especially early, made everyone's lunches, smiled and joked with Annie and the kids. He asked if I wanted to jog to school with him. I told him to wait while I put on some running clothes. I stuffed my school things into a backpack and came out into the living room to find Zak and Annie kissing. I smiled and put the lunch Zak had made me into the bag as well.

On the jog to school, Zak was animated and affectionate, touching my back while he pointed things out, the way he used to do when I'd first moved to the City.

"Look," he said, coming to a dead stop. "There," he whispered, pointing with his chin. "Do you see it?"

A bird's nest was precariously perched on a ledge beside a window box of purple and red flowers. I could even see a small, light blue egg sitting snugly inside. Zak took my hand, pressing my knuckles to his lips. I smiled and we started running again.

After school, I went to the teacher's lounge. Zak was talking with Malika; after he was supposed to keep an eye on my things while I met with her. We both had some grading to do.

Zak came into the lounge and gave me a guilty smile. "Would it be OK if I left you here? I finished grading during my free period and I'm kind of tired."

"Sure," I said, disappointed. "See you later, then."

Zak stepped forward and kissed me full on the lips before heading down the hall.

When I told Malika my decision about the summer, she was visibly upset. "You're deserting me too?"

"There must be others you can ask. What about Jon?" Malika began to respond when I realized what she'd said. "What do you mean *deserting too*?" I asked.

"I mean Zak. After all these years I thought I could count—"

"Malika, I gotta go. I forgot something. Sorry about this."

I left the building at a run, searching the street for Zak. I looked east and thought I saw him a few blocks ahead. I ran in that direction. As I got closer, I confirmed it was him. He was walking at a leisurely pace, turning his head from side to side like a tourist. Was I wrong about my fears? He didn't appear agitated, but why hadn't he said anything about not teaching this summer? I decided to follow him.

When Zak was nearly at the subway, I was half a block behind. He moved towards the entrance to the station. Zak almost never took the subway. He said he liked being in the open air—though the F and G train lines in this part of Brooklyn were elevated. Should I call out to him? I heard the sound of a train approaching and glanced up. It was headed east, towards home.

"Zak!" I called.

He glanced over his shoulder in alarm and began to run. I took off after him. Inside the station, Zak vaulted over the turnstile. I followed less gracefully, accelerating as I chased him up the stairs to the platform. *Shit, shit, shit* I said, damning myself for hesitating. I glimpsed the nose of the F train as it began to enter the station. Zak, meanwhile, was clearing the top of the stairs. There was a crowd of teenagers ahead of him. He quickly maneuvered around them but I had no compunction about shoving anyone in my way. I grabbed for Zak's shirt just as he tried to fling himself onto the tracks. There was a tearing sound. A whoosh of air. A shout.

I fell backwards onto the platform, sliding across the bumpy yellow buffer zone. My fist was full of Zak's shirt. My other arm tugged reflexively at what it held. Zak's waist. I tightened my hold, hauling him and myself further back from the train as the car filled with passengers. The doors hissed closed. Curious, unconcerned eyes stared at us through the scratched windows of the subway car as it moved past us. I got to my feet, pulling Zak up with me. With a sudden, violent movement, he twisted around and punched me in the face. I staggered backwards, letting go of him, then managed to tackle him to the ground. I brought us to our feet again, pinning Zak's arms, as a new crowd of people streamed up the stairs. Zak struggled, screaming at me to leave him the fuck alone. He twisted again and I managed to wrap my arms around his arms and torso from behind.

"Take it easy," I whispered.

The people on the platform mostly ignored us, merely edging away while continuing to listen to their headphones or stare at their screens. A few gave us furtive glances, but only one—a women of about forty in work clothes and purple spiky hair—spoke up.

"Are you OK?" she asked Zak directly. "Should I get help?"

Before Zak could answer, I said, "He's my brother."

"You don't look like brothers," the woman said, eyeing us in turn.

"Brother-in-law, I mean. He's gone off his meds."

"Liar!" Zak screamed. "I took my meds! You saw! Let go of me, Jeremy, let go!"

Zak threw his body one way, then the other, but I had him in a good hold now, and Zak's own words had eased the woman's suspicion. She now addressed me instead of Zak. "Do you want me to call 911?"

"That's OK. I want to get him home, let my sister decide what to do."

"Get your fucking hands off me!" Zak screamed, still struggling.

"Quiet, now," I said, loud enough for those around us to hear. "Do you want this nice woman to call the police? Get transported to the hospital in an ambulance?" Zak quieted. "Thank you," I said to the good Samaritan, and dragged a more passive Zak towards the stairs.

I didn't have a concrete plan, but I felt the need to keep moving. As I walked Zak down the stairs, I heard the train to Manhattan coming into the station across the tracks from where we'd been. I hurried us up the other set of stairs and managed to push him into the car as the doors of the train began to close. I still had my arm wrapped around his chest to restrain him. A few people gave us sideways glances, but if there's one thing most New Yorkers can be counted on to do, it was mind their own business.

The train was headed away from home, a few stops from my apartment in DUMBO. We got off at York Street. Zak didn't resist. He seemed to be in a daze and obeyed my small shoves to walk in the direction I indicated. We soon arrived at my old building. The doorman buzzed us in, saying he hadn't seen me in while. "Are you taking the buy-out?" he asked.

"Probably, but right now we're here to get some things I need."

I guided Zak into the building. The elevator arrived and I pushed him gently inside. As soon as the doors closed, Zak sucker-punched me, then began pummelling me with his fists. At first, I was too shocked to react, then I merely shielded my face and stomach as best I could. When I felt the elevator slow and the doors open, I grabbed him again in a wrestling hold. The fight seemed to have gone out of him as I dragged him to my apartment.

I pushed him into my daughter's bedroom. Maybe I subconsciously hoped seeing Kyra's old toys and clothes might quiet him; mostly I was focused on how the room's one small window was equipped with heavy-duty window guards.

When Zak became conscious of his surroundings, he dropped to his knees and began to sob. I stood protecting the door. With the beating I'd taken in the elevator, I was wary of getting too close, but listening to the desolate sound of his cries, I couldn't stop myself from taking him in my arms. I spoke soothingly, waiting for him to settle down or fall asleep, something that usually happened following one of his episodes, but this time he wouldn't be comforted, so I simply held him while I watched the Supergirl clock in my daughter's bedroom tick off the minutes. The numbers turned over 43 times before Zak quieted and finally slept.

I maneuvered us towards my daughter's small bed and grabbed her blanket. It was too small for a grown man and smelled dusty, but it was soft and warm, so I wrapped it around Zak's middle. Only then did I assess my own damages. I had a fat lip, and my right eye was swollen half closed. My tongue tasted the blood that had trickled down from my nose. It could have been worse. My nose didn't seem broken, none of my teeth were loose, and at least I could see out of my left eye. Still, I hadn't taken a beating like this since I was twelve and had fought a bully two years older than me. I reached for my daughter's pillow and removed the pillowcase, using it to clean the blood from my face.

I sat with Zak's head on my lap and thought things through. I should have seen this coming. All the signs were there: Zak's sudden cheerfulness following months of depression, the special attention he'd paid everyone this morning, his shows of affection, the change in routine. I'd wanted to believe he'd finally turned the corner, so I'd let myself be deceived.

I needed to contact Annie. I texted her, saying something had happened and

179

we might spend the night in my old apartment.

Annie texted back. What happened? Is Z OK?

He's safe. I'll explain when I see you. He's sleeping, so don't call.

R you sure he's safe? Promise to call if anything happens.

I promise. See you in the morning.

When that was done, I had no energy for anything else, even for thinking. I waited for Zak to wake up, hoping it wouldn't be too soon.

It was dark when he began to stir. "I'm here," I said.

Zak pushed himself to a sitting position. I asked how he was feeling.

"My throat hurts," he said, his voice hoarse.

"You had a pretty long crying jag. But otherwise?"

Zak was silent. "I can't do this anymore. Three times you've stopped me."

"I'm just trying to ..."

"To control me. And you're doing it for yourself, not for me."

"That's the depression talking. When you're better—"

"No! It's me talking, and you're not listening. It's *my* body. *My* life. You don't own me. You say I'm the one who's being selfish, and I know you think I'm a coward—"

"No, it's the opposite. I think you're incredibly brave."

"Shut up and listen! I can't do this anymore. Please, J. Let me go."

Zak reached out in the darkness of the small room and put his hands on my face. I winced. He froze, then clicked on the lamp beside us. I tried to turn away, but he held me fast to examine my injuries. With the gentlest of touches, he stroked my swollen eye, my bruised nose, my cut lip. "J, oh J," he said, his eyes filling with tears.

"Don't, sweetheart, please don't cry. Your crying hurts more than ... than that does."

Zak released me and brought his legs to his chest, pressing his face to his knees. I let him be, resisting the urge to fill the silence with useless words of comfort.

"Jeremy," he finally said, regarding me with dry eyes. "You think you know me, but you don't. The person you're trying to save—he's a stranger to you, and he isn't worth saving. He's the person who beat you while you never even lifted your arms in your own defense—"

"No, that's not who you are. You're—"

"Stop. You don't know me. If you knew what I'd done—"

"Tell me. I'm listening."

Zak shook his head, but it didn't come across as a refusal—more like a hopeless gesture of negation. He gripped his right wrist with his left hand, hard enough that the taut muscles and tendons of his arm were clearly visible.

"Let me call Dr. McQueen," I said.

"No, please. I can't talk to anyone right now. I ... I swear, I don't remember anything. Just that ... Everything you think you know about me is a lie!" He stopped talking abruptly and put his head to his knees again. I put my hand on his shoulder to comfort him, but he shrugged it off. After a time, he lifted his head again. "What you're doing is wrong. I have the right to end my own life. There's gotta be a limit to ... to this pain. I can't bear the idea that there's no limit. Please J, I beg you. If you love me ..."

I looked away, unwilling to meet his eyes and see the anguish there, but there was no escaping it. My consciousness of his pain was a heavy misery weighing down my chest and throat, making it impossible to breathe normally. And this was merely a reflection of what I imagined he was feeling.

"What are you asking of me?" My fear made my words sound choked, weak.

"There needs to be a time limit. I'll do everything you and Annie say, everything Laisha says. But at the end, if I still want to die, you have to promise not to stop me."

"How long a time limit?"

"Until ... 'til the end of the year," he said, and I panicked, worried he meant the end of the school year, which was just around the corner.

"New Year's Eve," I said quickly, before he could clarify.

Zak pressed his lips together and, after a moment, nodded.

"That's ... that's plenty of time," I said, making my voice sound sure and

181

positive. "By then, you'll be fine. You're much better now. I know it doesn't seem that way, but I've been doing a lot of reading about ... what you're going through, and it's always darkest before the dawn. It's not just a cliché. We've already learned much about what's at the base of your problems, and Dr. McQueen has a better sense of your body chemistry, and ... and your cognitive state. A breakthrough is just around the corner."

"Do ... do you really think so?" Zak regarded me with his dark eyes, so trusting.

"Of course I do. I wouldn't have agreed to this so easily otherwise."

"But J, if you're wrong, you still need to promise me—"

"You have my word. I'll do as you wish. I won't interfere."

Zak let out a breath, relief smoothing the tightness of his face, the rigidity of his muscles. With the relief came exhaustion; he was clearly at the end of his strength. I pulled him into my arms and he clung to me. "I love you so much," he whispered. "If not for you and Annie ..."

"Shh, I know. We love you too."

Poor Annie, I thought to myself. What was I going to tell Annie?

CHAPTER 27

I told Annie about the suicide attempt but not what I'd promised Zak. Her expression said she knew I was hiding something, but she didn't push. I was relieved, though the burden of the withheld information weighed heavily on my conscience.

Perhaps Annie sensed something had changed; certainly she could see I was close to a breaking point. She offered to make me an emergency appointment with Dr. McQueen as she'd done for Zak, but I was already seeing her the following Saturday. Annie and Zak both took the rest of the week off and I went to school, understanding more clearly how Zak could be so functional there when he was coming apart at the seams—something about the routine, the support of our colleagues, the need to hold it together for our students.

Still, it was difficult to get through the work week. I was an experienced enough teacher to deflect my students' curiosity and jokes, but it was harder to do the same with my friends. Naturally, they wanted to know what happened, with Zak out sick and me walking the halls like a zombie, the mark of his fists still fresh on my face. Robyn and Khalil both asked if I wanted to talk, Jon awkwardly patted my shoulder, and Malika told me her door was always open. I couldn't bring myself to confide in them. Their concern warmed me, but like sunshine in January, I appreciated the rays of light but knew I was deep within winter. I thought again of my promise to Zak and shivered.

Saturday afternoon, I arrived at Dr. McQueen's office ten minutes early. I huddled next to the water cooler in the waiting room and considered taking a drink. My eyes moved from the dull white plastic spigot to the tiny, cone-shaped paper cups. I closed my eyes instead, wondering what I'd say inside that familiar office while I stared at the painting with the three orange suns. Dr. McQueen's voice woke me from my reverie. She wore an unusual necklace fashioned of wire and wood that reminded me again of that painting.

"I'm sorry. I know I'm early," I said. "I'll sit here until it's time."

"Please come in, Jeremy."

I followed her inside. She took her seat behind the desk while I stood a moment longer. I usually sat on the chair by the door but today I chose the couch where I'd sat beside Zak that first time and Dr. McQueen had laughed and told me she wasn't going to eat him. Now her face was sober and I was weary to the bone. She prompted me. "I know you stopped Zak from jumping onto the subway tracks. And you've been injured. Do you want to talk about it?"

I rubbed my good eye with my knuckle and thought about where to begin. With our run and how he'd showed me the bird's nest? I recalled how he'd brought my hand to his lips and the warmth that travelled up my arm and into my chest and made it so I couldn't keep from smiling. I didn't have the strength to relive how that day had ended, but all of Dr. McQueen's kind attention was on me.

"Can I tell you a story instead?" I asked.

"Of course."

I stared at the carpeting and began. "Once upon a time, there was a happy family. A mother, a father, a girl—she was eleven— and two boys, one eight and one four." I took a deep breath. "One day, the parents left the two boys with the babysitter. The sister was dropped off at a friend's house. The babysitter—her name was Emily."

I looked up at Dr. McQueen. She nodded her encouragement.

"Emily had dark curly hair and big, beautiful eyes—slanted a little like ... like an Egyptian princess in a storybook. The older boy, he liked storybooks. And he liked Emily. She ... she could do anything—make puppets out of socks, bake cookies, play baseball, do algebra. The boy decided he was in love with her, not only because she was smart and beautiful or even because he thought she might be a princess. It's because when she looked at him, he felt ..."

I glanced again at Dr. McQueen.

"Go on," she said softly. "What happened when she looked at ... at the older boy?"

"Only that she made him feel special. When he talked, she listened as though ... as though what he said mattered. I ..." My shoulders slumped. "I needed that, I

184

guess."

Dr. McQueen smiled. "Go on, Jeremy."

"At home ... I felt invisible. My sister, Jennifer, she was at an age where everything was drama. And my little brother got all the attention. He was a beautiful child. Sweet, good-natured, and so smart and ... " I swallowed. "Emily was my first love. You're probably thinking it was just a crush, but it felt like love. I knew I was too young—she was fifteen—but I was big for my age. I figured she could wait for me to grow up." I laughed and rubbed at my eye again.

"Emily usually kept us indoors, unless it was warm and sunny. My brother—he got sick easily and had asthma. Jennifer and I were both pretty robust." I tried to recall my brother's features; instead, I saw Zak's bright eyes and sweet smile.

"One day, Emily took us on a hike to the river—almost a mile from where we lived."

I remember holding my brother's hand and walking slowly so he wouldn't get out of breath. I sighed and continued.

"Down by the river, there were some trails. I asked if we could walk in the woods, but Emily said no. She promised we'd play games. My brother and I loved all kinds of games.

"It was April but cold. It started as one of those days when the sun keeps peeking in and out of the clouds, but by the time we got to the park, the sky was completely overcast. I was afraid Emily would take us home. She didn't. At some point a teenager joined us. She introduced him as her boyfriend, Terence.

"My parents put a lot of stock in good manners, so I shook Terence's hand automatically and said 'pleased to meet you.' Inside, I was furious. I thought she should have told me she had a boyfriend, as though this were the kind of thing you mentioned to ... to the eight-year-olds you were babysitting. But I felt betrayed, like she'd lied to me.

"It's weird. Adults don't tend to take kids' emotions seriously. As though the strength of their feelings should correspond to their smaller bodies. But it's not like that, is it? A young child can hold a huge amount of emotion inside. As a parent, as a teacher, I try not to forget that.

"That day, my feelings kept growing, getting more complicated. I was angry at Emily, but when she got upset about something Terence said, I wanted to punch him. This surprised me. When I found out Emily had a boyfriend, I'd decided not to be in love with her anymore, but I learned it wasn't so simple to turn my feelings on and off.

"Emily asked if I'd be a big boy and watch my brother for five minutes while she and Terence talked. She promised to bring us both candy bars if we behaved.

"They walked off. I wondered if they'd kiss, like in the movies. The idea enraged me. It occurred to me that maybe Emily hadn't taken us to the park to please me but to meet up with Terence. It turns out I was right—Emily's parents wouldn't let her date, so this was a way to see Terence secretly. By the time I found this out, though, I no longer cared.

"Waiting for Emily, I got even angrier. When I thought five minutes had passed, I decided to run away. My brother tried to stop me. He was very obedient. Maybe that's why I thought he'd stay on the picnic blanket until Emily got back."

I brought my hands to my face, wondering if what I'd just said was true. Did I really expect my four-year-old brother to sit there all alone and wait for his babysitter to return? The only thing I was sure of was how the woods smelled when I entered them—like something wild and rotting and long frozen was coming back to life. I felt free and powerful. I'd run away and do as I pleased and they'd all be sorry they hadn't paid more attention to me.

"I thought he'd wait there. I ... I think that's what I thought. But a few minutes later, I knew he'd followed me. I could hear him behind me on the trail. And he called my name. 'Jemmy!' he called. 'Wait for me, Jemmy!' I ... I ran faster so he wouldn't catch up.

"After a while, I couldn't hear him anymore. I figured he'd turned back. I was relieved but also disappointed. By following me, it was like he'd taken my side. Plus, it would be more fun running away with someone else. We could play games, make a shelter out of tree branches. And I liked the idea that I wouldn't be the only one getting into trouble, though even at eight, I understood it would be worse for me as the older one. I nearly went back for him, but it was getting cold, and I didn't

186

want him to get sick. In my mind, he was back in the park with Emily.

"I ... I don't know how much time passed. I'd crossed a few foot bridges because I like bridges, and it felt like I'd gone far. I noticed that the trails were less well-maintained; some of the bridges were missing planks or rotten. Once or twice, I almost fell. Eventually, I stopped and sat on a rock. It was cold and I was getting hungry. I decided to go back, telling myself that my brother would miss me and my parents and sister too. As I retraced my steps, I thought I could hear my dad calling my name. I thought I heard some shouts too.

"Even now, I can still picture the scene. My mom, my dad, and some other adults I didn't know were bent over something by the river bank. Emily was crying. I ran down the slope. My father saw me, intercepted me. I didn't know what they were bending over, but maybe I did. I fought him while he held me and told me not to look. I got loose for a minute and dove between the adults' legs and caught a glimpse of my brother's face. It was so white, his light blond hair plastered to his forehead. 'Zack!' I screamed."

Dr. McQueen's head shot up from her notes.

"Yeah. My brother's name was Zack."

CHAPTER 28

how me how to make the castle-piece move, Jemmy.

My brother's small, white face gazed up at me from the other side of the chess set. I shouldn't have been able to see him in the dark of my room in the middle of the night, but his face was luminous, like the moon that was missing from the sky. That's how I knew he was really dead, that my baby brother was a ghost.

Now show me how to do the knight, Alright Jemmy? Jemmy?

"Jeremy? Are you alright?"

"Yeah," I told Dr. McQueen, shoving my hands under my armpits as I shivered in her warm Manhattan office. The smell of icy mud filled my senses.

"Can I get you something? A glass of water? A tissue?"

I shook my head. My throat was dry and my eyes burned with unshed tears, but it had taken me twenty-five years to find the courage to tell this story, and I needed to finish it. I held the image of my brother in my mind, and beside it, one of the living, breathing Zak whose life I'd do anything to preserve.

"There's more I need to tell you," I said to Dr. McQueen.

"I'm listening," she replied, tension underlying her usual aplomb.

"The day Zack ... my brother died, something else happened."

I struggled to recall the details of the day, but everything was fuzzy, fragmented. The crying. The wails of the ambulance. My father—how he held me so tight it hurt my ribs.

"It was night. I woke up and instead of my dad sitting by my bed, it was my brother. I thought I was dreaming. I closed my eyes. When I opened them again, Zack was still there. He told me not to be scared. That he just wanted me to finish teaching him chess. So ... so I did. When my dad came in the next morning, he thought I was playing myself."

Dr. McQueen opened her mouth to speak, but leaned back, putting her pen down.

"After that, Zack visited regularly. We'd play chess or run around in the backyard. My parents figured out what was going on and sent me to a therapist. He tried to convince me Zack's death hadn't been my fault. But of course it was my fault. If I hadn't run off, he wouldn't have died. Plus, it seemed inconceivable something this ... this horrible could simply be an accident. As for his ... his visits, I'd considered the idea that it was all in my head like ... like an imaginary friend. I'd even tested the theory by trying to make Zack appear and disappear, but he came and went as he pleased, not when it suited me. I decided this meant he was real, because otherwise, I should've been able to control it, right?

"How my parents must have suffered! I mean, what could be worse than losing a child, and one who was so well-loved? And to think your other son had gone crazy, to have to hear him talking to his dead brother as though he were alive ...

"After about six months, my mom told me if I didn't stop pretending I could see Zack, I'd end up killing my father like I had ..." I swallowed. "Anyway, I got scared. My dad had totalled the car the week before. I suppose he'd been drunk. He was always nervous, especially that something would happen to me. The thing is, right after Zack's death, it was my mom who fell apart and my dad who was strong, but after, it was the other way around.

"So, I lied. Told the therapist it had all been make-believe. The hard part was pretending I couldn't see Zack anymore. When other people were around I'd ignore him. If I were alone, I'd whisper to him to go away, that it was making Mom and Dad sad. Each time he came he was more ... more transparent. I ... It was like I was killing him, all over again."

I pressed the heels of my hands against my eyelids, pushing back the tears. My injured eye throbbed. I dropped my hands. Dr. McQueen seemed worried, like my father always did.

"I know ... I know I must sound crazy. But even now—even now I can't totally convince myself it was all in my head. And when I met Zak in college ..." I trailed off.

"Don't worry how you sound," Dr. McQueen said. "Tell me about meeting Zak. You both went to UC Boulder, right?" She smiled as though this were a normal conversation. I relaxed.

"That's right. I met Zak there my junior year. He was a freshman. The night before, I'd dreamt about my brother for the first time in years. In my dreams, he always looked the same—down to the jeans and grey jacket he'd been wearing the day he died. I guess when you're dead, you don't have to change." I laughed, but it was a hollow sound. "Well this time he looked different. He was tall and slender, looked about sixteen—the age he would have been if he'd lived. He said he needed to tell me something, but I woke up before he had a chance. My phone was ringing. It was my sister. I was supposed to fly home after finals, but Jennifer said it wasn't a good time, that Dad wasn't well—which probably meant he was drinking again. I hadn't seen my parents in two years. There was always some excuse—money was tight, Dad wasn't well ... "

"You told me they'd died in a car accident. Was that after you'd finished school?"

I nodded and swallowed a few times before daring to speak again.

"Anyway. I met Zak later that day. For a minute, it was like I'd seen a ghost. He reminded me that much of my brother. I even called him by my brother's name before realizing he didn't look a thing like him, though he appeared to be about the age my brother would have been—in other words, not quite old enough to be in college.

"It's weird. Zak didn't ask how I knew his name. Instead, he invited me to go running with him. It was a crazy idea with all the ice and snow and night coming, but I had no desire to study, and nothing else I needed to do.

"While we ran, we talked. He didn't say much about himself, and what he did say sounded unreal—except the part about wanting to be a teacher. He suggested I become one too, but that was later, when I'd gotten very drunk and ... and burned my psychology books."

I closed my eyes, remembering the heat of the fire on my face when the books blazed up, how it was like the words had escaped into the sky. I told Zak about my call with Jennifer and he put his hand on my shoulder, asking if I was alright. I shrugged. Zak squeezed my shoulder and waited. I was surprised. Other friends might have asked how I was doing, but none of them would have waited me out for a real answer. Maybe that's why I'd told him the truth. "Not so good," I'd said. "Sometimes I feel like an orphan." After a moment he said, "Me too." "Really?" I asked. Zak nodded, eyes distant, then smiled. "Hey, seeing as how we're both kind of like orphans, maybe we could be like brothers while we're in college." Uncomfortable by the sudden intimacy, I'd asked him about his accent and where he was from. He removed his hand. My shoulder was warm where it had been. I wished he'd put it back there, but instead he'd flashed me a grin and passed me another beer. Zak never did answer my question.

"Burning your books. A pretty dramatic way to change programs," Dr. McQueen said.

"Yeah," I answered. "But at least I didn't drop out of school like I'd planned. Zak made me promise to stick it out, that we'd play chess and go on midnight runs. I thought someone so young, without family support or the good sense to realize that running at night in the snow was a bad idea, might need looking after. I had a fleeting thought he wasn't real, that I'd made him up along with my brother's ghost, but after that night, I kept seeing him. He knew everyone. I meant to take him under my wing, but it was the other way around. In his first semester, Zak made more friends than I had in the two and a half years I'd been at school."

I leaned my head back on the couch and almost smiled, remembering that time when Zak and I became instant best friends. "I don't know why I thought of my brother when I first saw him. He doesn't look a thing like him," I repeated. "But there's something ... something about his ... his enthusiasm. His sweetness. You want to please him. It's why I let him ... why I agreed ..." I took a deep breath, but still couldn't say it.

"Go on," Dr. McQueen urged. "You can tell me."

"It's hard." I slowly unclenched the fists I'd made of my hands and stared at them—hands that had held Zak's arm as he sat on my window ledge, hands that had pulled him back from an oncoming train ... hands that would become useless after the 31st of December.

"He made me promise. I didn't want to but I couldn't bear ... So we agreed on a

191

... a deadline, and when it's up, I have to let him ... let him kill himself if he wants. He said it was his life and his decision. That I was being selfish. And he's right, because losing him ... I think it might kill me."

I waited for Dr. McQueen's response. It was long in coming.

"Why did you agree?" she finally asked.

"Because he begged me. And in the end, I can't deny him anything."

"Jeremy—"

"No. I need to say this. I've failed him and I've failed Annie. My job was to keep Zak safe, and now I've promised to let him kill himself."

"Listen to me. You're not responsible for Zak's life. You are also not responsible for your brother's death, though it's normal you'd experience guilt about what happened. You've studied psychology and you're an intelligent person, so I'm not telling you anything you don't know." She caught my eye before continuing. "But Jeremy, there's a lot to unpack from what you've told me today. The magical thinking, let's call it. I want you to consider seeing someone yourself. Someone just for you. I can refer you to a colleague of mine. He's—"

"No. We've talked about this. If I need to see someone, let it be you. You know Zak. How can anyone help me who doesn't know Zak?"

Dr. McQueen didn't look happy. "Alright. For now. But at least tell me what help you believe I can give you."

I thought hard about this, my mind racing ahead to when I'd be home. How would I look Annie in the eye? How would I smile in front of the kids? I didn't know how to act, with a future so uncertain, with all this fear and pain and guilt inside me.

"Tell me how to live," I finally said.

"A tall order," she said, smiling gently. "How do you want to live?"

I shrugged, feeling overwhelmed.

"What's most important to you?"

"To ... to be there for people—my daughter, my students, Annie. And Zak, of course."

"But what about you, Jeremy? What do you want for yourself?"

"To do the right thing." Dr. McQueen waited. "This is important to me," I insisted. "But yeah. I also want to be happy. Like everyone."

"And what would that look like?"

I imagined being happy. What I saw was Zak smiling, his hand on my shoulder as we ran in the park; Kyra giggling, acting out a scene with her superhero figures; Annie, her leg pressed against mine as we talked late into the night; Sierra, throwing a curve ball like I'd taught her; Brooklyn, playing a new tune on the keyboard for me; my sister Jennifer visiting, telling me stories and listening to mine.

"I want to be surrounded by family and friends. And to be at peace."

"What's keeping you from this?"

"Fear," I said, and knew this to be the truth. "I'm afraid all the time. Of losing the people I love. I can't even think about the future without being scared."

"How often do you think about the future?"

"Every minute of every day."

"And the past?" she asked. I looked down. "What about the present?" she pressed.

I opened my mouth. Closed it. "I don't know," I finally said.

"Can I share an idea with you?"

I nodded.

"It's good to try to make sense of the past. And of course, it's a good idea to plan for the future, to be prepared, especially when ... when there are some challenges to face. But the present is important too, the capacity to live in the moment. If not, all that planning and worrying about the future is for nothing, for a time you'll never be able to enjoy."

To give my thoughts time to settle, I walked over the Brooklyn Bridge. I concentrated on taking in everything around me: the cyclists ringing their bells, the tourists using selfie sticks, a jogger weaving her way around the slower moving pedestrians. I thought about how I'd want to live if now was the only moment I had.

At the center of the bridge, I stopped to watch the play of light on the surface of the river, but my eyes were drawn away from the water to family groups enjoying the spring weather. An idea entered my mind that made me smile, then wince. I touched my swollen lip gingerly, then my eye, gauging how long these injuries might take to heal. My plan didn't absolutely require that I look my best, but it definitely wouldn't hurt. But first I had to tell Annie the truth. It would be hard, but it needed to be done. For all three of us.

CHAPTER 29

I was down on my knees in my good, tan slacks, beside the screened-off table I'd reserved at the back of the Japanese restaurant. Zak and Annie sat, menus untouched, listening to the speech I'd prepared. In my right hand, I held two rings—one small and slim, the other larger and thicker, but still smaller than the one in my right pocket, the one I'd wear if they agreed.

"What I'm proposing—I know it's non-traditional, but we can make it work. I love you both. And Kyra already sees you as family." I moved to the conclusion. "So ... so I hope you'll accept my proposal of marriage."

Annie held the red rose I'd given her, twin to the one Zak was twirling in his left hand. Zak's expression betrayed no emotion other than very careful attention. He turned to Annie. Her cheeks were flushed, perhaps from the sake. A few weeks ago, when I'd come clean with her about my promise to Zak, she'd gone very pale. She'd asked me the same question Dr. McQueen had—why? I gave her the same answer—that Zak had begged me. Annie's pale cheeks had darkened with anger. She asked me a second question, one Dr. McQueen had not.

"And do you intend to keep your promise?"

I was confused for a moment. Did she mean my promise to her to look after Zak, or my promise to him not to interfere if he tried to kill himself? It occurred to me the ambiguity was intentional. I wanted to tell her I didn't know, welcoming the anger and contempt I deserved, but I knew what lay behind the anger—the same desperation I felt—so I looked Annie in the eye and said, "I intend to keep all my promises."

Would Annie understand this proposal was part of how I meant to do that? She looked to Zak for direction, and he smiled, continuing to twirl the rose I'd given him. I knew that smile, knew therefore I might be on my knees for a while yet.

"You look handsome, Jeremy," Zak said. "Nice shirt. But how come no tie? You didn't think the occasion called for a tie?"

"I don't like ties. They're too ... constricting. Would you like me to find a tie?"

"No. It's sexy, very manly, the way your chest hair pokes out from your shirt." He reached out to stroke my chest. "Don't you think so, Annie?"

"I agree. It's very sexy," she said, her smile now matching his.

"Do you want to touch it too?" he asked.

"Well, if Jeremy doesn't mind."

"He's proposed marriage to us. I think he's gonna have to deal with it."

I concentrated on not blushing.

"I'll wait until we've evaluated his proposal," Annie said, clearly enjoying herself.

"Yes, his proposal. Listen, J, I've got some bad news for you."

My heart sank. "What?"

"This idea you have. You know polygamy is still illegal in this state."

"Like you give a fuck," I retorted.

Zak awarded me with a huge grin. "Tell you what. Annie and I need to 'evaluate your proposal' as she put it. Why don't you freshen up in the men's room?"

"For how long?" I asked.

"Well, this is a serious discussion. It's not every day a girl, or a boy, or both, get a proposal for marriage. Let's say fifteen minutes."

"OK, then. Fifteen minutes. I'll give you fifteen minutes."

Smoothing my pants, I stood and walked towards the bathrooms in a way I hoped was dignified. In the men's room, I gazed at my reflection, turning my head from side to side. I'd gotten a haircut and beard trim. I usually went to the barber but this time had tried a fashionable salon. The haircut was intended to be stylishly asymmetrical, but to me, it just seemed lopsided. The beard looked good, though. Something between scholar and lumberjack.

I washed my face at the fancy sink, the hot and cold water flowing through an elegant trench, and used one of the dark green towels stacked neatly in the bamboo holder. I checked my cellphone. Three minutes had passed. *Concentrate on now,* I told myself. Since my appointment with Dr. McQueen, I'd been working on living in the present. Zak, meanwhile, was being weaned off the old drugs. Dr. McQueen had changed her primary diagnosis to trauma, a decision I wholly agreed with. I'd always believed Zak's manic tendencies were more a natural part of his energetic personality than evidence of a mood disorder.

Leaning over the sink, I examined my right eye carefully. The last of my injuries to heal, the bruise had faded to yellow. In the days following the subway incident, Zak had agonized over the beating he'd given me. I resisted the urge to tell him not to worry about it. Instead, I thought about how I'd feel in his place and let him take care of me. This seemed to help him, and as for me, I enjoyed his attentions. I'd forgotten what a good caregiver Zak was. He iced my swollen eye and lip, cooked me large, healthy meals, massaged my sore muscles.

The nights were tender and electrifying. Though there was still no sex, each day brought us closer. One night we faced each other in bed, not quite touching, Zak's soft breath on my face, the heat of his body inches from mine. He leaned forward and kissed my throat as my heart beat rapidly in my chest. Another night, he rubbed his thigh against mine for long, luscious moments as a sweet ache blossomed low in my stomach. In the past, I might have found this frustrating, but I concentrated on living inside the pleasure of each unique 'now', treating it not as building towards a future act, but as a moment full and complete in itself.

Seven minutes to go. I tried to pee, but my daydreams made that difficult. I thought about Zak's fingers stroking my chest before and Annie's following suit, which didn't actually happen. I wondered if Annie was as horny as I was. We took turns going to bed early with Zak, the other waiting in the living room until the household was asleep. As far as I knew, she wasn't getting any real sex either. I followed that thought to an obvious solution, then faltered.

My mind wandered finally to last night. Zak had taken me in his arms, stretching the full length of his body against mine. His hand moved up and down on my hip in a lazy, arrhythmic motion. I slid my hand down his back to cup his ass. He kissed me, long and deeply, and I floated in an ecstasy of pleasure and longing. These weeks had been restful, healing, but tomorrow Zak began a new regiment of therapy and medication. Time was moving forward and living in the moment was not the same thing as failing to act.

I gave up on peeing, zipped my trousers, and returned to the elegant sink.

Checking my phone, I saw that exactly fifteen minutes had passed. I exited the bathroom. Back at our table, there was no sign of Zak. The roses I'd given each of them were gone as well.

"Where—"

"Zak had to go somewhere but come sit. There's avocado sushi. Edamame too."

I stood where I was, appetite gone. Annie began to speak again, then smiled at something behind me. I turned and there was Zak, a swirl of red and green rotating before him. He was juggling—juggling red roses.

"Zak," I said, breath slipping out in one relieved sigh.

"Hey, J, you didn't get enough roses. What about the kids? They're part of this too."

I counted one, two, three, as he caught half of the roses in sequence in his right hand.

"And there's three of us," Zak continued, juggling the three remaining roses in a circle with his other hand. "You got one for Annie." He tossed one rose in the air. "And one for me." The second rose followed. "But you forgot to get one for yourself," he finished, tossing the third one high. Zak caught the first two roses in his left hand and, as the last rose descended, he bent his left knee, slid his right leg back, and tilted his head up, catching the last rose in his teeth. "For you, J," he pronounced with difficulty, mouth around the stem. I reached for it quickly, noticing the thorn a millimeter from his lip.

Annie clapped her hands, laughing with delight. Some customers from the closest tables joined in the applause. I smiled and waved the rose, lowering my voice. "Does this mean you've accepted my proposal?"

"Yes, but we have some details to work out," Annie answered. "Will you sit?"

I sat beside Annie, Zak completing our triangle, and reached for a piece of sushi.

"Well, for our honeymoon," I began, "there's this cabin north of Montréal, in the Laurentians. Remember that conference last year? I met this linguist and her wife and she—the wife, that is—teaches at l'Université de Montréal and runs this research project on local flora and fauna. There's a cabin on some land that's been set aside as a preserve and they invited us to stay sometime. I got in touch with them—just in case—and they said we could have it for the entire month of August while they're in Europe. Don't worry, Zak, I haven't forgotten the kids. They'll love it—lake, meadows, trails—all totally private. We can swim, hike— just no motorboats or sea-doos. I know a month is long for taking off work, Annie, but like Zak said, it's not every day a person gets married, right?"

I reached for another piece of sushi and Zak, who'd been grinning happily at my description, took the opportunity to grab more edamame, sucking out the beans and licking off the salt before adding it to the pile of empty pods on his plate. The server came to take our orders. I chose tofu teriyaki, deciding all at once that I could get used to eating vegetarian.

Annie poured the remains of the sake into my cup and turned at me, eyes twinkling. "This honeymoon idea sounds lovely, Jeremy. But we're getting ahead of ourselves."

"What do you mean?' I asked.

"There's the wedding itself."

"Oh. I thought we could have a small ceremony at the cabin, write our own vows."

"What about my family? Our friends? They'll want to be there. A marriage is more than our personal vows, you know; it's a public declaration. And an opportunity to have a big party."

I opened my mouth to speak, but Zak put his hand on my arm.

"Sounds like Annie has a proposal. She should get down on her knees, like you did."

"That's not necessary," I said. "Annie's wearing a skirt and—"

"I don't mind," Annie insisted, pulling back her chair.

"Wait," I said. I placed my jacket on the ground.

"So gallant," Annie said, grinning.

"That's our J," Zak agreed, complicit in the fun they were poking at me. I decided I didn't mind. I liked when they were both paying attention to me.

"OK," Annie began. "I propose we have a party. A very big party. And that there be music and dancing and ... and champagne. And I propose we hire a babysitter."

"You want to leave the kids out?" Zak said.

"No, they can come, but with someone else to watch them. I'm going to be dancing. With you. And with Jeremy. Or with you and Jeremy at the same time."

Zak laughed. "Yes! Let's do it! What do you say, J?"

"I ... I don't dance. I'm a very bad dancer."

"Should we make Annie go to the women's room while we discuss it? Or you and I could go into the men's together." Zak winked at me.

"The idea of dancing with both of you is about as much excitement as I can handle right now. Fine. A big wedding party. But don't have high expectations about my dancing."

"Oh, I don't know, Jeremy. Zak's said some nice things about your ... your moves," Annie said slipping back onto her seat. She reached over to the plate of sushi and carefully arranged the three remaining pieces in a close triangle. I quickly looked away.

"So Zak, how about you, do you have a proposal too?" I asked, to change the subject.

Zak went still before sliding to his knees with a gravity that supplanted the whimsical mood of Annie's proposal. "I want to stop taking medication," he said.

"Zak—"

"Please, J," he said, laying his head on my lap.

"Don't. Don't do this." I took hold of his shoulders and pushed him off me.

Zak remained kneeling, head down, left hand resting lightly on the table. I couldn't help noticing his gracefulness, even on his knees. When I knelt to make my marriage proposal, I felt awkward and must have looked that way. But I was following a tradition whereas Zak was really begging. I didn't like to see this.

"I can't give you permission to go off your medications," I finally said. "I don't have that right. This is your decision. Yours and your doctor's."

Zak turned to Annie in mute appeal.

"Jeremy is right. You should discuss it with Laisha."

"It's just ... I don't want you to think I'm giving up."

"Are you?" I asked him.

"No. I want this. All of it," Zak said fiercely, spreading his arms. "Only ..."

"Come sit with us, love," Annie said. "We can talk about it together."

Zak remained where he was.

"I won't discuss it while you're on your knees," I told him. "I won't do it."

Zak considered my words and regained his chair in one smooth movement.

"Why do you want to stop taking your meds?" Annie asked.

"I ..." Zak chewed on his lower lip. "I don't want to do what we've planned all drugged up. I want ... I want to be myself. To be able to feel the world, to feel the two of you, without going through a thick layer of chemicals. The drugs, they're hurting my mind, they're hurting my body, and I wouldn't even care if I thought they were helping me."

"Medications like these have saved a lot of lives—"

"I know, Annie, but in my case ... they're poisoning me from the inside, like the last time. Everyone keeps talking about finding out what happened to me. How can we do that when I'm so medicated I can hardly think? The things you've helped me to remember, J, when you hypnotized me—Laisha's been helping me put it together."

"And?" I asked.

"Sometimes I remember things, but ... I'm not sure they're real. Like what happened to my mother. Or going to school, hiding my bruises. I know this was normal for me. Constant. But I can't remember the beatings themselves. When I try to, I see things that ... that scare me."

"It's OK," Annie said. "You're safe now."

"I'm not afraid of being hurt. I'm afraid none of my memories are real. Because when I do remember, it's me who's using his fists. It's me who ..."

Zak began to tremble. I grabbed his hand, noticing Annie had done the same.

"No. You haven't done anything wrong," I told him. "Someone messed with your mind."

"Don't worry. Everything will be alright," Annie added.

"I ... I don't know," Zak said.

"I know. Annie knows," I replied, releasing his hand to put my arm around him.

"And we're both here to support you."

Annie put her head on Zak's shoulder while I rubbed his back. Little by little, the tension left his body. I sensed his spirits lift again, the darkness drain out of him. I turned to him and he smiled, and it was as though the room had grown lighter.

"I see how it's gonna be now," Zak said, "with the two of you teaming up on me even worse than before. Fine. I'll talk to Laisha about the meds. But ..."

"But what?" Annie asked.

"I get another turn. To make a proposal, I mean."

"I guess that's fair," Annie said.

Zak slid back down to the ground, but this time he was smiling, buoyant.

"I propose ... that there be three flavors of ice cream at our party. If there's gonna be a wedding and dancing and a big party and I'm off my meds, I'll be high as a kite. So I won't be drinking. But I deserve a treat too."

I glanced at Annie. She nodded her head. "Agreed," I said.

"There's one more thing." Zak turned to me. "You have to invite all your friends to the party. Including your entire basketball team."

"I thought I'd invite Khalil—"

"All of them, J. The center, the guards, the forwards, the backwards—"

"You know very well there's no such thing as a backward—"

"Every fucking one of them, J. You understand me?" I nodded quickly. "And your sister," he continued. "I want her there too."

"Jennifer's in San Francisco."

"I know. The two of you keep alternating coasts. You tell her we want her to stay with us for at least a week. At the end, I want her to be Annie's sister and my sister too, and I want you to spend quality time with her, you hear?"

"Yeah, fine," I said, wondering how Zak had managed to turn his proposal into a command. But truthfully, having an excuse to spend time with my sister was something I very much wanted. I felt a sudden surge of joy. I grabbed one of the three remaining pieces of sushi, dunking it in wasabi and soy sauce. Annie picked one up too, and I handed the third one to Zak. "Eat this," I said. "The oil in the avocado's good for your skin and hair."

Zak smiled and popped it into his mouth. "Whatever you say, J."

CHAPTER 30

If there were a paradise on earth, it would be just north of Montréal in the Laurentian Mountains by a beautiful lake hidden from the world. This is what I was thinking on the tenth day of our honeymoon vacation. While the rest of the family prepared for supper, I lay in the warm sun with Zak in my arms, the smell of grass and wildflowers filling my senses.

I wondered how I ever could have thought being with Zak was anything other than perfect. When I wrapped my body around his, he fit exactly within the spoon I made for him; when I faced him as I was doing now, thigh to thigh and chest to chest, all I desired was within easy reach of my hands and lips. I listened to the lapping of water in the nearby lake, the chirping of birds and frogs, the sound of wind in the grass. Zak's voice in my ear was the melody this gentle music was meant to accompany.

"Let's stay here forever," Zak whispered, and I pulled him still closer to me.

The depth of peace and privacy I'd found in this place was exactly what I needed following what had been like a continuous, wild coming-out party for me and my new family. As much as I'd been trying to live in the present, I couldn't help obsessing over everything that might go wrong, including each potential awkward moment. With all the talk at the Japanese restaurant of my sister and basketball buddies, we all knew which conversation I was really dreading—the one I needed to have with my ex-wife.

The strategy I'd decided to follow was to spill everything to Tara at once—like pulling a band-aid off a wound. I told her I'd been sleeping with Zak for over a year and that he and Annie and I had decided to become one family.

By now I'd gotten used to the fact that not everyone was shocked by the news that Zak and I were lovers. Robyn hadn't been the only one of my friends who'd suspected, and my sister actually asked what had taken me so long. Despite this, I wasn't prepared for Tara to be so unaffected by the news. "Why do I have the impression you're not surprised?" I asked her.

"You've always loved Zak more than me. It's why our marriage didn't work out."

"How can you say that? It broke my heart when you asked for a divorce."

"You were more upset about losing your family than losing me. So now you're getting a new family. Congratulations. I have one question. Are you sleeping with Annie too?"

"Tara, that's really none—"

"Hah! You're not, are you? That's what I thought."

I bit down angry words. Clearly, the idea that I wasn't having sex with Annie pleased Tara. I wasn't sure if this was because she wanted to think I liked men more than women or because she thought I wanted Annie but couldn't have her.

"Well, anyway," I said. "Thanks for being so ... understanding." She regarded me carefully, probably wondering if I was being sarcastic. "Look, Tara, I'd be pleased if you came to our wedding party. But I'd rather you didn't tell Todd. He's not as, um, open-minded as you are." That was an understatement. Todd was a raging homophobe.

In the end, Tara didn't come to the party, which I took as a sign she'd honor my request to leave her creepy, controlling, bully of a boyfriend out of the loop. She did send us a gift, though—king-sized bedsheets, maybe her idea of a joke. Most importantly, she'd agreed I could have Kyra for the entire month of August so we could go on our family getaway.

We'd taken the train to Montréal, a trip of more than ten hours that Zak observed wouldn't have taken him much longer by bike. I sat with Kyra, who at first was so over-excited she couldn't keep still and then so cranky she had a meltdown. This wasn't like her. She was usually a good traveler, happy to read chapter books or color while gazing out the window.

Annie saved the day by suggesting we play musical seats. She spent the next hour with Kyra beside her, the two of them designing 'wedding clothes' for Kyra's superhero dolls.

Sierra and Brooklyn each took a turn too, playing Go Fish and eating gooey Amtrak pizza together. Finally, Kyra sat with Zak, chattering non-stop about everything under the sun. When they were finally quiet, I peeked over the seat, ready to take her again, but she was fast asleep in Zak's arms. I decided every kid should have at least three parents.

Annie's idea to take turns spending time with each other was how Zak and I managed to find ourselves alone today. At first, we'd done everything as a family so the kids would know this marriage was about them too. Sierra continued to show me in small ways that I'd sabotaged her normal family life, but I was surprised to find Kyra acting out too. I even texted Tara, who told me she was going through a stage. In the end, I chalked it up to all the excitement of the marriage. In fact, Kyra had become obsessed with weddings, playing out scenarios with her action figures and directing the whole family in reenactments with lots of kissing, to Brooklyn's hysterical laughter. So when Annie suggested Kyra might feel insecure about her place in a new family, I decided to spend more one-on-one time with her.

Walking through the woods holding Kyra's hand, I reassured her that even if Sierra and Brooklyn were now my kids too, that didn't mean I loved her any less. I concluded by saying: "Not only do you have me and Mommy to love you, but you also have Annie and Zacky as another mommy and daddy."

"What about Todd?" she asked.

"Todd," I said, in what I hoped was a neutral tone. "I'm sure Todd loves you too."

It crossed my mind at that moment that hoping Todd wouldn't find out about my non-traditional family life was ridiculous—unless, of course, Tara broke up with him. Tara did seem less enamored with him lately. I hoisted Kyra onto my shoulders, feeling more cheerful.

"Hey," I said. "See how tall you are!"

"Daddy, don't be silly. *You're* tall. I'm just a little girl."

"What do you mean, *just a little girl*. You're Supergirl!"

I lifted her high above my head and ran as fast as I could to her squeals of delight.

The next day, I'd insisted on taking all three kids for the day so Annie and Zak could enjoy some time together. With Zak medication-free, his sexual appetite had returned in full force; yet, despite officializing our threesome, our couplings hadn't

206

changed: Annie and I were still having sex exclusively with Zak. There was a new intimacy, though. I was less self-conscious making love in front of Annie and allowed myself to experience pleasure when watching the two of them together. That didn't mean some alone time wasn't appreciated too.

I rolled carefully onto my back in the grass. Zak was dozing with his head against my chest. We'd stayed up last night to watch "les étoiles filantes"—the Perseids meteor shower this region was famous for—then woke early to hike up the ridge in time for the sunrise. It was chilly; I'd zipped up my sweatshirt, shivering as the sun began to lighten the sky. Zak had moved behind me and wrapped his arms around my chest. "Cold?" he'd asked. "Not anymore," I answered, Zak's body heat both warming me and igniting a responsive heat in my own limbs.

We'd resumed our hike. Before long, Zak, who tended to run hot, had removed his own sweatshirt, gradually shedding clothes until he was running through the woods naked. I'd pursued him, stuffing his discarded clothing into my backpack, and caught up to him at a clearing deep in the woods. He lay on his back waiting for me, knees in the air and slightly splayed. Though the rest of the family was far off and my professor friends had assured me this land was closed to the public, I still wasn't sure about making love out in the open. But I was too excited. I knelt between his legs, spreading him further. I kissed and stroked and finally entered him, his feet on my shoulders and his strong legs pushing and releasing, setting the rhythm of my thrusts.

We'd continued to hike, run, and climb our way through the day. Each new discovery filled Zak with joy—the wild raspberries whose thorny branches lined the paths, the family of rabbits who'd bounded off into the woods, the orange caterpillar that tickled his arm, the tiny purple flowers we noticed everywhere. I've never seen a person smile as much as Zak smiled that day. I asked him if he was happy just to hear him say yes. Instead, he'd tackled me to the ground, saying he'd be happier if I took my shorts off. I pinned him against the soft, moss-covered ground, the smell of pine and rich earth filling my nostrils.

Now, as Zak roused, the sun began to sink in the sky, turning the air cooler. "Do you want to get dressed?" I asked him as he nuzzled me sleepily.

207

"What for?" he replied, nibbling at my neck. His teeth were alarmingly sharp.

"You're like a wild animal," I breathed, grabbing his shoulders.

"You're the one who's all furry," Zak countered, rubbing the thick thatch of hair on my chest and stomach. "Hey, what happened to that belly of yours?"

"I lost it. Chasing you all over the fucking place."

"We need to get it back. It was comfy."

"I like myself this way," I told him, gasping as he used his teeth to pull at my waistband. I pushed him away so I could open my shorts.

"I like you this way too," he said, slowly taking my whole length into his mouth.

When we were done, he spoke again, picking up our conversation where it had left off. "I'm gonna cook you a big, fattening supper."

"Annie's cooking tonight, and I happen to know it's steamed broccoli and grilled tofu."

"But tomorrow's my turn and I'm making homemade pizza and ice cream sundaes."

"I guess Annie and I will plan on having an active day," I said, smiling.

"Like the one we had?" Zak grinned mischievously.

"Not quite," I answered, thoughtful. I flipped onto my side to face Zak once again. "When you and Annie were together yesterday, did you—"

"Fuck?"

"Of course you did. That's not my question. I was wondering if you talked about me."

"While we were fucking?"

"Zak, be serious for a minute. I'm worried that ... I mean, since I proposed and now we're, well, married, maybe she thinks it's odd that ..."

"You're not fucking?" Zak said, grinning.

"You're not going to make this easy for me, are you?"

"You don't like when things are too easy, don't you know that about yourself? Alright," Zak said, using his thumb to stroke my beard. "You're wondering what Annie thinks about the two of you not having sex. Well, I'm sure Annie knows you well enough to understand you have reasons for the things you do—or don't do.

Sometimes, these are really good reasons. Sometimes they're really bad reasons."
He laughed. "But does Annie know what your reasons are this time? How would
she, if you haven't told her?"

"I wouldn't want her to think I didn't love her, or that ... I wasn't attracted to
her."

"Well if you really want to know what she's thinking, or want her to know what
you're thinking, why don't you quit using me as an intermediary and talk to her
yourself. Being in a *ménage à trois* doesn't absolutely require you to have sex with
both of your partners, but I think you ought to have an open and honest relationship
with both of us. And as it happens, you'll have the perfect opportunity tomorrow,
when the two of you spend the day together."

CHAPTER 31

I helped Annie over the huge, moss-covered tree trunk that lay across our path. She took my hand with a smile that suggested she was doing me the favor, and maybe she was. Once over the trunk, Annie slipped her arm around my waist. I slowed my pace to accommodate her shorter legs. It was nice hiking with someone who was slower than me for a change.

"Did you have fun yesterday with Zak?" she asked me.

"Yeah, I did."

"Zak told me all about it. Sounds like you had a pretty active day." She winked at me.

I cast my eyes down to the path and thought about what I'd cook for dinner when it was my turn. Thinking about mundane tasks was one of my strategies for stopping my mind from wandering off in unhelpful directions.

"How about you?" I asked after a moment. "Did you have fun with Zak the day before?"

"It was great. We swam, kayaked. And spent a lot of time in the cabin." Annie laughed.

My vision of innocently sautéing vegetables morphed as I imagined Zak entering the kitchen, rubbing up against me, and leading me into the bedroom where he'd let me slowly take his clothes off as Annie watched and ....

"What are you thinking about?"

"Our wedding night," I answered semi-truthfully, recalling Annie's heavy-lidded gaze as I undressed Zak. "You looked so sexy, Annie. I hope you don't mind me saying so."

"Of course not. You looked pretty good yourself."

"Not like the two of you."

We stopped talking for a few moments as the path steepened. I pictured the silvery dress Annie had worn that night, low-cut on top, with strips of different-colored fabric sewn onto the skirt. Each time she turned, the strips swirled in the air, adding a magical quality to her graceful movements. And Zak. He had a violet sapphire in his left ear that glittered against his black curls. His pants were a soft grey and hugged his thighs, and his purple, silk tunic was so sheer I could feel the heat of his skin and the shape of his muscles right through it.

"I liked what you wore," Annie repeated, out of breath. "Brown and green ... suits you. You reminded me ... of a tree."

"What is it with the two of you and trees? Zak's always comparing me to one."

"Trees ... are nice," she panted. "I'd like ... to be under one ... right now."

"Do you want to rest?" I slowed my pace. "Or we could start back. It's getting late."

"No ... I want to make it to the top." Annie put her hands on her thighs and took a few deep breaths. "OK. This way." Annie left our roundabout trail and mounted a steep incline towards the summit. I wondered how she could find climbing easier than walking uphill.

"Wait a second, Annie!" I called out, but she was already far above me. I followed, searching carefully for secure handholds and footholds.

After ten more minutes of steady climbing, I was practically at the top, my head and shoulders above the highest trees. Annie grinned and reached her hand out to me. I took it, feeling humble, and walked with her towards the precipice.

Gazing at the view with Annie, I thought of the bike ride in the Palisades I'd taken last summer with Zak. He'd pushed me towards the lookout point, his hands on my shoulders, my heart beating rapidly from panic and exertion. The two views were very different. In the Palisades, I'd glimpsed sharp cliffs and water, imagined breaking our bodies on the rocks or drowning far below. Here everything seemed soft—the cottony clouds almost reachable, the treetops rounded by the distance. But the height was still dizzying. As though reading my thoughts, Annie asked if I were afraid of heights.

"Not really." She raised her eyebrows. "Well sometimes," I admitted. "When I'm with Zak, anyway. Not now. Not here with you."

I realized this was true. I was happy and relaxed, the vast expanse making me feel not scared but merely small—like the world was bigger and wider than I'd thought, but also simpler. I found myself thinking that maybe somehow everything would be alright. Especially if I kept my promise to be honest with Annie.

"Listen, I want to ask you something. Do you ever wonder why we haven't ... I mean, here we are married, so to speak, yet in bed ... "

"Yes?" Annie prompted.

"Well, you're probably glad I've been keeping my paws to myself."

"You know that's not true. I tease you enough."

"You like to tease me. I don't mind. That's always been part of our friendship. But seriously, Annie, what have you been thinking about ... about my reluctance in bed?"

"Well, I know you're a bit—I don't know—old-fashioned maybe? Or shy? That's why it's so much fun to tease you. Plus, despite your polyamorous marriage idea, ironically, you're the most monogamous person I've ever known. When you were married to Tara, and even after, you were obsessed with her. And now you're obsessed with Zak. That kind of love doesn't leave much room for other ... love affairs."

"You're not wrong, but there's more to it. Honestly, I've always had a thing for you."

"You don't have to say that."

"You're right, I don't, but I've decided to make a habit of telling you the truth. Do you remember the night of Dez's memorial, how Zak and I came home wet from the rain and he was so ... so strange? And later I told you I'd made him cry?"

"Of course. I gave you my appointment with Laisha so you two could talk about it."

"Well the thing was, Zak had been asking me how I felt about you and was encouraging me to, you know, be intimate with you. At some point, I realized Zak had this idea I could replace him. He could kill himself and I'd step in as your lover, help you raise Sierra and Brooklyn. He had it all worked out. So when I imagine being with you, I worry about how that might translate in Zak's messed-up head."

"Oh God, Jeremy. I wish you'd told me this sooner."

"I should have. I thought I could handle it myself and I didn't want you to be

212

upset."

"But what about this polyamorous marriage thing? Why did you propose it, then?"

"For all of the reasons I gave. For love. For family. Because it feels right. And when Zak made me promise ... it was time to go all in. I don't know what's going to happen, but this marriage makes me happy and it makes Zak happy. I hope it makes you happy too."

"It does. Whether or not the two of us have sex."

I moved back from the edge and sat down on a rock. I enjoyed the sight of Annie's agile, shapely body as she gazed fearlessly into the distance, eyes level with the clouds.

"C'mere," I said. She walked towards me. I reached for her and she let me pull her onto my lap. "I don't know what the future holds, and what we'll decide to do about the physical side of our relationship. But I wanted you to at least know what my body thinks of the idea."

Annie grinned as she adjusted herself on my hard lap. I put my arms around her, resting my chin lightly on the top of her head. "I do love you, Annie."

"I know. I wouldn't have agreed to this polyamorous marriage thing otherwise."

"We should call it our PMT."

"Better than PMS," she agreed, laughing.

We sat together quietly. I felt happy. Safe. But I also knew this was due, in part, to the fact that Zak would soon be coming with the kids to meet us by the lake. Annie again seemed to follow my train of thought. "Let's go down," she said, standing.

We walked down the mountain, side by side, chatting easily about my sister's visit, the mayoral primaries, the differences between the countryside here and in upstate New York, what Zak was cooking us for dinner. When we were almost at the lake, we discussed his progress, searching for that perfect balance between hopeful and realistic.

"Did he talk to you about his Skype session with Dr. McQueen?" I asked.

"A little. It sounds like she may actually resort to hypnosis when we get back.

That's how important she believes it is to recover those repressed memories. Zak's made some progress, but he's blocked."

"I still think someone purposely messed with his head."

"That's a bit far-fetched. But I suppose the hypnosis could help either way."

"I wonder if Dr. McQueen would let me do it," I said.

"I doubt it, and that's probably for the best. Let's let Laisha do her job. You and I have a different role to play. This PMT idea of yours—it's made him very happy. And, with time, maybe it'll give him the security he needs to face his past."

I nodded but thought about that end-of-year deadline. It was like a ticking bomb.

When we arrived at the lake, it was still early, so we settled on the grass to wait, speaking of other things. Kyra would be starting kindergarten in the fall. Since she wouldn't quite be five when she started school, I'd considered holding her back, but Tara vetoed the idea, arguing that Kyra was already reading. I supposed she was right but was uneasy with how all the changes in Kyra's life were affecting her.

Zak and the kids finally appeared over the rise. Kyra was sitting on Zak's shoulders and Brooklyn was holding his right hand. Sierra walked on Zak's left, tossing a ball in the air. They looked like the gang from Peter Pan. All four of them were barefoot and Zak and Brooklyn were shirtless. Kyra had on her favourite sundress, a faded green, the hem dusted with dirt and grass. Sierra wore a light blue tank top and cut-offs, her baseball cap turned backwards on her head. What struck me was how Zak looked like a kid too, a sweet, innocent expression on his face, his pockets filled with weeds and wild flowers.

When they were within a few feet of us, Kyra squirmed to be let down and ran to Annie and me. "I have brought you the Fairy Prince!" she announced in a loud, theatrical voice. "Fairy Prince, here are your bride and groom—the queen and king of the forest."

I caught Annie's eye, smiling in tired defeat, but Zak seemed happy to play along with what was shaping up to be our seventeenth marriage reenactment.

"First, your makeup, Queen Annie!" Kyra approached with two large dandelions and rubbed them over Annie's face until the yellow powder stained her cheeks with a weirdly-tinted natural blush. When it was my turn, Kyra had me close my eyes so she could apply the dandelion to my eyelids, nose, and the tops of my cheekbones, thoughtfully avoiding my beard.

"Now you may kiss the bride!' Kyra said to Zak.

Zak took Annie in his arms and kissed her. I could tell he used some tongue.

"And now you may kiss the groom."

This time, Zak took me in his arms. If Sierra's eyes rolled any further, I wasn't sure she'd be able to look straight ahead anymore. I placed my hands on Zak's shoulders. His skin was sun-warmed, and he smelled like wildflowers. I let him push his tongue into my mouth too.

"How did Annie taste, Fairy Prince?" Kyra asked.

I started but Zak hardly missed a beat. "Like wild strawberries."

"And how does Daddy taste?"

"Like hot apple pie, of course," he said, grinning at me.

"Todd tastes like cigarettes. It's yucky." Kyra said.

All at once, everything seemed to go silent, even the birds. Sierra, who'd still been playing catch with herself, froze mid-toss and turned to me. Zak was the first to recover.

"Kyra, sweetie," Zak said. "Maybe you and Daddy would like to take a walk together. That way you can have a private talk about Todd."

I took a few steps towards Kyra, ready to scoop her up in my arms.

"I can't. It's a secret." Kyra backed away from me, terrified.

"You could go to the enchanted meadow. It's magical there. You can tell your secrets and nobody will know," Zak explained.

"I can't tell Daddy 'specially!" she said, near tears.

"Go with Annie, then," Zak said quickly. "If it's a girls' secret, you could tell her."

Kyra hesitated, but shook her head. "You, Zacky! 'Cause you're a magic fairy."

Zak met my eyes. "Alright," he said gently. "We'll be back soon."

Kyra took Zak's hand and the two of them walked slowly towards the rise again. Zak glanced back over his shoulder. I saw that Peter Pan had plummeted to the ground leaving a beautiful, wounded child with the eyes of an old man.

CHAPTER 32

The others returned to the cabin while I waited for Zak to bring Kyra back. I paced because when I stood still, I was too conscious of my heart pumping blood into my arms and legs, filling me with the urge to smash and pummel, or simply run. When the pacing could no longer contain my nervous energy, I went to search for them. I had a general idea of where the 'magic meadow' was from Zak's description this morning of where he planned to take the kids.

I followed the wide, rocky path away from the lake. When I came to the turnoff that would take me back to the cabin, I went left instead, towards the woods. I walked briskly, trying to imagine some innocent explanation for what Kyra had said. My imagination failed me. I called out, "Zak, Kyra!" There was no answer but the wind.

The path came to a fork. I went left again, where the grass was flattened. The trail soon narrowed to a barely discernible track. There was no meadow, no obvious signs of where they might have gone. I kept walking, all my senses as alert as I could make them, but I was no woodsman—simply a city dweller who liked to be in nature sometimes. My mind travelled back again to that day when I was eight years old and ran off into the trees. My little brother had been four then, exactly Kyra's age. I quickened my pace.

I noticed a large stone ahead, to the left of the path. There was something odd about it, like it was covered in yellowish moss. When I got closer, I saw that what I'd taken for moss was a pile of wilted dandelions. I examined the area carefully. Beside the stone, there was a small opening in the foliage at about the height of a four-year-old child. I ducked down low, using elbows to widen the opening. A hidden path was revealed.

I pushed through the brambles to follow this path. The woods were quiet, very still. The path went straight, followed by a sharp turn to the right. The land opened up to a small meadow framed by white birches and covered in a sea of wild flowers colored chicory and dandelion. The dramatic beauty of it seemed surreal. At the other side of the meadow, Zak was moving along the edge of the trees, Kyra in his arms. I cut across to them, stepping high over the grasses and flowers. When I was closer, I saw that Zak had wrapped his t-shirt around Kyra. Her small, dusty feet peeked out, making her seem even more vulnerable.

"Zak," I called.

He shushed me with a finger to his lips and gestured that I should follow. Rocking Kyra in his arms, Zak continued walking at a brisk pace along the edge of the meadow.

I jogged to catch up. "Zak! Where are you going?"

"I'm walking the perimeter," he said without slowing. "We need to keep Kyra safe."

I quickened my pace, reaching out to grab the back of Zak's shoulder. His skin was slick and hot, like he'd been running hard. "Perimeter? What are you talking about?"

There was a howling in the distance. Zak trembled.

"The wolves. We have to keep them from Kyra," he whispered.

"Those are loons," I told him. Zak tried to pull away to continue his patrol but I held him fast. "Give Kyra to me, Zak. Right now."

Zak obeyed, carefully lifting and placing Kyra on my own shoulder. She stirred, so I rocked her as Zak had. "Did she tell you what happened?" I asked quietly.

Zak nodded, gazing towards the entrance to the meadow as though to satisfy himself no one was there. "She's fine but scared. I had to promise. Not to tell anyone. You especially."

"But you're going to tell me." Zak chewed on his bottom lip. "Zak!"

"I can't break my promise. If I do—"

"Fuck that! She's my daughter. Tell me what that bastard did to her."

"J, he said he'd kill you! I had to promise him not to tell ... "

"What are you talking about? *You* had to promise him? Promise who?"

Zak seemed confused. "I mean Kyra had to promise ..."

I cupped my hand around Kyra's head, rocking her some more, while Zak stood wringing his hands, taking quick glimpses towards the opening in the trees and looking sick with panic.

"Zak, focus now. For Kyra's sake. Tell me everything she told you."

Placing his hand on Kyra's back, Zak's confusion seemed to clear at the same time as his resolve hardened. "Kyra only told me because I promised this was a magical place, where secrets are safe. I won't betray her trust." I opened my mouth to argue, but Zak put his finger on my lips. "I know I have to tell you what happened. I know that. And I will. But in my own way."

Zak removed his hand from Kyra's back and wrapped his arms around us both. He smelled of perspiration, of fear, but his arms were steady. "Do you trust me?" he whispered.

I hesitated, focusing on the warm weight of my daughter's head on my shoulder. This, along with Zak's strong embrace, anchored me. "Yes," I answered.

"Good," he whispered. "Because I'm going to tell you a story. About kissing. And not kissing. I can't tell Kyra's story but I can tell my own. At the end, you'll know what happened to her. And what didn't. Not because my story is Kyra's story, but because it isn't. Do you understand? That's the key. This is *not* Kyra's story."

I nodded with an assurance I didn't feel. Zak began his tale.

"My father never kissed me. Most fathers kiss their children. Maybe to say goodnight. Or when they go to work. But other fathers. Or … stepfathers. Maybe they kiss their children inappropriately. Sexually, I mean." Zak glanced at me to see if I understood. I nodded slowly.

"But that's not my story. In my story, the father never kissed his son. Not to say goodnight. Not on my first day of kindergarten or when I was sick or got straight A's or won a contest or … or a baseball game. My father never showed me any affection. You understand, J? There are fathers who kiss their children—or their girlfriend's children—in a bad way, and maybe this happens once—only once—and then someone puts a stop to it. That's *not* my story."

219

Zak looked at me significantly until I nodded again. Not his story. Kyra's story.

"My father didn't kiss me. Sometimes he didn't even talk to me. Instead, he beat me. With his fists. Or if we were alone outside and I did something he didn't like, he'd grab a stick and hit me with that. Sometimes he used a belt and when he did that he made me ..." Zak trailed off, gazing into the distance again. His look was so intense, I turned to see what he was staring at, but there was nothing.

"My father never kissed me but he did other things to me. I couldn't remember all the things. But now I have to. For Kyra. To make it not be her story. You understand?"

"Yes," I said reflexively, keeping my eyes on him. Since beginning his tale, Zak's nervousness had returned. On top of that, his voice had changed. It had gotten brighter, younger. And though he was staring straight at me, it was like he was seeing someone else.

"Sometimes ... Sometimes my dad wouldn't talk to me. Not even to say 'pass the potatoes.' That was worse ... worse than the beatings. Once we went a whole month like that. I went a little crazy, alone in that house on the edge of town and him paying me no mind at all."

Suddenly Zak grinned happily. "Hey, did you know I was a pitcher? Like Sierra."

The grin slipped from his face.

"My dad ... was our coach. We were the Wolf Cubs. One day—it was the day I pitched the no-hitter. I was nine. Someone called me a long-haired wolf 'cause I wouldn't get my hair cut. I'd used the money to buy me and my friends ice creams. I knew that'd make him mad. I ... I did it on purpose—so he'd have to talk to me. I didn't care if he beat me. I needed him to stop acting like I wasn't there.

"At the game, he let me pitch. 'Cause I was the best and dad always wanted to win. So everyone was there watching me pitch with my long hair. I knew Dad'd be mad but I thought he'd be proud too. I pitched real good that day. But he said I'd humiliated him. 'Cause I looked like a girl. That's what he said when ... "

Zak went silent, still staring at someone who wasn't there. I held Kyra close to me.

"When we got home, we went into the house and his eyes ... My father's eyes,

220

they were like wolf eyes. Red and mean, like he'd tear my throat out and I was so scared I did everything he said and he made me drop my pants like when he used the belt, or when I was little and I bent over his knee to be spanked, but I was too big for that so he bent me over a big old chest instead and I heard him taking off his belt and I braced myself but he did something to me and I didn't know what it was except that he'd figured a way to hurt me inside as well as outside and it hurt so bad I screamed and he told me if I wanted long hair like a girl he'd treat me like one but I didn't get what he meant 'cause why would you treat a girl like that?"

It was a warm summer day sliding towards evening, but Zak stood panting and shivering in the middle of the meadow like he'd been running in the snow. I'd wrapped my arm around Kyra's ears to block her hearing even though she was fast asleep and I shivered with Zak, sick to my stomach. I reached for him, shifting Kyra higher on my shoulder.

Zak stumbled back. "No!" And then more quietly, "You shouldn't touch me right now."

I stayed where I was and watched Zak carefully, wondering what I'd do if he tried to hurt himself while I held my sleeping child in my arms. After a moment, Zak calmed.

"I'll finish the story now. My father never kissed me, but he raped me. Again and again. From the time I was nine until ... until it ended. Getting my hair cut didn't matter. He said I was too pretty to be a boy. That I looked like my mother, who was beautiful but in the end was just a dirty gypsy. The mother I'd killed when I was born. But no, that was later ... "

Zak seemed confused again but he shook it off, squarely meeting my gaze.

"My story isn't and will never be Kyra's story because we won't let it. I'll do anything to make sure this will never be her story."

CHAPTER 33

Be careful what you wish for. I'd longed for a breakthrough that would help Zak remember and face his childhood trauma. Now that breakthrough had happened, but with it came deeply disturbing revelations—along with a threat to my daughter's well-being. I brooded upon all this as we took steps to keep Kyra safe.

There was the difficult call to Tara, her initial shock and denial slowly yielding to the truth. There were the numerous Skype sessions with Dr. McQueen—including one with Zak lasting three and half hours. There were the late evenings in front of my laptop writing and rewriting statements for the police; the multiple phone interviews with Child Protective Services; the notifications and paperwork that had to be done for Kyra's school. On top of that was the art and play therapy Annie and Dr. McQueen had collaborated to create, and the many long hours indoors the rain afforded us to do this therapy. We spent so much time in that cabin that I dreamed at night about the pattern of the carpet in the living room, and each knot and whorl of the wooden beams were likewise branded into my brain.

Without understanding everything, Sierra and Brooklyn instinctively rallied around Kyra, drawing and playing and singing songs with her. And we three adults spent every waking moment with them, playing and drawing too, though the singing was beyond what I could manage.

Kyra sat in Annie's lap clasping her Supergirl action figure while she told off a large, plastic stegosaurus for trying to kiss her without permission. Brooklyn joined in the scolding, rolling his own action figure—Bicycle Boy—to Supergirl's side. I thought about joining them, but glimpsed Zak on his hands and knees reaching for a toy unicorn with a purple mane. I turned away, asking Sierra if she wanted to play chess.

After six days of this, I was beginning to go stir crazy—though Zak was preternaturally calm. Since the rain wasn't letting up, Annie decided we should go into town. We treated ourselves to poutine and pizza; then Annie suggested Zak take the kids and do the shopping since we were short on groceries.

"Let's all go," I objected.

"No, Jeremy. You and I have a date with a couple of cups of coffee."

I thought about arguing but knew Annie well enough to recognize that tone of voice. I squatted down to close the top snap of Kyra's rain jacket while she squirmed impatiently, then watched them walk off before reluctantly following Annie up the street.

We slid into a booth with blue vinyl seats just across from the old-fashioned soda counter. The place was about two-thirds full, bustling without feeling crowded. Soon, we were blowing air across steaming cups.

"Why do I get the sense I'm in trouble again?" I asked.

"Not in trouble, but what's going on between you and Zak?"

"I ... What do you mean?"

"You've been avoiding him. As much as it's possible to avoid someone inside a small cabin we've been pretty much trapped inside since Monday."

"It's only that I need to spend time with Kyra right now."

"You've spent every minute with her for a solid week." I didn't respond. "She's going to be fine, Jeremy. Laisha says so and you can see it yourself. There was only the one incident and the worst part for her was how he'd scared her into keeping it secret. Now that it's out in the open, she's her old chatterbox self. No more obsession with kissing. No more acting out. She was even able to talk about what happened with her mom."

"I know and I'm relieved. Especially that Tara got an order of protection so fast. I was afraid she wouldn't believe me."

"And she wouldn't have if Zak hadn't taken the phone and talked to her."

I sighed. "I know."

"So why are you pushing him away?"

"I keep thinking about how if I'd been a better father, this wouldn't have happened. I'd sensed something was wrong. Maybe if I hadn't been so wrapped up in Zak—"

"That's not fair. You never neglected Kyra. And not only did she get all your paternal love and attention, she got a double portion because she got it from Zak too."

"Maybe that's true, but ..." I sighed again, struggling with how to explain it. "It's like I ... unknowingly made some kind of a Sophie's choice. To save Zak by letting Kyra be hurt. I wanted so badly for Zak to have a breakthrough. I would have done anything—"

"Jeremy," she said, putting her hand on mine. "That's magical thinking. Your worst thoughts are still just thoughts. They can't make bad things happen."

She was surely right, but I was unconvinced. Annie shook her head in frustration.

"Blaming yourself for this—I don't mean to be harsh, but it's childish. The universe isn't weighing what you are and aren't worrying about and deciding to teach you a lesson. The universe doesn't give a shit about us. Because why else would children like Kyra have to go through this? And why would someone like Zak have to suffer ... suffer the way ..."

I slid out of the booth, bumping my knee on the edge of the table, to take her in my arms as her eyes filled. "Shh, Annie," I soothed, "Shh, it'll be OK."

"Qu'est-ce que t'as dit pour faire pleurer ta blonde?" a young guy at the next table asked.

"Rien du tout, je vous assure," I said, not sure how to respond.

Annie reached for a napkin and blotted her eyes. "What did he ask?"

"He just wants to make sure you're alright," I temporized, frowning.

"It's cool you can speak French, Jeremy. Sometimes I forget how smart you are."

"It's no wonder with how stupid I act."

"Don't say that. You'll make me feel guilty for saying your guilt was childish."

I laughed, and we silently sipped our coffee. It's true I'd been pushing Zak away, not just because I felt guilty for not protecting Kyra better, but because I was freaked out about what had happened to him. I wondered again if there was something unhealthy about our relationship, especially how I let him provoke me into hurting him. I pushed my thoughts back to my daughter.

"How do you think I should act around Kyra now?"

"You need to be present and reassuring but you should stop fussing over her. She can sense your worry, and it's bound to make her nervous."

This made me wonder how my own father's constant worrying had affected my parenting style. Emulating his overprotectiveness rather than my mother's distance was surely a better choice. But did I have to emulate either of them?

"What about Zak?" I finally asked. "Should I give him some space too?"

"No, exactly the opposite. He needs a strong man in his life who won't hurt him."

"Maybe I'm not that man."

"Of course you are. Stop being so hard on yourself!"

Annie's confidence reassured me. She squeezed my hand before taking out her cellphone to check her messages, signaling the end of our conversation. I eyed the door, anxious for the rest of the family to return. The steady sound of the downpour calmed me. After a while, the rain tapered off, the water on the glass front window of the café already drying. The sun filled the café with rays of light as Zak appeared at the entrance with the kids. They were carrying ice cream cones. As they walked towards our table, Zak dipped his face towards an untouched cone of melting chocolate and licked it all the way around. He offered it to me with a shy smile.

CHAPTER 34

Zak and I sat facing one another in the 'N-chanted meadow,' as Kyra liked to call it. I thought about how to break down that wall of unspoken fears keeping us apart. As usual, it was Zak who jumped into the breach, placing his hand on my shoulder. "How you doing, J?" he asked. I smiled, remembering a younger Zak who made that same gesture.

"How am *I* doing," I repeated.

"With what happened to Kyra? Yeah, how you doing?"

"You're really something. Well, I'll tell you what. I'm not doing so great with that. But there's this other thing I found out, which is that my best friend, who also happens to be the love of my life, was raped by his father when he was nine years old. And now he's sitting here asking me how I'm doing, even though I've been shutting him out all week."

"You're upset. It's a lot to deal with."

"Zak," I sighed, pushing a lock of hair from his eyes. My body longed for him, but I pulled back, troubled. "I ... I need to tell you something. That day, when Annie and I were waiting by the lake for you and the kids? You came down the hill and I ... I couldn't get over how young you looked. If I didn't know better, I'd have taken you for a teenager. And yet, I was so hot for you. At the same time that I thought you looked like a kid."

"It's alright—"

"No. How am I different from Todd? Or from your ... your bastard of a father? I want to kill them both. Yet there I was, turned on by how you looked like a kid. What's wrong with me?"

"There's nothing wrong with you. You're the best father in the world. The best friend. And as your lover, I'm glad you're turned on by how I look." Zak stroked my beard before grabbing my hand and placing it against his own cheek. "Tell me what you feel."

I ran my hand up and down the side of his face. "You need a shave," I announced.

He smiled. "Yeah. Because I'm not a boy. I'm a man, just like you."

"Maybe you're not a man and you're not a boy either. Maybe you're a magical fairy." Zak made a sound that was something between a laugh and a sob. "You're so beautiful," I whispered.

Zak ducked his head, but I saw the pain in his eyes and remembered how his father used his beauty as an excuse to abuse him. I thought about what Annie had said. "I would never really hurt you. You know that, right?"

"I know," he said. "Sometimes ... Sometimes I wish you would."

"Why would you want that?"

"I don't know," he murmured, bringing his knees up to his chest.

"You're probably just confused," I told him gently. "Because of how your father treated you. Sometimes victims, they think they deserve to be hurt."

"No. It's not that."

"Then what?" I waited, but Zak stared at the ground, looking unhappy and frightened. "Talk to me, sweetheart. Tell me what you're thinking."

"Maybe ... Maybe I need to see that you're stronger than me. So that ..." Zak swallowed.

I put my hand on his shoulder, squeezing gently. "So that what?"

"So I know I can't hurt *you*," he whispered.

"There's only one way you can hurt me, and you know what that is."

Zak shrugged, a shrug that was like a door closing.

"Don't shut me out, Zak. Dr. McQueen— she said it's important for you to try to ... to process what happened to you. I'm here. I'm listening. Please, just talk to me."

"It's ... hard to talk about. To think about."

"What can I do to make it easier?"

Zak sighed. "I don't know. Maybe ... maybe if you ask me questions—"

"Sure. I could do that."

Zak lay back, the high grasses hiding his face. I lay down too, reaching for his hand. I thought about what I should ask. The only thing I really wanted to know was whether Zak's father was still alive, and if so, where I could find him so I could

227

remedy that problem. But this was the one question I'd already asked him, and Zak had shut down so fast and so hard, I dared not ask it again.

"Can you tell me how many times he ... he raped you?"

"Can you tell me how many times you took a shit last year? No? Me neither. But I know it was a lot." Zak laughed and it was a bitter sound, so unlike his usual laugh.

I told myself his anger was good, far better than the self-loathing he'd felt without understanding why. "How did you bear it?" I asked.

Zak was silent, but I waited him out. "I would count," he finally said. "The first time I remember doing that, I counted to 669 before it was over. Funny I can remember that number but not ..." Zak took a deep, slow breath before continuing. "I liked to count by threes. I was good at it. I could've counted to a million that way. But I never had to. See, there was a limit. The pain wasn't infinite. It would end, as long as I could count it out. The numbers—they protected me."

I remembered the night in the ski lodge, Zak's panic that the blank scrabble tile meant infinite. I squeezed his hand. "Did no one try to help you?"

I felt his shrug. "There was a teacher. I ... It didn't work."

Now I thought about Dez. That "didn't work" either. But things were slowly starting to make sense. The math. Being a teacher. Dez.

"You must have had a lot of friends. Did any of them ... Did they suspect ..." Zak's hand went limp in mine. I hung on, rubbing his knuckles with my thumb. There was no response. "Zak, it's OK. You don't have to answer. I won't ask any more questions." I turned onto my side, flattening the grass so his face was visible. He was swallowing convulsively; his face was wet with tears. He didn't seem to be aware he was crying.

"J," he said, trying to smile. "Look how blue the sky is. How did it get so blue?"

I reached over and wiped his face with my hand. "I love you," I said simply.

"Sometimes I wish you were ... " Zak chewed on his lip and looked away, as though embarrassed. "J, do you think he loved me at all? Even though he didn't kiss me? Even though ...Maybe he couldn't help himself. Maybe he did it because he loved me."

I wanted to tell him the truth, that his sick bastard of a father probably didn't love anyone but himself, that if he were in front of me right now, I'd put him out of his misery without a second thought. Zak seemed too vulnerable to hear this, yet he deserved my honesty.

"Rape isn't about love. It's about violence and ... and power. The beatings, the silence, the rape—it was all abuse, plain and simple."

Zak's eyes filled with tears. Did he not know this already?

I reached for the silver ring I'd given him which he wore on a chain around his neck. I held it between my fingers and kissed him lightly on the forehead. Zak smiled slightly and I kissed him there again. "Close your eyes," I told him and when he did, I kissed both his eyelids, then his nose and his chin, wishing I could give him all the gentle, platonic kisses he never received as a child. I turned him over and rubbed his back, then pushed up his tank top up to reveal his tattoo. I kissed the one, two and three squared, those nines, so twisted and tortured. The bottom half of the tattoo included symbols I still didn't understand. A fist, the number twelve surrounded by its integers, a fire that seemed to blaze up under my lips. I pictured a parched dessert, my kisses like water, seeping deep into the sand, turning it into rich, dark soil where something beautiful could grow—like those purple flowers we kept seeing.

Zak drowsed in my arms. "You can ask me the two questions now," he murmured. I hadn't hypnotized Zak since Dr. McQueen asked me not to, and I hadn't intended to now. I opened my mouth to say he didn't need to answer questions, but an idea occurred to me.

"Think back to when you were small. Forget the bad things for now. Instead, concentrate on your good memories of your father. Times when he was loving, kind. Alright, Zak?" He murmured his assent. "Sort through all those good memories and find the best one. The one that proves your father loved you." I paused to give him some time. "Have you found it?"

Zak breathed in and out, his arms locked around my chest. I waited, but he didn't answer. When I'd concluded he was sleeping, he said, "I'm little," and indeed, his voice sounded very young. "I'm ... four. I don't go to school yet. It's winter and it's cold."

"Where are you?"

"I'm in the woods with Dad. There's snow on the ground and on the trees and everywhere. I'm being very quiet. So Dad won't get mad and hurt me. Dad has his gun and I'm carrying a stick and pretending. But I don't want to shoot anything. I ... I see a bird. It's blue and beautiful!"

"What happens next?"

"I show Dad the blue bird. I point to it without talking. Like he taught me. Now Dad's looking at the bird too. I stretch my neck and wish I were tall like him so I could see it closer up. Dad sees me trying to be taller. He lifts me up in his arms and points to the bird. It's blue and so beautiful and it's cold but Dad's arms are warm and there's smoke coming out of our mouths and I watch the blue bird."

"And then what?"

"Dad puts me down. I walk behind him again, good and quiet, thinking about the bird and how Dad picked me up to see it."

I waited, but that was all. Zak looked at me with sleepy eyes and repeated, "He picked me up. So I could see the bird better. That means he loved me, right?" he asked, uncertain.

"Of course," I said, pulling Zak's head against my chest so he couldn't see my tears—tears for my poor friend whose very best memory of his father was this small, sad tale. I swallowed, my voice steadying. "Sleep, sweetheart, sleep and think of the blue bird. And while you're sleeping, I also ... I want you to know how much I love you. And I can love you any way you need. I can be your brother. Your lover. I can ... I can even love you like a father, like you're my own precious child." I kissed the top of his head. Zak sighed in my arms. "But whatever happens, I will always, always be your best friend."

"J," he murmured into my chest as I held him close.

When Zak was deeply asleep, I settled him onto the grass and laid back. The clouds were moving fast in the sky, forming pictures that dissolved and reformed and dissolved again. I heard a bird singing, reminding me of Zak's blue bird. I searched the skies but saw only a cardinal of a startlingly bright red that made me think of blood.

"J!" I heard Zak cry out. I sat up with a start.

"What is it?" I said, but Zak was still asleep, his eyes closed and his chest moving up and down in slow rhythms.

"J," he repeated. Only his mouth moved. "I need to tell you a secret. You think you know everything now, but you don't know the worst. You need to stay away from him."

"From who?" I asked without thinking.

"From Zak. He'll kill you. Like he killed the other J."

His voice gave me goosebumps. It wasn't the voice of an adult, nor the childish Zak from before either. Something between the two, but with a nasty edge.

"What other J?" I asked, despite a creeping fear.

"The first J. His best friend. He killed him dead. When he was only twelve."

The fear leapt into my throat. I swallowed it.

"Zak would ... You would never kill anyone. Why are you saying this? "

"You're too soft," he said, contemptuously. "I'm trying to give you a chance. You're good to him but he doesn't deserve it. You should have let him die. Now he's gonna kill you."

To hell with not waking a sleepwalker. I couldn't listen anymore.

"Zak," I said, my voice soft but urgent. "Wake up now."

"Run, J," he whispered. "Run, J, Run!"

"Zak!" I took him by the shoulders and shook him hard.

Zak sat up. "J?" I released him. He touched my face with his hands. "It's you."

"Sure. Who else would it be?" I paused. "You OK?"

"I feel wrecked. Let's head back."

Zak stood. We walked across the meadow. I breathed deeply, trying to calm myself. I rested my hand on Zak's shoulder. He leaned into me and I was reassured.

231

"You sure you're OK? You were saying some weird shit in your sleep."

"What did I say?"

I hesitated but decided to forge ahead. "Something about killing me. That when you were younger you killed the first J and—"

Zak hit the ground with a thud. He'd blacked out, arms and legs splayed on the grass.

"Zak!" I said, one hand on his shoulder, the other on his face.

He opened his eyes, sat up slowly.

"Can you stand?" I asked.

"Sure I can stand. Why are you asking me that?"

I helped him up. "What's the last thing you remember?"

"I was sleeping. I ... I had a bad dream?"

"Yeah. Maybe. How do you feel now?"

"A little cold."

I unzipped my sweatshirt and helped him put it on. We left the meadow and started back to the cabin, Zak shivering despite the sweatshirt. "I don't feel so good, J ... Jeremy," Zak said.

I slipped my arm around his waist, but he pulled away.

CHAPTER 35

Zak began avoiding me. At first, it wasn't obvious, but when we returned to the City, he was not only increasingly skittish in my presence, he also began having terrible nightmares that left him sobbing and shaking but unable to articulate what was wrong.

At least this time I didn't hide anything from Annie. I told her what had happened, repeating Zak's nonsense about killing the 'other J' and how I was next. Like me, Annie didn't believe Zak had killed anyone, but she suggested perhaps Zak was secretly afraid of me—that his crazy idea about me not being safe around him was some form of protection. Her words wounded me. How could she think Zak feared me, even subconsciously?

I'd hoped the truth of what was really going on would come out in Zak's sessions or during hypnosis, but Zak had done an about-face. He refused to be hypnotized by Dr. McQueen, had closed himself off not only to me but to his memories.

I shouldn't have done it, but the Saturday of Labor Day weekend when we were all in Prospect Park, I'd heard birdsong and thought of Zak's sad story. I gazed at the sky, searching for a blue bird, but again saw something red. This time, it wasn't a cardinal but a maple leaf— a sign that autumn was coming. It made me afraid. Soon it would be the end of the year. The deadline I'd agreed to would be here, and with it, the end of my ability to save Zak from himself.

The next day, after bringing Kyra to Tara's, I returned to the apartment to find Sierra and Brooklyn out. Zak was putting away some groceries and Annie was folding laundry.

"What's for supper?" I asked. Zak started at the sound of my voice, though he'd seen me come in. "Can I help?" I asked him, approaching the kitchen.

The cucumbers Zak was holding slipped from his hands. "It's OK, I'm good."

"You're not good. You're nervous as hell." Zak recovered the cucumbers and placed them on the counter between us. I reached for his hand, noticing that it was shaking. "Zak, maybe it would help if you knew the thing you're nervous about never happened—"

"Jeremy—" Annie warned.

"He needs to understand. You never killed anyone, Zak. You're not going to kill me—"

Zak's knees buckled and he collapsed to the floor, his head smacking the linoleum. Annie ran into the kitchen. Zak was out cold, his forehead bleeding. He opened his eyes and I moved to his side. Zak shrunk from me.

"Go ... go get a towel, Jeremy. And some ice. I'll get Zak to the couch."

I grabbed a tray from the freezer and twisted it in my hands, dropping the cubes onto a clean towel. Zak lay on the couch, turning his head from side to side as though feverish or in pain, while Annie knelt beside him. I approached them with the towel full of ice.

"Easy does it," Annie said to Zak, flashing me a warning look.

I stood where I was, reaching out to Annie with the icepack I'd made. She placed her hand on Zak's forehead. "He's burning up," she announced. "Go see if we have some Advil."

There was nothing in the medicine chest but children's Tylenol. I returned empty-handed. Zak was having trouble catching his breath. "We should go to emergency," I said.

"Please, no hospitals!" Zak begged.

Annie placed her hand on Zak's chest and turned to me, her expression grim. "Jeremy, would you go to the pharmacy? Pick up some ibuprofen. We'll see if that helps."

I returned to the apartment with the pills in a small, white paper bag. Annie said Zak was resting comfortably now, but I insisted on checking on him. As soon as he saw me, he became agitated again. Annie told me to wait in the living room. I watched her leave the bedroom and return again with a glass of water and some pills. I waited for her, pacing nervously. About ten minutes later, she came into the living room and motioned for me to sit.

"His temperature was over 104. Now it's back down to 100."

234

"So fast? That's gotta be psychosomatic," I said.

"Of course it's psychosomatic. I didn't even give him the Advil. I gave him the children's Tylenol. Which expired last April."

"He's making himself sick. He's found a new way to kill himself."

"But only when you're in the room. He's fine now, but if you walk in there, I guarantee his fever will shoot up again," Annie said.

"Because of that bullshit. He's convinced he's a danger to me."

"Jeremy," Annie said. "Why did you say what you did in the kitchen?"

"You mean about him thinking he was going to kill me?" I asked. She nodded. "To show him what was actually going on," I explained.

"You told me you tried that in the meadow. So you knew how he'd react."

"I didn't think he'd black out again. Or hit his head. I thought—"

"No, you didn't think. And when you don't think, you're a danger to him."

"Annie—"

"Jeremy, I'm sorry, but it's best if you leave."

"Leave? What ... what do you mean?"

"You should sleep in your old apartment tonight."

"Annie, please. I'm sorry. I was just trying to help."

"I know what you were trying to do. But if you love him, you'll back off right now."

I argued, but in the end, I did as she asked, because when it came to the complexities of our entwined relationships, it was Annie who had the moral high ground. I'd done all kinds of things—both right and wrong— because of my love for Zak. Annie, on the other hand, had always acted in Zak's best interests. I wasn't sure I loved Zak enough to let him go, but I knew she did. Otherwise, she'd never have encouraged Zak and I to become lovers. I understood now that she'd done this because she thought it was good for him. If I wanted to come back, she'd still have to believe this.

The night Annie banished me from the apartment, she'd been angry, but she'd reassured me that it was only temporary—until Zak's shock in remembering his father's abuse wore off and he began to come to terms with it. Instead, things with Zak got worse. The first day back to school, he stood as far from me as he could at the teacher's assembly. He was nervous and clumsy in my presence, unable to stand still or complete a conversation. Yet, he seemed fine when I wasn't around—or so I was told. After two weeks of this, Annie and I decided it would be best if I took a sabbatical, ostensibly to work on my book. Malika agreed to find a replacement for me and Zak didn't argue.

We settled into a new routine. I stayed clear of Zak, though we spoke every night. If I was lucky, we'd Skype. To avoid depriving Kyra of her new family, I was forced to further divide my time with her. During the weeks I had custody, she spent some nights with me in DUMBO, others with Zak, Annie, Sierra and Brooklyn. The kids were puzzled, of course, but seemed to accept what we told them about my needing time alone to finish my book. And if my landlord thought I'd returned for good, I might be offered a bigger settlement in exchange for giving up the apartment. We held out the promise that if all worked out, we'd soon be able to move as a family to a bigger place.

As time passed, my separation from Zak felt more and more like a bitter punishment. I told myself not to be selfish. Wasn't my sacrifice worth it for Zak to be whole and happy? But that was the problem. He wasn't whole. He wasn't happy. A vicious lie had taken hold of his mind and he wouldn't be well until that lie was rooted out and replaced with the truth.

October was dark and unseasonably cold. Halloween, a holiday I'd stopped enjoying after my brother's death, was the perfect close to a dreary month. Annie and Zak were taking all three kids to the parade on 7th Avenue. They wanted me to see their costumes, so we arranged to Skype early in the evening. Sierra was dressed as a major league baseball player, her uniform regulation perfect; Brooklyn was a dragon that blew bubbles instead of breathing fire; and Kyra was the Invisible Woman from the Fantastic Four, her flashy blue spandex making her anything but invisible. After I admired their costumes, the kids filed into the kitchen for supper and Zak came to the phone, turning off the video.

"How are you?" I asked.

"OK. You?"

"I ... I miss you."

After a moment, Zak asked me how the book was going.

"I completed another chapter. I'm about 75% done now."

"That's what you said last time."

The tease in his voice made me smile. "It was true then too."

"That's impossible. Another chapter's gotta bring you closer to 100%."

"Not if the 100% is changing. I mean, if the book keeps getting longer."

"Ah," he said. "A moving target. Well, I have faith in you. You'll finish it eventually."

"Yeah, I'll finish it and come back to school and give up this apartment finally. And we'll all live happily ever after," I insisted.

Zak didn't respond. If I could see him, I could at least read his expression.

"Zak? Would you turn on the video? Please?"

I waited. The screen remained dark until I saw what looked like a white oval in the middle of a dark background. It resolved itself into a face that was unearthly pale. My heartbeat accelerated as I recalled the image of my dead brother. "What the hell?" I whispered. I gazed at the screen more carefully, saw it was Zak dressed in all black, his face eerily whitened. "What ... who are you supposed to be?"

"Death," he answered, his voice flat.

"Fuck death," I retorted. "You're the opposite." I reached for the screen, placing my hand on the image of Zak's face, uncertain if my gesture was meant to block or caress. "Let me see you, Zak. In person. Please. Let me hold you for a few minutes."

The screen went blank. I heard a muffled sob. The video came back on, but it was Annie's face I saw. She was made up to be a clown, but she wasn't smiling.

"You can't do that to him, Jeremy."

237

"I'm sorry. But this is like my first divorce times three," I said, feeling ashamed.

"You know why we're doing this."

"Can I see *you* in person, at least?"

"You'll see me on Tuesday when we're having pizza with the kids."

"I mean alone."

She hesitated. "Of course. The two of us will go somewhere afterwards. Alright?"

"Good. As long as it's not another coffeeshop."

We met at 'Whine Bar' on Fifth. The interior was faux art deco, all metal and glass and too brightly lit. I chose two wines from the Finger Lakes region: a Riesling for Annie and a French-American hybrid for me. Annie took a sip and smiled. "You always choose well, Jeremy."

I shrugged, not willing to let a compliment change my mood. "How are the kids?"

"You just saw them."

"They seemed ... anxious. Unsettled maybe."

"They're fine. Kids are amazingly flexible. Capable of accepting all kinds of situations as normal and adapting to them. Maybe you're projecting," she said.

"You love that word, don't you? Maybe they're feeling what they seem to be feeling."

"Maybe they're reacting to how you're obviously feeling. Kids are sensitive. They pick up their parents' emotions."

"Make up your mind, Annie, are they flexible or are they sensitive?"

"You're angry."

"I miss Zak." Annie waited, her expression patient. "OK, yes, I'm angry too."

"What are you angry about?" she asked.

"That you don't trust me."

"You're wrong. But trusting you and agreeing with you are different. You think you understand what's going on with Zak and that you can ... do things to him without consulting his psychiatrist, or me. Maybe I'm just a more cautious person than you are. People say you're the cautious one, but I know you better. When the stakes are high, you go with your gut, and because you're smart and have good instincts, you can usually get away with it. But when you're ... overwrought, you can be ... Well let's just say I'd rather play it safe and follow Laisha's advice."

"It wasn't Dr. McQueen who threw me out. It was you."

"I didn't throw you out. I only—"

"Look, I don't want to fight with you."

"Then why are you?"

I picked up my wine. Sighed and put it down again. "You told me if I loved Zak, I'd back off. So I did. But then I asked myself a deeper question—whether I could give Zak up completely if his well-being depended on it. I've decided I could, even though it'd leave a hole inside me big enough to ... to drown this city in. As long as he was well and happy. But here's the thing. We've been apart now for two months. Is he well? Happy?"

"First of all, this separation, it was supposed to be temporary—"

"*Was* supposed to be?"

"Is supposed to be. Until he's better."

"Until he's better," I repeated. "And how's that going?"

Annie took a sip of her wine, not meeting my eye. "It's true he's low energy. A bit depressed. But there's no suicidal ideation, no self-harm. He isn't shaking or dropping things or waking up screaming. He's functional, at least."

"Functional. That beautiful genius who's always had more energy than three people combined is functional. That's great. I'll stay out of it then."

"You can't be with him right now. He'd fall apart. With some more time, maybe—"

"We don't have that luxury. Right now, he's not trying to hurt himself. But what if that changes? What if in the new year his depression worsens, becomes dangerous?"

"He's coming to grips with sexual abuse. Depression is a normal reaction."

"And his fear he's going to kill me? Is that normal too?"

"I don't know. Maybe it's related to the ... the particularities of the abuse. And the complex way he views you. He's projecting—"

"He's not projecting! He's introjecting! Annie, Zak's been gaslighted. His father put these ideas in his head. It's obvious! You know the movie—"

"I know what gaslighting is. And introjecting. I'm a clinical social worker, remember?"

"So you understand what I'm saying. What I think is that Zak had a childhood friend—J or whatever his actual name was— and he confided in this friend, who then tried to help him. And something happened. And Zak's father convinced him he'd killed his friend."

Annie was silent, but it was obvious she was thinking through what I'd said. This was one of the things I loved about her. Other people—me, for instance— might be listening carefully, but only in order to figure out how to counter the other guy's arguments. Annie, on the other hand, was actually considering whether I might be right.

"Do you think ... Could his father have killed this other child?" Annie finally asked.

"I doubt it. Probably no one killed anyone and it's all bullshit, part of what an abuser does to isolate and frighten his victim. That's why this forced separation ... It's not good for him."

"In the long run, I agree. But right now, when he sees you—his reaction is too extreme. Like Laisha says—sometimes you need to treat symptoms before getting at the cause."

I sighed. "I understand. And I agree to stop pushing so hard to see him."

Annie glanced at me in surprise. "I was afraid you'd try to change my mind."

"No. But there is something I'd like you to do. Explain the gaslighting theory to Zak."

"I suppose I could suggest that his father may have manipulated him into believing certain things. Or ask Laisha to talk to him about it."

240

"That'd be great," I said, coming to a sudden decision. "Listen. In the meantime, I won't be seeing Zak or you for a while."

"Why not?" Annie asked.

"I'll be travelling. It's time I visited Nebraska."

CHAPTER 36

The worst moment is just before takeoff. You're strapped into your seat, phone on airplane mode, laptop tucked away. It's too late to back out but too early to order a whiskey. All you can do is wait and think, and wait and worry, and wait some more until the thrust of the airplane pushes you into your seat and the pressure makes your ears ache and you're hit by the realization that even the air can be your enemy. Air. Time. Distance. Truth. They all can be your enemy.

Flying to Nebraska, I'd been determined, even hopeful. Now, on my way home, I was clinging to the memory of that hope. What would I say to Zak about what I'd learned? I closed my eyes, remembering the Skype conversation we had just before I boarded the plane.

"We'll be together soon," I'd said. "Whenever you tell me you're well enough."

"I may never be well enough."

I wanted to contradict him, but a more honest response was that I'd take him exactly as he was, well or not. "I'm here for you," I said instead. "In sickness and in health."

"We didn't say those words."

"It doesn't matter what words we said. There was a reason I got down on my knees and it wasn't to beg. I was pledging myself. To you and to Annie. No matter what."

"I don't deserve it. You're ... you're too good to me."

"That's not true," I said, louder than I'd intended. A waiting passenger sitting in one of the rows of black, bolted-down seats jerked his head up from his paper, but I was too worried to care. What Zak said reminded me of the eerie voice that had come from his sleeping body in the meadow—-*You're good to him, but he doesn't deserve it. You should have let him die.* "Listen to me, Zak. Do you see where I am?" I lifted my computer and rotated it slowly, 360 degrees, as I attempted to suck every last bit of Wi-Fi out of the airwaves of the Western

Nebraska Regional Airport. "Recognize this place? You must have been here when you went off to college."

"No. I didn't fly, I ran. And when I'd run far enough, I hitchhiked. I never went back."

His candor and clarity surprised me. When I first met Zak, he'd told me he was an orphan, but not where he was from. I don't believe he's ever once lied to me. Not knowingly.

"I'm never coming back either. We're done with this place, with the past. I know everything I need to know and ... you don't have to worry anymore."

"What ... What did you ..." Zak trailed off. I heard his rough breathing.

"Everything's alright. Turn the video on—I need to see that you're OK."

After a long moment, Zak complied. He sat alone, elbows resting on the kitchen table, the other family members undoubtedly still asleep at this hour. He was wearing one of my flannel shirts; the cuffs had slipped past his wrists and were covering his hands to the knuckles. He looked thin, the shirt hanging loose from his shoulders, but I told him it looked good on him.

"It's a bit big," he responded. "But I ... I like how it smells."

Zak rubbed his cheek against the fabric, wrapping his arms around himself. I cradled the computer which held his image, my chest aching.

"They'll be boarding the flight any minute now so I'll have to fill you in when I'm back, but one thing I can tell you. Your friend—the one you also call J? He doesn't look a thing like me. I mean, his hair's brown and wavy, and he's fair-skinned like me, but he's not even that big. It's just that he was older than you. But now ... I'd be surprised if he's even six feet." I watched Zak's face as I spoke. "And sure, his name starts with 'J'. You called him Jack but his real name was John, right? Like his dad. Like your own dad—John Wolf."

As I babbled on, Zak's expression went through a series of transformations—from terror to uncertainty to a cautious hope. He'd stopped chewing on his lower lip to stare straight into the camera. "But Jeremy, are you saying you ... you found Jack?"

"Of course I found him. Though I had a hell of a time of it. No Facebook account, no LinkedIn or Instagram. I had to use old school records. I can show you when I get back, but ..."

"But what?"

"It's only ... Well, I'm sure he'd want to be in touch with you. But sometimes people need to forget the past, to move on, even to run—as far as they can. Hey, did you know they had a social media interface for people doing international solidarity work? Peace corps, woofing—some of those places don't even have Wi-Fi! And—" I stopped to listen. "*This is the pre-boarding announcement for flight 3069. Those passengers with small children or who require special assistance ...* "Zak I gotta go. I don't want to miss my plane."

As we said our goodbyes, I reiterated my promise to answer questions when I got back. He looked like a man who'd received an unexpected death sentence pardon but wasn't sure he deserved it. I gave him a confident smile. After a beat he smiled back. As always, it was his look of trust that undid me. I'd do anything to deserve it. Anything but throw him to the wolves.

I now had six hours to figure out what I'd tell Zak had happened in West Lupe, Nebraska. How much truth could he stand? When does an omission equal a lie? And what about fiction—couldn't that be a kind of truth? I rehearsed three different versions of my story.

The first version was the most believable—that I was completely stone-walled. At 13,494 people, the town where Zak grew up was a fraction of the population of the college we'd both attended in Boulder. Folks in small towns can be kind to strangers, but they rarely air their dirty laundry. And the laundry we were talking about was as dirty as it got.

The stonewalling extended from one-on-one encounters to inquiries at government offices. Birth records, death records, police reports, property sales—everything was missing, archived, or otherwise unavailable. As soon as I mentioned the name 'Wolf,' it was like a metal gate had been pulled down between us. The worst was at the hospital.

"We can't give you that information," a man with a toupee and tortoise shell glasses told me. "Federal law requires ..."

"I know about HIPAA. Zak's doctor sent all the authorizations."

"We never received anything." The man shrugged, his face impassive.

"Fortunately, I've brought another set." I handed him the documents.

The hospital administrator reluctantly took the forms from my hands and glanced through them. "This is a photocopy," he said, triumph in his voice.

"No, it's an original." I pointed to Dr. McQueen's signature in blue ink at the bottom.

"The information on the forms has been photocopied, even if the signature is original, so that makes it a photocopy. I'm sorry," he said, sounding not at all sorry. "You'll have to submit an original to obtain those records. And it will take sixty days. How long will you be in town?"

"HIPAA requires that you process the request within thirty days."

"We're allowed an additional thirty days for good cause."

"This is a small hospital. How hard could it be to find these records?"

"They're more than fifteen years old. When you try to dig up old histories, there are bound to be problems." He looked me straight in the eye. "I'd advise you to keep that in mind."

I had better luck at the schools. West Lupe, Nebraska boasted two elementary schools, two middle schools and one high school. One of the middle schools was adjacent to the high school; the other was on the outskirts of town on a flat, dusty road, directly across from a dry riverbed. It was there I found Zak's seventh grade math teacher.

Millie Field wore a powder blue pantsuit and pearl earrings. Short grey hair curled around her small, almost triangular face. "I have photos from the math team from the last forty years," she enthused, clearly flattered that a teacher from New York City was interested in her school's math program. I bent over the photos with her, making appreciative noises. About halfway through her collection, I was rewarded with a photo where a young Zak's dark eyes stared back at me from the middle of a small group of neatly dressed students.

"Do you remember this boy?" I asked Ms. Field.

Her expression became guarded. "Why do you ask?"

"Zak and I teach together," I said, grinning.

Her face relaxed into a smile, exposing a gap between her two front teeth. "I'm not surprised he became a math teacher. He was a gifted student."

"Are there other photos of Zak? He'll get a kick out of it when I tell him I met you."

We walked down the hallway, empty but for the janitor and a middle-aged man wearing a bow tie who hurried past us. Ms. Field showed me the 'Wall of Honor,' a photo display of school teams that had won championships. She found a photo of the track and field team from one year earlier than the math team photo. On the far left was a slim Zak with dark curls; a bigger, fairer boy was beside him, his arm casually thrown around Zak's shoulder.

"Who's that?" I asked, pointing to the bigger boy.

She leaned forward, pushing her glasses down the bridge of her nose. When she saw who I meant, she pulled back abruptly. "You can't expect me to remember every child I taught."

"No, but you remember him, don't you?" She set her mouth in a firm line and I sensed that gate coming down again. "Please," I said. "It's important. Just his name. That's all."

She gazed up at me, taking my measure. "You're not a math teacher, are you?"

I hesitated. "No. But I am a teacher. And Zak is my friend."

She sighed. "Jack. Jack Philips. Now I need to get back to grading."

"Jack Philips," I repeated, the boy Zak believed he'd killed when he was twelve.

I returned to the hospital twice more but made no progress. On my final visit, a dark-haired woman looking about forty-five approached me in the parking lot. I'd noticed her watching me during a previous visit.

"Why do you want Zak's medical records?" she asked.

"Zak's not well. Having his complete medical history could help him."

"You've been asking questions in town. About his family life, friends. About his father."

"Yes."

"No one's going to talk to you about John Wolf."

"Why not?"

"Who are you?" she asked, ignoring my question. "Who is Zak to you?"

I didn't answer. She began to turn away. "Wait," I said, grabbing her wrist. She wrenched her arm away, fear in her eyes. I stepped back and apologized, horrified I'd frightened her. "Please. I'm ... I'm his best friend. If you could help him ..."

The woman rubbed her wrist, but the fear was fading from her expression. She seemed to measure me with her eyes, the way Millie Field had, but in a way that felt more intimate. "I'll try to make sure they send the medical records," she finally said. "But the sooner you leave, the better. Your coming around just makes things difficult."

I hesitated. "What about John Wolf? Do you know him?"

"I ... I knew him. He's dead now."

"Dead?" I was surprised. I figured everyone was stone-walling me because they were afraid of Zak's father. That was certainly the vibe I got. "How did Wolf die?"

"He died at home, in bed." I opened my mouth to ask another question but she cut me off. "Isn't the important thing that he's gone now? Your friend can have the closure he needs. And you can leave the rest of us in peace."

With that, she turned on her heel and left me in the parking lot. I decided she was right. It was time to go home. I went back to my room and packed my bags.

Another version of the story begins like the first, but this time, prior to returning to the hospital, I meticulously filled out a new set of original forms for obtaining Zak's hospital records. I overnight expressed them to Dr. McQueen, and three days later, I received the signed originals at the Airbnb where I was staying, about sixty miles from town.

Back at the hospital, I threatened to show up every day until the records were produced.

"You can hold your breath until kingdom come," the toupeed supervisor said, shoving the new request under his arm. "It won't make one whit of difference."

I noticed the fortyish woman, dark hair in a neat bun, watching me from down the hall. When I returned to the parking lot, she was waiting for me, a cigarette in hand.

"Do you have a light?" she asked as I walked towards her.

"Strange habit for a doctor," I remarked.

"I'm not a doctor."

"A nurse, then."

"I'm a social worker."

"My ..." I stopped, unsure how to describe what Annie was to me. "Someone I'm close to is a social worker," I said, feeling the inadequacy of my words. "I don't smoke," I added.

"I'm trying to quit. Tell me, what's your connection to Zakarya Wolf?"

"Zak Heron," I corrected. She seemed surprised but nodded as though she understood. "He's a friend," I said. The woman waited, expectant, her unlit cigarette pointing at me. "More than a friend," I said quietly.

She nodded again, thoughtful. "I'd just started working here when I was given his case. His father wasn't happy."

"That you were so new?"

"No, that a social worker was assigned to his son."

I waited, but she said nothing more. "Can you help me?" I finally asked.

"That depends. What are you looking for?"

"Zak—Zakarya's medical records. And to find out what happened to his friend, Jack Philips. And to see Zak's father, if he's still alive."

She sighed, rubbing the back of her neck. "I'll do what I can about the medical records. It's the least I can do after failing him when he was a child. But the rest— you know, sometimes it's best to let sleeping dogs lie."

"Zak needs closure. I'm here to make sure he gets it."

"You may end up finding out things you wish you hadn't."

"Been there, done that," I replied.

"John Wolf is a dangerous man."

"Is?"

"You're not afraid of him. You should be."

"The only thing I'm afraid of is losing Zak. Anything else, I can handle."

248

She regarded me for a few moments without speaking. I stood alert, arms hanging loosely at my side—a fighter's stance, I realized. Finally, the social worker—whose name I still didn't know—ground the unlit cigarette into the gravel of the parking lot and approached me, shaking my hand before walking off briskly. I turned to find my rental car, not opening the paper she'd slipped me until I was far from the hospital. When I got back to my room at the Airbnb, I checked the address she'd written. It was about seventy miles northeast of West Lupe.

The next day, I checked out, drove to the airport, and returned the rental car. I walked the three miles to Scottsbluff and rented a room at a sketchy motel where real names were neither required nor expected. I shaved my beard and bought some new clothing including a blue knit cap, then rented a bike and camping equipment, saying I planned to cycle to the National Forest and hike there for two weeks. Instead, I biked the forty or so remaining miles to where Zak's father lived and began hanging out at stores and restaurants closest to the wolf's den, as I thought of his place. I spotted him my third day in town.

He was tall and wiry like Zak, though with none of Zak's graceful fluidity. He could be a charmer too. At the diner, I overheard him flirt with a waitress half his age, then praise the cook, a florid man with a pot belly who smiled with real pleasure at the compliment. Most times, though, he seemed a bitter, belligerent man, his expression often a sneer as he pushed past people on the street. He was especially nasty when he'd been drinking—something he did frequently—picking fights with men twenty years his junior and winning them through sheer viciousness.

I waited three more days before making my move, following him home from a tavern where he'd been drinking and brawling. He lived in a small house—more a cabin—well off the main road. I knocked and he opened the door without hesitation. I said I was Zak's friend. He narrowed his eyes, asking me what the hell I wanted. When I didn't respond, he looked me up and down and gave me a filthy smirk. "Never mind. If you're my son's friend, I can guess." Then he turned his back on me like I was beneath his notice.

There was a wooden baseball bat leaning against the wall. I picked it up. The grip was worn, the bat smallish—a kids' bat. Perhaps he still coached. Perhaps he still hurt children. I held it in my hands and waited. When he finally turned to face me again, I bashed his head in. I thought about taking his wallet to make it look like a robbery but couldn't bring myself to touch him. Instead, I took the bat and left him crumpled on the ground, elbows and knees pointing at different angles.

The next thing I knew I was biking, my mind as blank and empty as the land I was riding through. The flatness of the road made the 72 miles to the National Forest less difficult, but the ugliness of it hurt my soul. Not a mountain in sight and no woods either, save the forest itself, which I'd read was man-made. It made me wonder about Zak's story of the snowy woods and the blue bird. Had it been real, or a wishful, childish vision? I decided it had been real—there'd been so much detail. I imagined his small hand on his father's neck, the way Kyra placed hers on mine when I held her and she wanted my attention. Then I imagined Zak's father raping him five years later, Zak screaming, his skinny arms braced against the chest. I pulled over to the side of the road and threw up.

I stayed in the park for a week, enough time to grow back a short layer of beard, burn the clothes I'd been wearing along with the bat, and repeatedly wash non-existent blood from my hands. The guy at the place where I'd rented the equipment asked me how the camping had been. I told him it was important to get away from people sometimes. It turned out he knew a lot about wildlife. I asked him the name of the blue bird I thought I'd glimpsed in the trees.

"Sounds like a bluebird," he told me, laughing.

"Are they common in Nebraska?"

"They're endangered now, what with all the shopping malls destroying their natural habitats. There's even a society to protect Nebraska bluebirds."

"Doesn't development endanger other birds too?"

"Yeah, but bluebirds are less aggressive, more vulnerable than other species."

"Do they migrate or stay in Nebraska for the winter?"

"Some migrate and some stay. Some of the ones who stay die from the cold, but others make it through. Brave little birds."

I nodded my head. "It's time for me to head home. I just got married. I gotta start looking for a bigger apartment."

"Well good luck to you. And don't forget the bluebirds."

"Not a chance."

In the third variation of this story, the social worker is still waiting for me in the parking lot. Like in version two, she warns that sometimes it's better to let sleeping dogs lie. I tell her that as long as we're trading clichés, she should remember that the truth will set you free. As in the other versions, she asks who Zak is to me. I hesitate, then surprise myself by telling her the truth: that he's everything to me. The social worker, whose name is Ronnie Taylor, decides to open up.

"When I studied social work, it wasn't only to help families. I wanted to change how people—especially children— are treated by social institutions. Zak was one of my first cases. He ended up being a brutal lesson in how naive I was."

"You have another chance to help him now."

"I'll do what I can about his medical records."

"What about Zak's father? Can you tell me anything?"

"He was the most terrifying person I've ever met."

"Was?" I ask her.

"He passed away some time ago," she explains.

"So why is everyone still afraid of him?"

"Because of John Wolf, people did a lot of things they're ashamed of. When people start lying, it's hard to stop. Even when the main reason for the lying is no longer there."

"How did he die?"

"Why does that matter?"

"I won't know until you answer my question."

"Maybe it doesn't matter. Water under the bridge."

"Zak's standing on that bridge right now, threatening to jump, and I need to know what's under it. Water or blood or hard concrete."

251

We argue for a few more minutes, and she finally gives way. She tells me Zak's father died in a fire. His home burned to the ground in the middle of the night, with him sleeping inside. I ask her when this happened and she tells me: It was the summer before Zak left for college and never returned. He was still a minor, but no one tried to hold him back. It was six months later that I would meet him for the first time, his back freshly tattooed.

The plane was starting to lose altitude. I could sense it even in my sleep. My dreams were full of the sensation of falling while alternate versions of Zak's story played themselves out like a lurid film. What would I tell him? The only thing I knew for sure was what I'd say about Jack. Zak and Jack—that's what they used to call them, like one name: ZakandJack, and always Zak first. Though younger, he was the leader—charismatic, always full of energy and ideas. They were like brothers, and then they fought, and Zak's brother was gone. But now the lost brother was found and everything would be alright. The big, bad wolf was dead, somehow or other, and Middle-earth would finally be at peace. It was time for a happy ending.

CHAPTER 37

As soon as we landed and the seatbelt sign went off, I grabbed my things and stood bent over, the clogged aisle making me dance from foot to foot with impatience. I fished out my phone and took it off airplane mode. A chorus of messages chirped for my attention. I scanned through the texts and missed calls—three from Tara, two from Annie, and one from Zak. Tara and Annie both asked me to call back; Zak's message simply said "Come home J."

Inside the airport, the news screens were reporting a major blackout in lower Manhattan. That probably explained the multiple messages. My head told me to return Tara's call first, my heart wanted to choose Zak, but my finger was already speed-dialing Annie.

"Jeremy? Where are you?" she said, picking up on the first ring.

"On my way out of the airport." I stepped onto the escalator. "What's the matter?"

"Did you speak to Tara?"

"Not yet, but I heard about the blackout."

"Yeah, well Tara got stuck downtown and there was a mix-up and ... It's Kyra, Jeremy. The school released her to Todd."

"What! Are you saying he has her?" I seized the escalator's handrail.

"Try not to panic."

I made for the exit with my carry-on luggage, hands shaking. "The school has strict instructions on who can pick up Kyra! How—"

"I don't know. Something about new staff and the computer going down. When they realized their mistake, it was too late. But Zak thinks he can intercept them."

Outside, I got into one of the cabs waiting at the curb. "Head to Brooklyn," I told the driver. He grunted his assent and started the engine.

"Tara wants you to come over," Annie continued.

"That's the last place he'd go."

"Call her at least. And call Zak. He's worried."

"Where are Sierra and Brooklyn?" I asked. "Are they OK?"

"They're fine. I'm on my way to pick them up."

I called Tara and learned the police had put out an Amber Alert. "They have both of their descriptions," she told me. "I'm supposed to stay here in case Todd tries to contact me. There's a police car across the street."

"I don't understand how this happened. And why did Todd choose today?"

"I ... I don't know," she said, but her tone said otherwise.

"What aren't you telling me, Tara?"

She sighed. "Todd found out about you and Zak. And Annie. When I met with him—"

"You met with Todd?" I shouted. The driver glanced towards his rear-view mirror.

"At a public place. He told me he was going to counseling. Kyra was with Zak and Annie. I told him that so ... so he'd know he wouldn't be able to see her. But he went nuts when I explained about your arrangement with the two of them—"

"It's not an *arrangement*, Tara, it's my family. My fucking family. And now my daughter is in danger because of your ... because of Todd."

"You don't think he'd hurt her?" I didn't respond. "Jeremy, answer me!" she wailed.

"I'm going to find her," I said. "Call me if the police learn anything."

I hung up. My hand gripped the inner door handle of the taxi. I wanted to rip it off.

"Keep going west," I told the cabbie. "I'll let you know where exactly."

"It's your dime," he said, turning up the radio. I put on my headset and called Zak, my eyes scanning the digital traffic billboards for news of my daughter.

"J, where are you? Don't worry. He can't have gotten far." Zak's voice was clear and sure.

"In Queens, en route to Brooklyn. Where are you?"

"Headed for the Williamsburg Bridge."

"Why there?" I asked.

"Because it's his first opportunity to cross into Manhattan. It's total chaos

254

there, which he probably figures'll help him. Plus, he lives in Jersey."

"I'll call the police. They could block off the bridge."

"I wouldn't count on the cops," Zak said.

"I know you don't trust them but we could use their help." He didn't answer. "I'll call Tara—she's in direct communication with some police officer—and call you back. Better yet, stay on the line. Can you hold the phone while you bike?"

"I don't need my hands to bike, just my legs."

"Put on your headset. That's what I'm doing."

"Don't worry, J—you can count on me."

I put Zak on hold, told the cabbie to head to the Williamsburg Bridge, and called Tara. She was very subdued, agreeing Zak could be right about what Todd would do. I had her describe his car and what Kyra was wearing, then hung up so she could call the police.

I got Zak back on the line and learned he'd been turned back by riot cops at the other side of the Williamsburg Bridge. He was now on his way to the Manhattan Bridge instead. I told the driver to stay on the Expressway to downtown Brooklyn.

I clung tightly to my phone. This bit of plastic and electronics seemed too small, too delicate, to be a lifeline to my family. If only I could reach through it and bring Kyra to safety. When Tara and I divorced, I'd insisted Kyra have a cellphone so I could talk to her when we were apart. I wondered if she had her little phone with her now. I tried composing a message but my auto-correct kept changing the nonsense I was typing into worse nonsense. I cursed the manufacturers who marketed cell phones to children but couldn't create a keypad that would accommodate my thick fingers, clumsy with nervousness. Finally, I read what I'd written:

Daddy and Zacky are coming. Look out your window. Wave if you see us.

I hesitated, unsure if such a text would help or put her in greater danger. At the end, I pressed send, deciding to take advantage of Kyra's early literacy skills.

I put the phone to my ear. "Where are you now, Zak?"

"Nearing the entrance to the Manhattan Bridge."

"I told Kyra to watch for us—sent a text to that little cellphone I got her."

"She has her cell with her?"

"I'm not sure. Possibly."

"But if she has her cell, she can be traced!"

"You're right," I said, coming to this myself. "I'll call Tara. The police can trace it."

"We can do it ourselves. Do you have a tracking app for her? If not, we'll use the 'find my device' function. What's the password? I know her number."

"Supergirl. You're doing this while you're biking?"

"Quiet, J.... OK, got it. They ... They're on the Brooklyn Bridge. Right now."

I told the cabbie to head to the Brooklyn Bridge and tried to phone Tara. I got a message saying all the lines were busy. I called Annie—same result. Shaken, I dialed '911,' which is what I should have done to begin with, but got the same "all lines are occupied" message. Shouldn't there be an exception for 911? But if cell usage had overloaded the system, I supposed it would affect emergency services too.

I composed a brief message to Annie and Tara saying where we'd pinpointed Kyra and asking them to inform the police, hoping it'd get through even if a call couldn't. I sent it as the driver got off the highway at the Cadmen Plaza/Brooklyn Bridge exit and brought the cab to an abrupt stop. "This is as far as I go," he said. "Nothing's moving on the bridge."

"But my daughter's on that bridge with a ... with a crazy man! We gotta keep going!"

"If you think I'm getting stuck on that bridge, you're crazy too. You'll be faster on foot anyway," he concluded, his bushy eyebrows a thick, immovable line.

I handed the driver most of the money in my wallet and climbed out of the cab, realizing he was probably right. I dialed 911 once more before switching to Zak on the other line.

"I'm at the bridge, on foot now," I told him. "Where are you?"

"Coming up on you."

I heard Zak's voice in stereo—through my phone and behind me. I turned. He was biking towards me, gesturing towards the path with his chin. I put the phone

256

away.

Like the roadway, the bike and pedestrian path was mobbed. With the power out, the subways down, and the communications systems overloaded, people—some of whom must have experienced 9/11 and the 2003 blackout—were in crisis mode as they fled the City. We were faced with a loud, anxious wave of humanity, and Zak and I—headed towards instead of away from Manhattan—were swimming against the tide. Zak kept to his bike, standing on his pedals to maneuver around everyone. I used my arms to clear a path, engulfed by a heady mixture of sweat and perfume as I pushed up against briefcases and shoulders.

Progress was nerve-wrackingly slow. I peered down at the roadway to the left of our elevated path to see how fast the cars were moving. The three lanes going into Brooklyn were bumper-to-bumper. The Manhattan-bound traffic to the right of us was faster but more chaotic. They'd opened one of the three lanes to eastbound traffic to allow more people to leave Manhattan. The middle lane was closed entirely, orange cones forming a buffer between the unaccustomed two-way traffic.

"Give me your phone, Zak. I need to see where Kyra is now."

The blue dot was two-thirds of the way across the bridge.

Zak peered over my shoulder. "This is too slow. Hold my bike." He pushed his way to the far right of the path, hoisted himself over the side railing, and climbed down, hand over hand, to the roadway below. He reached up for his bike and I passed it to him.

Zak took the unused middle lane, slaloming around the orange cones. I continued my slog across the bridge, but a surge in the crowd corralled me against the side again. I looked at the tightly packed path, then down at the stop-and-go traffic. I tucked the phone into my pocket and climbed after Zak.

Darting in front of the eastbound lane of traffic, I made it to the middle lane and began to jog towards Manhattan. A woman dressed in a suit, seeing what I'd done, climbed down as well. Soon, the roadway began to fill with pedestrians. Drivers honked their horns and screamed obscenities out their windows. I pushed past people walking in the opposite direction, craning my neck to see how far Zak had gotten. When I was more than halfway across, I felt a vibration in the right pocket of my pants. Still jogging, I took out my phone and checked it, hoping it was Tara or Annie saying the police were on their way. It was a text:

Back off fag if you ever want to see your daughter again.

The message had come from Kyra's phone.

I went from a jog to a full-out sprint, pushing aside anyone in my path. I tried 911 again. The same mechanized voice told me all the lines were busy. There was a vibration in my other pocket. I'd forgotten I'd taken Zak's phone. I picked it up and checked it—a failed call from Annie. The screen still showed the map. I searched for the blue dot that represented Kyra. It moved towards the middle of the East River before winking out.

CHAPTER 38

n Manhattan, about half a mile past the Brooklyn Bridge, a uniformed woman with a whistle conducted traffic in the dark street. "You gotta come with me," I told her, explaining about Kyra and Todd and the blue dot in the water.

"I'm not a police officer," she said. "Just a crossing guard, trying to help out."

I now saw that she wasn't wearing a police uniform and that she held a child's scooter in her hand. "Can I borrow that?" I asked. "Here, take my wallet. My contact info is inside." She was still hesitant. "Please. This is your kid's, right? So you understand. Please."

With a reluctant nod, she handed it to me. "Good luck finding your daughter."

The scooter was much too small, but I hunched over, pushing hard and fast with my foot. Manhattan was dark and eerily peaceful after the chaos on the bridge, but at South Street, small groups of young men were shouting and laughing near the docks. I scootered towards them, nearly tripping over something. I saw with horror that it was Zak's bike, the front wheel twisted. Approaching the nearest group, I asked what happened, pointing to the bike.

"You shoulda seen it!" a husky teenager in a hoody said. "This dude on a bike comes outta nowhere and rams the car. Boom! Lands right on the roof and rolls onto the car's front window." The kid spins around as though to demonstrate the roll. "Driver can't see nothing so he stops and opens the door. Bike dude pulls him out and starts beating on him."

"Was there a little girl?"

"A girl? Nah, man. Just the two guys fighting, closer and closer to the water. Right at the edge, bike dude punches the big dude with his left—boom, boom— and he flips over the side into the water. And you know what bike dude fucking does next?"

"What?" I asked, stomach in knots.

"Jumps in after him!"

I rushed across the dock to the railing, my eyes scanning the water. Two forms, both adult-sized, were moving in the steely gray, the darker one dragging the bigger one to shore.

"Kyra!" I shouted.

The dark head looked up. Zak. "Look in the car, J!"

There were dozens of cars parked or abandoned below the overpass, and all of them appeared navy blue in the dark. Sirens swelled and faded, lights flickered in the periphery, and my heart thudded in my chest. I approached the closest car and examined it methodically, went on to the next and did the same. The third was a blue Honda that fit the description Tara had given me. The driver's door was dented and partly ajar. I opened it all the way and peered inside. Nothing. I reached over the driver's seat and unlocked the back door. All I saw was a crushed juice box, and beside it, a booster seat hanging askew over the edge. I gently pulled it into place. A small form was curled on the floor.

"Kyra," I whispered.

"Daddy, can I come out now?"

I lifted my daughter into my arms, dizzy with relief. I looked up. Someone was shining a flashlight into my eyes. I used an arm to block the light and a voice barked, "Don't move!" Two cops were standing in front of me, guns drawn. I cupped the back of Kyra's head with my hand. "Put the child down and raise your hands up slowly," a second voice, female, said.

"You're making a mistake." I held Kyra tight. "You think I'm—"

"He's not Todd," Annie's voice said behind them.

The first cop spun around, pointing the gun at Annie. "You! Come into the light."

She moved forward, Sierra and Brooklyn clinging to each hand. "You're looking for Todd. He took Kyra in violation of a court order. This is the child's father, Jeremy Singer."

"Who are you? How do you know this man?" the first cop demanded.

"Kyra's my step-daughter. And Jeremy is my husband."

They say you can never find a police officer when you need one, and today had certainly been proof of that, but now the area was crawling with them. Three police cars pulled in, their headlights making brightly lit circles that put Kyra and me in the center of a three-ring circus, the spectators watching the show from a safe distance. Two other cops dragged a wet and battered Todd towards the perimeter of our circle of light, and Zak was behind them, looking wobbly but triumphant. Last of all, a fourth police car pulled over and stopped. Tara climbed out the back and rushed towards us.

"Kyra!" Tara cried.

"Momma!" Kyra answered, but didn't let go of my neck.

A police officer got out of the car Tara had arrived in, but the one who'd pointed the gun at Annie spoke first. "We're going to sort this out right now." He turned his attention to Kyra. "What's your name, young lady?"

Kyra buried her face in my neck. I kissed her head and whispered, "Don't be afraid. You're Supergirl, but you can tell them your secret identity."

She lifted her head. "Kyra, and I'm not a young lady, I'm a big girl."

"Alright, Kyra. Can you tell us who you know here?"

"This is my daddy," she said, patting my head. "And that's my momma—Tara. Right there is Mommy Annie with my big sister Sierra and my big brother, Brooklyn. Where's Zacky?" Zak limped out of the shadows. "Zacky's my best friend and my other daddy. He's also a magical fairy and he saved me from ... from Todd. He's the bad man with the two polices holding his arms." Kyra buried her face in my neck again. I tightened my hold on her.

"Thank you, Kyra. That makes the mud a little clearer. I'll be taking statements, starting with the magical fairy." The officer's face twisted in a sardonic grin as he turned to Zak.

I moved to follow too, but Annie put her hand on my arm. Tara was watching me. She hesitated, then put her arms out for Kyra. I turned away from her.

"Jeremy," Annie said softly. "Maybe Kyra would like to go to her momma."

"I can't." I held Kyra still more tightly. She squirmed.

"You can. If that's what's best for Kyra."

My husband, Annie had said when the cop asked who I was. I gathered my strength and passed my daughter to her mother. Two days until I had custody again.

Little by little, teams of officers left to respond to emergency calls coming through their radios. When all our statements had finally been taken, Tara and Kyra went into one of the police cars, but not before I'd torn the booster seat out of Todd's car and installed it there.

"Where's Zak?" The last pair of cops had left, shoving Todd roughly into a squad car.

"He said he was tired," Annie answered. "You know how he is about cops. Hey kids!" Sierra and Brooklyn were taking turns on the scooter I'd borrowed from the crossing guard. I found Zak sitting in a dark corner, propped up against a railing.

"Time to get the hell out of here." I told Zak. "The blackout's spreading." I gazed out over the water as another swath of lights went out further uptown. "The subways aren't working so we're going to have to hoof it back to Brooklyn."

"I don't feel so good, J."

"What is it?" I reached for him, then stopped, remembering what happened the last time Zak said he wasn't feeling well and I tried to touch him.

"My stomach hurts. And I'm dizzy."

I laid a tentative hand on his shoulder. He didn't flinch from me. His skin was cold and clammy. But then again it was November and he'd taken a swim in the East River. He needed to get out of his wet clothes. His jacket, normally a light grey, was black with moisture.

"You should change. I'll lend you something of mine. Shit, I left my suitcase in the cab. Wait. I have a sweatshirt." I reached over to help him with his jacket. He cried out in pain and my hand came away wet. Wet and sticky. "Annie!" I shouted. "Annie! Zak's hurt!" For the umpteenth time that day, I dialed 911. Annie carefully opened Zak's shirt and jacket, quickly taking off her scarf to press it to his stomach. Zak moaned.

"You called 911?" Annie asked.

"I can't get through. All the lines are busy."

"Try again. Use my phone too. No, wait, switch with me. I need you to press down firmly on the wound to stop the bleeding. I'll make the call."

I did as Annie said. Zak tried not to cry out again. Sierra came over on the scooter. I heard Annie explain that her dad was hurt and she should play with Brooklyn until help came.

"Did you call 911?" Sierra asked.

"The line was busy."

"Maybe you can text them," Sierra said.

"That would be a good idea if ... Wait—the call's going through."

Annie answered questions calmly. At some point she came over and knelt next to us, placing her fingers on Zak's neck. "A little rapid," she said. "I think he's in shock .... Yes, I have some medical training .... We're trying but his clothes are wet .... We're trying ... Yes, just east of South Street, near the pier .... We'll stay right here."

"What did they say?" I asked when she'd hung up.

"They'll send an ambulance, but there are a lot of emergencies, including a 37-car pileup on the West Side Highway. They say the hospitals are overrun."

"I have a sweatshirt in my backpack Zak could wear."

"Do you have a clean t-shirt?"

"No. Just the one I'm wearing under this. I left my bag in the cab."

"It'll have to do. We'll use it as a bandage and tie my scarf around it."

I removed my t-shirt and helped Annie bind Zak's wound. We wrapped him in my sweatshirt and jacket, settling him on his back with knees bent.

"What happened, Zak?" Annie asked.

"I don't know. Todd and I were fighting. He had a knife, but ... I didn't feel anything. The knife—it fell in the water."

"Alright. Rest while we wait for the ambulance."

"Annie, I swear. I didn't feel anything. Not at first."

"I believe you. You were in shock. Rest now. You need to conserve your strength."

Zak lay quietly taking shallow breaths, more and more so as time passed. Brooklyn, and Sierra especially, kept circling near us, nervously glancing towards their dad. Annie checked the wound, checked Zak's pulse, touched his skin. Her calm demeanor began to fray.

263

"Let's call again," I said. "It shouldn't take this long."

"This is New York."

"Maybe they forgot about us." I took out my phone.

Annie bent over Zak, tightening the scarf around the wound. Zak hissed out a breath.

"The call's not going through," I said. "I'll try again."

"Fuck it," Annie said. "I can't sit here and watch him ... watch him suffer," she finished. "I'm going to find help."

"I could—"

"No. Stay with Zak. In case ... If we need to carry him."

"What about the kids?"

Brooklyn had come to a stop not far from us, balancing on the scooter and pretending not to eavesdrop on our conversation. Sierra didn't bother with such a pretense. "Brooklyn, you go with Mommy. You're fast on the scooter. I'll stay here with Daddy. And Jeremy."

Annie reluctantly nodded. "Are you ready, Brooklyn? I'm going to run and you're going to scoot. Stay close by me." Before leaving, she put her own jacket over Zak, bending to whisper in my ear. "Take care of him. Get him to hang on until I get help."

At first, I didn't disturb Zak, afraid I might hurt him. I'd had one glance at the long, deep slash in his stomach, and it was enough to make me queasy. I sat holding his hand and looking out into the distance, willing the flashing lights of an ambulance to appear. Sierra walked back and forth between where Zak lay and the street above, like she was on patrol. On one of her forays towards South Street, I bent over Zak.

"Are you in a lot of pain?" I asked.

Zak swallowed. "I could bear it better if I wasn't so cold."

The temperature had dropped. I was cold myself in just my long-sleeved shirt. Zak couldn't stop shivering. I wondered if we could do anything about his wet clothes. We'd removed his wet shirt and jacket before applying the makeshift bandage but removing his pants would require a lot of shifting, which could make him bleed more. We could take off his wet socks and shoes at least—I'd heard keeping extremities warm was important.

Sierra returned as I unlaced his sneakers. "Do you want to help?" I asked.

"What should I do?"

"Take your dad's sneakers and socks off and dry his feet so he's warmer."

Sierra dove into this task, obviously relieved to be doing something to help. She rubbed Zak's feet, placed them in her lap, and covered them with her jacket. Taking my cue from Sierra, I partially draped my body over Zak's, careful not to touch the wound. With my arms around him, his trembling diminished, but his breaths were quick and shallow. "Tell me if I'm hurting you," I said.

"You could never hurt me," he whispered.

Minutes passed, each longer than the last. In the distance, there was noise, and across the water, light. In my corner of the world, the only sound was Zak's breathing, the only light the faint glimmer in his eyes.

"I want to ask you something. Why did you jump in after Todd?"

Zak was silent. I wondered if he'd heard me, but then he answered in a whisper. "All the time I was chasing him I thought about .... about Kyra. I imagined killing Todd. Killing ..." Zak swallowed. "But in the end, I didn't want it ... didn't want him to die. To have caused him to die."

I rubbed Zak's shoulders and arms, his chest, his face. I did this every few minutes to keep him warm. "You were really something. Some guy on the dock told me how you rammed Todd's car. How you used your left hook to knock him out. "

"Left, right, left left, right," Zak whispered, trembling. "Jeremy, tell me the truth. Did you really find him?"

He was talking about Jack. Or did he mean his father? "Of course I did," I answered, stroking his face. "I told you, there's nothing to worry about. It's all behind you now."

More long minutes passed. Zak lay very quietly but for the shivering which took all his strength. Even breathing seemed to be an effort. There had to be something I could do. I felt I'd explode from inaction, but I couldn't leave Zak's side.

"Sierra, run up to South Street and tell me what's happening. Can you see your mom? An ambulance? Anyone who could help?"

Sierra sprang to her feet and took off. I rubbed Zak's arms and kissed his face.

"J," he said, as though just waking up. "Am I gonna die?"

"No," I said. "I won't let you. Not after everything we've been through."

"I don't want to. I want to be with you and Annie and our kids. J—"

"Jeremy! Jeremy!" Sierra was coming towards us fast. I realized she had the scooter. "Mommy says we have to get to the next pier. There's a ferry boat. They'll take us across to Brooklyn. An ambulance there will take Daddy to the hospital. Can you carry him?"

"Yes. Where's your brother?"

"He's up at the street, waiting for me."

"Go to Brooklyn. I'll be right behind you."

I lifted Zak carefully into my arms. He cried out. I took a few tentative steps holding him, got a better grip, began running. Sierra had put Brooklyn on the front of the scooter and was somehow balancing the two of them while pushing it. "Careful, careful," I panted, not sure if I was talking to myself or to Sierra. I ran next to her; she glanced at me sidelong to make sure I was keeping up. I accelerated. Zak should have been a heavy weight in my arms, but it was as though he'd grown weightless.

Annie was waiting at the dock with two men who helped carry Zak into the small boat. Sierra took Brooklyn's hand while he climbed in, then jumped down herself. I held Zak in my arms and tried to keep him warm, heedless now of his wound that had already begun to bleed freely during the run. He was shivering violently. Annie sat with us, holding Zak's hand and blocking the wind as best she could.

"Annie," Zak gasped. "Are we ... going home now?"

"Hang on, baby, just hang on. We're almost there." She bit her lip and stood to look across the water, perhaps trying to spot the ambulance.

The blood had soaked through the layers of t-shirt, scarf, sweatshirt and jacket. I held him, trying to warm his shivering body. "We're almost there," I said, repeating Annie's words.

266

"Jeremy," he whispered. I put my ear to his mouth. "Wait for me. Wait for me, Jemmy."

His violent shivers began to abate, though he was no warmer. "Zak, don't," I begged, shivering myself. Something cold had entered me as our boat passed from darkness to light, now from light to darkness. Had we remembered to pay the ferryman?

"J ..." Zak said, and his voice was all air. And when the air ran out, there was silence. Silence and cold and an unbearable emptiness.

All this time as Zak struggled with depression I'd thought I could imagine his pain, but it was only now, with his cold, lifeless body in my arms, that I knew what it felt like to want to die.

CHAPTER 39

They were trying to take my brother from me. This time I wouldn't let them. I held on to him tightly, felt the sharp sting of a slap across my face.

"Let him go!" a familiar voice cried. I looked up, confused.

"You promised, Jeremy," Annie said. "The children, they need you. *Our* children."

Sierra. Brooklyn. Along with Kyra, they were my children now. My arms trembled. I forced myself to release Zak. Two EMT workers shifted him onto a gurney as Brooklyn began to cry. I lifted my son into my arms and held him against me, where I'd held Zak moments before. Annie spared one brief glance over her shoulder as she climbed into the ambulance where they'd placed Zak's body.

"We're supposed to follow them." Sierra's voice was hoarse. She pulled on my sleeve and I walked up to the next street. "Taxi! Taxi!" she called while I stood there like a dumb beast. After a time, a car pulled up. We climbed inside. I tried to put Brooklyn down but he clung to my neck and I didn't fight him. His warm weight was a reminder that I needed to keep going when all I wanted to do was curl into a ball and howl.

The car stopped. Sierra nudged me and I reached for my wallet. Where was it? There'd been a woman. A scooter. It all seemed very remote. Sierra dug into her backpack, handed the driver some bills. "Don't worry about it," the cabbie said, returning the money to her.

We entered the hospital. Everything about it terrified me—the chemical odors, the green color of the walls, the too-bright lighting, the combined sounds of machines and suffering and mundane conversation. I found Annie and stepped into her arms, still holding Brooklyn.

Time passed though I couldn't have said how much. I sat close to Annie. Sierra was on her other side, Brooklyn's head on my lap. We were a small island I tried to inhabit with my mind blank, emotions unplugged. I could do this for a few blessed moments before I'd remember some gesture of Zak's or the sensation of his body against mine and I'd begin to tremble again.

"What's taking so long?" Sierra cried.

"It may be a good sign," Annie said bravely, pulling Sierra closer.

I did not believe this. They'd probably forgotten about us, about Zak. I pictured his body lying on a slab, a sheet thrown carelessly over his eyes. Maybe they were harvesting his organs. I imagined them taking his heart. It was larger than normal, a deep red, pulsing still. They needed to put it back; they could have mine instead. I walked towards the swinging doors.

"Jeremy, where are you going?" Annie called out, alarmed.

"To give them ... to tell them ..."

Sierra stared at me, her face blotchy. Brooklyn was asleep, curled up on the seat. *You promised, Jeremy.* I walked back and sat down.

'Ms. Roisin? Annie Roisin?"

A balding man in blue scrubs approached us. Annie stood. "Zak?"

"He's out of surgery," the man said.

"Then he's alive?" Annie replied.

"Yes. He's stable now."

Suddenly there was air in my lungs, blood in my veins. I could feel my heart beating. Annie took my hand. "Please, doctor, can you tell us more?"

He glanced at the kids meaningfully. Annie asked Sierra to watch her brother and we moved down the hall. "The surgery went well," the doctor said. "We were able to save his spleen, to repair the damage, but it was touch and go for a while. He lost a lot of blood."

"He was so cold," I said.

The doctor turned to me, mouth slightly open. I realized my teeth were chattering.

Annie put her arm around me. "Jeremy's little brother died of hypothermia."

"I see. In this case, it may have saved the patient. The cold constricts blood vessels, which kept him from bleeding to death. So far, we've given him three units of blood, but depending on how he's doing, we may need to give him another transfusion."

"He can have my blood," I said, holding out my arm. "I'm A positive."

"When can we see him?" Annie asked, simultaneously.

"His condition is still serious, so only next of kin, and only briefly. You're his spouse?" the doctor asked Annie.

"Yes, but so is Jeremy," she said, gesturing to me.

"He's ... he's whose spouse?"

"I'm trying to say that Zak and Jeremy and I are one family."

The doctor turned to me, looking doubtful. I nodded.

"Please," Annie said. "If Zak doesn't see us both, he'll be upset."

The doctor hesitated. "Alright, but the children need to remain outside."

Zak lay still, his skin greyish, under a blanket that looked like a thermal sleeping bag. There were tubes coming out of his arms and one taped under his nostril. His eyelids fluttered when Annie took his hand. I knelt beside her so he wouldn't have to turn his head.

"Annie, J," he breathed.

"We're here." I gently squeezed his shoulder.

"The ... kids?"

"Sierra and Brooklyn are outside," Annie said. "And I spoke to Tara. Kyra's fine."

"How are you feeling, sweetheart?" I asked him.

"I'm a little cold. Can you and Annie come to bed now?"

Before I could frame an answer, Zak's eyes closed. I watched his chest move up and down, then turned to the doctor. "Why is he cold? Can't you do anything?"

"Don't be concerned. His body temperature is satisfactory."

"Zak runs hot. His normal body temperature is higher than average."

The doctor lifted his eyebrows, looking dubious.

"Maybe it's blood loss," I persisted. "I'm ready to donate. Take as much as you want."

"That won't be necessary, Mr. ...?"

"Singer. Jeremy Singer."

"Mr. Singer, your friend ... partner is stable right now. If he needs another transfusion, we'll see to it that he gets one."

"I want to donate my blood," I insisted stubbornly, unable to accept these assurances, certain in some odd, superstitious way that a blood donation from me could somehow help Zak.

The doctor looked uncomfortable. "Mr. Singer, let's step outside for a minute."

I stood. Annie lingered by Zak's bed, her hand resting lightly on his chest.

In the brightly lit hallway, the doctor's bald spot gleamed, but his smooth, pinkish cheeks made me realize he was younger than I'd assumed. "As I was trying to explain," he began, "a blood donation from you right now is neither necessary nor useful. The blood would first have to be tested, catalogued. That would take time. And, in any case, there are certain restrictions. To avoid the possibility of ... tainted blood," he finished.

"Tainted? I don't understand," I said.

Annie, who'd joined us, placed her hand on my back. "Jeremy, he's talking about HIV. "

"But I'm not ... I ... I've given blood. Lots of times! Look, there's nothing to worry about. The only ... man I've ever been with is Zak."

"Hasn't the ban on gay and bisexual men donating been discontinued?" Annie asked.

"Yes," the doctor told her. "As long as the donor hasn't had sexual relations with a man in the past year." He turned to me.

"I ... This is bullshit. You test all the blood anyway. You just said that."

"Mr. Singer, right now, what the patient needs is rest. Why don't you return tomorrow?"

The thought of leaving Zak made me sick with anxiety. My eyes found Annie's. "One of us will stay at the hospital," she said. "That way, if there's anything we can do ..."

"There's nothing you can do for him right now, I assure you," the doctor told Annie.

"I'm going to stay here," I said. "I won't get in anyone's way."

The doctor gave me his third dubious look of the evening.

Over the next week, we worked out a schedule so one of us could be at the hospital while the other was with the kids. When I was home, I worried about Zak; when I was away from the kids, I worried about them. It was worse when I didn't have Kyra. After all that happened, I was considering suing for full custody. Annie said I should ask myself whether I'd be doing this for Kyra or because I was angry with Tara.

I wanted to discuss it with Zak. I had a million things I wanted to talk with him about, but though his wound was healing well and his color was better, he often appeared confused, and he continued to complain he was cold. I was uneasy, as was Annie, who was haunted by her memories of the nightmarish time she'd had Zak hospitalized.

I spoke about our concerns with Zak's surgeon—whose name I learned was Dr. Brandt. I asked whether Zak's confused state could be caused by hypothermia or blood loss, and brought up the issue of donating blood again.

He shook his head dismissively. "Please, Mr. Singer, I assure you we're using our best medical judgment in the patient's treatment."

"Zak. His name is Zak."

Meanwhile, Annie and I conferred with Dr. McQueen. She wanted to speak with Zak's attending physician about his psychiatric history, particularly his adverse reaction to certain drugs—but had not succeeded in reaching him. Dr. McQueen eventually went to see Zak, like any other visitor. I asked her how he seemed.

"Somewhat disoriented. He didn't seem sure where he was. Then, at the end of the visit, he got very tearful and asked me to tell the doctors that ... he was being good."

"What's going on?" I asked, alarmed.

"Have you ever heard of hospital psychosis?"

I shook my head.

"It can happen during a medical stay. The stress, the unfamiliar surroundings—

272

some people react by breaking with reality. There can be confusion, hallucinations, paranoia. The good news is that they usually recover once they're home."

Dr. McQueen promised me she'd keep trying to reach Dr. Brandt. I was reassured by this until the next evening when Zak asked me to help him plan a prison break. I couldn't tell if he was kidding or not.

A couple of days later, I arrived to find Zak thrashing from side to side. A nurse was bent over him, speaking softly. To my horror, they'd strapped him to the bed.

"Take those straps off," I said, rushing to Zak's bedside.

The nurse stood, a patient expression on her face. "They're—"

"Take them off now!"

"I'll get the doctor," she said, moving towards the door. "He's down the hall."

I pushed Zak's blankets aside, fumbling to release the belt-like strap around his chest.

"They're to keep the patient from hurting himself," I heard Dr. Brandt say.

I undid the other straps. Zak threw his arms around me, burying his face in my chest.

"Mr. Singer, what you're doing is unwise. He's agitated. He may injure himself."

"It's OK, I got you," I said stroking Zak's hair and ignoring the doctor.

"Mr. Singer, please. He needs to lie back so I can examine the wound."

I held Zak in my arms a moment longer, then pushed him gently onto his back. I held his shoulders while Dr. Brandt removed his bandages, examined the wound, and put on fresh dressings. Zak stayed perfectly still during the whole procedure.

"Next time Zak becomes agitated, please call me or Annie. If I see him in restraints again, I'll sue the hospital for abuse."

"Abuse?"

"Malpractice, then. Whatever."

The next afternoon, when it was time for me to leave, Zak's eyes followed me out of the room. I told him not to worry, that Annie would be there soon. He nodded, but his hands clutched the sheets nervously. At the bus stop, I glanced up at the dark clouds moving in and felt a wave of apprehension. I decided to call Annie and suggest she leave the kids with Robyn and meet me at the hospital. This way, Zak

273

wouldn't be alone while we switched places. Unable to reach her, I left a message and returned to the hospital.

I knew something was wrong even before I entered Zak's room. Two male orderlies were rushing down the hall while the nurse outside Zak's door spoke anxiously into an intercom. I slipped in as the orderlies neared. A quick glance at Zak's empty bed and my eyes were searching for him. Zak was crouched behind a chair, holding a dripping syringe like a dagger.

"J!" he called when he saw me. "We're outnumbered." I rushed to Zak's side. "Get behind me, quick," he continued. "I disarmed one of them. They were trying to stick me with this. Be careful—they may have other weapons!"

"Try to calm him," the nurse said, "The doctor is on his way with another sedative."

"What happened?" I asked the nurse, slipping my arm around Zak.

"He refused to take his medication," the nurse said.

"I'm OK, J," Zak said. "I can still fight."

One of the orderlies began to creep forward.

"Don't come any closer," Zak said, pointing the needle at him.

"Easy does it, Zak," I said. "Why don't you give me that? You're hurt."

Zak put his hand to his side and seemed surprised it came away with blood.

"But do you know how to use it, J?"

"Sure. You and I are brother knights, right?"

Zak handed me the hypodermic needle. The tension in the room went down a notch. Then Dr. Brandt arrived, another syringe in his hand. Zak began to tremble.

"Don't come any closer!" I said, brandishing the needle. The nurse smiled uncertainly. I winked at her, but when Dr. Brandt stepped closer, I took a swipe with it and said, "I mean it!"

Dr. Brandt backed off. Then Annie's voice said, "What the hell is going on?"

She was in the doorway, wet from the rain, an umbrella in her hand.

"Annie!" Zak said. "Everything's gonna be OK now. The three musketeers are together!"

It took some time for things to calm down. While we couldn't coax Zak back into bed, he agreed to lie down on a blanket on the floor as long as Annie and I remained 'armed.' So I hung on to the syringe and Annie raised her umbrella.

Annie asked what they'd been trying to give Zak. She had a letter from Dr. McQueen which included a list of counter-indicated medications. Unable to speak to Dr. Brandt, Dr. McQueen had called Annie, believing it was critical that Zak's physician understand his psychiatric history. This belief had been confirmed earlier today when she'd received a package at her office—Zak's medical files from Nebraska. The social worker, Ronnie Taylor, had come through.

CHAPTER 40

've never seen Dr. McQueen angry before," I whispered to Annie.

"Yeah, well she's pretty frustrated."

Annie and I sat side by side on Zak's hospital bed. Zak had fallen asleep on the blanket on the floor despite the conversation in the hall outside his room that had erupted into raised voices.

"It was completely unnecessary for you to come here," Dr. Brandt was saying.

"If I'd been able to reach you ..."

"So, he didn't even call her back?" I asked Annie quietly.

"He says he tried, but Laisha phoned him like ten times."

"Do you think he's racist?" I asked. "Or sexist?"

"The two aren't mutually exclusive, you know. It's called intersectionality."

"Either way, I've never met such an arrogant prick."

"Try to keep in mind that he saved Zak's life," Annie said.

I grunted. In fact, Dr. Brandt was using that argument right now.

"My treatment decisions saved his life. I don't appreciate your second-guessing—"

"I'm not doing that. I'm merely offering you additional information about your patient so that you take it into account. Up until now, the greatest threat to Zak's life has been suicide, something he's attempted three times in the past two years. That's what *I'm* working on. The benzodiazepines you gave him are dangerous to his mental health."

"That man, Mr. Singer, tied my hands. He told me he'd sue the hospital if I restrained Mr. Heron. I had no choice but to sedate him instead."

"Fuck him," I murmured. "Even if he did save Zak's life."

"I get that you're angry, Jeremy, but isn't that a bit over the top?"

I let out a slow breath. "I'm just scared. The anger makes me feel less ... powerless."

Annie turned to me and smiled.

"What?" I said.

"You've changed. You're more honest now."

"You probably still shouldn't believe anything I tell you," I said, smiling back.

Annie laughed.

"No, really—"

She hushed me. Dr. McQueen had lowered her voice but was speaking urgently.

"... to have prescribed those kinds of drugs to a twelve-year-old!"

"Was a psychiatrist in charge of his case?" Dr. Brandt asked.

"As a matter of fact, he was a pediatrician. Dr. John Wolf. Zak's own father."

Annie gasped. "Zak's father was a doctor? I ... I can't believe it." My heart pounded with the same shock. "No wonder he had a total breakdown that time I hospitalized him. And no wonder he's losing it now. We gotta get him out of here, J."

Dr. Brandt and Dr. McQueen entered the room, waking Zak. He pushed himself up.

"Are you here to take me home?" Zak asked Dr. McQueen.

"Dr. Brandt is your attending physician, Zak. He believes you're not well enough yet."

"But I am!" Zak tried to stand. Annie and I both sprung towards him. We tried to help him into the bed, but he refused to lie down. Instead, he collapsed into one of the chairs.

"I can't in good conscience discharge a patient in this condition." Dr. Brandt said.

"You shouldn't keep Zak here against his will," Annie responded. "Discharge him AMA."

"What does that mean?" I asked.

Dr. McQueen replied. "A patient can ask to be discharged against medical advice."

"If he has the capacity to make such a decision," Dr. Brandt retorted. "In this case—" He glanced at Zak. "There are clearly mental health factors to consider."

"There are, but those factors may point to early discharge," Dr. McQueen

277

responded.

"Dr. McQueen is his psychiatrist," Annie said. "Shouldn't she be the one to decide about Zak's mental capacity?"

"No," Dr. Brandt said, his jaw jutting out. "This is my prerogative. If he's discharged and harm comes to him, that would be my responsibility as his treating physician."

"Dr. Brandt is right." We all turned to Dr. McQueen in surprise, Dr. Brandt included. "He can only discharge Zak if he's convinced Zak understands the medical risks. That's why it's him and not me who should discuss this with Zak now," Dr. McQueen concluded.

"I ... Yes, thank you Dr., uh ..." Dr. Brandt stopped, looking embarrassed.

"McQueen," she supplied, smiling.

"Yes. Dr. McQueen." Dr. Brandt squared his shoulders and turned to Zak. "Mr. Heron, it's too soon for you to go home," Dr. Brandt said in an even tone. "If I discharge you, your health could be at risk. Do you understand that?"

"Please," Zak whispered, unable to meet the doctor's eye.

Dr. Brandt repeated, "Do understand the medical risks?"

Zak bit his lip but didn't answer. Dr. Brandt shrugged as though to say, "You see?"

"So tell him," I said. "He can't understand medical risks you haven't explained."

Dr. Brandt sighed, turning back to Zak. "There's the risk of infection, first and foremost. The wound may reopen. You could start bleeding, internally or externally. Your blood pressure could drop. You could need another transfusion. There are many risks."

Zak wrapped his arms around himself and continued to stare at his own lap.

I went over and knelt by Zak's chair, putting my hand on his shoulder. "Dr. Brandt just explained the risks of leaving the hospital now. Can you tell us what they are?" Zak remained silent. "Just tell us what he said." I whispered, rubbing his shoulder blade with my thumb.

Zak lifted his head. "There's the risk of infection, first and foremost. The wound may reopen and ... and start bleeding again. Internally or externally. Blood pressure could drop. Another blood transfusion might be needed. There are many risks."

"Good," I said. "He knows the risks."

"This is ridiculous. He just parroted my words."

"What would it take to convince you?" Annie asked.

"Ms. Roisin, I'm not unsympathetic, but his mind is confused."

"Why don't you ask him questions," I said. "Test his mind. You could, I don't know, give him math problems."

Dr. Brandt seemed exasperated but shrugged as though willing to humor us. He gave Zak a few simple addition and subtraction problems while I sat back down on Zak's bed with Annie and Dr. McQueen settled herself into the remaining chair. Zak answered Dr. Brandt's questions easily, actually relaxing as the problems became more difficult. Annie slipped her hand into mine, smiling. Dr. McQueen's expression was hard to read. When Zak continued to respond correctly to problems I would have taken longer to solve with a calculator, Dr. Brandt consulted Zak's chart. "What is it you do for a living, Mr. Heron?"

"I'm a math teacher," Zak said, grinning happily.

"I see," he said. Dr. Brandt turned to me, furious. I shrugged, unrepentant.

"Do you think this is some kind of a game, Mr. Singer?"

I stood, tired of all the bullshit. "What I think is—"

"Jeremy," Dr. McQueen said, with a warning look.

"No, let him speak," Dr. Brandt said.

"You're the one who isn't taking this seriously," I said. "You couldn't be bothered to return Dr. McQueen's calls and you don't seem to give a shit what's in Zak's hospital records."

Dr. Brandt flushed. "You're wrong, I do care and I've tried to be flexible with your ... unusual demands, but there are limits. It's time to follow the appropriate rules and procedures." He turned to Zak. "I need to ask you a few questions if you insist on being discharged against medical advice." He waited until he had Zak's attention. "First question, what is your name?"

"Zak Heron," Zak replied.

"I mean your legal name," Dr. Brandt said.

Zak looked up towards Annie, a frightened, pleading look on his face.

"I've always known him as Zak Heron. People can change their names," Annie said.

"Zak Heron is not the name on his files," he said, stealing a glance in my direction. "The medical files from Nebraska that you claim I don't care about."

Before I could respond, Dr. Brandt turned back to Zak. "Second question, do you know where you are right now?"

Zak seemed to shrink under Dr. Brandt's gaze. "Please," he said, his voice barely above a whisper. "I want to go home. I'll ... I'll be good. I promise."

Dr. Brandt glanced at me again and I clenched both my fist and my jaw, resisting the urge to either throttle him or shout at him. He jotted down something in his files before turning back to Zak once more. "Just a few more questions. Can you tell me today's date?"

When Zak didn't reply, I prodded him, saying, "Come on, Zak, you know this. Remember the kids dressing up for Halloween? Remember my trip afterwards? To ... to Nebraska?"

"November," he softly, and then, "Is it ... is it my birthday?"

"Your birthday's in July," Dr. Brandt said, double-checking Zak's medical records.

I exchanged a look with Annie, realizing with horror what today's date actually was—November 13th, the date Zak's mother was killed, the day he used to claim was his birthday until I ambushed him with his own birth certificate, triggering a late-night suicide attempt.

"Today's date," I said quickly, "It has significance to Zak. It's not a good question. He—"

"Fine, I'll ask something else," Dr. Brandt said. "How old are you, Zak?"

"How old?" Zak asked, licked his lips nervously.

"Yes, tell me your age—a simple question for a math teacher."

"That's enough. Leave him alone," I said, stepping forward.

"You mean how old am I now? Or before? Or ... Or before that?" Zak stammered.

Dr. Brandt looked as triumphant as a television show lawyer. "You don't have to answer. But Mr. Heron ... that is, Mr. Wolf ..."

Zak stared at Dr. Brandt with panic, fingers digging into his own thighs.

"I said leave him the fuck alone!"

"A patient who has the capacity to discharge himself against medical advice should at least know his own name and age, don't you think?"

I lunged at Dr. Brandt. Annie and Dr. McQueen each grabbed one of my arms.

"Call security," Dr. Brandt said to the nurse.

I considered apologizing, but before I could form the words, two men burst into the room and grabbed me. When they tried to drag me outside, I began to struggle.

"Don't hurt him! Don't hurt J!" Zak threw himself to the ground at Dr. Brandt's feet and wrapped his arms around the doctor's legs. "I'll do whatever you say. I won't tell. I won't let him tell either." He pressed his face against the doctor's crotch.

Now Dr. McQueen pulled Zak away from Dr. Brandt. "Look at me, Zak. You're not where you think you are. He's not who you think he is."

"J!" Zak wailed. "Don't hurt J!"

I freed myself from the guards, shoving one of them. The other grabbed hold of me again. Annie moved between me and the second guard. Dr. McQueen stood too.

"Wait," Dr. Brandt said to the guards.

Everyone froze. After a moment, I tugged my arm out of the guard's grasp. Zak flew at me and I caught him in my arms. "It's OK, it's OK. No one's going to hurt anyone." Zak's body was drenched in sweat and he was shaking. I took his face in my hands. "Zak, listen to me. You're thinking of Jack. Your friend, Jack Phillips, from when you were a kid. He found out, didn't he? He found out what your father was doing to you and threatened to tell."

Zak went very still. The room went quiet too, including the security guards waiting for Dr. Brandt's next instruction. Zak reached up and touched my beard, his other hand straying to my chest. "Jeremy," he said. I nodded. "Jack ... he tried to help me. I begged him not to—that if he did my father would ... " Zak swallowed convulsively. "Jack wouldn't listen. We fought. I remember. I see it sometimes in my sleep. Left, right, left left, right. He fell. His head hit a rock. I killed him. That's why they locked me up in the hospital."

"No. It didn't happen that way. Yes, you fought, but a schoolboy fight. That's all."

"Traumatic brain injury. My father told me—"

"Your father lied. Pathologically. You weren't the ... You never killed your friend."

"But my father ..." Zak said slowly.

He gazed into my eyes for the truth. I met his gaze wordlessly. I've been told I have a good poker face. I imagined the hand I was holding now. Two jacks, one of hearts. A queen. The ace of spades riding his white horse of death. And a fifth card, unknown. Zak moved his hand from my beard, touching my lips with his fingers.

"J, I need you to stop lying to me."

I trembled, my eyes filled.

"Jack's dead, isn't he? You let me believe he was alive, but he's dead."

"Yes," I said, my voice breaking with my heart. "I'm so, so sorry, Zak."

Zak began to weep. I pulled him towards me, my cheek against his head, remembering all the other times I'd held him while he cried. I was tired, tired of fighting all this sorrow, all this pain. Instead, I let it engulf me. I cried with him—for my brother, for Jack, for Dez, for all the children hurt and abused and killed by the adults who owed them protection.

I don't know how long I cried, but when I quieted, Zak was still crying softy so I hummed to him—the same tune I'd hummed so long ago when he'd woken with night terrors, the melody he'd hummed to me the first time we'd made love. I imagined his mother had sung this song to comfort him when they were on the run from his father. It comforted me too, but an even greater comfort was Annie's hand on my shoulder, her other arm encircling Zak. And Dr. McQueen's presence was comforting too—calm and wise as she told Zak it was good to let out the hurt. When he was depressed, when he'd tried to kill himself, his cries had been laced with despair, with self-hate; he'd sounded lost and alone. But this time, his weeping seemed like simple grief—and if the grief was laced with anything, it was relief.

CHAPTER 41

Wearing pajama bottoms along with my flannel shirt and jacket, Zak walked out of the hospital on his own two legs, supported on either side by Annie and me. Dr. McQueen was waiting in her car. We helped Zak into the back where he lay across the seat, head on Annie's lap. I rode in front with Dr. McQueen for the short trip home.

After all that had happened, Dr. Brandt still refused to discharge Zak, insisting he was neither medically fit to leave, nor mentally fit to make that decision. Dismissing the security guards, he'd taken me into the hall. "Mr. Singer, my professional judgment is that Zak belongs in a hospital." He paused. "But this isn't a prison. Patients have been known to leave without permission. If such a thing were to happen, well ... at least have it happen when I'm off-shift."

I turned to him in surprise, noticing for the first time his fatigue, his reddened eyes.

"Thank you, doctor," I said. "For everything you've done." We left that same evening.

"What are you thinking about?" Dr. McQueen asked me, while Zak dozed in the back.

"Dr. Brandt," I said. "In the end, he was a decent guy. And if he hadn't been a bit of a jerk, Zak wouldn't have had his breakthrough. And ... I wouldn't have either."

"I'm glad you're feeling positive. But Jeremy, I wouldn't want you to think that Zak is all well now, that his mental health challenges will suddenly disappear."

"I know. Annie and I will look after him. And naturally he'll keep seeing you, but ..."

"Yes?" Dr. McQueen slowly maneuvered the car around a pothole.

"The thing is, of course I don't want Zak to suffer from depression or hurt himself, but if there were a pill that would make him ... more like everyone else, someone with an average amount of energy who doesn't scare the hell out of me one second and make me laugh the next—that person wouldn't be Zak. I don't want him to change. I just want him to be happy."

"Well, I wouldn't worry about it."

"Because he'll never change?" I glanced at Annie in the rear-view mirror. She smiled.

"Because he'd never take your magic pill. I only hope the two of you can get him to take his antibiotics, let alone his other medications."

Over the next few weeks, Dr. McQueen's remark proved prescient. Zak refused all pain medication and took the antibiotics only after we'd bribed him with a probiotic frozen yogurt party with friends. This solved a second dilemma—the huge number of people who wanted to see Zak. Initially, we'd said no to visitors, concerned it would exhaust him. The party idea meant a small group could visit briefly once a day. We gave one of the first precious invitations to Tara. Kyra had been begging to see her 'poor Zacky' and it was Tara who'd had custody then.

The parties were a success. Zak was happy socializing and seemed relaxed, his head clear. I'd even had a civil conversation with Tara. She'd been shocked to see how badly Zak had been hurt and it appeared to affect her deeply. She was helpful during the party and treated Zak with tenderness. Kyra fed him frozen yogurt in bed with a tiny spoon, telling him, "If you eat all your ice cream, you can have dessert." Both seemed to think this was the funniest joke ever.

After that particular party, Brooklyn went home with Robyn for a playdate with her kids while Zak napped. Annie said she'd clean up if I'd take Sierra to the park. I hesitated.

"Go on," Annie said. "Some fresh air will be good for you. Besides ..." She gave me a significant look. "Sierra needs to practice her *layups*."

I wasn't sure what 'layups' was meant to stand for, but I put on my sneakers.

Sierra seemed preoccupied as we walked to the basketball courts behind the nearby middle school. It was wet and chilly enough that we had a court to ourselves.

"Think fast," I said, shooting her the ball. She caught it and drove left to the rim. "Nice. Now let me see you do it on the right side."

"I'm a lefty. Why do I have to practice right-hand layups so much?"

284

"Because this way, you won't have a weak side. Let's see you hit twenty. If you do well, I'll show you how to go up the right lane and slip it in on the left."

"Sweet!" Sierra said. "After can we play HORSE?"

"Sure, but just one game. I want to get back to your daddy."

Halfway through the game of HORSE, I got a glimmer of what was on Sierra's mind. She'd made some crazy shot which involved spinning around and tossing the ball underhand and backwards over her head. To my chagrin, it hit the board and went in. "Your turn," she said.

"No way I'm doing that. It looks ridiculous," I told her.

"Ha! Then you have 'H-O-R' and it's my turn again," she taunted.

"Pass me the ball. I'm not giving up that easily."

"That's one of the things I like about you, Jeremy. You don't give up."

"There are things you like about me?" I grinned.

"It wasn't that I didn't like you. It's just ... You know."

"Uh huh," I said, figuring that was a safe response.

"I guess I've decided it's OK," Sierra confessed. "That you're in my family. You can help me with baseball and basketball and stuff. You're like me—you wanna win. It's so frustrating when Daddy doesn't even try or makes up his own rules."

"Yeah, tell me about it."

"And now I know you really love him. 'Cause of how you cried. And the way you carried him. Mommy couldn't have done that. She's not big enough."

"You didn't think I loved him?" I carefully copied her spin move.

Sierra avoided my eyes. "I figured you were some kind of a sex maniac. When you decided to get married to Daddy and Mommy, I read up on polygamy. It sounded sketchy. All those guys with harems. But I figured out it was mostly Daddy you wanted to have sex with."

My arms jerked and the ball went wild, soaring up and over the backboard. "Sierra, I've asked you not to speculate about my sex life. If for some reason you can't stop doing that, at least have the good manners not to talk to me about it."

"That's H-O-R for you," Sierra said, retrieving the ball. She walked to the free throw line, stepped back, and shot a three-pointer.

285

I carefully placed my feet where she'd placed hers.

"I read some more stuff online," Sierra continued. "I found out a polyamorous marriage doesn't have to be like that—one guy having all the fun. Everyone could be equal."

I bounced the ball twice, carefully eyed the hoop, and brought my arm up—

"So that's why you should start having sex with Mommy too."

—and air-balled it.

"Sierra! What did I just say?"

"That's H-O-R-S! One more and I win."

Sierra considered her options, then dribbled to center court. From there, she threw the basketball one-handed, like a baseball, towards the hoop. Luckily, it missed.

"My turn now," I said.

I took the ball to center court too and eyed the rim. "I'll be honest with you," I said, dribbling the ball. Sierra watched me carefully, memorizing my moves. "I love your father like crazy, but I love your mother too. She's the best person I know. And on top of that," and now I made a run for the basket, "she's beautiful." Boom, I dunked the ball right through the rim.

"No fair!" Sierra said. "I'm not big enough to dunk."

"You're also not big enough to advise me about my sex life. Think fast!"

I passed Sierra the ball again, and when she caught it, I grabbed her, lifted her into the air, and let her slam the ball through the hoop.

"Yes!" she said.

"I guess we'll call it a tie. Come on, your mommy and daddy are waiting."

We walked side by side, bouncing the basketball between us.

That night, I went to bed late. I was thinking about my book—something I hadn't done since early fall. Though my research focused on language acquisition in children, I began to consider the non-linguistic ways children learn—through sports and music, games and numbers. Children also learn from pain; still other truths from love and loyalty. There was something tickling my brain—something about alternate pathways that related to my thesis concerning how children exposed to multiple languages experience choice and identity. I decided to jot down my ideas, raw as they were, before they slipped away.

It was past midnight when I entered the chilly bedroom. I stripped down to my boxers, thinking longingly of my flannel pajamas, but Annie said skin-to-skin contact was the best way to keep Zak warm. I kicked my boxers off too and burrowed under the covers. Annie was right. Zak's skin where it pressed against mine was deliciously warm. It was like stepping into a bath—no better than that—a hot tub with Zak and Annie already inside.

Annie was facing Zak, her thigh pressed against his, their faces close together. I curled my body around Zak's back, hoping not to wake him, but a few moments later he stirred, grunting softly with pain. Zak hid his discomfort well during the day, but the nighttime was harder. Being in pain all the time was exhausting, yet sleeping through the night was difficult for Zak. I put my arm around his shoulders hoping he'd fall back asleep. He quieted, but I could tell by the rhythm of his breathing that he was wide awake.

"Can I get you anything?" I whispered into his ear.

"Just trying to find a comfortable position."

"Some Tylenol and codeine would take the edge off."

"I'm taking enough meds as it is."

"I don't like to see you in pain."

"If you want me to feel better, why don't you stick that big dick of yours up my ass."

"I .... I'd be more than happy to. When you're better."

"You know you want to now."

"I can wait. It's enough to be sleeping next to you again."

"Your mouth's saying one thing, but your dick's saying another."

"Are you two talking dirty without me?" Annie mumbled sleepily.

"If you guys would only have sex with me," Zak said, "I could make painkillers inside my own body! Annie, tell him about endorphins."

"Annie, tell Zak he needs to lie still if he wants his scar to heal in a straight line."

"I won't move. I promise!" Zak pleaded.

"I guess no one's going to get any sleep until this is resolved." Annie reached over to turn on the bedside lamp. Her cheeks were flushed. "Jeremy's right, Zak. If you thrash around, your wound could reopen. But Jeremy, Zak is also right about endorphins released during sex. They can serve as a natural painkiller."

"So ... What are you saying?" I asked.

"Zak claims he can stay still. Let's test him."

I smiled, surprised and excited by this game Annie seemed to be proposing. "I doubt very much that Zak is capable of staying still."

"I am!" Zak insisted. "Please! Test me!"

Annie nodded so I pulled off the blankets to expose Zak's nude body. He was laying on his side, and already had an erection. I stroked his nipple with my fingertip. Zak shuddered. Annie brought her hand between his legs and caressed his balls. Zak gasped. "No fair. You're ganging up on me."

"Yes," I agreed. "And you're going to love every minute of it."

Annie laughed, a sexy sound from deep within her throat. She kissed Zak, her breasts pressing against his chest. From behind him, I brought my lips to Zak's neck, breathing him in. Zak's distinctive scent was not just an aphrodisiac, it made me feel alive and happy. I nibbled on his earlobe, cupped his ass in my palm. His skin was feverishly hot.

"I'll take the front of him," Annie said.

"And I'll take the back." I dug into the bedside drawer, finding the lubricant.

Annie and I took turns stroking and caressing Zak. He panted, muscles rigid, his struggle to remain perfectly still taking on a heroic air. Using liberal amounts of lube, I pushed one, then two fingers inside of him. He moaned, muscles tightening. Annie slid her upper leg around Zak's hip. I grasped the back of Zak's shoulders and pushed myself inside him an inch and pulled out again. "Please!" he panted. I paused and pushed into him again, a little more deeply. Annie was rubbing herself against Zak's cock. His chest heaved for release.

"Wait," I said. "I'm going to make this easier. Zak, don't you dare move a muscle."

"I won't. I swear."

I slid my right arm under his shoulder from behind, wrapping my left around his chest. Slowly, slowly, I turned onto my back, taking Zak, whose body remained stiff and straight, with me. As soon as I had Zak settled comfortably on top of me, my dick still partway inside him, Annie straddled us. She guided Zak inside her while thrusting her hips forward. Zak cried out with pleasure. She pulled back and slid forward again, each thrust of her hips pushing me more deeply into Zak. I grasped his forearms to ensure he didn't move and knowing that being restrained would add to his pleasure. I felt his muscles flex with each thrust, could barely keep my own body from the frenzied movements it wanted to make. Not only was I fucking Zak, but it was like Annie was fucking both of us. I let go of one of Zak's arms and reached for her hip.

Later, washing in the bathroom, I recalled the moment in the hospital when I'd given myself over to grief. Did I have the courage to embrace the joy the way I'd embraced the pain? I once told Dr. McQueen it was fear for the future that kept me from being happy. Somewhere along the way, this fear had lessened. I could imagine a future now, something possible enough for me to reach for with hope.

I saw myself finishing my book and returning to school to teach side by side with Zak and Robyn, Khalil and Malika, and our other colleagues. Zak would keep seeing Dr. McQueen and perhaps I would too. With three adults working and the buy-out from my landlord, we could rent a bigger place, with more room for the kids as they grew. Maybe Annie would get the transfer she was hoping for—to work in Brooklyn with homeless youth.

Or maybe after I finished my book, I'd start another one which explored ideas about learning both stranger and deeper than the first. Annie could go back to school and study medicine and become a psychiatrist like Dr. McQueen; maybe she'd focus her practice on kids who've been abused. We'd stay in this apartment to save up for medical school. The kids would be happy as long as our home was filled with love and trust and they were free to be themselves.

Or maybe our future would be something I couldn't imagine—something wonderful or difficult, something challenging or amazing, and completely

289

unexpected.

In the meantime, there was now. The now where pleasure had momentarily taken Zak's pain away, smoothing his features until he drifted off to sleep. And Annie. Annie who was stronger and wiser than the two of us put together. She was like an island refuge in the middle of an ocean during a storm that had lasted my whole life.

I returned to the bedroom. Annie was still awake, the soft light from the lamp on the night table making her hair into a red and gold halo. I paused at my side of the bed to watch Zak breathing evenly on his back, a sweet smile on his face. I hesitated, then walked around to Annie's side of the bed. My head and heart were too full to speak, but I needed to find a way to express how I was feeling.

"Annie—" I began.

"Yes," Annie replied. "Yes."

I fell into her arms. It had been two years since I'd been with a woman but everything was easy and familiar. Annie's skin was soft and she smelled like strawberries. She also smelled of Zak, which made being with her both comfortable and transgressive. I wanted to taste her, inside and out. I filled my hands with her breasts, her nipples going hard under my palms, and I kissed her heart-shaped face, feeling safe and happy. Her legs were long and muscled and when I slipped inside of her, I marveled at how wet and hot she was. She bore down on me and I could feel her waves of pleasure, prolonging and intensifying my own.

After, she lay against my chest, one hand idly outlining the shape of my ear. My hands were learning her form as they slid down her flank to her hips. Her skin cooled more quickly than Zak's, so I reached for the blanket and pulled it over her.

Annie touched my cheek. "You're a dear person, Jeremy, and I love you very much."

"I love you too."

"I know. But I also know you'll never love me how you love Zak."

"Annie, that's not—"

"Don't tell me it's not true. You've promised to be honest—with me and

290

yourself."

"Alright. Yes. My love for Zak is ... it's special. But my love for you is special too. To compare the two kinds of love, I wouldn't say it's apples and oranges, but it's less a question of degree and more a question of ... of color."

"Color?" she asked.

"Do you remember the winter day we sat in that café on Seventh and you convinced me it was really fine with you if I slept with Zak? You reminded me how Sierra used to be jealous of her little brother. There was a book you had me read her when I babysat—about the two brothers who asked their mom which one she loved the best. It was called *I Love You the Purplest* or something like that."

"I'd forgotten all about that book!"

"It left an impression on me. Anyway, like in the book, my love for each of you is a different color. For Zak, it's red. Red like blood. It ... It flows through my veins—hot and ... and intense. Sometimes dangerous. But it's also red like an apple—the first apple of the season, bright and sweet and juicy and just plain good."

"And me?"

"My love for you is yellow. Warm and bright like the sun. You know that feeling when it's been raining all day and suddenly the sun comes out? You lift your face to the sky and there's all this amazing sunlight—generous and ... and warm. Or after a long, dark night you thought would never end, but there it is, there's the sun, stronger than your fears and brighter than your hopes. That's you, Annie. And here's the good part, the part that makes it perfect. I don't have to love in primary colors. I have you both, which means I have orange."

Annie laughed.

"No, really. Red and yellow make orange, my favorite color. It's the color of autumn, the most beautiful season—my favorite time of year, when school starts. For me, orange is the color of new beginnings. And my love for the two of you is like that too— a new beginning."

I heard a sniffle and turned. Zak was awake, his eyes bright.

"Beautiful," he sniffed.

"Then why are you crying, sweetheart?" I asked.

"Because I'm happy. And because if I laughed instead, I might tear my stitches."

I leaned over to kiss Zak's face, tasting his tears. They did taste happy.

Zak tried to talk us into more sex. Annie and I negotiated him down to kissing and cuddling. Soon, we were all drowsy and heavy-limbed. As I drifted off, Zak whispered into my ear.

"Do you think there'll be a baby?"

"A baby?" I repeated softly. I had no idea where Annie was in her cycle, but it's true no one had used protection. "Is that something you'd want? Or most important, that Annie would want?"

Zak gazed at Annie who was snoring softly. "We always wanted another one, but after Brooklyn was born ... I wasn't well."

"Let's concentrate on helping you to get better, alright? In any case, if Annie got pregnant now, we wouldn't even know whose baby it was."

"Sure we would," he said, and whispered the answer in my ear.

I kissed his neck and his hair and wrapped my limbs around him. He took my hand and rested it, along with his own, on Annie's stomach. She stirred, drowsily sliding her own hand into ours and we slept peacefully through the rest of the night.

EPILOGUE

I sit in the park and watch the child who was the product of these past events climb up the slide, his curls bouncing against his browned back. The early summer sun shines on my face and there's nowhere in the world I'd rather be. In a little while, I'll lift him to my shoulders and carry him to the baseball field where Sierra's team will be playing the first game of the semi-finals. He'll wrap his arms around my neck and call me Papa and beg me to please run faster, and even if I'm racing down the path with my heart pounding in my chest, I'll somehow manage another burst of speed just to hear him laugh.

It's hard to believe that next year Sierra will be going to college. She's decided to become a school guidance counselor—combining teaching, social work, and psychology, thereby convincing all the adults in her life that she's following in their footsteps. I lift my head to see beyond the fence of the playground, wondering if Brooklyn's piano recital went well. Two figures are coming down the path looking more like brothers than father and son. Though they're still far off, I recognize Zak's distinctive bouncy walk and the familiar way he tilts his head. Even after all this time, the sight of Zak coming towards me fills my chest with warmth. Annie's not with them, which means Kyra managed to convince her to help choreograph the play she's written for class—probably a good thing. These one-on-one moments with a parent were a key part of how Kyra finally got over her jealousy of her younger brother. And the important thing is we'll all be together later for Zak's birthday party.

I fetch our little boy from the climbing structure where he's helping another kid up to the top. There's no mistaking he's Annie's son with his natural generosity. There's no mistaking Zak's mark on him either. He's a beautiful, active child, full of life, whose flame burns hotter and brighter than everyone around him.

We named him Raphaël—God has healed—though Zak is an atheist and his healing is, at best, a partial, fragile thing with frightening scars that will never completely fade.

When Raphaël was born, everyone wondered if he were mine or Zak's. I told them I didn't care, that it didn't matter. Despite this, friends and family members continue to search for signs of paternity. Some draw attention to the fact that he's big for his age, but Zak's tall too. My sister points out that Raphaël's an early reader, like I was, like Kyra was, but with three parents and three older siblings all competing to read him bedtime stories, it's no wonder. And if Rapha's love of words runs deep, it's no more so than his love of numbers and puzzles.

Of course, if we wanted, we could have him genetically tested and perhaps resolve the question of paternity. I've explained why we have no need to do this, but people are slow to understand. The truth is, I know whose child Raphaël is, have known it from the start. It was Zak who told me the very night Raphaël was conceived. "He's our child," he'd said. "Yours and mine and Annie's."

After cleaning up from the birthday party and ensuring that the kids are all asleep, I find Zak and Annie standing by the bed making out. I wait in the doorway and watch them. I do this now not as the confused, anxiety-ridden man who'd been unsure of his place, but simply because I enjoy the sight of the two of them together. Zak puts on a show for me, and Annie, though less exhibitionist, still enjoys teasing me. I fold my arms over my chest, not wanting to give in just yet, until Zak says, "Get your ass over here already, J."

I move towards the two of them and take Annie into my arms, leaving Zak to watch, not above a little teasing myself. After a few moments, Annie says in a husky voice, "Let's not neglect the birthday boy."

"No, we wouldn't want to do that," I answer.

I turn towards Zak and gently take his face in my hands. I kiss him tenderly then roughly as I respond to his frenetic energy rising to the surface. Throwing him onto the bed, I pin him down as I say to Annie: "I'll hold him while you tear his clothes off."

294

Annie, anticipating this, already has his shorts down below his hips.

"What about your clothes, J?" Zak says. "You need to take them off too."

"Quiet," I say, grabbing fistfuls of his dark locks. "Or I'll use my teeth on you."

"I'd like that," Zak says, unperturbed, "but tonight it's your turn to be pinned down. Help me, Annie," he says as, with a sudden movement, he twists out of my grasp to begin a counter-attack.

For a while, I successfully evade their four grasping arms; then Annie manages to kneel on both my legs and Zak gets me into a wrestling hold that I, myself, taught him. After they have successfully stripped me of my shorts and button-down shirt, I grudgingly admit defeat.

"What's my consequence?" I ask.

"You have to go down on both of us," Annie answers immediately.

"Fine," I say, thoughts of this 'punishment' making it hard to hide my smile. "But don't think I've given up. There will be a next time."

Zak laughs in my face while Annie shakes her head in mock exasperation.

The truth is, I'm not thinking about next time. I am here, with them, in this moment. Now and now and now.

ACKNOWLEDGEMENTS

Thank you to the whole gang at Renaissance Press for your support, and especially to Nathan Caro Fréchette for believing in this story early on. Merci beaucoup aussi to the awesome editing team, including Marjolaine Lafrenière, Myryam Ladouceur, Philippe Vallée, Evan McKinley, and Nathan Fréchette.

I would never have had the courage to write and ultimately try to get this book published if not for my two writing groups, who took the story seriously and intelligently commented on work that might have been outside of their comfort zones. Much love to Sivan Slapak, B.A. Markus, Cora Siré, Deanna Radford, and Sharon Lax; and to Philippe Vaucher, Alexandre Rochette, and Joey Bongiorno, Jessica Patterson, and Emilie Moorehouse.

Thanks also to fabulous beta-readers Charles Roburn, Ahmar Husain, Matt Lee, Cameron McKeich, Marla Rapoport, Cora Siré, Scott Sokol, and Maya Merrick. Thanks also to Chase Quinn for reading an early draft and giving me confidence about Zak.

Very special thanks to the amazingly talented Lin-Lin Mao for the fabulous front cover art and to the super-polyvalent Nathan Fréchette for the back cover art.

Finally and as always, thanks to my wonderful family and friends for nourishing my heart.

ABOUT THE AUTHOR

Photo by Matt Lee

Su J. Sokol is an activist and a writer of speculative, liminal, and interstitial fiction. A former legal services lawyer from New York City, she immigrated to Canada with her family in 2004 and now makes Montréal her home. Su works as a social rights advocate for a community organization where she speaks French (and English) with a New York accent.

Cycling to Asylum, Su's debut novel, was long-listed for the Sunburst Award for Excellence in Canadian Literature of the Fantastic and has been optioned for development into a feature-length film. Her short fiction has appeared in a number of magazines and anthologies. When she is not writing, battling slumlords, bringing evil bureaucracies to their knees, and smashing borders, Su curates and participates in literary events in Canada and abroad.

Renaissance.

Diverse Canadian Voices

Renaissance was founded in May 2013 by a group of friends who wanted to publish and market those stories which don't always fit neatly in a genre, or a niche, or a demographic. We weren't sure what we wanted to publish exactly, so like the happy panbibliophiles that we are, we opened our submissions, with no other personal guideline than finding a Canadian book we would fall in love with enough that we would want to publish and sell.

Five years later, this is still very true; however, we've also noticed an interesting trend in what we tended to publish. It turns out that we are naturally drawn to the voices of those who are members of a marginalized group (especially people with disabilities and LGBTQIAPP2+ people), and these are the voices we want to continue to uplift.

To us, Renaissance isn't just a business; it's a family. Being authors and artists ourselves, we are always careful to center the experience of the author above all else. We involve our authors in every step of the process, and trust that they know how to best market their labour of love, though devoted committees take on the difficult tasks of copy editing, designing and marketing to achieve professional results.

At Renaissance, we do things differently. We are passionate about books, and we care as much about our authors enjoying the publishing process as we do about our readers enjoying a great, professional quality and affordable product on the platform they prefer.

renaissancebookpress.com
info@renaissancebookpress.com

If you enjoyed this book,
you'll love these other Renaissance titles!

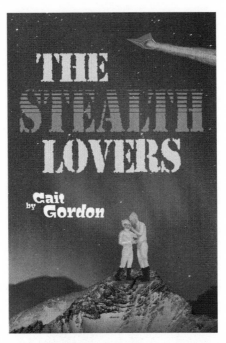

LGBT/Science-Fiction

MANY YEARS BEFORE THEY LANDED ON CINNEH, TWO YOUNG MEN STARTED BASIC TRAINING, ALSO KNOWN AS "VACAY IN HAY."

Xaxall Dwyer Knightly might only be a private, but his sergeant is fascinated by him. During a combat exercise, Private Knightly wins the distinction of being the first-ever trainee to throw an opponent through a supporting wall. The teen has the strength of five Draga put together.

Vivoxx Nathan Tirowen, son of General Tirowen, stands tall with a naturally commanding presence. A young man of a royal clan, the private has an uncanny talent with weaponry. The sarge is convinced that Private Tirowen could "trim the pits of a rodent without nicking the skin."

When the two recruits meet, Vivoxx smiles warmly and Xaxall speaks in backwards phonetics. Little do they know the bond they immediately feel for each other will morph into a military pairing no one in Dragal history has ever seen.

THIS IS THE STORY OF THE STEALTH— LEGENDARY, FORMIDABLE, AND FABULOUS.

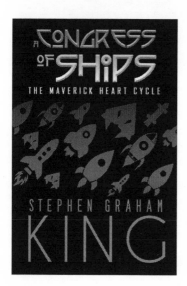

BY STEPHEN GRAHAM-KING
Science-Fiction

In a desolate system on the outer edge of Pan Galactum, the skin of the universe has ruptured, tearing open a portal to an alternate reality. Witnessed only by the sentient science vessel N'Dea, a massive, battered ship falls through, housing a community of refugees fleeing an enemy that has pursued them across the cold reaches of space for decades.

But have they come alone?

Summoned by N'Dea while en route from a reunion with dear friends on the Galactum's capital, the mystery is a lure that fellow Artificial Sentience, the Maverick Heart, cannot resist. It's now up to Vrick, along with humans Keene, Lexa-Blue and Ember, and allies old and new, to come to the aid of this ship of lost souls. Together they must find a way to seal the breach for good, before a ravening hunger can spill through and rip the Galactum apart.

SOME ASSEMBLY REQUIRED
NATHAN CARO FRECHETTE

Graphic Novel / LGBT

How well do you ever know someone?

Louis has been in love with his best friend Laurent for years. Unfortunately, Laurent is in a happy relationship with Lily, another one of Louis's best friends. After they graduate high school and start feeling the pressure of adult life, however, Laurent begins exhibiting really odd behavior, and it seems Louis is the only one who can help.

43253123R00184

Made in the USA
Middletown, DE
24 April 2019